The
BLUE HELIX

The
BLUE HELIX
William B. Eidson

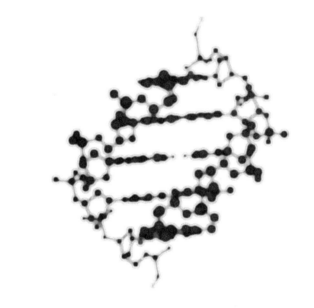

A NOVEL

William B. Eidson

VIENNA BOOKS LIMITED
HAMPTON FALLS, NEW HAMPSHIRE

THE BLUE HELIX
Copyright © 1999 by William B. Eidson

Cover and interior illustrations © 1999 by Rick Berry
Book design by Stephen Bentley
Author photo by Bill Eidson

All right reserved under International and Pan-American Copyright Conventions.

IS THAT ALL THERE IS?
By: Jerry Leiber, Mike Stoller
© 1966, 1969 (Renewed) Jerry Leiber Music, Mike Stoller Music
All rights reserved. Used by permission.

FIRST EDITION

Vienna Books is an imprint of
Donald M. Grant, Publisher, Inc.
POB 187, Hampton Falls, NH 03844
http://www.grantbooks.com

Library of Congress Catalog Card No. 99-071124
ISBN 1-880418-47-9
Printed in the United States of America
        10 9 8 7 6 5 4 3 2 1

Dedication

This book is dedicated to the two very different women who have taught me what it is like to live with and love a woman.

Are either of them a prototype of Sara in this book? Absolutely not. There was never a drop of Sara in either of them.

Yet—if my wife, Mary, whom I lost some seven years ago to breast cancer and my present companion, Nell, had not existed, then this book would never have existed.

Acknowledgements

You probably have seen the name of Bill Eidson on the covers of five different novels. Great books, each of them—but not mine. They were written by my son, Bill, who keeps making me feel lazy as he keeps writing new and very different novels. I acknowledge him here because he has been such a major help with *The Blue Helix*. Bill has read the manuscript many times, finding a little flaw here, and making a good suggestion there.

Thanks to Richard Parks, agent extraordinaire, as well as Richard Berry, Robert Wiener, Stephen Bentley, and Frank Robinson. I would also like to express my appreciation for the continued support of my family, including Catherine and Albert Sinkys, Martha and Bill Hansen, John and Amy Eidson, and Bill's wife and son, Donna and Nick.

INTRODUCTION

I can't help but feel that storytelling is the family business of the Eidson family. In particular, my father always related most everything of importance to us through stories.

My father's boyhood around Georgia's lumber mills in the 1930s are images in my head: building his own rowboat to drift down the Thunderbolt River; during the Depression, his father taking aim at a rabbit and saying, "We've only got one bullet. I make this shot, or we don't eat tonight."

Then there's the story about my father being late to his own wedding. His car died in Boston on his way to the church in Arlington, Massachusetts. Here he was, this largely unknown character from the south, a veteran of the Battle of the Bulge, and no one knew what to think. Could he simply have taken off? He finally arrived, grease on his hands, to find my mother, the former Mary Cullinane, pacing in the vestibule, her train flying at head height...

My father is not only a natural storyteller, but a writer. Soon after my oldest sister was born, he and my mother decided he should quit his job as an editor in Boston. They loaded the car and moved to Saint Petersburg, Florida. My father tells of typing his short stories in 100-degree summer heat on the front porch of a rented house while cradling and entertaining my sister, Catherine, with his bare feet.

OK, so she's been a little strange ever since, but he sold a handful of short stories to regional publications, before landing a national mainstream success with a story in *Colliers*. Nevertheless, there wasn't enough money in short stories, then or now, to keep a growing family going, and he and my mother eventually brought us all to Rhode Island. He put writing fiction into the realm of "someday" and, with his partner, built a successful 25-30 employee advertising agency in Providence: Goodchild and Eidson Advertising, Inc.

My father always remained a voracious and insightful reader. A little over ten years ago, he applied his expertise in helping me reshape my first novel, *The Little Brother*. To say that no one could have been happier than he when I secured a contract with Henry Holt & Company would be a tremendous understatement. He beamed then, and he has beamed ever since with the subsequent publication of my following books. He's always the first person I call with good news or bad in the book business.

Somewhere along the way, I remember him looking at one of my novels, and saying, "It's high time I got my own book started..."

I was delighted to see him begin work, approaching it as something he wanted to do whether or not the story ever became published. Nevertheless, I worried—what exactly was I going to say if it wasn't any good?

Thank God, his writing was up to his storytelling. I was so damned relieved when I read the first few chapters. Better still, I was able to sit back, just dig into the story and lose myself.

When I finished, one could even say I was beaming.

The Blue Helix is told with energy, style, and remarkable intelligence. That's not to say *The Blue Helix* is a light, happy story. *The Blue Helix* is fascinating, it's entertaining, it's a story with characters who live and breathe...but it is also a very personal story.

My father first drafted this book while my mother was dying of breast cancer. Though Andy and Sara Camp are clearly not thinly disguised versions of my parents, there's little doubt what motivated my father's interest in the story.

Seven years have passed since my mother's death. My father has embarked on a new phase in his life, including finding the love of a woman we all feel is simply wonderful, Dr. Nell Morsch.

With the kind of irony usually reserved for fiction, just months before Vienna Books accepted his first novel, my father was diagnosed with lung cancer. So he's begun in earnest the battle for life itself which is so powerfully highlighted in *The Blue Helix*.

Andy and Sara Camp, you'll soon see, become superhuman. My father's thoughts, views, and storytelling will take you on this superhuman ride while addressing the most human questions of all: why do we live if just to die? And what would we do with our lives, if we could do absolutely anything we wanted?

It's a great story. Well told. Just the way my father has always told them. Welcome to *The Blue Helix.*

Bill Eidson, Jr.

Author of:
The Little Brother
Dangerous Waters
The Guardian
Adrenaline
Frames Per Second

 chapter one

I watched Sara struggle, each small breath a triumph. "Heart failure," her doctor had said. "The lungs fill up with fluid. She could drown."

What was her sickness? A mysterious everything. A general dissolution of kidneys, heart, lungs. Her vital functions were slowing, each body system seemingly killing the other. What was her prognosis? Death. What was the cause? Age.

"It's just the way it is," the green-coated doctor had said. "Some of us hit a hundred and play golf every day and others are old at sixty. Actually, eighty is about right."

Right for him, maybe, but not for Sara. This dying business was for other people, not for us.

The doctor (Christ! Why do they wear those sickening green coats? Don't they know they look like death themselves?) tried for reassurance but he wasn't blessed by great insight so his message was trite: "We'll keep her as comfortable as possible," he said, meaning sedated. "She won't suffer."

But Sara was in terror and she could hear the doctor as well as I could.

I knew the theory: that as death approached our circle of consciousness grew smaller, until the outside world ceased to be, and only a small area around the deathbed existed in the mind of the dying. Then, as the circle drew even smaller there was an acceptance of death, maybe even a welcoming of the dark angel, and the chosen one slipped away to die in peace.

So much for theory. Sara would have none of it. She was terrified, holding onto life with a grip that used every ounce of her strength, a grip that she knew was slipping.

I stood in the darkened room, smelling the hospital smells. conscious of the arthritic ache in my own back (after all, when one is seventy-nine...) and peered intently into Sara's eyes.

They were alive and beautiful still, those eyes. Deep and lovely and vital. Young eyes in a bed of old flesh. And never mind what

Sara herself had always thought about those same eyes. Sara could be wrong, was wrong about those lovely eyes.

Her once raven black hair was wispy and white, a white that was shocking to me. Her face was swollen, with long remembered features almost overwhelmed by the soft flesh of her sickness. The body, the glorious body that I had kissed and loved over the years, I hardly knew now at all.

But the eyes. Somewhere deep inside this disaster of a body was my lovely Sara. Age and sickness. Age and sickness. Age is the ultimate sickness.

"Keep her alive," I said. "Just keep here alive until I get back. A week at the most. Maybe less. Don't let her go until I get back."

"We'll keep her comfortable," doctor green-coat said, soothingly.

"No, damnit! Keep her alive. Whatever it takes, keep her alive. If she's not alive when I get back I'll sue your ass off. I want her alive. Do you hear?"

He was affronted by this foolish and demanding old man. So, let him be affronted. I turned to Sara: "I'll be back…" glancing at the doctor, searching for a code word that Sara would know and he wouldn't. "I'll be back with the goods. Soon. Hang on."

Her eyes filled with impatience. She knew exactly what I meant and emphatically didn't believe it. Husbands are never respected in their own land.

"Stay…hold my hand…tell me lies…don't go, don't go," she breathed, barely audible as she forced the words around a thick and swollen tongue that had once, not so long ago, been as alive as a grass snake as it explored the inside of my own mouth. For we had been an active couple.

I kissed my fingers and placed them on her lips. "I'll be back with… something. You'll still be here. It will be all right. Really."

The doctor gave me a disapproving glance and left us. I fumbled under the sheets until I found Sara's hand and gave it a squeeze, then followed the doctor out of the room.

"God damn, I hate old age," I said to him as I walked by.

"Consider the alternative," he replied idly, flipping through a chart on a metal clipboard.

Oh, I am. I am. More than you'll ever know, I thought, walking quickly away, down the corridor towards the elevator. "If you ever in your sweet life knew what I was up to," I muttered to myself, "you'd mess your pants like an infant."

 chapter two

Sara was not an easy woman. But then, I was not a man who liked easy things.

I let the memories of our fifty years together run through my mind like a silent movie during that late afternoon drive from the Connecticut hospital to our Rhode Island home. I thought about all the dozens of our friends (friends?) who had seen me as either a fool or a saint for putting up with Sara.

Fools themselves. I had been married to a magical creature who was also a tangle of contradictions, and I never, even once, "put up with" Sara. I had always been endlessly fascinated by her intelligent and painful discontent.

Sara had always wanted things so vividly. I had watched other wives, other husbands, who seemed content to have just the hand that fate had dealt them; satisfied to live a peaceful, uneventful life; happy with little pleasures. Admirable people, so I've always been told, and have perhaps believed.

But Sara was not one of these. And in my own very different way, neither was I.

As I drove the familiar sixty-odd miles toward our Rhode Island home I passed close by a better-equipped and more convenient hospital along the way. Why hide Sara in another state?

I had my reasons.

Rhode Island is such a cozy little place. You think you can hold it in the palm of your hand and examine every inch of it. Yet, after half a lifetime I could still get lost in this small state, speaking either geographically, socially, ethnically, or historically.

I crossed the new Jamestown bridge and then the Newport bridge and turned north, threading through an almost garden-like landscape as I headed for our town, our home.

As I pulled into the driveway I thought that this house that Sara had loved was a traitor to her now. It was still so peaceful, so serene in its soft tan and white trimmed colonial design as it crouched on its small hill and gazed out over Narragansett Bay.

Where was the urgency, the sense of panic that I felt? Damn you, house. Don't you have the slightest feeling of concern for Sara, after all she's done for you?

Silly old man.

The neighboring homes were also mostly colonial in design.

Trees and green grass gave a sense of privacy, so you were never overly conscious of other homes.

A pleasant, upscale neighborhood. It was our seventh home in some fifty years of marriage and one that Sara had loved.

We'd long ago outgrown it financially, but why move? It was all we needed, it was home. Besides, we had friends here. Or, if not friends, then at least familiar acquaintances.

I listened to the chatter of two teenagers next door, who were tossing a ball back and forth.

I'll bet they did that in ancient Rome, I thought. *And sounded exactly the same.*

I tried to remember the first names of the two teenagers, who after all, had grown up no more than one-hundred and fifty feet away from us, but their names escaped me. "Sara would know," I told myself.

Consciously shutting out the sound of the ball-tossers, I pulled off most of my clothes and went to bed and tried to sleep because I knew I'd need it later. The shades were drawn and I wore a sleep mask against what light was left but I turned and tossed and felt the old-age disease, arthritis, twinging up and down my neck and spine and I couldn't relax, couldn't sleep. Thoughts of Sara were too strong. I kept seeing her there, fighting for each breath, and I cursed every wrinkle in my sheet for keeping me awake even though I knew it wasn't bed wrinkles but fear, fear of old grinning death itself that kept me rigid.

I glanced continually at the bedside clock. Time was my enemy. For Sara, time was too short. For me, since I had to wait until after midnight to get into the Germ Factory, time was too long. How to wish away my time without wishing away Sara's life?

"Calm down, now." I kept saying the words aloud to myself because I had to have my wits about me when I went to work tonight. I had told Sara to hang on for a week or maybe less, but I had lied. It was tonight or it was maybe, probably, almost certainly, never.

Soon after it got dark, long before I could hope to get into the Germ Factory, I got up, dressed, made my peanut butter sandwich and stuck it, with an apple, into my lunch box and then carefully washed my thermos and sterilized it with boiling water and packed it into the lunch box, empty and ready.

And then I still had four hours to kill.

"Don't let yourself get into a frenzy," I said, aloud. "Sit down. Breathe. Think calm thoughts. Try to imagine something peaceful."

What I had to do that night was not work for a frenzied old fool. I had to concentrate, to use delicate, sure hands, or I would kill any chance Sara might have. Kill Sara, really.

I got up and wandered around the living room, switching on the TV, then switching it off as soon as I heard the sound, before a picture could appear.

"So, this is how it will be if Sara dies," I said to myself. "This empty. This lonely. You'll just rattle around, moon around, until you die, too. Well, the hell with that!"

I one-fingered a few notes on Sara's piano, cheered by the familiar sound but dismayed, as always, by my total inability to play.

"Hang on, Sara," I muttered. "Keep breathing." I glanced at my watch. Now I had only three hours and forty-four minutes to kill.

I forced myself to review the situation, to take a step by step look at who I was and who I had been and what I intended to do tonight. I got up and found Sara's old photo album and started leafing through it, not looking for anything in particular, just remembering.

We did go back, Sara and me. Over fifty years of mostly happy marriage.

Looking at the pictures I could remember the day when Sarah announced that henceforth she was dropping the final "h" and becoming a more exotic (she thought) "Sara," instead of the dowdy and biblical "Sarah."

"It's got an India-indian sound," she said. "Suits my nature, don't you think?" And with her brilliant black hair, ivory skin and flashing brown eyes, perhaps it did suit.

I was born in 1915 and Sara a year earlier, though she'd never admit it. She on Cape Cod (just "the Cape," you know) and I in

6

Baltimore. I got out of college with a degree in chemistry just in time for the Great Depression. Finally got a job in a paint factory. Quality control. There's reality for you: fifty paint samples every morning, waiting to be analyzed. Twenty-three eighty-five every week after takeouts and glad to get it.

I went out one night to a cheap nightclub, a roadhouse, they used to call them, with a sweet little blond girl who kept telling me that I was wonderful, while I smiled and beamed and tried to look even more wonderful for her. We were celebrating my new job in the paint factory. Then the spotlight came on and a singer, a fantastic brunette with a loud and melodious, but somewhat out-of-control voice came on and sang and sang until people began to shuffle and talk and walk to the bar for drinks. I was transfixed, my nice blond forgotten. I had met Sarah, soon to be Sara, soon to be mine as soon as I could find a way to make it happen.

Always after that, always during our long married life, I would introduce Sara to people we met as, "the girl I snatched away from success on the stage," and always Sara would smile and simper as though it were exactly so and I would wonder yet again how much she understood about how badly she had sung but how beautiful she had looked doing it.

chapter three

Sara's old album was getting brittle and tattered. I wondered why she hadn't replaced it, but the photos were still intact. I remember how impatient I had been when Sara took them—or made me take a snap of her.

But now, how precious every one of them seemed! They brought back the years so vividly. I thought now, "Only a few dozen faded black and whites in a lifetime. Why didn't we take more?"

Here was a photo of Sara before we were married. It was our third or fourth date, not very long after that nightclub business. Sara was beside a lake in New Hampshire, where we'd gone for the day because a friend of mine had a cabin. Sara in shorts and halter, posing on a rickety dock beside a tied-up row boat, a massive black-and-white sunset spreading into the background behind her.

I gazed at that photo and smiled as only a lover can. I had thought she was gorgeous. Gorgeous without reservation. As I looked now, I could see some of the things I had been too blind to see, some of the things Sara had always hated and tried to hide. So foolish. Such little imperfections, but mountainous to her.

She had those perfect voluptuous lips, like Rita Hayworth. I remember so clearly how those lips had excited me. Does anyone look at anyone today with the same intensity? Is it really possible?

The thought that she would actually let me press my own lips against those magical red and soft female parts was almost more than I could believe.

You laugh. Things were different then.

I remember being anxious because the sun was setting and we were miles from our two homes and Sara was a nice girl and I wanted to stay beside this lake but I knew we had to go and I was so surprised that Sara didn't seem upset by the coming darkness.

"Well… we could spend the night… " she said, smiling archly. "After all…there's plenty of room."

"For each of us," she added.

I remember that I was beside myself, caught among such a complex of hopes and fears and embarrassments that I could hardly breathe.

After dark, after we'd scraped up a small meal from our left-over lunch and a couple of candy bars, we sat on the porch of the cabin in a glider and looked out over the moon-glittery lake and smelled the clean, warm, air of New Hampshire and listened to the crickets and other summer sounds and we kissed.

Sara was still in shorts and if my hand or my knee or any part of my body happened to brush against her upper leg it was a shock to still my heart with guilt and longing. I wouldn't have dreamed of touching her there on purpose. Really, I wouldn't.

We kissed and fumbled in that glider and I tried desperately to put my arms around her in just the right way, so that I was holding her, caressing her, loving her, yet not touching anything forbidden (like a breast, oh, God help us, not a breast!) and we kissed and kissed, so expertly, it seemed to me, so tenderly, so sweetly, yet so excitingly. We were in a fever of creative imagination with our kissing.

Our kiss was the object of our lovemaking, not just a waypoint to something else. I see people today in the movies who open their mouths about four inches and go for each other like a pair of hungry alligators and I think, "Oh, you fools! I know you're trying to portray excitement but actually you know nothing about kissing. Nothing!"

After the longest time, Sara whispered something to me in her low, throaty voice, so softly that I couldn't hear, so that I had to ask her to say it again and she said, just a little louder, "You can get on top."

I pretended that I didn't understand, that I didn't know what she meant. I was so much in awe of Sara, so much in love, as I knew love then, that I simply couldn't. How could I sully this marvelous creature with my dirty needs? Even then I was aching painfully and I was oozing a sticky mess into my shorts but I was admitting nothing about the grossness of my desires.

Sara looked at me in a strange way. Looked directly into my

face. Then I remember how she quirked her full lips into a tight little smile and said no more.

After a moment she slid out of the glider and said, "Well … let's find a couple of nice places to sleep tonight.

So, this was one photo. One quick snapshot of a pretty girl at a lake. One small window into my memory of the magical few months before we were married.

Another photo: Sara walking in the backyard of our second home—the three bedroom ranch we'd bought just after I got out of the army. It was summer again and Sara was in shorts (Sara loved shorts but had begun wearing them a little longer) and she had her black hair tied up in a pony tail and she was sticking her tongue out at me as I took the picture.

There she was, after all those years, tongue out, one foot slightly off the ground, one finger pointing at me in a comic coquettish way, forever young on this piece of shiny paper.

I remember that when she first saw this picture she had wailed, "Oh, look at those fat, dimpled thighs. What can I do about them, Andy?"

So foolish. She had, at most, two ounces of extra weight on each upper thigh. Sweet, carnal flesh. I loved it.

Sara was moderately tall, with vivid black hair which she constantly worked over with rinses and thickeners because it tended toward a thinness when she wanted it thick and luxuriant. "The curse of womanhood," she would say, "Thin hair."

She had beautiful white teeth, (she spent a lot of time flossing and brushing them and smiling into her mirror) but they had a small gap in front that she hated. She railed about this gap. "Couldn't I have just one damned thing that's perfect? Couldn't I?"

Her eyes. Oh, her lovely, dramatic eyes, (I thought) Oh, her too-small undramatic eyes, (she thought). When I first met her I thought her eyes were huge because she had used every trick of eye shadow, eye liner and false eyelash to emphasize them, even in broad daylight, so I accepted it as just the way Sara looked.

Looking at the photos I was struck by the way we'd gone through life defined by our seven homes. First, there was the little

10

red rented cape where one of us had to stand back to let the other go through the door to use the one bathroom.

Then there were the apartments Sara had rented to follow me around in the army during World War II. Then the small yellow ranch house where the neighborhood BYOB parties began in summer backyards. Then the better neighborhood with the larger ranch. Then… ever upward as Sara looked for her happiness in homes, furniture, clothes and in more and more successful friends. But then… didn't we all? Let's not be snotty about it.

Another photo: a party scene with neighbors. Sara dressed as a pirate, with a wooden sword and red sash, heavy lipstick and makeup, with a painted-on mascara mustache, black velvet pants and a cocked hat she worked for hours to make from paper.

From the way she stands, from the expression plastered on her face, from the hands thrown akimbo in free abandon, I know that Sara had had more than her share of the martinis. But then, so, I'm sure, had I. So had everyone. That was what we did when we partied in those days.

Was it that night? Or another night just like it? There were fifteen or twenty of us crowded into someone's kitchen because that's where the food and booze were and everyone was talking too loudly until there was one of those unaccountable sudden silences and Sara's voice was raised so that everyone could hear her say, "…after all, Andy and I don't play golf or tennis or collect stamps, so sex is our only hobby."

This brought appraising looks from the men, who from then on always looked at Sara a little differently, and exasperated, who-do-you-think-you're-fooling looks from the women.

I turned the album page and saw a few of our wedding pictures. Only a few. People didn't hire photographers and rent tuxedos in 1936. Friends took snapshots. And you didn't honeymoon in Bermuda, either. You spent ten dollars for the best hotel in town and then the next day you went home. Sara and I splurged. I had saved up so we could have a whole weekend.

But here is Sara in white, black hair shining, red lips bursting with a sweetness that was to be mine alone, breasts high and prominent but not on display, ankles slim above her white pumps.

11

Absolutely lovely, I thought. But Sara would have torn up this photo if she had had others because her smile showed the small gap between her front teeth that she hated. And even in this old black and white photo you could see that her eye makeup was heavier than was considered "nice."

There were no more than a dozen people at our wedding, most of them people who worked with me at the paint factory.

I remember Sara's tight-lipped, almost silent mother, a bitter-seeming woman who looked enough like Sara to give me the willies. Her eyes kept boring into mine as she seemed to search out the depths of my soul—or maybe the depths of my depravity.

If our wedding was something of a blur to me our first night together was forever etched into my psyche. I would relive it over and over again and never tire of the memory.

I've always thought that making love was like eating: there are so many varieties of such a simple and basic activity. There are those who like to nibble on a lettuce leaf or a carrot stick (in a figurative sense) and there are those who want to dive immediately into a greasy roast pork swimming in gravy. And I've often thought how awful it would be for a carrot nibbler to marry a pork roaster and spend a lifetime arguing about what was "normal."

With Sara, the two of us fell together right into a savory pot of bouillabaisse and reveled in it. It seemed that all those months of passionate but virginal kissing had finally brought us their reward. Oh, we were clumsy, all knees and elbows, but vigorous and happy and eager to learn.

I remember it all so vividly. I remember the sexual smells; the glimpses of her in the dim light, naked and sensual and so unlike my "nice girl" image; the feel of her flesh against my flesh and the soft, sweet and almost greedy sound of her voice as she told me what she was feeling; and the warm, sweet smell of her breath and her underarm deodorant and face powder and even the faint whiff of foot odor at one point.

I remember also that there was no blood, no pain and some small evidence of experience beyond my own and I told myself that it was not my business if she wasn't a virgin and it didn't matter at all. After a while the very thought of it almost left my head.

I remember the next morning when I woke to find Sara crawling out of the bed and I had just a glimpse of a smeared, bedraggled woman with lipstick and mascara streaked and with smaller eyes than I remembered looking at me in an anxious way as she streaked for the bathroom.

There were smudges of an orangey powder and other makeup on the pillows and sheets and I realized that she had gone to bed without removing it, but I remember thinking, "How do you know what women do? What they're supposed to do?"

She came out again in a few minutes and gave me a brilliant smile, looking beautiful again, with huge eyes, and said: "You'll get used to the way I look. I'll make you love me."

Of course my heart went out to her. "How could I not love you?" I asked.

I soon learned that I would always have to put her toothpaste cap back on, blow away the dust from her powder box, recap her shampoo. Little things. I thought of it as, "taking care of Sara," and I enjoyed doing them, but I could never quite take care of her insecurity.

"If you were even more beautiful I couldn't stand it," I would say to her.

"Tell me the real truth. What do you hate the most about me!" she would plead. "Talk to me, Andy. What can I do about my looks?"

My beautiful Sara. Never happy with herself. Never believing that I really believed. Constantly searching for a new cosmetic, a new artifice to make her as perfect in her own eyes as she already was in mine.

I was about to close the photo album when I saw one last snapshot turned backwards and slipped into the lining of the back cover. I turned it over and caught my breath with surprise and heartache to think that Sara had hidden this picture away for her own personal need after all these years.

It was a photo that I had taken of a naked Sara when she had been seven months pregnant. She had her secret smile because the photo was in profile and she was holding out her stomach proudly for me, and me alone, to see.

We had had two miscarriages before, and while we didn't know it at the time, this was to be the third. It was a little boy with all his equipment, fully ready for life at seven months, but born without it. I had thought that Sara had forgotten him by now, but here he was hidden away in her photo album as he had been hidden away all those years ago in her belly.

chapter four

Half a decade in the paint factory. I had worked up to forty-eight dollars a week and had already found a few gray hairs. "Premature," I said.

"Better you than me," Sara said. But I knew about her bottle of color in the medicine cabinet.

Then came World War II. Useless years in Chemical Warfare teaching uncounted thousands of GIs to put on a gas mask and run through a tent filled with tear gas. A waste, but I wasn't dead, and many were.

The GI Bill put me back in school (say, you're kind of old for this, aren't you, buddy?) and bought me a doctorate in biology. That's right: a PH damned d. I couldn't believe it and neither could Sara. "Show me some of your biology, Doctor," she would say, and I would show her, with great enthusiasm.

So, I got my first job in biological research. Much better than sniffing paint samples. Now I could sniff unbelievably complex mixtures of organic soup. We were eager to unravel what we thought were the secrets of life. How naive of us. We knew nothing, absolutely nothing, back in the early sixties. But thank God, we tried.

Then, after a few years, I moved into a university, combining research and teaching with medical studies until I got another degree, this time in medicine. I never practiced, never served an internship, just got what I needed out of it. I was becoming very interested in the human animal and his intricate microbiology. My special interests at the time were hematology and immunology.

When Sara saw that she had married an educational junkie, saw that I would bounce from chemistry to biochemistry to medicine to molecular biology to whatever interested me next, she turned toward something similar. She specialized in "Language, Literature and Lust," as she put it, and she became very good at all of them. The "Lust" wasn't what you think... it was the study of history. The Lust was man's (and woman's) wars, land thievery, religious persecutions and almighty ambitions. More and more I looked inward towards smaller and smaller particles to find my truth while Sara looked at the largest issues she could find to search out her's.

The next fifteen years were the glory years. I went to work for a company that made toothpaste, deodorant and tampons. The company wanted to make a name in ethical pharmaceuticals so they were happy to let us mess around with enzymes and plasmids and snippets of mouse DNA. "Just keep us informed," they said. And for the longest time, they were patient.

And Sara? Was she also patient? Not always. I've loved her and watched her for over fifty years and I still don't know exactly what goes on inside. To me, this is part of her fascination. Sara is like the DNA model, endlessly complex and endlessly unknown. You unravel a bit of her emotional gene sequence and find there's always more to unravel, *ad Infinitum*, up the spiral staircase that is Sara.

She was the perfect mate for me. But was I perfect for her?

Once, and only once, at an overcrowded neighborhood cocktail party, I looked up to find Sara leaving a bedroom where the coats were piled and she had a certain look of guilt and defiance on her face and I knew immediately that something, perhaps something not so bad but something against the rules, had happened.

I first thought I'd wait a moment and see which man straggled out with the same expression, but then I thought better of it and turned away and fetched a drink for the two of us and walked Sara into the garden for a look, as I told her, "at the romantic moon."

Then it was home, bed, and my three AM staring-at-the-ceiling contemplation of this latest wrinkle in Sara's moral DNA.

I knew it was only a chance encounter, fueled by boredom and curiosity, but even so, I knew that I'd had a warning and before the night was over I had made plans to take time off from the laboratory and travel with Sara to Rome, Paris and London.

Sara loved Paris and Rome. I loved Paris and Rome. I loved Sara and Sara loved me.

But then we got to London and it hit the fan. Because London was even then one of the world centers of the biotech business and I had people and places to see that weren't listed in the Michelin guide.

Oh, well. I should have gone to the Tower of London instead of to CXC, Ltd., where they were doing pioneering work with bacteriophages, those unthinkably small viruses that infect bacteria and give us clues to doing the same.

But what harm in just a look? It was only a morning. How could I have known they'd ask me back the next day and then I'd be so caught up I'd spend practically a week monitoring their techniques? After all, important is important and staying on top of the biotech business is like riding the lead bull in a stampede. You just don't get off to smell the wild flowers.

And we adjusted. In a long marriage the incident was just one of those surface cracks, barely noticed, almost forgotten.

Almost.

*   *   *   *   *

Another glance at the watch. Now I had three hours and two minutes to kill. Time! We're such a prisoner of time. Looking back over our long life, the scenes seemed to develop so slowly. I was impatient with my own memory as year followed year in my mind. I could see us as a young couple, could remember a glimpse of Sara combing her hair and smiling into her mirror as vividly as if it were yesterday, and I could see us getting old, losing our freshness, squandering our time when we should have hoarded it. And yet, here I am now, an old man with little time left to hoard, and I'm burning with impatience to see it pass.

Two hours and fifty-eight minutes. Good! I'm past the three hour barrier.

So, what do old men do to pass the time? Right. I'll go pee and make a pot of coffee.

*   *   *   *   *

Back to the research lab where the toothpaste chemists and money people had almost childlike faith in us. They were delighted with the papers we were publishing and they liked to show us off at annual stockholder meetings. But after a couple of years, when it became obvious that the task of prying out the secrets of life could also be a slow road to bankruptcy they gradually began to choke off the money. Could you blame them? They'd dropped millions and all they could see was a group of guys standing around clinking glassware and talking about reaction buffers and gels.

So I wrote out a twelve page prospectus full of biological jargon and Sara typed it for me with two fingers at the kitchen table and I went to Wall Street and worked out a private placement of stock with several venture capitalists that gave me a new company legal shell and plenty of seed money.

In an old brick building that had been a shoe factory I started the research lab and manufacturing facility that would, within a few years, become the Germ Factory. A few years later we went public and became a hot new issue on the stock market. Sara and I became moderately rich before our company made a dime.

In fact … our new company made a startling new advance in gene-splicing, and lost money. Our company built one of the finest P3 containment labs in the world (soon to be obsolete), and lost money. Our company developed a new vector, or plasmid, that had the scientific community standing on chairs applauding, and lost money. Our company had a secondary stock issue that sold out in spite of losses. Because microbiology was still a hot button for investors and that year we lost a really impressive amount of money.

And with the inverse logic of Wall Street, these years of losses led to ever-rising prices for our company's common stock because the investing public was still excited about biotechnology, so that Sara and I grew steadily richer on paper.

I refused to look at the financial pages every day, so it became a ritual every Sunday afternoon. Sara would hunt through the weekly stock tables and multiply our stock holdings, plus options, with her hand held computer and announce the results grandly.

"At this very moment, Andrew and Sara Camp are worth exactly $40 million *and* $378,764.00 ," she would announce with a flourish, and we'd smile and beam in the fantasy of a wealth that seemed unreal. And on those odd weeks when the total would go down we'd both be in the deepest depression for a while, talking

18

bitterly about the money we'd lost until the next week's accounting would have the stock price up another 1/2 or 3/4 , bringing our holdings up another half-million or so.

So it went in the glorious eighties if you were well-connected in the high tech world. After a time, we drifted up near the fifty million mark, but when we heard someone say, "the rich," we always thought it referred to someone else, never ourselves, and we never sold a share of stock during that time, never spent a penny of it.

But that was also the year that I designed the Germ Factory and actually broke ground for the buildings, using the money from the secondary offering.

Excitement! It was marvelous to see it go up. And soon afterwards we had our first really profitable product on the market, a human growth factor for use against burns.

But then the money began to run out faster than it could possibly run in and Wall Street had decided it wasn't as thrilled with DNA as it once was. So that's how we were sold. A merger, they called it. My old toothpaste and tampon company had been watching us struggle through scientific success and financial failure and decided it was time to pick up a bargain in technology and straighten out the business end.

It wasn't so bad, being part of the big corporate world again. Sara and I were still mildly rich. Our almost fifty million had dropped to a sobering fourteen million after the takeover and Sara and I felt really poor for a while, talking about how we'd "lost thirty-six million," until we finally realized that the fourteen million was real money that we could actually spend if we wanted.

So Sara bought clothes until her closets were stuffed and I started carrying a wad of twenties in my wallet to ease my way through life. Otherwise, nothing changed.

The Germ Factory was completed. My career was at its height. I published one paper after another and honor followed honor. I was suddenly "somebody."

Did you ever see your own face looking back at you from the cover of TIME magazine? Even Sara was impressed. You know what we did? Bought ten copies of TIME and Sara lined the bed with them and we jumped in and used them. Somewhere today there is a trunk with a bundle of TIME magazines bearing my face, many of them still scrunched up from our grinding knees and buttocks. So, that's the way it goes among our leading citizens in the privacy of their own homes from time to time. And we were well into our sixties at the time. No dignity among the elderly.

I want you to understand something: when I talk about Sara and I remember some of our intimate times that's because now I'm seeing her helpless and old in a hospital bed and remembering how alive she used to be. But there was always more to Sara than fun and games. She was always a step or two ahead of wherever you thought she would be and she had a brutally honest sense of self. She knew her own importance and my importance—and she knew our overwhelming smallness, too, in the cosmic sense.

That's why the TIME magazines in the bed. It was not to put me down, not to diminish my natural pride in seeing my face on every newsstand, but simply to say, "we know … we know the fine line between fame and failure. We know how to revel in it even to the point of physically rubbing ourselves in this recognition (shall we say, wallow in it?) but we also know that next week will bring another face on the cover and life's little drudgeries will go on.

* * * * *

"Hold on, Sara! Keep breathing! I know every moment is awful, but the grave is worse. Hold on!"

Every now and then the enormity of it would hit me. I'd get up and pace around, check the time, shout fierce instructions up to a god I didn't know, telling him to keep my Sara safe a little longer. Then I'd work at getting my emotions under control again. Calm, that's it. Calm and peaceful amidst the tumult. Caaaaallll-llmmmmm!

* * * * *

So, there I was at the height of my fame, as fecund with new biological ideas as a shad and totally pleased with myself when they gave me a young administrative assistant whom I quickly labeled "The Wiseass" because he was, and pretty soon they gave him a young assistant and by and by wherever I turned I found that someone had his young elbow pointed at my nose and there just wasn't room for me to stand or sit or be. I had gone from complete competence to complete redundance in about the time it takes to visit the men's room.

*   *   *   *   *

Then... oh, then... that awful moment with the board chairman when I saw the full fruit of corporate politics in action... "You know, old man, we think you're absolutely brilliant, but hell, everyone's brilliant around a place like this and these young guys don't carry around a lot of unnecessary mental baggage. Right?"

So there you have it. The story of my life in a few pages, ending in a bad joke. Because the "young guys" he mentioned were the Wiseass and his friends. Together, playing their dirty little political games, they had stolen my Germ Factory from me, and from that moment on, I despised them for it.

 chapter five

To hell with them. To bloody hell with them all. I did not choose to vegetate or to lapse into golf-playing senility. Had I spent over seventy years frantically digging for knowledge only to throw it away because someone said it was time?

I bought myself the biggest computer I knew how to operate and set up an office and small lab in the basement of our home. "You just watch me," I told Sara. "I'm going to make us a pill. One pill for you and one for me. And we're going to take those pills and sail off straight for La La land."

"You've finally blown it," said Sara. "You're over the edge. Let's take a trip to Greece."

Instead, I took my computer and modem and began searching the medical libraries and research laboratories until I was sure I'd sucked up about ninety-eight percent of the knowledge the world had about the process of aging.

And in a few weeks I had all this information organized in my computer and in my head.

You know what it amounted to? Almost absolute zero. Much of it worse than zero, because it was so obviously wrong. No one knew anything worthwhile about the aging process or how to reverse it.

You know why? Because no one who called himself a scientist would believe it could be done, so they never gave it a thought. Oh, they gave it lip service now and then, but no real work.

There were a few valid clues. Example: researchers at the University of Aarhus, Denmark, found that as our cells age the level of enzyme activity inside the cell recedes and protein synthesis begins to be inefficient, probably because elongation factor 1 alpha doesn't do its catalytic job as well as it should.

So this was the type of thing I thought about. I grew human cells (borrowed from Sara and myself) in a culture medium and confirmed what researchers had already noted: cells from an older person take much longer to reproduce themselves than they used to. So, what else is new? Everything about my body took longer than it used to.

This was the genesis: research and quiet contemplation, all on aging. I had not yet become frantic.

Sara and I did go to Greece and to many other places she picked out. We did have vacations, almost like normal people, and I think it was a good time for her. I worked only eight or ten hours a day and took most weekends off.

When I think of those years I remember especially our happy times with Sara at the piano and the two of us trying to sing an off-key and wandering duet with half the words forgotten and filled in with "hmmm, hummm, dedummms."

Sara played rather mechanically, remembering what little she had been taught decades ago when she was a girl on the Cape. Her left hand would pump up and down like a piston while the right hand fumbled for the tune, but then she knew this as well as I did and to me it was brave of her to play at all when we both knew she didn't play well and really it was glorious, the two of us making bad but sweet music together and to hell with technique.

And sometimes we'd put on a record and dance around the living room and out back onto the patio with Sara humming in my ear and that was our business, too, and no one else's and if it made us an average, stumbling couple, it made us happy, too, and that was what was important.

So it went, for several years. I never once visited the Germ Factory (I knew I wouldn't be welcome) and my own little basement lab may have looked pitiful to an outsider but my computer and I were moving right along, following my own ideas, and I didn't have to argue or justify or explain anything to anyone.

I could have injected Sara with collagen to smooth out wrinkles or developed a hormonal cream for her, but why? Sara could still turn heads on the street even in her seventies. Maybe she wasn't a young girl anymore, but my Sara had style, so what's a wrinkle or two?

It came down to this: out of the two thousand or so different kinds of protein found in the living human cell, at least one of them, more probably a group of them, cause us to age. I was out to find that bit of protein and zap it with something to eliminate it or change it. It was a nice theoretical exercise and I was well along with the work, fairly happy with my progress and wishing I could publish about ten papers on various aspects of aging I had already worked out. But of course I was too far outside the professional establishment to do that now. And then something happened.

Sara got old. Just like that, it seemed to me. In one blink, I who had expected to live with Sara in bliss forever saw the end of life and saw that it was near.

She was sunning herself beside the pool when I came up out of my basement lab for lunch one day, eyes closed and peacefully relaxed, I thought, until I realized that Sara was asleep.

In her sleep, in the bright sun, I could plainly see what I had not allowed myself to see for some time now: Sara was not the girl I had carried in my mind for over fifty years. Something had happened.

I began, deliberately, as any scientist would, to study her as she slept. I noted the pouched belly, the slumped shoulders with a bit of a hump in back, the wattled neck, the deep lines around the mouth, the purple veins, the knobby knees, the thin rough skin at elbows and heels, the thousand little flaws of skin she normally covered with makeup, the yellow teeth that showed as she slept, mouth slightly parted, the irregular sound of her breathing, the black hair now white and so thin that pink scalp showed.

I looked at Sara, I thought about my years of orderly and unhurried theoretical work on aging, and I said to myself, "Oh, you fool!"

Sara woke. She opened her still-beautiful eyes and looked directly at me, knowing that I had been staring. "Now you know.," she said. "How do you like being married to a crone?"

Soon after, Sara began to get sick. That winter she caught a cold that wouldn't quit, then slid into pneumonia. Hospital. Oxygen. Gradual recovery, but little sparkle left.

After that, a broken hip. A slow mend, using an aluminum walker. Then another illness, then another. The two of us lived in doctors' offices, filled prescriptions, bought thermometers and bedpans, hired nurses. No matter what the season, life became winter for us.

"But you're a doctor, doctor. Why don't you do something useful!" said Sara.

Sara's problems drove me back to the Germ Factory, back to the one place where there was a chance to lick this thing, even though any responsible scientist would tell you it was completely impossible.

I knew it was impossible too, of course. But I had one thought that gave me slim hope: this thing that Sara had didn't seem like a natural condition to me; this age business acted more like a disease. And a disease could be cured.

$$*\quad *\quad *\quad *\quad *$$

I checked my watch. Just over an hour now, and it would take me thirty minutes to drive there. Oh, the hell with waiting! I'll go now, spend the rest of the time fooling around near the gate.

So I grabbed my lunch box, turned off the lights, and headed for the garage, filled with tense anticipation and hope.

chapter six

I had traded my Buick for a Ford van and now, two years later, still wasn't used to it.

So, aged seventy-nine and trying to pass for a young sixty-three, I drove away from our suburban home, then a dozen miles down a secondary highway that was deserted at this hour, and then off an exit ramp to a private road with clipped shrubbery on each side (I had insisted on spending the money for this beautiful approach road years ago and this evidence of 'waste' was one of the things the Wiseass had used against me) and then to the final dramatic turn in the road that revealed the full view of the magnificent group of hi tech buildings I called "the Germ Factory."

There was still a few minutes to wait until the magic hour when I would be admitted. Then I would have time to take fifteen years off my appearance and get to work on the graveyard shift.

So first, as I did every night, I parked the van on the road shoulder at that last dramatic turn and admired the Germ Factory.

It was almost exactly as I had dreamed it, years ago, poring over architectural drawings. Beautiful. Clean. In scale. It filled the landscape. Eleven buildings, all connected by covered walkways and corridors, totaling just over a million square feet of research and manufacturing space.

Inside were miles of stainless steel piping, acres of fermentation vessels, media vessels and harvesting systems. After a lifetime of work in the field I could never completely believe that our cumbersome equipment could really touch and control the microscopic bits of human matter that were our raw materials. But of course we could control them in a crude sort of way, and every day, every month, our abilities to change and control life forms grew less crude.

Do you remember the race to clone and reproduce human insulin? It was a two year effort for teams of scientists willing to work all night, to sleep an hour on a sofa and work again, to scheme and compete red eyed and unshaven against other teams

26

in other labs and to finally win when winning meant merely to have the single drop of clear fluid in the bottom of an Eppendorf tube need hours of testing before anyone could prove it was actually human insulin. An extremely undramatic appearing revolution. But a real revolution, nonetheless. A major revolution.

And today that whole two year struggle could be reproduced in two weeks. Today we have super computers to model the newly desired product and gene machines to help us construct it.

Human genes. Monoclonal antibodies. Recombinant DNA. Marvelous pharmaceutical materials. The stuff of dreams. Also the stuff of hard, cold, manufacturing cash, because we at the Germ Factory had finally developed a product line that was the envy of the biotechnology world. We even had stockbrokers memorizing the names of our products so they could talk learnedly about the market prospects for alpha vs gamma interferon.

The "Germ Factory." Oh, how that name bothered the brass. And I understood them. I even agreed with them. But to me it was a term that cut everything down to size.

There was the company PR man whom I knew dammed well had been sent to see me by the Wiseass. It was almost funny to see the poor bugger try, against all his PR training, to disagree with a superior.

"Dr. Camp," he said, rubbing his lips nervously, "About this ... term ... this name of yours for the, ah, facility here ... we feel ... that is the management (then realizing that I was management, too) that is the corporate management feel rather strongly, sir, and they've asked me ... to inform or rather to request that you refrain in public, particularly in public but in private too if you don't mind, that is to say it is imperative, sir, that you do, or rather do not, use that term (I'm sure it is just a joke of yours, sir, but you realize how it may sound to the uninitiated) Germ Factory."

There. He finally had it out. And I knew. It was a PR man's nightmare. It was the word, "germ," that bothered them. The "factory" part they probably liked. With a public already scared witless by every mention of biotechnology (but with the same public as hungry as misers for the benefits) it was totally irresponsible for the senior scientist of the facility to use a scary, old fashioned and unscientific word like "germ." But, somehow, I liked the sound of it.

Is that one of the differences between young and old? Would a young man immediately adapt, start using whatever jargon management wanted? Perhaps. But it wasn't just dumb inflexibility. I remembered when everything microscopic was a "germ." When there were simple names for simple concepts and there was the illusion that knowledge was both true and permanent.

I was so conscious of how things change today, of how the words this young PR man so desperately wanted me to use would soon be superseded by other words, other concepts. I had invented many of the things he wanted me to say, and knew that he barely understood them, yet I resisted using his words because I knew how temporary this new knowledge would be, how soon new changes were to come. How much easier to put all this newly bloomed science into its proper perspective with one sweep of the hand by calling this the "Germ Factory."

The Germ Factory glowed brilliantly in the dark. It was like the model I had pored over years ago, tracing with my finger where each research lab would go, how the manufacturing space would be arranged to give us both efficiency and flexibility, deciding where critical reagents would be stored and even where broom closets would be needed.

Broom closets. How clever of me to know about them now.

chapter seven

I had a sudden flash of Sara on her sick bed, choking on her own saliva, her eyes frantically searching for her husband of more than fifty years, crying the eternal wifely cry: "Where is he when I need him?"

Because she knew … she had spent a lifetime watching the slowness of progress in research labs.

Oh, yes. Sara understood it all. And she understood that her dying body wouldn't wait.

But I knew a thing or two she didn't. Certainly I had skipped a lot of steps and assumed a lot of assumptions and guessed a lot of guesses to arrive at the pale blue liquid I had bubbling away in a fermentation vessel down below in the back corner of Building Sixteen, but I had reason for hope. After so many years of doing this, I knew what I knew. Or, if I didn't, I knew that I'd never know.

I gave the ignition key a twist and the van obediently began to carry me down the hill to the guard house, where I had to show my pass.

The guard, with his blue uniform and blue and gold hat (oh, how we submit to authority even when we know the authority is only a rent-a-cop) leaned out of his little building and took my pass for a quick but thorough examination. I kept my face in the shadows of the van. There was no need to impress him with my age even if I did have a valid pass.

The guard gave me back my pass with a quick smile and a jerk of the head that said "enter, friend," because the pass had a light blue background and that meant I was a blue collar worker, like himself. A scientist would have had a white paper pass. My blue pass with my new name, Armond Champignon (taken directly out of the phone book because it resembled my own closely enough for me to remember it) and my new profession, janitor, and my new age, sixty-three, got me onto the grounds of the Germ Factory every night for the 1AM to 5AM shift, when there were very few eager young scientists at work.

I drove to the employee parking lot and found a spot in the shadows, away from the nearest street light.

Then I unpacked my lunch box, leaving the peanut butter sandwich and the apple on the seat beside me. I took the empty lunch box and its empty and carefully sterilized vacuum bottle with me as I left the van to head for Building Sixteen.

That lunch box and vacuum bottle had carried away months of work. Each morning I took samples directly home for evaluation and testing with my fruit flies and mice.

Just before 1AM I was in the employee locker room, crouched in a toilet stall with my makeup kit trying to remove the last fifteen years from my face, when the outer door opened.

A voice I recognized immediately said: "That you, Armond? That you foolin' around in there?"

It was Fred. Fred Rainy, Master Janitor and financial opportunist.

"You know what day this is, Armond? You know why I'm smilin' and grinnin' like an ape, Armond?"

"Sure, Fred. It's payday. Just give me a minute." I finished my makeup with a few deft swipes and stepped out of the toilet stall. There was Fred, as he was every week at this time, with his hand out and with a look of almost voluptuous greed on his face.

I put the small stack of twenties into his hand and watched his fist close on them like a snake swallowing a frog. "It's nice, Armond, it's truly nice to have you do that!"

So, Fred got paid at the Germ Factory and he got paid again by me. What he did with the extra money was his own close-lipped secret. Did he have a woman on the side? Was he a hunting freak? A fisherman? Who knows. Maybe he just liked to have a wad of greenbacks in his jeans.

Fred took out a pack of Camels and shook one cigarette up and stuck it into a corner of his mouth and lit it. Then he squinted at me above the smoke and said what I knew he would say because he said it almost every night.

"Don't tell me!" he said, "I don't want to know, you know? You could just be an old guy playing with his chemistry set for all I know, you know? But you be careful. I need this job, even if you don't.

30

"I tell you, Armond, the powers-that-be around here would shit a squealing worm if they knew you were foolin' around with the equipment. They truly would, they'd shit a squealing worm."

That was his big expression. I heard it almost every night and twice on Fridays, which were paydays.

I left Fred, still shaking his head in awe at the size of my transgression. Truth was, the powers-that-be would have been almost as appalled by his cigarette but there was no way to make him believe that.

He would do my part of the sweeping and cleaning. That, and his silence, were his part of our bargain. It left me free to "Play with my chemistry set." And for my part of the bargain, I had promised feverently that, if caught, I'd swear that I never saw Fred before in my life.

"Just you remember, Armond," he had cautioned me, "They catch you foolin' around I'm going to swear I never laid eyes, you understand what I'm saying? Oh, that's right. Who he? I'll say. Who the hell is this guy, what's he think he is, breaking in like that? That's what I'll tell 'em, Armond, you just bet I will, so you just watch your ass, Armond."

And then again: "You know what you're doing in there? You're not messing up any of the chemicals, are you? OK, you say so, I believe you. I do believe you. How about handing over another couple of those twenties just so my mind'll rest easier!"

Laboratory Number Six was dark except for a few red night lights but there was nothing unexpected about a janitor flipping on a light as needed and I could get around very well in the half dark, anyway.

For I had become the phantom, not of the opera, but of the Germ Factory. Armond, the ghostly janitor/biologist, flitting here and there, as it were, with all facilities under his control.

I watched the production reports, the personnel files, the vacation notices, the laboratory assignments and particularly the progress reports of various scientists and used them all.

What's this? Visiting Doctor Oconawa is coming from Japan on the sixteenth to spend six weeks with us on the oncogene trigger project?

31

Why this means I can safely tie up the three 10-liter fermenters I've been needing. All I have to do is scrawl L. Oconawa and the notation, Project MT-56786, on the card attached to each fermentation vessel, and no one would dare touch them.

Oh, I knew who was doing what, and exactly how I could fit in. I could even order special reagents or plasmids or special lab equipment if needed. One night I'd fill out a request form, using a likely name and project number, and the next night or so, there would be my requested product, waiting for me. Very efficient. Very nice.

Thank God they pamper research scientists, I thought. In any other industry each request would be reviewed by a moneyman or committee, but here, no one who was not a scientist knew enough to challenge those who were and they were all afraid to try.

I was deep into the night's work, totally engrossed, when the door opened suddenly and Fred shuffled in. "Hey, Armond, I want you to watch it tonight, there's trouble, maybe."

"Oh, Christ, Fred, you're smoking that cigarette in here again. I've told you, this is a clean room. It's special. You just can't imagine…"

"Clean, shit. That ventilator takes it all away. See?" He flicked the ash into a nearby lab sink and held the cigarette up for an exhaust fan to pull the smoke away.

"Listen, anyhow, I saw a guy wandering around and he wasn't a worker. I mean he had a suit and tie on, what's he doin' here, two-thirty in the goddamned morning with a suit and tie?"

I didn't discount the danger. But my blue liquid was dripping steadily into a beaker and I was literally finished.

If I had nothing, Sara was dead and I was an ancient. But if I had what I thought I might have … ?

The blue liquid had become an end in itself. The holy grail of biochemistry. There had been indications from previous attempts. Exciting indications. Exciting enough to put my face on TIME magazine again if I had been a legitimate researcher with time to prove my claims.

Watching the slow drip, drip, drip, I fished in my wallet and found a couple of twenties for Fred. "Go find him for me. Go see where he is and keep an eye on him. Give me a few more minutes and I'll leave for the night, OK?"

Why tell Fred that his cash cow was leaving, not for the night, but forever, no matter what happened?

He took my money, gave me a huge conspiratorial wink and left to bird-dog the suit and tie man.

Do you have any idea how complicated the cloning process is? Let me give you a quick look. First off, you have to know you're working blind. You're like a person who goes into an absolutely dark and soundproof room, then sticks his hands into a black velvet box, and tries to assemble a watch, using tools he's never seen before. Oh, yes, he wears thick gloves, too. Can't feel a thing. It has to be done by sheer reason, with none of the senses involved. And no one will ever tell you when you go wrong. In fact, no one will even agree you've assembled the watch until you prove it to them through a series of tests.

No. No. That's crude. Let's try again. Forget the watch allusion. Let's talk simple molecular biology.

Start with DNA. That's short for deoxyribonucleic acid—or the molecule that hides inside every one of our cells and gives us our genetic blueprint. Then, break the structure of this DNA molecule into its chemical sub units and you get adenine, thymine, guanine and cytosine. Call them A T, G, and C for short. You can call these 'bases' too, because they form a structure—the arms of the famous double helix described by Crick and Watson only a few decades ago.

The bases (the A,T,G,& C) form part of the nucleotide. Surprisingly enough, the A joins only with the T and the G only with the C. But simple or not, these four sub units combine in different combinations with sugar and phosphate to form a minute part of the structure of the double helix shape that is DNA.

So, there are maybe two or three billion base pairs of DNA in every human cell and a small segment of this DNA, which contains the coded instructions for making a particular bit of protein, is called a "gene."

Now the important thing to a genetic mechanic like me is that these base pairs are joined together by a chemical bond that can be broken and rejoined.

33

You can cut-and-paste. Or you can zip and unzip the double helix and tack on a particle to create something new.

Let's say you want to join one gene to another to create a new hybrid. First, you "cut" by adding a chemical, say cyanogen bromide, that will cut the links in your amino acid chain. Understand now, you don't see them cut, you can't measure them cut, you have to take it on imagination and faith.

Then, you do what's called a "sticky-end procedure." Every molecule of RNA has a tail of at least a hundred Adenines, or "A's" and if you present this to a long string of "T's" the "A's" and "T's" grab each other like "sticky ends" and form a new bond. That's pasting.

Now comes the fun part: you can take these cut and pasted snippets and insert them into special bacteria (called plasmids) that will grow and reproduce whatever you inserted. The bacteria has to be specially engineered itself, of course, to do just this one job. A science in itself.

Finally (and remember, this is just a short, oversimplified explanation) you can put your plasmid, with the newly engineered gene inside, into a culture medium and it will reproduce billions of times and reproduce whatever you have implanted in it.

I can hear Sara now. "Oh! Do give it a rest, Andy! Who wants to hear that kind of heavy technical stuff? I don't know how you stand it, but I know I don't want to stand it, so let's knock it off. Talk about something real for a change."

Maybe Sara's right. I've told you enough to bore you and not enough to do you any good. So, let's move on.

Tonight's pale blue liquid was my last chip in this mortal game.

Three times in as many months I had taken home a new protein that I had been certain was the final solution to Sara's problem. And three times my final solution had failed.

Oh, I had created enormously healthy fruit flies, all living well beyond expectation. I had old white mice in a cage in the basement who weren't old at all, from the way they frisked around, twitching their whiskers and chasing after young girl-mice.

But nothing I had brought home had touched Sara's illness.

"Are you sure?" I had pleaded with her. "Don't you think you feel a little better? I think your color's better. Don't you? Aren't you breathing easier?"

She had used all of her carefully controlled breath to answer, pushing the words out in a rush. "You should have married a mouse," she said. "Or a fruit fly."

And yet, everything I knew, everything I'd learned in all my years, told me I was on the right track, and after each failure I had carefully built up new hope in my mind for the next trial, because without hope all was finished.

And now I had convinced myself that this time success was indeed certain, that all I had needed was time to make small adjustments. Time to examine and refine. Time for trial and error and retrial. Time to make sure of each of the many, many steps in the process.

Time.

As I came closer to the end I had become secretive, with elaborate visions of someone finding a trace of my work and duplicating it—as they well could if they found it and knew its importance.

So, I had gotten into the habit of elaborate cleanups, starting with the soaps and rinses provided in the lab and ending with a wipedown of the complete lab area with a strong solvent I had brought in weeks before.

My blue liquid had finished dripping. All I had to do was take it and go, as soon as I finished the final cleaning. First, the reactor vessel, then all the glassware, and then...but damnit, there was Fred, at the door again.

"Fred? What is it this time? Well, come in. Don't just stand there." I was scrubbing the lab table top with solvent from a big beaker.

"YOU!" It was a top-of-the-lungs scream. There was nothing else to call it. "You old bastard!" I knew I'd find you in here!"

I whirled around, cleaning cloth in hand, and there in the doorway in his suit and tie was the Wiseass.

The Wiseass! At a time like this! My thoughts flew to the blue liquid. Protecting it, getting it safely away, became my only concern.

I reached for my thermos and turning my back on the Wiseass, began, as carefully as I could, to pour the blue liquid into it, even as he walked into the room.

I knew the Wiseass would stop me if he saw. I knew it, because in the world where he and I had lived for so many years the sight of a man pouring a liquid from one glass laboratory container to another was ordinary, nothing to stop the eye. But the sight of a laboratory liquid being poured into a thermos, well that was something else. So, I was hoping to get, oh just the few ounces that Sara and I would need into the thermos quickly, while he was still walking towards my sheltering back, then I would do whatever I could with the remainder later. Desperation time.

"Well, Clifford, how are you," I said, as he approached. I had my few ounces of blue liquid in the thermos, my insurance ounces and I quickly put the thermos aside and turned to face him, hoping that the beaker of blue liquid wouldn't attract his eye because to me it was the precious child in the presence of the hungry wolf. I could only save it by misdirection.

The Wiseass, a.k.a. Clifford Gilbert, was still incredulous. "You! It is you, isn't it? Even though I knew I'd find you here I still can't believe you'd be so stupid as to be here. What in the hell are you doing?"

The Wiseass was medium tall and slim, just slightly round shouldered, had legs that bent backward at the knee and locked when he stood and had curly dark brown hair with a small bald spot in back. Long, drooping nose, blue eyes behind rimless glasses, and there you have it. Except you really don't. You don't know the Wiseass until you look at his mouth. It droops. His lower lip hangs and quivers when he talks. It looks as if he could suck it up if he wanted to, but he never seems to want to.

When I first knew him, when he was my meek-appearing slave assistant, before he became my assailant, I used to say to him constantly, "Suck up that lip. Suck it up or something will light on it."

I thought briefly of saying this again, just to get him so agitated that I could pour the rest of the blue liquid into my thermos, but thought better of it.

For once in your life, take it easy, Old Man, I thought. Go along with him. Mollify.

What followed was a sort of short, nasty old-home week. The Wiseass wanted me to know that he had done well, which I already knew because I had followed his progress like everything else in the Germ Factory.

He was now a group vice president, in charge of not only the Germ Factory, but six other plants.

Asked what I was doing, I grew vague. I wanted nothing, absolutely nothing of value to be left behind with the Wiseass. "Oh, I've been working on aging," I finally said.

"And doing a damned good job of it, to," he said, in one of his few attempts at humor. "You look like a goddamned arthritic turtle. Bent back, beaky nose, watery eyes, old wrinkled skin. Man, you've got the old age disease and you've got it bad."

Actually, I thought he had said it exactly right: the old age disease. I had taken the point of view from the first that age was not a natural condition to be borne but a disease to be cured.

"If you want to see old, I'll show you old," I told him.

"Look." I took wad of paper toweling and began wiping the makeup from my face and neck, then I turned and gave him a close-up profile.

"Disgusting!" He drew his breath in sharply. "You ought to go hide."

"Its all right," I told him. "People are so used to the way old people look they don't even see us anymore. We become invisible."

Then, to stall for time while I thought, but also because I was truly curious, "Why are you here? Did you come looking for me?"

"Yes," he answered. "At first I couldn't believe it was you. But then I used pure inductive reasoning. You know, if you find ape droppings, you look for an ape. QED. And, old man, did you leave your droppings! A few months ago I thought I picked up your scent, but I said, Oh, naw ... it can't be. But lately ... well lately it was as if you didn't give a damn, you just left your sign all over the place and we couldn't miss it."

"Perfectly harmless, Clifford," I said, "You know I'd never do the company harm."

"No harm? No harm! You've been dabbling, Old Man," said the Wiseass sternly, in that adult-to-child tone of voice that those under fifty use to those over seventy. "You've been sticking your damned old nose into our affairs, you've been playing God with our work (he began to get short of breath at the thought) and you've done it for the last time. The last time, do you hear?"

I tried to demur, but he wouldn't have it. He wasn't through. He made an effort to be calm, rational, to explain it to me in a way that my simple-minded old-man brain would understand.

"Do you remember the postdoc, Henry Fowles? Remember his neuropeptides project? What was it, the memory hormone, ACTH? It was only two weeks ago, remember?"

I tried again to mollify. I didn't give a damn about Fowles and his Adrenocorticotrophic hormone. It was childish, anyway. Fowles was simply stumbling along. They used to say a few years ago that I had golden hands because of my touch in the research lab. There are about two dozen things that can go wrong with the cloning process, most of them so subtle that you don't even know when you've screwed things up. And I seldom did. My hands seemed to know the right thing to do, even with impossibly delicate lab procedures. But if my hands had been golden, Fowles' were made of lead and he had a brain to match.

"Oh, sure, Clifford. Good man, Fowles. What's the problem?"

"The problem? The problem! The problem is that you stuck your dirty finger into his project, didn't you? Didn't you, Old Man? You're the one who left that written critique in his workbook, didn't you? Don't say you didn't! Think I don't know your style by now? Think I don't know exactly how you say things? How almighty pushy you can be?

"You did it to Martin Beck, too, with his Lymphokines project. You have been behind the scenes spying and tinkering with other people's work like some kind of goddamned super scientist, getting in the way (the Wiseass was working up to a fine rage by now) and actually changing things. Why, poor Martin was just about to make a breakthrough in macrophage activating factor when you had the gall to pour his work down the sink and substitute some crap of your own."

Well, he did have me on that one. But what's the harm? My own research had already taken me way beyond what Beck was trying to do, so why not give him a little boost? I liked Martin.

"Perfectly harmless, Clifford," I said. "You know I'd never do the company harm. Besides, you'll be glad to know, this is my last night here. I was just about to take my things and walk out."

"Your last night? Your things? You old fool, you had your last night here years ago! What do you think you're doing here, anyway?"

I glanced at the pale blue liquid. It had become ineffably precious as I heard the Wiseass talk, because I knew, absolutely knew, that he would never let me simply take it and go.

"What am I doing here?" I turned my back on him again and reached for the thermos and the blue liquid, "Why, I'm just mixing up a little medicine for my wife. You remember Sara?"

I began, carefully, to pour, hoping he'd talk just a few more seconds. He did.

"Mixing up … what do you think this is, a goddamned cough drop factory? Oh no, I know what you used to call it: a Germ Factory. Well, that was stupid, but today, who cares?"

Then he switched his thought. "Do I remember Sara? Of course I do. Raunchy old girl. How is she?"

"Dying. Just days away, hours maybe."

"Well then, my God, she must be about eighty, like yourself, so I can't get excited. Besides, I used to have to kiss her ass because I had to kiss yours, but no more, old man, no more. Now, let's get you out of here before you get us both into trouble. My God, just imagine it, a senile old man here messing around with the most delicate, most important … hey! What're you doing? You think I'm too dumb to know you've been sneaking that stuff into your thermos? Think I'm blind or something? Now, what you're going to do is pour it out. All of it. Into the sink. Its just crap anyway, didn't you know that?

"Look at me," said the Wiseass. "I want you to see my face when I tell you. We found what you were working on. Oh, yeah, you thought you were so damned clever, but we found it and we fixed your wagon the same way you've been fixing ours."

I could feel an icy finger run down my spine. "Fixed my wagon?"

"Damned right, just like you did it to us. I went around this afternoon to Henry Fowles, he was the one who had been raising the most hell about your snooping, and I said, 'Henry, give me whatever crap you've got handy,' and he did. You know those garbage proteins? Those mistakes we all throw away? Those funny-looking structures with tails of human DNA on them? Those who-the-hell-knows-what-they-are things?"

I was beginning to sweat and feel dizzy. My ears were taking it in but my brain was refusing to process the information.

"So this afternoon, just before I left work, I poured a few ounces of Henry's junk into your culture. Who knows what it actually was that I put in? Who knows what you've got now? Whatever it is it certainly isn't what you think it is, so why don't you just pour it down the sink before I do it for you?"

My brain had reached a logical compromise: one half of it would listen, think, understand, know that my blue liquid had been violated and that Sara was dead. The other half, remembering the months and years of work, would refuse to understand anything. Whatever the blue liquid was or wasn't, it was all there was. So, very deliberately, I took the flask and began to pour the remainder of it into my thermos, ignoring the Wiseass.

"What are you doing, man … didn't I tell you? Are you getting so senile you don't you understand plain English?"

"Listen," said the Wiseass, as patiently as though he were explaining something to a child, "you've got to understand. I could have poured cyanide into your flask. I didn't. That would have been murder, don't you see? Besides, it could have caused me trouble. So I did what was right. I just erased the wrong you were doing. D'you understand?"

"You have no idea how wonderful my blue liquid was, Clifford. Did you even guess what I was trying to do? Did you know how close I was? Did you know what you destroyed? Maybe a cure for aging?"

He was filled with impatience.

"I don't care shit! The more wonderful you think your stuff was, the worse it was for me. If you were just a dabbling old fool it wouldn't matter, but you used to be good enough to be dangerous, and maybe you still are."

"Hey, listen. Think about it. Let's say you did have something. How would it look? We spend over a billion dollars a year for research here, you know? We've got our four main research teams, each with a major project, and they're broken down into sub groups and their goals are defined and we've got weekly progress reports and we've got corporate goals to meet and by God we're meeting them and we've got a system that employs hundreds of the world's best molecular biologists to say nothing of hemotologists and endocrinologists and God knows the long list of other specialists and we've got competition snipping at our heels and this is the real scientific world, man, where things are done and done right, with all the right paperwork and controls ...and here you come along a worn out old man, sneaking in at night and working as a goddamned janitor, a janitor yet, if you can believe it, and suppose you did come up with something? Suppose you did? What are we going to say? How do you think that makes us look?

"Are we going to hold a press conference and say, "Oh, by the way, our eighty year-old janitor just discovered a cure for aging? Is that what we're going to do? Huh? Can you just see me doing that? Can you see me going to my management and saying that? Do you think I'm stupid or something?"

"But, Clifford, the world needs..."

"Needs? What the hell does the world need? Another hundred million old people made to live longer every year? Do you know what death is? It is the wonderful way nature has of taking care of birth, the cleanup of the trash at the end. Don't you know that? When you get old and ugly and can't cut it anymore you die and that's it. Don't mess around with it.

"Of course I know that whatever you think you've got there can't really be real, but let's just pretend for the sake of argument that it really was whatever you thought it was and not just some old fart's dream, then it would be the most dangerous thing a man ever did. Understand? And besides, it was done outside our system, our establishment. So no matter what it was, to me it was nothing. Understand?"

"So, Clifford, if your management had asked you to work on a cure for aging, if it had been a real project on your agenda..."

"That would have been different. Stupid, maybe, but different. We could have put a team together, maybe had a little gradual success. It would have taken years, there would be papers published, lots of news items, Nobels awarded, that kind of thing. Sure, in the proper way it could have been legitimate. Still can be. We can work on it. Maybe we will. The stockholders would love it. A lot of them are old bastards, too rich to want to die, so they'd love it."

"Just no overnight success, eh, Clifford? No big break-throughs to change the world?"

"And not by any goddamned over-age janitor sneaking around at night! Now, that's it. You understand me? Now, I want that stuff. I want to pour it down this sink with my own hands and I want to see you walk out of here.

He came for me, arm outstretched to take my blue liquid. *"Give it to me!"*

But I whirled around, keeping my back to the Wiseass in a game of keepaway and continued pouring the last of the liquid into my thermos.

"Here! Gimmeethat! Whatever crap that is, its *our* crap, not yours, understand? You're *stealing* it, and I won't have it!" He danced around me and I kept shuffling around in a tight circle, one shoulder raised in protection as I poured the final bit of what should have been Sara's life into the thermos.

"I'm getting mad, now! I said *give* it to me," and he made a lunge as I whirled the thermos just out of his reach and screwed the cap down.

"You old bastard!" he screamed, "*Give* it to me" and this time he shoved my hip into one corner of the lab table and made a grab over my shoulder.

My hip hurt like hell. I went sick with pain and slumped to the floor, momentarily completely helpless. But I had the thermos tucked safely into the fold of my stomach. The Wiseass grabbed the second beaker I had left on the lab table in a fury and snatched it over my head so fast that a few ounces went flying behind him, while most of the remainder poured down over his head and over his shirt front.

"What *is* this?" he yelled. "Its strong. It stinks. What *is* it?"

"Acetone," I said. "I use it to clean the…"

"Acetone? You brought *acetone* into this biology lab? What are you doing, regressing? You think you're a paint chemist again? Is that it? Your second childhood?" He was practically screaming now. Outraged beyond endurance.

I was struggling off the floor, the pain receding but still for-midable, when the door opened and there was Fred, popeyed with anxiety, looking from one to the other of us, saying, "Oh, Jesus, oh, Jesus...," with the inevitable cigarette dangling from his lip, shedding grey ash.

"You!" Ordered the Wiseass. "Get him out of here! Get this old man out of here! And put out that stupid cigarette. Go on! Put it out! Right now!"

Fred was on automatic. He took a quick, nervous puff, then dropped the cigarette in a shower of sparks and poised a foot over it, then let out a little "ehh!" of astonishment as blue flame ran from the cigarette to the spilled acetone and then down the floor along the path of the spill, then up the front of the Wiseass to the top of his head.

Nice blue Wiseass, shimmering in silent flame.

For the first few seconds it looked as innocent as a home magic trick as the Wiseass glowed with the blue flame. Then his hair began to burn with a yellowish, crackling flame and the Wiseass began to beat himself over the head and around the face with frantic hands. When his clothes exploded in smoky red flames the Wiseass began to make muffled noises.

"Don't breathe," I told him. "Don't suck it down your lungs."

Useless advice. How do you not breathe when you're burning alive and filled with panic?

"Uh, Uh, Uh," choked the Wiseass.

"Oh, Lordy, Lord... do something, Armond..." said Fred, beside himself with anxiety, not knowing whether to take charge or run now that we'd both been revealed as suit-and-tie guys.

I did something, all right. I washed the last beaker in soap and then left it under the lab faucet with the water running, then I took the last of the acetone and poured it down the sink (oh, if I had only had the guts and the good sense to pour it over the burning Wiseass to finish the job, but I didn't. Frail humanity intervened over good judgment) then I searched the area carefully, patted my pocket for my note pad, which was there, and finally, absolutely certain that I could leave with no trace of my work left behind, I turned my attention to the burning Wiseass.

Ripping off my white lab coat (feeling the sharply painful arthritis in each shoulder and the neck as I did) I threw it around the still burning head and smothered the flame, then moved it down his body and smothered the last of the flame there. I think it was easy to put him out because his fire was about to burn out anyway. The human body does not a good torch make unless you keep adding fuel.

Soon the Wiseass was just a smoking, writhing, moaning body. He had fallen, first to his knees, then flat onto the floor, where I stripped off the remainder of his clothes.

Fred was still goggling. "He alive? Whatcha goin' to do?"

Good question, Fred. My plans for the evening had no place for this white, now pitifully vulnerable body with the blackened, greasy welts of burned flesh.

The face was the worst. After all, heat rises and flames shoot up and hair provides fuel. Eyebrows and eyelashes had gone with the rest of the hair and the facial skin had that soft, slippery look that said it could easily be wiped away, leaving raw meat.

Damn you, Wiseass, for leaving me with an ethical problem when I had other business.

"Look at me," I demanded, peering into his tightly closed eye slots, and when the Wiseass dutifully opened his lids the eyes appeared to be filmed over and useless. But I asked,

"Can you see me?"

First a moan, then rising terror. "Nooooo.....can't...am I? Am I blind? Glasses. Put my glasses on. Maybe…oh God, is there still a light on …?"

I really should have left him. Tragedy is all around us and even good people suffer agonies, so what's one more?

But I didn't. A fool is a fool is a fool.

I told Fred to go get my makeup case, in the locker room. I gave him the combination to my locker and told him I had something in the case that would help. This got rid of Fred, particularly because I had given him the wrong locker combination. He would be there, two buildings away, frantically twirling while I did what I had to do with the Wiseass.

I found a glass rod, and, opening my thermos, dipped into the blue liquid and removed a drop of it. "Hold still, you pitiful bastard," I told him, then used my thumb and forefinger to pry open first one eye, then the other, putting five or six drops into each eye.

Then I recapped the thermos and washed the rod carefully at the sink with some soap, all the while watching the Wiseass carefully.

I was not just trying to be kind. I had spent years despising the Wiseass and I had watched him burn in a cold fury, unwilling to help this man who had stolen my Germ Factory from me and had now destroyed the one chance Sara had to live. I was still the researcher doing an experiment. Would my blue liquid help? I no longer knew what it was. As I had originally made it, it contained a powerful growth factor that would have helped to cure burns, although that wasn't its purpose. But now? After the contamination? Who knows?

"Too bad you screwed up my stuff," I told the burned and writhing Wiseass. "It could have cured you, you know. I've got fruit flies at home that've been alive for months and they're so strong I have to keep them in a steel cage. I was really onto something and then you came along with your wiseass ways and ruined it."

His answer was a muffled grunt. Then he began to shake as if he were very cold and make little "Uh, uh, uh" sounds.

I peered at him intently, the old researcher watching his test subject for signs of change. For several minutes I saw nothing but burned and groaning Wiseass, but after a while my heart sank as I began to see his hair fall out, burned skin slough off, and a general worsening of his condition. "Another screw up," I muttered. *Must be that crap of Fowles' that he added.*

"You look like hell," I told the Wiseass quietly. "I'll make a phone call, get you into a burn center, they'll fix you right up, most likely."

I almost turned to go but out of the corner of my eye I caught the sight of several new brown hairs pushing their way up through the burned scalp like a patch of crocuses in the spring and saw what seemed to be new young flesh under the surface mess of blistery burned skin, and saw the milky white scum slide off the surface of each eyeball and collect in a small puddle in the corner of each eye, then run down the side of the nose as new eye-flesh glistened.

I realized I was seeing rapid, impossibly rapid, change as new flesh grew under the old flesh and pushed the burned skin aside. Black, greasy welts disappeared. Eyes opened and obviously saw. The body sat up and spoke to me.

"What the … what the … what have you done with me? Is that your stuff you gave me?"

45

Then I saw something completely upsetting. That lip, that dangling Wiseass lip, began to tighten and there was a subtle change in the entire mouth area that gave it a well made and pleasing look.

I felt fascination, holy joy, and complete terror, all at once. I was still a frail and arthritic old man with a secret that was no longer a secret. I was seeing my enemy grow stronger by the second and I understood even in that early moment that it would do no good to hit him over the head and run.

"You're naked," I said. "Its embarrassing for a vice president to be naked. Stay there, I'll get some clothes."

I grabbed my thermos and scuttled away as fast as I could scuttle. Would my remark hold him there? Of course not. But maybe it could buy me seconds, while he was still confused.

Besides, in the dark, with red night lights everywhere, I knew how to get around and knew exactly where I was going. He didn't.

I turned down corridors, seemingly at random, but always heading for the parking lot and freedom.

I ran, shuffled, stumbled my way through the complex until I opened the last door and was into the parking lot heading for the van when I heard the Wiseass's voice boom out from a dozen loudspeakers located throughout the complex: "Stop the old man! Stop and hold the old man!"

I made it to the van and crawled in like a grateful animal to its lair.

Hands shaking, almost brain-frozen with fear and anxiety, I poured about a spoonful from tonight's thermos of blue liquid into my palm. I had the strongest urge to toss it down my throat, but knew better. The stomach would digest this complex manmade protein as easily as it would a small bite of steak. This had to go directly into the blood and I had no hypodermic.

"*Stop the old man! A thousand dollar bonus to the man who stops the old man!*" The loudspeaker was at it again.

I threw back my head and half-poured, half-snuffed it up my nose where a complex of tiny surface blood vessels would absorb it.

My long sought blue liquid. Could it possibly do what I had already seen it do?

"*Stop the old man!*"

At first, I felt hunted, glancing around the parking lot, waiting for a door to burst open as they came after me, cringing at the voice from the loudspeaker, feeling my own body aches and conscious of my old-man vulnerability. But then, after a few minutes, I began to forget the outside world. I was like a man slipping into terminal drunkenness as I fell into a vortex of my own mind, my own body. I became totally occupied with self, a self in the midst of rapid change.

Outside reality disappeared completely as I began sloughing off old flesh. I put my hands to my head and felt the scalp give way, with my mat of gray hair coming loose like a cheap toupee. Oh, my God! I thought. *I'm peeling away to my skeleton!*

But then there was a massive itch all over my body as new flesh, new hair, sprouted under the old, and new muscles twisted and stretched.

Thank God I watched the Wiseass, I thought. *Or I'd die of terror before it was over.*

I was being reborn, and knew it. I was participating in every nuance of the change... a spectator at my own re-creation. But amidst all the wonderment, I was almost sickened by the smell and feel of the old flesh I was discarding.

After a time, things stopped. Is this *it?* I asked myself. Then let's find out what *it* is.

I got up from the floor of the van, oh, so lightly, and slipped into the front seat, behind the wheel, and sat there absolutely reveling in my new sense of wellness and strength, which still grew, moment by moment.

"You've died and gone to heaven, but you haven't died." I was chattering nonsense to myself. I had to chatter. I had to tell someone how I felt and there was no one to tell but me. I sat there describing to myself how my feet felt, how strongly my head sat upon my neck, (the neck that had just recently ached with calcified bone) and how my hands clenched and unclenched with obvious strength. And, strangely enough, as I began touring my body, feeling and testing every bone, muscle, nerve and piece of cartilage, I began rattling off their Latin names, learned almost forty years ago in anatomy class and I had thought, forgotten. My brain was whirling, whirling, thoughts flying impossibly fast, but in a chaotic, disjointed way. I was flying apart, I was coming together in a new whole, my brain catching up with my body in rapid change as I became a new being. I was a human kaleidoscope.

Hunger! Suddenly I was ravenous. There is no other word. It was not a weak-starving, but a strong, almost cruel demand for food. I wanted to eat the world.

I twisted the key to start the van and it came away in my hand, a limp lump of warm metal. Experimentally, I pinched a small part of the steering wheel and it, too, came away like unbaked dough.

Andy, you're impossibly strong, impossibly! My mind was running like a driven thing, sorting through possibilities in a way it never could before. I was in a fever of excitement, yet coldly analytical, and I felt that the change was still far from over. A small flash: thirty seconds ago I was the "old man," now I was "Andy." So, attitudes were changing, too. I was growing, growing, into…something.

But the hunger! It ruled me now. Quickly, I stripped away the ignition wires, twisted together the ones that energized the engine, gave the wheel a quick turn to break the ignition lock, then touched the ignition wires with the one that spun the starter and the van was alive, as well as ever.

How did you know how to do that? A flash of thought, then the immediate answer: *Oh, you always did. You just never needed it before.*

Carefully, carefully, telling my hands and feet to treat the van gently, I drove to the gate and the guard, where the order to "*Stop the old man*" still rang out from the loudspeaker on the outside post.

I drove up to the rent-a-cop, held up my blue paper pass with a finger carefully covering the photo and stuck my face out of the window and let him have a good look as I stared him down. I was prepared to deal with the guard if I had to, but he simply looked, shook his head and said: "Don't know who you are, young fella, but you sure as hell ain't no old man!"

He waved me on. I drove through the gate, up the winding road to the highway, and into the big world. When I was alone on the highway, in the middle of the warm black night, I began to howl in absolute delight. I turned on the overhead light, swiveled the rear view mirror to show my new young face, and simply revelled in what I saw. I stared at the backs on my hands, my muscular arms. I ripped open my shirt front and felt my body. It was hard. Hard and muscular. An absolute delight when one has been forced to accept aging flesh. I was driving wildly, howling, thumping myself, screaming just to hear the force of the scream, but above all my delight I felt that overwhelming hunger. I had never known anything like it.

Hunger! It demanded to be satisfied.

chapter eight

My right hand, searching across the seat of the van like a grazing animal, found the peanut butter sandwich and the apple I'd left there earlier and began to stuff them into my mouth as I drove.

Ahhh! That taste!

Every grain of peanut butter, every morsel of bread, every crunch of apple found their way into my senses, there to be registered, analyzed, savored and remembered, particle by particle. The smell! The texture! The very appleness of that apple!

More importantly, I was so aware of this peanut butter, this bread, this apple, becoming a part of me. As I ate I could feel the food going through a change in my stomach, could feel it rushing through my veins and creating new bone, flesh, sinew and skin. And that, I knew now, was the source of my terrible hunger: I was still in the process of rebirth.

My need for food was voracious, desperate. It was the hunger of absolute compulsion as the million-billion-trillion cells in my body each cried out for food.

My mind raced as I drove, trying to understand my new self. Experimentally, I pinched my thumb and forefinger together as hard as I could and saw the finger bones break, felt the broken ends grinding together.

Then, moments later, I saw and felt the bones knitting together again. So, my muscles were stronger than their supporting structure. I knew I would have to feed those bones. My body was crying out to me: "Yes, you're strong, but you're merely starting."

I floored the van. It was black night. Where would I find food? A few car lights came toward me, whooshed past, were swallowed up in the blackness. The van screamed, its endurance tested. My newly found hand-and-eye coordination kept it on the road when it would sooner have left and found a tree to crash against.

I howled from time to time. I howled just to hear the force of the howl. I couldn't get enough of my new self. I was starved for further revelation. It was maddening that I had to waste time driving.

The lights of Newport grew stronger. I veered off to the right, avoiding the city, then over the mile-long bridge to the island of Jamestown, then over the next bridge to the mainland, heading always west, toward Route 95 and Sara's Connecticut hospital.

Boring! How can I sit here and drive while I starve? No, not boring, maddening! Tedious! Where can I find food in the middle of the dark night? Should I jump out, run into a field and graze on the green grass like a cow? Stop at a farm house and break into the kitchen? Drive, Andy, drive! How fast will this box of sheet metal go?

Finally! The entrance to I-95. Lights. Cars and trucks zipping by. Civilization of sorts. Fooooood, damnit!

Then, up ahead, the soft glow of many lights. A truck stop! An all night truck stop. There will be food. Where there are truckers, there has to be food!

The van tore through the cool night air, shooting me as straight as an arrow towards that odoriferous grease-splattered kitchen that my mind and body craved.

I slid to a stop beside a herd of tractor trailer behemoths, then untwisted the ignition wires and let the van die while I raced to the door of the truck stop. It was a large one, well lit. Inside were perhaps two dozen truckers and a couple of late driving tourists gathered around a horseshoe-shaped counter. There were tables in a room to the side, but only one was occupied—by a couple with a small child. Three white-aproned waitresses toiled in the center of the horseshoe.

One of them glanced up as I slid onto a stool near her and I saw a small start of pleasure replace the weariness on her face as her eyes took me in. My mind, racing, racing, noted in passing that now I would always have this effect on women—and perhaps men, too. It would be the sheer animal strength and vitality that would attract them.

For my part, my racing brain saw this room full of eaters and servers almost as wax figures, moving impossibly slowly, seemingly impossibly slow-witted.

"Hamburgers-homefries-eggs-toast-coffee-steak-donuts-jam-jelly, whatever you've got, whatever's fastest, hurry, hurry, please move, honey, don't stand there why don't you move?" I blurted it out and she didn't move.

She slowly, slowly poised her pad and pencil "What did you say?" Smiling prettily, anxious to please, but confused. "Could I have that again, one thing at a time?"

"Hamburgers. Hamburgers," I said, getting off the stool. "Whatever the cook has on the grill. Whatever he can put on the grill. As many as you can, as fast as you can. And milk. A gallon of milk. I need lots of milk."

"He needs milk for his ittle bones," said a trucker across the horseshoe, smirking to his neighbor.

"Damned right," I muttered. "My bones need milk. Please hurry!"

The waitress was writing, ever so slowly, lips pursed in concentration.

"How's about I give you five or six *glasses* of milk? I wouldn't know how to charge for a whole gallon."

It was too much. I couldn't wait like this. Everyone was looking, now. Jaws had stopped masticating. The truckers had a show to watch. Show, hell. I'd give them a show.

I turned to the trucker on my right, who was about to fork in his first bite of scrambled eggs until I stopped his hand as gently as I could.

"Wait, friend. I need this," I told him. I can still see his look of astonishment. It was a red, wind-roughened face with features set in a scowl of permanent aggressiveness. Here was a man who had looked at the world and decided that he would need to fight it all the way. And perhaps he did have that need. But not tonight.

His scrambled eggs were overlaid with bacon. Glorious, greasy, nose-wrenching bacon. Eggs covered with carefully spaced flecks of black pepper. Dancing little grains of salt still visible where he had sprinkled them. Toast, soaked in melted butter and cut into triangles and stacked on the rim of the plate.

To him, it was breakfast. To me, it was my hope of heaven. I had to have it and I took it, tilting the plate towards my mouth and pouring it in, guiding the flow of food with my fingers as my jaws worked faster than the trucker could watch. My whole movement must have been a blur to him.

"Thank you, I said to him, "Thank you, thank you." I gave a little nod and a smile as I handed him back his empty plate.

Then I found myself going from man to man around the horseshoe table, giving a smile and a short apology to each man as I took his food and sucked it in. "Sorry," I muttered over and over, like an incantation, trying to mollify the truckers so I wouldn't have to hurt them when I took their food.

They watched, first fascinated, then angry as I went from man to man, shoving whatever food they had into my eager mouth, chewing, swallowing, smiling, taking, moving on to the next, feeling the food become me, each bite crying out for a new bite, each gain in strength demanding new food for new strength.

I realized suddenly that I was covered in truckers. They clung to my back, pulling at my clothes, kicking my legs, hitting the back of my neck with balled fists, swearing as creatively as they could, and as I moved from place to place scooping up food they moved with me in an ever-growing pileup of outraged men.

"Sorry," I told them again and again, and "pardon me," as I caught yet another trucker with food and gently took it from him, trying not to damage what I already thought of as frail, tender humanity.

It was over soon. Everything around the horseshoe had been eaten. Shouting, "I thank you all!" to the truckers who still clung to me, I started for the kitchen, dragging them behind me like a walking football pileup.

On the way, I saw the couple with the child and thought, Spare them. Let them eat in peace.

But then I saw the expression on the child's face, a little girl of about eight or nine, and what I saw there made me walk toward them. Because she absolutely reeked of pouty self assurance. The man, her father, shrank back, his eyes filled with confusion as he saw me dragging my weary but still violent clutch of truckers towards them. The wife's face was the mirror of her child's, with the same greedy self assurance. In it I could see the look that I had already come to understand. She was attracted. I was repelled by her look of cunning.

Why do you bother? I thought. *Leave them. Snatching food from a baby is beneath you. Leave them.*

But somehow, I couldn't. Something in that eternal spoiled brat face demanded that I answer it, so as gently as I could I bent, putting my face directly into the child's face as I ran my fingers gently down her small arm to her hand and pried open the fist that held a hamburger.

"Thank you, Missy, thank you," I said, eating the hamburger with the same blinding speed as the rest of the food, then smiling directly into her now red, screaming, outraged face I gave her a long slow wink and left her to her fury.

Then I continued on my way to the kitchen, where I brushed aside the cook and started clearing off the griddle with a spatula, raking eggs, steaks, hamburgers, homefries and bacon all into large platters.

While this cooled, I found the mashed potato pot and threw in a pound of butter, a shaker of salt and another of pepper. Then I stirred it with a wooden paddle and began to eat. Oh, God, it was good! Spoon it in, spoon it in, a full pot of mashed potatoes went down the hungry red path, disappearing faster than my hangers-on could believe and digested and made a part of the new Andy just as quickly. I glanced at my belly. No bulge, it was as flat as ever, no matter how much I ate and there was always room for more because my body digested it immediately.

My audience grew very quiet and one at a time they began to back away and watch the eating, anger forgotten, replaced by fear as they understood that they could never understand what they saw. The speed and the sheer volume of food eaten were totally beyond them.

I finished the potatoes and turned to the heaping platters of partly grilled foods. "You don't have to watch"' I told my truckers. "This will be messy."

But they did watch, just as a gang will watch a fight or a rape, the more disgusting the better. Their eyes were wide and their jaws clamped shut in silent awe as they watched the platters of greasy food disappear.

Oh, I was growing inside! It was lovely!

The storage room! There was a ton of food I hadn't eaten!

Luckily I had the van. While my gawkers gawked I ran out of the back door of the kitchen, ran to the back of the van, picked it up by the frame and dragged it, wheels protesting, to the back of the kitchen. Then I opened the van's back door and began loading up cases of canned goods and crates of vegetables from the store room.

"Don't worry," I shouted to anyone who wanted to hear, "I'll send you a check tomorrow. What do you think? A thousand? Two thousand? I'll send a check. Go home. There's no more food. Go home. I'll send a check."

I loaded every scrap of edibles I could find. The van was sagging. I did leave, purposefully, the freezer full of raw meat. I was not yet ready to see myself gorging on raw frozen meat like a jungle predator. Maybe it would come to that. I hoped not.

"Thank you all! Thank you all! Sorry for the trouble! I'll send money!" I was babbling, I knew. They stared, eyes round, every man, every woman as quiet as a corpse, watching this strange man as he moved, almost a blur of speed to them, packing his van with their food.

I put a case of fresh, ripe tomatoes on the seat beside me, then ripped off the top of the crate, got a gallon of mayonnaise out of the back of the van, spread handfuls of this on the tomatoes, shook on salt and pepper, then licked my fingers clean and selected a big, juicy tomato, well smeared with mayonnaise.

I popped it whole into my mouth and sat there in the front seat, my audience just outside the van and still staring at my every move, and savored the taste.

Oh, my God it was good! Tears streamed out of my eyes. Until now I had eaten for the sake of filling myself, noticing the taste but subordinating it to the satisfaction of life-building fuel flowing down my throat. Now it was pure sensation. Greed fulfilled. I allowed myself no other thought but that tomato taste. I shut out my staring audience, shut out the lights, the warm air, the sight and feel of the van and the very earth itself to concentrate on each tomato alone.

I ate and I worshipped.

After a long while, I gave a wry smile and a wave to my still attentive audience and started the van again. Slowly, letting only a small part of my mind and body control the van, I drove onto the highway and continued south toward the city where Sara lay in her hospital bed. I drove at a reasonable eighty miles per hour through the warm and pleasant night air, eating tomatoes. Glorious tomatoes. Devoting my vast and growing consciousness to the tomato at hand, I ate one after another after another until the crate was empty and the lights of the city ahead were upon me.

Suddenly I was assailed by guilt. How could I keep forgetting Sara like this? How could I trade her life for a tomato? How could I take hamburgers from little girls? I floored the accelerator and let the van scream its way from a comfortable eighty to a quavering ninety-four, which seemed to be all the engine could possibly do.

What could be wrong with me? "I'm coming, Sara!" I shouted into the wind, knowing it sounded melodramatic and childish, but needing to hear myself say it anyway just to cut the guilt. It seemed to me that as I grew stronger, faster, younger, other people grew less important in my mind and Sara, even Sara, became a dream-person who was outside my new reality.

"Nooooo!" I shouted out of the window of the racing van, "I'm coming, Sara!"

But my mind said to me softly, almost sneakily, "What's all the shouting about? A sick old woman?"

"Shut up, Andy!" I said back. "Don't even think it!"

I swerved the van into an exit ramp and then onto a bypass road to avoid the city and floored it once again, hearing the anguish of its engine, feeling the grip of its tires on the road, feeling the fragile sheet metal body flutter and sway. The need for speed was a reflection of my own need to use my new body, my new mind, to escape the pace of the world as I had always known it. And it was a frantic need to get to Sara's hospital room before she slipped away … or before my own tricky mind found a new thought to play with and despite all my resolve forced me to desert Sara altogether while I followed my mind's new eye. I was beginning to be like a man in a dream, made to follow a sequence that made no sense… except possibly to the master-dreamer.

Who the hell are you, Andy Camp? What have you done to yourself? Are you some superman out of the mind of Fredrich Nietzche? Are you straight out of the funny papers? Or are you just a vastly improved model of old Doctor Camp?

 chapter nine

The moon was gone. The night was aging. The van roared through blackness on an almost empty road. A loom of lights glowed on my left as I circled the city. I was headed generally in the direction of Sara's hospital bed, but I was once again losing the strong sense of urgency that had driven me for so long. Sara's sickness receded into the background of my mind as I began to lose control. It was as though a light bulb had been turned off, whether I liked it on not.

I found a wide shoulder in the road and slid to a stop, killing the van's engine, knowing that to have driven even a few more moments would have been to risk disaster.

I opened the door and fled into the darkness, finding an open field, where I stood, spraddle-legged, head whirling, as confused as a falling-down drunk. I began to fly apart like an exploding nova and then come back together again only to repeat the explosion.

What? What? How could this be happening to the superman I had recently been? I fell to my knees, uncertain now even of standing upright, and fumbled around in the dirt until I found a fist-sized stone, which I crushed into a powder with one hand.

So, I was still strong. But then, what? What was happening? Why had I stopped? Why had I had to stop? How could I desert Sara like this? Exactly, now ... who is Sara? Of course! Don't be stupid. Sara. Of course you know Sara! Even in a dream you know Sara. Why are you stopped here in the woods?

Without seeming to will it, I stood up, then began to jump in the open field. I jumped from place to place to place, all about the field, like some crazed giant flea, going perhaps fifty feet up and a hundred feet forward with each jump. Each time I left a ragged hole in the ground where the force of my jump dug my feet almost knee deep into the soft soil.

One jump landed me near the van and my right hand reached out and grabbed the front bumper and without seeming to even think of what I was doing, I shook the van like a terrier shakes a rat, with all four wheels off the ground, until the bumper came loose in my hand and I tossed it away. The van bounced up and down violently, springs squealing and squawking, then settled down. Deep in the back of my mind a voice said: "Don't worry. It doesn't matter. You don't need a bumper."

Then I ran. I ran short dashes, a quarter mile this way, then a quarter mile that way, from fence row to fence row, then I began to run around the four sides of the field in an ever increasing blur of speed, wearing a rutted path that got deeper with each circuit.

I stopped suddenly. Why? Why are you doing this? What do you need to prove? Why not just get back into the van and drive? But while I was still debating I found myself pinching handful after handful of living oak wood out of the nearest tree. Soon I had cut the tree in half with my hands and began to rip off branches and throw them into the next field. "You primitive bastard, what are you doing?" I shouted to myself, then found a fence post and pounded it into the ground with my fist.

It seemed to me that my body had cut loose from my brain and was running amok, doing strictly physical things to please itself.

Yet, I knew that my body was not really tested. These were childish things: running, jumping, crushing, pounding. What was I then, a child, being reborn, learning to live with its body and brain in a new world?

I became intensely aware of the earth. It was soft to my feet. Trees, all living things, were soft, insubstantial. Yet the fragile earth and all that was in it seemed immeasurably complex and interesting.

I became intensely aware, bathed in sensory perceptions. I heard ants crawling at my feet, each of their many footfalls making a distinct noise. I smelled rotting vegetation all around me and it was a sweet, natural smell. I kicked the earth to expose fresh soil so I could inhale the rich aroma.

My ears caught a new sound, something walking with soft, deliberate steps. My brain searched its memory and identified it: a housecat on the prowl. Ahead of the cat, a field mouse, scurrying quickly, then hiding, then scurrying again. The cat walked inexorably on, hunter after hunted, in the age old game that hunter usually won.

My head flew back, seemingly of its own volition, and I stared at the stars and planets overhead. "Vega," I murmured to myself "Arcturus, Antares, Enif, Diphda, Mirfak, Srika, Suhail, Canopus, Miaplacidus."

Stupid, the names man has given to these glorious whirls of burning gases. I'll have to learn more about what these stars really are when I get around to it.

Oh, to learn! Suddenly I was aching for it, as starved for new knowledge as I had been, only an hour ago, for hamburgers. My busy, busy mind seemed to reach out and soak up facts, any kind of facts. It was indiscriminate and totally selfish. I took in the temperature, felt the direction of the breeze, measured the sponginess of the earth with my feet, felt the texture of the clothes on my body with my skin, sniffed the air and sorted and labeled each of a thousand smells. There was a covey of quail in the next field. I could smell then and hear them walk quietly in the grass.

Then, abruptly, I stopped. All sensory perceptions were cut off as my brain took a new direction. I began to remember. A flood of memories.

"Joey Applebaum! Harry Sedon! Fred. Fred Noyes! That little snot, Angie Roy! The one who stuck her finger into my cake. It was my birthday, seventy-four years ago, when I was five.

Then...one perfect moment ...a summer morning, with my father, sixty-five years ago, fishing on the pond where we had a one room cottage. The water was a mirror. Our skiff was anchored by an old piece of clothes line attached to a rusty auto flywheel. My cork had just bobbled ever so slightly, a small upward movement, then a pause, then a series of downward jerks followed by a sharp pull under the surface as I raised my cane pole to meet and connect with the fish.

Then the game of tug between fish and boy, feeling the life struggle of the fish, all the excitement of conquest on the boy's part, with almost none of the pity because we were not only different species but lived in such different elements.

Then, with the fish landed and flopping around in the boat, I looked up at my father with a triumphant smile and as he smiled back I saw clearly that he was small-shouldered, bald, with a natural tonsure, and he had a tentative soft sweet smile that may have endeared him to a friend but which repelled a son who wanted a hero to emulate. I had always known that he was hardworking, that he was almost desperately driven to make a living in a hard world for his little family. I was grateful, but I was also growing scornful.

I felt again the guilty fear I'd known those years ago as I looked at his flaws and knew I might inherit some or maybe all of them.

The hell I will, I thought then. *I'll be what I want to be.*

And I saw a sweet and smiling mother. Too sweet. Too smiling. Too willing to sacrifice and scrimp and save and make do and spread family love around the house like marmalade.

I saw again the boy who had muttered to himself sixty-five years ago: "One thing I know…I don't want a girl just like the girl who married dear old dad. And I don't want to *be* dear old dad, either."

Then…oh, God, then…one Saturday afternoon fifty years ago when Sara and I had raked leaves all morning and she had gone in to shower and change and I was reading the newspaper, waiting for my turn in the shower and she called to me from the bedroom, "Oh, Andy…come in here a moment. I want to show you something…"

And what she wanted to show me was her own naked self, lying on the bed like Venus on the halfshell.

But later, when all should have been bliss, there were tears running down her cheeks, followed by big, heaving sobs as she remembered the stillborn boy I had thought she'd forgotten.

From that day on, whenever I saw autumn leaves I thought of Sara. Sara and dead babies and love intertwined with grief in a way that made love deeper and richer. And now that vision was so real that momentarily I felt transported to the scene, almost overwhelmed by the vividness of it.

And some part of my brain said: "Go to Sara, now, you fool. You're running out of time." But the thought faded. I had lost control again.

The memories: I was suffocated in them. They flooded in, good and bad, with no seeming order: *3.141593…enthalpy is directly* *proportional to mass...Fritz Haber received the Nobel prize for the synthesis of ammonia from nitrogen and hydrogen...*scraps. Pieces of the past. What did I give a damn, now, for entropy or enthalpy or geometric isomers?

Memories. Am I going to have to live forever with every detail that's ever happened? Am I to be buried in trivia? I see page after page of encyclopedias and text books I've studied. I can recite the names, addresses and phone numbers of all the pages of all the telephone books I've ever opened. The newspapers! Do you know how many thousands I have read? To remember every detail of every one! I seem to remember absolutely everything. It is overpowering. I am suffocating in the vivid memories of the cracks in the pavement of the thousand streets I've walked.

Bad memories, too. Here's one I hate, and it flooded in on me and refused to leave until it had played itself out in every detail: the Germ Factory, fifteen years ago, time to go home and it is already dark on this winter evening. I am walking by a row of offices when I hear a muffled sound of distress and open a door. There is a man, his back to me, and standing, grappling with the man, is a woman and she is giving off the muffled sounds I've heard. The man is obviously forcing himself upon her. I walk in, grab him by an arm and whirl him around to face me and it is the Wiseass with that wiseass lip dangling and the blue veins showing in the wet inside of it and I think, *How disgusting to have that lip pressed against yours when you don't want it.* And then the Wiseass is sputtering with rage and his eyes are blazing behind their glasses and the woman, a secretary I barely know, is cowering, showing both relief and shame and wanting desperately to be away from both of us...

Oh, good sweet Christ! I had forgotten the Wiseass! Had my brain hidden him away this last hour? Had I purposefully hidden from myself the fact that I had created a monster before I recreated myself?

The Wiseass! Was he, even now, going through the same type of change? Had he had the same eating binge? Was he equally as strong? Had he jumped and crushed and smelled and heard and felt and remembered just as I had?

What would he do with what I had given him? What would I do about him? What could I do about him?

62

Then, as suddenly as it had come, thoughts of the Wiseass were pushed aside. I could almost hear my brain say, "later."

Because my brain was quickly and systematically taking over, creating order out of disorder. I stood there in the open field and turned my thoughts inward, my brain watching my brain at work.

It seemed to me that I had been like a computer that had almost crashed with a sensory overload. My head had to get it all under control again.

You know what? I thought, *You had something like DOS or UNIX in your head all along. A controller of some kind. And this flood of thought was too much for it, so your brain had to build a new operating system, like a new DOS. Does that sound right? It feels right.*

Take driving the van. Up until now, if I didn't watch it every moment I'd tear chunks out of the fragile metal, twist off the steering wheel, destroy the brake pedal with a careless foot. But now with my new "controller" in control I can apply exactly the right of pressure on the gas pedal, grip the wheel with only the amount of force needed, and drive as easily as I could before I took the blue liquid. Yet, any time I want, I can pick up the van and toss it over a house.

But you can't pick it up by the bumper, you damned fool, I told myself scornfully. *You've already torn that off!*

After a while, I turned and began walking towards the van. When I reached the highway I stopped and cleaned my muddy shoes and flicked the soft dirt from my pants.

How long had my mental rebirth taken? Maybe only a few minutes? Maybe longer? I had no idea. I had been totally out of control, all urgency gone. But now urgency was back. How could I have wasted Sara's time like that?

I slid behind the wheel of the van and was twisting the ignition wires to start it when my nose picked up a scent and my eyes found the source: on the floor of the van, on the passenger side, there was a leaking, crumpled pile of plastic and glass. The thermos! My silly van-shaking had broken it.

The thermos. The blue liquid. Sara's life.

Stomach-sick with guilt, I grabbed the still-intact thermos cap and holding the wreckage of the broken thermos, let what remained of the blue liquid drip into the cup. When it had dripped what seemed to be the last drop, I squeezed the plastic sides of the thermos together and felt broken glass crush to a powder inside, but I did get a few more precious drops to drip into my cup.

How much? A spoonful, altogether? Maybe just a little more? Enough? Enough for Sara? It had to be.

I looked at the wet mud that the rest of the blue liquid had made on the floor of the van and cursed my unconscious stupidity.

Never mind, Andy, I told myself. *You've got enough for Sara tonight...and surely you can always make more if you need it.*

But...why would I need more?

"I don't know!" I argued with myself. "Just shut up and drive. And don't screw up again!"

Holding the thermos cup in a steel grip, palm of left hand firmly clamped over the top to prevent another spill, I did drive, as fast as the van would take the curves.

The hospital was no more than fifteen minutes away.

 chapter ten

When you've been married as long as Sara and I have, things build up. There are a thousand little cuts and scratches to remember. A hundred little faults. A dozen mannerisms to overlook. A few terrible disappointments. Even a couple of wild hatreds. But there is also love.

Strange thing, love. What is it? How do you know you've got it or that you're in it, or whatever? How can you be sure?

All I can say is that for more than fifty years every time I saw Sara coming toward me in a crowd I had a happy little start of pleasure. Whenever I heard her voice it went directly to my inner self, completely unlike any other voice.

It would have been easy to find another woman now. After all, isn't fifty years enough? Why carry all the old baggage with me? All I had to do was wait a few days, a few hours, even. Nature would solve the problem for me and who could cast a gleam of blame my way? "Poor man, he lost his wife."

I could have searched the world for the perfect mate, then made her even more perfect: immortal and supernaturally beautiful.

I never gave it a moment's thought. I could no more give up Sara than I could give up myself.

Why not? Was it fear? Fear that for one brief moment Sara would look me right in the eye and know that I had betrayed her?

Perhaps.

Was it habit? Was the living pattern of fifty years too strong for me to reject? Was it the comfort of knowing exactly what Sara thought about every subject and how she'd react to any situation? Knowing exactly how we fitted together so that the two of us made one whole?

Perhaps.

Was it simple loneliness? Was it that I didn't want to live in a world where no one knew my innermost thoughts and understood and accepted me the way Sara did, despite my faults?

Perhaps.

Was it passion? Certainly Sara and I had had our share of that and in our case, passion had lasted.

The common cold is a complex of more than 200 different viruses, so two people seldom have exactly the same disease at any given time.

So it is perhaps with love. Who knows what the ingredients are? Who knows that your love is like my love? All I can say for certain is that I had caught a dose of love over fifty years ago and it still has me in its grip.

*　　*　　*　　*　　*

The hospital was in a valley, ringed by small hills. I left the van at one of these, at a scenic overlook that had also become an unofficial trash dump, and walked down to the hospital, springing into the air with my toes at each step in a way that seemed comfortable to me, taking loping steps about twenty feet long.

In one careful hand I carried the thermos top with the spoonful of blue liquid for Sara.

The "Blue Pill." That's how I thought of it. So, it wasn't a pill but a liquid. So what? When Dr. Paul Ehrlich invented the "Magic Bullet" against syphilis years ago, was it really magic? And was it a bullet? Of course not. But it certainly did shoot down the disease.

The hospital was in semi-darkness, with a blazing light only at the door to the emergency room. I walked in quickly and looked around me. Even at this hour, the chairs were half filled with the sad sick and wounded of the area. One man, heavily bearded, bald, about forty and plumpish, sat in a chair beside the admitting nurse's desk and held a bloody towel to his ear as he answered questions about his health and accident insurance.

The admitting nurse glanced up, obviously intending to tell me to take a seat and wait, then took in my muddy pants legs, the torn shoes that barely hung on my feet, the split shirt where my newly muscled chest and shoulders had broken through, and decided that maybe I was a problem.

"Wait!" she said. "I'll be with you…wait!" But I ignored her and strode off down the hall to a coin operated candy machine I saw there.

There was a dollar bill changer and I used it, but the damned thing kept returning my dollars, one after another, over and over. I hated to destroy property. I really did. The habit patterns of almost eighty years of law-abiding citizenship protected this balky machine from my need.

But I had a powerful reason to want that candy, so I tucked the fingers of my right hand into as small a spear as possible and reached through the sheet metal into the guts of the candy machine, where I triggered the release of a column of candy bars into the bin below. I was proud of the relatively small hole I had made. "They'll fix it in no time," I said over my shoulder to the admitting nurse, who had left Mr. Bloody Ear to his own devices while she ran to protect private property from the marauder.

"Stop! What're you *doing*? You put that back!"

But I ignored her and strode off down the hall to an open elevator door. I punched the button for the fourth floor just as the nurse got there, yelling, "Wait! You can't go up there!"

But neither I nor the elevator mechanism agreed with her, so we went up to the fourth floor, where I got off and walked quickly to the nurse's station. There was something there I had noted on other visits and now I needed it.

Two nurses were at the station. One was updating charts, her back to me, while the other had a pair of tweezers and a magnifying mirror and was busy pulling an ingrown eyelash out of the corner of her eye.

"Yes?" she said, still intent on the mirror, not really looking at me but aware that I was before her. "What can I...then she glanced up, took me in, decided I was not a hospital employee, not a proper visitor at this time of night, and definitely not the right sort at the right time at the right place. Instant alarm.

"You! Stay right there! You have to go! What are you doing?"

The other nurse turned now and the two of them would have ganged up on me, but I ignored them and reached over the counter to the utility cart I had remembered and opened a sterile plastic package and removed a clean hypodermic syringe and needle.

Their eyes became huge. This was the ultimate proof of my wrong doing.

"You put that back!" the first nurse said, with stern authority. The other quietly picked up her telephone and trying to be unobtrusive, began talking to someone, perhaps a guard or policemen.

"Thanks," I said to them both, brightly. "I'll only be a minute. Don't get yourself upset. Don't follow me, now, I know the way."

I turned, and walking faster than they could believe, reached the end of the hall and the door to Sara's room. Then, slipping inside, I pulled a chest of drawers to the door to block it against the nurses and swung around to greet Sara.

All my senses were assaulted. I was almost overcome by nausea. I had always hated age and sickness but had grown to accept it. Now, in my supreme wellness, I was even more strongly repelled by it. If the whole momentum of my life had not so long been directed toward saving Sara, I would have fled.

Her condition had worsened. She could have no more than moments to live. I felt like forcing open the recently blocked door and yelling to the pair of nurses, "Get in here, you bitches...my wife is dying!"

Of course the nurses were not to blame. They could do nothing, and I could. But I was so sickened by the sight and the smell and the feel of Sara's dying flesh that I was almost stunned into inaction.

I bent over her soft, puffy face, almost allowing myself to believe that I had the wrong room, the wrong woman, when she opened her eyes just a slit, saw me, then opened them further, then wide open in wonderment. They were Sara's eyes, no escaping it, her lovely brown eyes.

"YOU...(a soft, almost lost voice) what have you done to yourself? (a raspy whisper) You never looked this good. Never. Is it you? Am I (pause) am I dead and dreaming?"

Her voice brought me out of my funk. What I had to do was so simple.

The two nurses were beating on the door now. "What are you doing? We've called the police! You let that patient alone! Do you hear!"

I reached into my pocket and brought out a Baby Ruth candy bar and peeled it. "You'll want this in a minute. You'll see," I told Sara. Her eyes were following me as I tilted the thermos cup to fill the syringe and pushed the plunger down slightly to push out the air. Then I bent to inject the blue liquid into Sara's arm.

It wasn't easy. Her veins had collapsed. Her blood had almost ceased to flow. I probed and drew back the plunger, making sure that I had found a vein, then I moved the plunger in and out until I had mixed some of her blood with the blue liquid and turned it pink in the barrel of the syringe. Then, finally certain that I had the needle in the center of the vein, I pushed and sent the entire pinkish, bloody mixture into her body.

Then I withdrew the hypodermic and crushed it between my fingers, leaving only a damp lump of plastic to throw down the toilet of the room. I wanted no one to be able to analyze what I had injected.

I began disconnecting the maze of tubes and monitoring devices that had been connected to every available part of Sara's body. You would think, to see me, that I was disconnecting Sara's life support system. I saw it otherwise.

I had already decided that I wouldn't watch, couldn't watch, the sloughing-off process that I'd already seen with the Wiseass and myself. Sara was too near death already for me to see her get worse.

So I stuck the Baby Ruth candy bar into her mouth and gathered her up in my arms, bedclothes and all.

"I'm checking you out of here," I told her. "No more sickness. You'll see. You'll be chomping on that Baby Ruth before you know it, and asking for more!"

A flick of the foot and the chest of drawers was shoved aside and Sara and I were walking out. The two nurses were on either side of us, talking, pulling, threatening, trying to block our way.

I ignored them, striding down the hall with Sara. I knew exactly how they felt, and applauded them for it. But how to explain? Why explain? Just keep walking.

As I turned the corner of the corridor I heard one nurse wail to the other: "Did you see what was sticking out of her mouth? Oh, disgusting! She couldn't have thrown up fecal matter like that. He must have put it there Can you imagine? Did you ever hear of anything so sick? Never in my wildest..." But we turned the corner, I leaped down the stairs and their voices were lost behind us.

As we neared the ground floor door to the service exit I felt Sara move strongly in my arms, and as I looked down into her face

I saw it in the midst of change and I saw that she was eating the evidence. In one gulp the Baby Ruth disappeared.

I could see that some of Sara's old flesh and hair was still caught in the bedclothes, but most of it must have dropped onto the stairs as we leaped down them.

God help the cleanup crew, I thought briefly, but then I was staring at Sara, recording every detail of her new self as eighty years of living disappeared.

I was staring at Sara, recording every detail of her change, and she was not staring at me but inwardly at herself, also absorbed in her change. Absorbed in wonderment.

Watching Sara was like watching a mirror of what had so recently happened to me. I saw her eyes swimming in a confusion that quickly cleared. I watched her face rearrange itself from puckered, almost transparent old skin to strong, firm flesh. I saw features change, become almost picture perfect, yet the features were Sara-features, not anyone else's. More Sara than Sara had ever been.

I saw teeth straighten and whiten, hair grow and become glossy black and silky, color appear on cheeks. I saw a hundred tiny flaws of skin disappear. At the same time, I could feel her body squirming in my arms as the body also rebuilt itself.

I could hear the two nurses, joined now by another, a male by the sound of him, pounding down the stairs after us, so I stepped out of the hospital door and into the night.

We had gone only a few steps into the darkness when Sara said, "Put me down. Let me walk."

I put her down, letting the bedclothes pile up on the grass, then fished another Baby Ruth from my pocket and peeled it. "Here. Stick this into your moosh. I know you want it."

"Yes, yes, I'm starved," she said. "Let's run!" and first hand in hand, then separately but close together, we ran. We ran beyond the van, ran down a still dark macadam road, ran over fields, through back yards where dogs barked. Then, when I said, "Look! Jump!" I jumped over a tall pine tree, but Sara simply ran around it.

"How did you do that!" she said. "Are you a ghost? Am I? Did I die back there? How can I be dead when I'm so hungry? Oh! I'm starved!"

"Let's run back to the van," I replied. "I've got it chock full of food. You'll see."

So we ran. I could hear the wind whistling by my ears at our speed. And nothing I could conceive of at that moment seemed more important, more worth doing, than simply running.

But Sara's hunger drove us back to the scenic overlook where I had parked.

Getting into the van, Sara inadvertently tore the door handle out by the roots. She looked at me in wonderment.

"I meant to tell you. You have to be careful with this world now. Everything will seem mushy. But you'll adjust. You'll see."

I was so hungry for her. I kept peering into the dark shadows trying to get just a flash of her face. Yet, I didn't want to look full on her yet. I was like a small boy licking delicately at a candy, trying to stretch it out, trying not to consume it in one gulp.

I reached into the back of the van and fished out a carton of cold hot dogs and a gallon of sweet pickles and put them on the seat between us before I started the van. "Eat. I know they look disgusting, cold like this, but you won't mind, really you won't. When we get home we'll cook up something hot."

The hot dogs were linked together and as I watched, Sara took a tentative bite, then another, then began to inhale them, link after link. It was like watching an anchor chain rattle down the hawser pipe of a boat. Now and then she'd stop and eat a handful of pickles, for variety.

My elegant, ladylike Sara. Where are your table manners now? Pickle juice was everywhere. The commercial sized case of hot dogs was empty. Sara burped, covering her mouth with her hand. "Delicious," she said. "I never ate anything more satisfying. But I'm still starved."

I drove toward home, wishing we could have used a hospital closer to home, but Sara had gone in under the name, "Sara Champignon" and had used the Blue Cross number from my janitor's job at the Germ Factory as well as a fictitious Connecticut address. It was the way I had planned it all along, hoping that this night would come out as it had, and that we'd need the anonymity when the police began searching for a stolen patient.

I barely noticed the familiar road as I drove toward home. Out of the corner of my eye I was memorizing every detail of the new Sara in her skimpy white hospital gown. And I noticed that she was watching me with the same concentration. We both knew that everything we had said to each other since leaving the hospital had been surface talk. Neither of us had know quite how to start.

Then, suddenly the dam of Sara's reserve broke and words began to flow out in an almost incoherent flood.

"Oh, you sweet man, you saved my life, you truly did. I was so tired of choking, so weary of trying to draw breath through my closed throat, so weak, and I had lost hope, you see. I didn't really believe, how could I really believe, I mean no one could believe that you could come up with anything like you did. I know you're smart, I believe in you, I truly do, I always did, but what you seem to have done is impossible. Absolutely. You know that, don't you? I'm not a fool, I know what can be done and what can't be, and this is, well this is a dream, a wonderful dream, but look at the world. You've not only changed me and changed yourself but you've made the world soft somehow, so this can't be. I must be dead but I don't remember dying, and somehow I don't think I am. Am I?"

Tears streamed from her eyes as she continued, her voice breaking and then recovering.

"I was at the end. Absolutely. I had been holding on because you told me to and because I was scared of dying, too, but I was choking and every breath was another choke and I was scared, scared almost more of choking than of being dead if that makes any sense. Yet I tried to hold on because you were coming back, you said you were and I wanted to see you one last time but I was getting so tired and so weak, so I said to myself, I'll just close my eyes and take shallow breaths and maybe I won't choke and maybe I won't be so afraid and yet I knew that if I kept my eyes closed long enough I'd slip away and die and that was terrifying, and yet in another way it didn't seem so bad, either, better than choking, you know.

"But then at almost the last possible minute, you were there, looking like a young god, better than you ever looked, better than anyone in the world ever looked except you were such a mess, your clothes, you know, and I said to myself, 'What is this, Sara? Is he real? Is this heaven? Shit, you never believed in heaven, how could you have been so wrong?'

"And then there you were sticking me with that needle and then you put that ridiculous candy bar into my mouth and I almost choked on it all over again…and then, out of the hospital we went like Zorro rescuing a fair maiden and you know the rest. Now tell me, what *really* happened?"

The van was nearing home, its engine screaming and the boxy body swaying and fluttering in its own breeze of passage. The long night was finally gone, with daylight creeping into the horizon, brightening the world moment by moment.

"I didn't set out to invent anything quite this wonderful," I told Sara. "I did think I had a cure. A cure for the aging, or at least partly. God! I never expected us to look young again, really young, I just thought we'd live a lot longer, look a lot better, be nice healthy old folks for a long, long time.

"But then there was an accident. I thought it was a terrible accident and everything would be ruined, but it wasn't, so I guess the accident wasn't really important at all."

"Then…we're real," she said, wonderingly. "Really like this. But what happened to the world to make it mushy?"

We wheeled into the driveway of our home and I untwisted the wires to kill the van's engine for the last time. Then I told Sara as much as I knew about our new condition. Told her everything I'd learned this long night.

But I didn't tell her about the Wiseass or Henry Fowles. Not just now. Why spoil a perfect hero story with an admission of stupidity?

"How long do you think we'll be this way?" Sara asked.

"I have no way of knowing. There were no directions on the bottle, you know, but I'm assuming forever."

"Forever? You mean like a thousand years? Or more?"

"Why not? If we've beaten aging, we've beaten it. Every molecule in our bodies has been changed. Why should they unchange?"

"Forever beautiful? Strong? Intelligent? Oh, Andy! This will take some thinking. Some heavy thinking!"

I leaned forward and kissed her lips lightly. "You go in. I'm going to unload the van and start feeding you the biggest hot breakfast you can imagine. Tons of it!"

So our first day began. The best day it is possible for me to imagine.

 chapter eleven

Sara ran eagerly into the house trailing her now-dirty hospital jonny behind her, long and beautiful legs flashing. I began to unload the van, stacking food all over the kitchen. It was a job I'd always disliked, but now I was a miser surrounded by gold. Every gallon can of peaches was a triumph, each sausage a delight.

Then I began to cook, so to speak. Trouble was, our pots were too small, our stove had only the standard four burners. How to cook a real meal on such pitiful equipment?

I washed a fifty pound sack of potatoes for a start, and stuffed as many as I could into our oven, then filled the microwave, then poured the rest into our biggest pot and filled it with water and put it on to boil.

Then I started ripping the tops off cans with my fingers and filling pots with peas, string beans, whatever came to hand. All the while my mouth was dripping with drool, which I kept wiping away with a wad of paper towel.

"Do you know what?" Sara shouted from the next room, "Old people lived here! Old! I can't stand it! Everything even smells old. And look at these granny dresses! How could I? How could I ever?"

"You never looked old, Saran, I said, loyally. "Never. I never thought you were. Besides, what's wrong with old?"

"Hahhhh!" she said. "Cook! Don't talk! I'm starved. Starved! Tomorrow, everything goes. Everything! Furniture, clothes, wall paper, everything! Start over. Everything bright, everything clean and new."

Electric frying pans! What a thought! We had two. I soon had one filled with sausage and one with bacon. Then—sheer inspiration—I took the guts out of our electric coffee pot and filled it with canned pork and beans and plugged it in.

Breakfast! Got to have eggs! I took our biggest pot, dropped in a stick of butter, turned the heat on under it, and began breaking eggs on top of the melting butter. When I had four dozen eggs shelled and dropped onto the butter I threw in some salt and pepper and took a wooden spoon to mix up the whole mess, then turned the heat down and let it cook slowly.

Bacon frying, sausage bubbling, potatoes boiling, baking and microwaving, beans bubbling, rice cooking, oatmeal heating, prunes stewing. I didn't stop until every pot we owned was filled and every cooking surface was covered by at least two pots.

I heard the shower go on and knew that Sara was washing away the hospital smells and there was a moment of pure domestic bliss as I thought of all the food I was fixing for the two of us and of Sara well again and showering and all that was right with our world. And there was the delicious anticipation of food and love and exploration.

Sara let out a scream of pure delight. I ran to the bathroom and threw open the door and watched.

Sara was naked, still damp and holding the wet towel she'd used to wipe a clear spot on the steam-covered mirror. She was simply staring at herself in the mirror as she turned this way and that.

"Oh, look at the teeth!" she cried, eyes burning with excitement. "Look at these perfect, perfect teeth with no damned gap!

"And the hair! Oh, the hair! D'you see how thick it is? Look at it! Will you just look at it!" she almost screamed at me, face split into a delighted grin as she ran her fingers through it over and over, caressing it, loving it. "I always knew I had this great hair inside me somewhere."

Catching the spirit of the occasion, I added my bit. "Just look at the neck. Look at the curve of the spine. Look at the flanks." I touched her back lightly. "Look at my whole beautiful woman!"

Sarah didn't disagree. "There was never a human being so lovely," she said softly, reflectively, with no trace of vanity. "It is impossible to be more perfectly made. This is so much more than an answer to my prayers, so much more than I could even imagine. Why, only an hour ago I would have sold my soul for just one deep lungfull of air. And now, look at me. What have I become?"

What indeed. What words can I use to describe the new Sara?

Start with her skin. It was smooth, tight, yet liquid in its movement. Seemingly without pores, it had a golden glow of inner color. You wanted to touch that skin. No, you ached to caress that skin. Your eyes and your hands and your lips reached out for it. knowing it would be alive and tantalizing.

Her body was slim, but not fashionably so. She would have been beautiful at any time in history, no matter what the fashion in beauty. Each limb and each part of each limb seemed made for its job, as if some divine sculptor had decided exactly how this finger should be made, how exquisitely turned that toe needed to be to grip the ground and spring, how deliciously nestled the small depressions of collar bone and pelvic hollows were.

And her eyes! The beautiful Sara eyes were now lit from within in a way that was both startling and compelling. They pierced you. They not only saw, they searched. These eyes would frighten children, draw men to her, and raise the neck hair of women rivals.

Sara's face was alive with constant, almost shimmering motion. There was never a moment of real repose, even thought, outwardly, her facial muscles were still.

"The two of us have really become…something else," Sara said.

"She walks in beauty," I said, softly, and I quickly stripped off my own clothes so that we stood, staring at each other and in the mirror at the two of us, close together, side by side.

It was the first time I'd seen myself naked and the sight was shocking, even though I expected it. I was as beautiful as Sara in my own masculine way. We had the same closed-cell, liquid skin. We had the same impossibly-alive look. You knew from a glance that the engines of our bodies were completely different from other humans. There were no bulging muscles, but our strength and agility were always apparent.

We were without age. Not young. Not old. Just totally non-connected with age.

It was disquieting. Like finding a person who cast no shadow. Age is always with us. We glance at a person, any person, and mentally estimate… "She's eighteen… he's thirty-two… she doesn't look a day over fifty…" It is an essential part of the way we describe people to ourselves.

We deny death, we describe old age as "golden years," we pretend, we pretend, but the knowledge and fear of age is with us constantly. Why, we can't look at a favorite pet without estimating how long it has to live in "dog years."

All that was missing from Sara and from me. And I think that if I had just seen Sara alone, if I had not been the same ageless way myself, I might have looked at her smooth perfection and felt, not only envy, but a small touch of fear.

To escape the treadmill toward the grave is...absolutely wonderful, but...unnatural.

I was just over six feet, Sara some four inches shorter. She was the brilliant brunette. I had thick brown hair with a slight wave and light brown skin. My features were much as they always had been, yet far more perfect. Fascinating to see yourself multiplied into the stuff of dreams.

We held hands. Sara had the same long fingered yet strongly knuckled hands I remembered, but I could feel those fingers now squeeze mine in a grip that would have made jelly of another man's.

"How lovely," breathed Sara again. "How lovely to be hungry and have food, to be in love and have a lover." We each began to caress the other, slowly, with soft exploring fingertips in a voyage of sweet discovery.

But then something even more compelling came up. With spontaneous and unspoken agreement we ran to the kitchen and started eating whatever our hands found. I watched my mannered Sara stuff down half-baked potatoes like peanuts; dip handfuls of string beans out of the pot; eat sausage, grease and all, with a bowl full of scrambled eggs.

"Oh, God, it's good," she muttered, raking more potatoes out of the oven and eating them skin and all, then drinking a gallon of milk before reaching out for a pot of peas.

I ate, too, and enjoyed. But my newly aware brain noted that I didn't have quite the frantic desire I'd had at the diner, nor the desire Sara obviously had right now.

So, I thought, this eating is for a purpose; to fill out our bones and complete our strength. Once we've fulfilled ourselves, perhaps it'll be back to maintenance eating, like other people, other animals.

But somehow, even then, I knew that our maintenance eating would always be enormous by usual standards.

Sara and I cleaned up the food between us. Not a scrap was left.

"What else is there?" she asked.

I found two cheesecakes in the freezer and put them into the oven and refilled the two electric skillets with pork and beans and opened all the soup we had on the shelf and put it into pots to heat. "That's it. Another snack coming up soon."

We drifted off towards our room, to the familiar conjugal bed that knew our bodies.

"We've had more than fifty years to practice this," Sara said. "Maybe this time we'll get it right."

And slowly, sweetly, with the most complete understanding and capability, we did get it right.

To tell you about our lovemaking would be to describe a sunset to a blind person. How to know the tactile sensation of live and sensuous skin against live skin from head to toe? How to smell the maddeningly delicious odors? How to feel the complex twist of muscles under the skin?

I couldn't get enough of the new Sara, nor she of me. It was the same intense hunger we had both had for food, but now it was body hunger, with almost all other perceptions wiped out, lost to mind and psyche.

Our very bodies changed to fit just this one purpose. We became sexual animals to the exclusion of all else, and were in perfect control, able to devote all our enormous energy, all our creativity, each to the fulfillment of the other's desires.

Sometimes it was slow and sweet. At other times you could only say that we mated like two sex-starved polar bears.

But always we were in control, guiding, shaping what we did, until finally we shared a mutual climax, the "little death" of other times, and I lost control. My mind a blank from an overload of emotion, I felt as though my vital inner parts were being torn from me in a rapture of sacrifice and renewal. Yet it was a sweet tearing. I felt that I was giving everything that was me to Sara, and she was giving the same to me.

Our bed was in splinters, a useless wreck sprawled in a slanted pile on the floor. Our mattress and bedclothes were soaked and ruined (for at some point we had brought the cheesecake and the soup to bed with us) and Sara said, "My God! We ought to sell tickets!"

It was still early morning and we were both anxious to explore our new world, so I said, "Bath time!" and we got into the shower together and washed each other with great abandon.

But as we got out and began to towel dry Sara wavered and then fell to her knees, looking weak and disoriented.

"I think you screwed up," she said softly from the floor. "I'm dying again. Immortality was sweet but short."

I picked her up and took her to the living room sofa and found a blanket and spread it over her. Then I took her into my arms as I sat on the sofa beside her.

"You're not dying," I said. "I know what's happening because it happened to me."

I tried to explain how the brain grew in complexity and ability along with the body and how she could now probably process information like a mainframe computer and how she needed to develop a new operating system in her brain like DOS or UNIX to handle all this and…

"Oh, do be quiet, Andy," she said. "Let me have my thoughts without all that yammering in my ear."

Of course, she was right. She had her right to privacy and self discovery. But there was nothing to prevent me from marveling as I watched her face and tried to read what went on inside it.

What was she thinking as she lay there in my arms, eyes sometimes closed and twitching in REM movements, like a sleeping dreamer, and at other times wide open and staring?

I remembered my own rebirth, as I now thought of it, and knew that she was in a helpless whirl of memory and sensory adjustment.

Would she go back to her childhood, as I had done? Oh, certainly she would. She would be seeing that difficult mother whom I had met at our wedding and a few times afterwards but barely knew because Sara had kept her away, out of some fear she never fully explained.

Her father? Sara had said that she never knew him because he had left when she was a baby, but I met her father once. I tracked him down and talked to him in a bar in St. Louis. A big man with a silly little mustache and a sly but engaging grin. "Oh, she remembers me," he had said. "After all, she was thirteen when I left. A big girl. Big enough. Oh, yes, she remembers me. Count on it!"

And piano lessons at Mrs. Dennis's. Wednesday afternoons, fifty cents a lesson in the hall next to the Dennis parlor, on an upright with yellow keys. She'd be seeing things like this. Of course.

Oh, but what did I know about what she would be seeing? How to know the real Sara mind? How to know what hopes, fears, guilts, what secret pleasures lived there?

Was the recipe for chocolate layer cake intertwined with a memory of first-lust in a porch swing with some far off and well-pimpled teenager? Or was this just my version of a Sara-memory?

She was twitching strongly, her nose sniffing like a hound on a trail. Is this the sharpening of the senses that I remember? The vivid smells and sounds of the earth and all that's in it?

I concentrated my own thoughts on smells and began immediately to pick up the choking miasma of dust motes streaming from under the sofa and the seductive but death laden smell of cut flowers in a vase nearby and the warm, multifaceted odors of Sara herself, and then the mown grass smell of the lawn and the always present earth smells...and oh, smells, odors, aromas without number, crowding in on my senses, and I knew that Sara was experiencing just such a flood.

But now! I could see her face change its focus. Perhaps now it would be sight or sound or...god no!...it was movement, just like my own crazed jumping around had been.

She was out of my arms, out of the house, into the backyard and running, running, running in a tight little circle around pool, kicking up sand and grass with every step.

She had gone almost before I could think and I could think very quickly now. I realized I was horribly embarrassed to see her run and jump. I would have watched with a smile of understanding, like a parent seeing his child learn an adult skill, but it was daylight, and we had neighbors on each side of our fence, people our own age, with grown children, people we'd known and talked with for twenty years without ever becoming real friends. On one side, a professor of history and his wife, on the other side, the owner of the local drug store and his wife, one of our would-be social queens. And Sara was not only impossibly, inhumanly active, she was extremely naked, just as I still was.

I remembered the huge jumps I had taken and I could just imagine how Sara would look from an adjacent backyard as she shot up from behind our fence over and over again to heights well above the house tops.

The inhibitions of a lifetime took over and I ran out and caught her and held her in my arms and tried to soothe her frantic activity.

It was like trying to hold a runaway machine. She was as strong as I was, or almost so, and her movements were not planned and predictable but erratic. It was like trying to hold a madwoman. She bit and scratched and hit me like a man, hissing through clenched teeth and staring with wild eyes. "Get off! Get off! Let go, you fool!"

I hung on grimly, wishing I had never started but too stubborn now to stop.

Then, as suddenly as she had started, Sara slumped, relaxed, looked at me with eyes now grown focused and intelligent, and said: "I'm all right now. Turn me loose."

And when I did, she sat perfectly still for a long moment, staring into space and twitching her lips in a series of silent grimaces.

Then she rose with one deliberate, fluid notion and went back into the house and flung open the sliding door to her closet. When one side of the door stuck, as it always did, she swept it away with the back of her hand and the door landed in splinters on the floor.

Sara began sorting through her clothes, throwing the rejects into a pile.

"Stupid flowered junky thing with the pads and the lace, what was I thinking of?" Riiiippp! It was destroyed and discarded, a dress that had once tried to make Sara look younger.

"Pitiful! Pitiful! Look at *this* one! And *this* one! And they smell of that awful lilac perfume…agghaah!

"I know you think you did the right thing back there," Sara said, flipping a purple pants suit onto the pile. "But sometimes when you do the right thing you do the wrong thing.

"It was far, far better for me to show my ass to those old fools next door and give them a thrill than it was for you to stunt my psyche, maybe forever.

"Do you know what you did back there? Holding me like that? You tried your damnedest to make me into a lady again. To make me into a nice girl. Careful and sweet and modest. Just what society did to me more than seventy years ago. 'Young ladies don't climb trees, Sara', she mimicked a voice from her childhood. 'Oh, now you've smeared your shirtwaist!'

"It's what the head doctors used to call 'repression'. Just ask any woman, she'll tell you all about 'repression'."

Making her selection, finally, I watched as she shrugged into underwear that no longer fit, tugged carefully at panty hose that wanted to tear, then pulled a simple blue dress over her head and began smoothing the cloth and giving it little twitches to try to force it to fit over her new body.

"You look nice in that," I volunteered.

"I look like a blue potato sack in this," she replied. "And you know it."

I found my own clothes and began to dress at the same time.

"Do you know what happened back there?" Sara whirled and faced me. "It was really something. Fantastic. Right out of a text-book. Good old Sigmund Freud all the way."

"Oh, save me from that old fraud, Freud," I answered. I've always hated his mysticism, his convoluted language. I'd rather think I had a new DOS in my head, a new computer operating system."

"No, no, look," Sara said, eagerly. "You've got to think about this. Really see it. Let's take the *Id* the *Ego* and the *Superego*," she continued, ignoring my groan.

"OK, let's start with the *Id*. It stands for confusion, chaos, jumbled thoughts, wild desires, anger, lust. A whirlwind of unguided thought and emotion. Just exactly what I experienced out there, and I'll bet you did, too." Without waiting for me to answer, she continued.

"Because my Id is supposed to be controlled by my Superego but my old Superego wasn't strong enough to control my new Id, so my mind had to create a new Superego. Are you with me?

"And now that I've got a new Superego controlling my Id, I've got a new Ego. This new Ego we have is essentially the new you and the new me. It's the you and me that people will see, that we ourselves will see. The you and me that's under control, that's civilized and rational and responsible. Make sense?"

"Sure," I said. "It's the brain's operating system, just like DOS or UNIX."

Sara gave a small wave of impatience and moved across the room with the liquid, gliding step that we both instinctively used now and slipped a cassette into our stereo tape deck. "For you its DOS and for me its Superego. Let's not fight about it. Listen!" she said, starting the music with a push of her finger. "I've always loved this."

The tape was a piano solo. A collection of the traditional fourteen waltzes of Chopin. "Do you know the name of this first one?" Sara asked. "The best Chopin could come up with for this beautiful piece was, *Waltz No. 1 in E-flat*. Isn't that terrible? Couldn't he think of a name? Pure musical snobbery, that!"

The tape rolled on, the clear, cleanly beautiful notes poured out, and my new brain took them in, savored their mathematical purity, and was startled after a moment to hear our own piano, with Sara at the helm, begin to overplay the tape.

At first, there was Sara's "thump de thump, de thump" of the too-heavy left hand, but after only moments that lightened to mirror-image the recorded music, and within a few bars she was performing exactly as the professional. Exactly.

I knew that I could have made an oscilloscope tracing of Sara's playing and placed it over as graph of the recorded music and gotten an exact match.

So it went for the first three of the Chopin waltzes. Sara matched the pianist note for note, rhythm for rhythm, expression for expression. Then she shut off the tape deck with another flick of her finger and began to replay the selections on her piano. To my ear, which was now very exact, she mirrored the now silent tape perfectly for a few moments. Then she began making subtle changes. Her timing became even more precise, her tones a little more intense, and her technique her own, not borrowed.

I was suffused with pleasure. I had no need to learn the piano myself. I was the listener, gratefully absorbing the aural pleasure that Sara gave me, knowing that I had my role and she had hers, and that there was an almost voluptuous need in the giving and in the receiving.

Abruptly, Sara stopped playing and found another tape, this one with popular dance music, which she turned up somewhat louder than I had expected. Soon she was humming along with the singer, and saying, "Let's dance," she held out her arms. I glided into them.

We became one with the music. Two newly made creatures, each with infinite strength and agility, with perfect pitch and timing, sharing a period of blissful togetherness, totally alone from the rest of the world.

We danced through the living room and out on the patio, then into the back yard where Sara's feet had so recently torn the turf around the swimming pool.

There were times when I would lead and times when with the merest suggestion of pressure, Sara would lead me, and it didn't seem to matter. We were immersed in the music together.

Softly at first, then more insistently, Sara began to sing along with the taped singer, just as she had with the pianist.

We danced then to Sara's singing, which became louder and more individualistic. Soon Sara was completely eclipsing the recorded music and was leading me in an acrobatic dance that had no name.

After a time the cassette came to its end and was silent but Sara sang and we danced, never tiring, never repeating the same step or pattern, always finding a new invention in the way we moved together to celebrate and illuminate the music Sara made with her voice.

"Look," I said. "Look who's looking." Because there were two heads peering over our back fence, then two more over our left fence and one head peering over our right fence.

"Too bad Sam couldn't make it," I said, nodding to Martha Sellars's lone figure to our right. "He'll never believe what the other five will tell him about us."

Sara was not amused.

She began to sing louder. And louder. I had to make a conscious effort to tune out her voice in my ear.

She turned up the tone again, then as the five began to put hands to ears and show pain, she stopped, suddenly. I understood: the love song she had been singing didn't lend itself to the intensity she wanted. After the briefest of pauses, she slipped into the old hymn, "Amazing Grace," and with it she could turn up the volume as high as she liked.

> *Amazing Grace, how sweet the sound*
> *that saved a wench like me.*
> *I once was lost but now am found*
> *was blind but now I see.*

Her voice grew louder with each word until the sound pouring forth was no longer music, and certainly no longer a hymn, but punishment for the listener. The five had looks of horror on their faces and they covered their ears and bent as in a heavy wind but they didn't look away.

Then, continuing to make small changes in the original to suit her own purposes, she sang:

> *Through many danger, toils, and snares*
> *I have already come*
> *Tis my Andy has brought me safe thus far*
> *and he will lead me home.*

"For God's sake," I muttered. "Why? What have they ever done to you?"

She answered in a burst of words that were so fast that no one except myself could ever have deciphered them and I answered with the same blinding speed, so that to our listeners there was scarcely a pause in the song.

"Do you remember that sister of Martha's? That frizzy gray, used-to-be-blond with the teeth? The one she invited to stay with her this spring?

"Sure. She was pleasant. Maybe a little over-friendly."

"She was a man-trap in action, brought in especially by Martha Sellers, and she was baited and set for you."

"*Me?* But that's stupid! I have you, Sara! Everyone who knows us knows that!"

"And I was about to pass out of the picture. Everyone knew that, too! So here is this perfectly good, well trained and wealthy husband about to come onto the marriage market again. Get your licks in quickly, ladies!"

"But that's ridiculous. Good God, she must be past seventy! Big, lardy ass, old ropy veins. Who'd marry that?"

"Maybe an almost eighty year-old widower with crippling arthritis and terminal loneliness. That's what they counted on. Everyone in the neighborhood knew what was going on; at least all the women did.

"How do you think I felt," Sara continued, "...with the grave hungry for my body and having to watch their little game to grab you?"

I thought briefly of my sixteen–hour work days, of my frantic Sara dominated life of the past two years and thought: *How pitiful. How trivial. How could they have been so small minded? So foolish in the pursuit of the unpursuable?*

"Let's forget it," I said. "That kind of stupidity just doesn't touch us. We're way beyond it. Always were."

"You forget it." Sara said. "I'm going to rub their noses in it like a puppy's in a wet rug."

She began to sing again, even louder, her own revised version of the third verse.

> *bright shining as the sun*
> *we'll have no less days*
> *our own hell to raise*
> *than when we first begun.*

The five watchers had progressed from horror to terror and as they turned to run, staggering and weaving toward their respective back doors, I saw a trickle of blood seeping from several ears.

Sara had finished her version of "Amazing Grace" and gave an operatic *Ha! Ha! Ha!* at their departing backs. Each *Ha!* seemed like a giant hand pushing them away from us.

Sara was on a new high of scornful glee. I was not. "It's not over, you know," I said.

"So, what can they do? What can anyone do? No one can touch us! Isn't that just delicious?"

I turned and went back into the house and took all the Encyclopedia Britannicas off the shelf and arranged them for easy reading. "I've always meant to do this, I said to Sara, and beginning with volume one, I started leafing through the pages rapidly, memorizing every word as I read. After a while Sara sat beside me and took each volume as I finished it and read it herself, just as rapidly.

"Big day out on the town," she muttered as she read. "Big encyclopedia-reading among the in-crowd."

So we sat for about thirty minutes, pages flipping as though blown in a wind, until each of us had finished the twenty-four volume set, plus the index. "So, how much corn do they export yearly from Nebraska?" Sara asked.

"Not nearly as much as they do from Oklahoma. Listen. Do you hear them outside?"

"Of course," she said. "Nothing escapes these ears. I can hear a parrot poot in Peoria."

"They called the cops, didn't they?"

"So? What's a cop to us?"

"But why disturb these people? Why not blend into the landscape, stay out of trouble until we know what we really want to do?"

"Why *not* disturb them? To hell with them. Compared to us, they're babies. Pitiful slow moving, slow thinking creatures. Let'em yammer all they want." Thus spake Sara. Obviously, we did have our little differences.

"They'll be beating on the door next," I said. "Let's go outside and face them. But listen… let's take it easy, OK?"

As Sara and I went to the door I realized with a passing thought that neither of us had reshelved the set of encyclopedias. We were both through with them, for all time, and they would go out with the trash tomorrow with the contents safely recorded in our heads.

With a glance at Sara I threw open the door and both of us stepped outside and took a couple of our quick, gliding steps to meet our audience just outside our front gate, on the sidewalk.

By now the neighborhood was gathering. I counted forty-six in the crowd and there were others still streaming out of houses and running forward with faces wearing expectant grins of excitement.

Two uniformed policemen led the group, with their idling cruiser in the background, lights flashing.

"What's the trouble here?" demanded one, looking from Sara to me. "We had a call saying there was a disturbance."

I said nothing. It was interesting to watch the crowd, most of them people I knew vaguely, having waved a casual 'hello' to them over the years.

They were watching us with intense interest. You could read their minds as they tried to read us. Who were we? What were we? Were we related in some way to that nice old couple who lived here? Did they recognize our clothes, perhaps?

"What have you got to say for yourself, mister?" The first cop demanded again.

Neither of us spoke and this flustered the cop more than a rude answer.

We were watching the crowd, even as they watched us. To me, the people before us looked inhuman, like a group of animated wax figures.

I could see their eyes focus first on me and then on Sara, then switching from one to the other of us. Every eye was intensely interested in what it saw, yet I'm sure no one would be able to describe what they saw. We were outside their range of experience.

By now, I felt that what Sara and I had become was simply normal, and that the rest of the world had become less than normal.

The people before us were infinitely tender and fragile, like so many living mushrooms. I would have been afraid to shake a hand, lest I inadvertently pinch it off. And they moved and thought and talked so slowly!

The people? Yes, but the dogs and squirrels and birds, too. Everything was so transitory. It was shocking. I knew we would have to readjust habit patterns, learn to live again in this fragile world without causing turmoil wherever we went.

Yet, this world was beginning to seem infinitely interesting also. It was as if someone had created a fantastic zoo just for Sara and me, peopled with fifty-million species of animals and insects, each of them so fragile as to be barely alive, yet each striding out, bravely working at the very limit of its ability to fulfill whatever destiny it saw for itself.

The police were a small but immediate problem. They felt that they had to do something and I felt that we had to protect them from their own egos.

Yet, I didn't feel like getting into a big discussion with them that would lead to evasions. Why should I let anyone make me become something I despised: a liar? So I said nothing, just a reassuring, "It's all right, officer. Nothing is wrong. Everyone can go home."

The second cop strode up beside the first, working up his belligerence with each step and placing his hand on his gun. "We'll tell you when things are all right! Now, what's going on here?"

Sara began to sing again, very softly at first, very sweetly. I watched the crowd of wax figures. Several began to smile and sway to her music. But our five immediate neighbors, the ones Sara had punished with her voice, were not amused. Yet, what could they say?

Sara's soft, sweet music was making a mockery of their complaint and her skill had already captured her audience.

I began to know what it meant to be a performer as I watched the eyes that watched us. Most of the men had their eyes glued onto Sara and never took them off.

Oh, you simpletons, I thought, watching them. *Here you are, ogling the ultimate female, thinking your scrimy little thoughts, never understanding that the sheer intensity of this new being would destroy you if your dreams ever came true.*

Woman, too, watched Sara. Some seemed to go along with her performance on a surface level and enjoy it, but others were piercingly appraising, examining Sara with an intensity that excluded all else.

WILLIAM B. EIDSON

"Danger! Danger!" you could read it in their faces. "There's a hungry female animal about! Hide the men!"

One young housewife I watched intently because she watched Sara so intently, but she watched her as the men watched her, with eyes glittering and tongue darting from slightly parted lips.

So, there are hungers of all kinds about, I thought. And then I wondered about myself. Why was it that I could watch the watchers watching Sara and read their naked desires and not give a damn? Was it because I just couldn't take these mushroom people seriously?

As Sara sang I could feel a little "hummmmm, hummmmm" from my own voice as I raised a quiet harmony to her lead, but no one could hear my sound but me.

So, Sara could be a performer, but I couldn't. Oh, I could sing, perhaps as well as she could if I put my mind to it, but not for an audience. I was the observer, never the observed.

Why should I run and jump and smile and sing and dance for this slow-witted group? What did I care for their adulation?

But then I had never needed people, except of course, Sara. I had certainly needed Sara. She had been my human race.

Sara did need people. She had always hungered for their approval… and the fact that she had seldom gotten it had been her abiding tragedy.

But now… now they would listen to Sara, and idolize what they saw in her if I knew anything about the world of mankind.

The two policemen shuffled forward, knowing it was time to resolve something, but not knowing exactly what.

"All right, folks. It's been fun, but let's break it up," said one. The other nodded and placed his hand on his gun holster in a unconscious gesture of authority and backed his partner. "All over now! Let's break it up!"

But then, soto-voice to me, "Something stinks here, Mister, and I'm going to find out what it is. You just wait."

The crowd drifted away, talking in small groups as they went, and as the police returned to their cruiser and Sara and I turned to go inside, I suddenly felt a small hunger pang. My God! Haven't you eaten enough? I asked myself. But then I glanced at Sara and

91

saw that she was licking her lips and smiling. "Go fire up the van and pick us up some fast food," she said. "Let's say a big bucket of Kentucky Fried Chicken, dinner for ten and don't forget the gravy, then swing by McDonalds for a sack of Big Macs, say about two dozen, and then pick up four dozen donuts and a couple of gallons of milk and whatever else strikes your fancy, maybe a few pizzas for breakfast, OK? And you'd better stop at the bank's ATM to get some cash to pay for it."

So here we were, back at the familiar husband and wife roles. Sara was in her heaven and all was right with the world.

 chapter twelve

The next morning after breakfast (boiled eggs, a few pizzas, milk, orange juice, oatmeal, pancakes with honey, corned beef hash and a pan of biscuits. Delicious!) I said to Sara: "Before we start living this new life we've got to kill the old one, make some arrangements."

So, after a quick discussion I got on the phone and began to run down our agreed-upon list, calling our banker, broker, real estate agent and lawyer, among others.

Within an hour we had put the house on the market, canceled our joint bank account and set up a separate account for each of us (at Sara's suggestion) at a new bank where our faces weren't known, sold all stocks and bonds with the proceeds to go directly into these two new accounts, canceled all insurance policies (*screams* from the agent. Do you *realize?* At age seventy-nine with no hope of buying a new policy you want to *cancel?* Do you *realize?*") and generally taken care of all our financial affairs.

Then we called a hauling and trash disposal service and a house cleaning team and made arrangements for them to take away all broken furniture (we'd killed another bed during the night—the one in the guest bedroom. Smashed it to splinters. "Have to learn some type of control or else start using the floor," Sara said) and clean the house to get it ready to sell.

Both of us had to fill out new signature cards at the new bank and we had other errands to do, so we put the van to work again, driving to town.

After the bank business, I dropped Sara off at her favorite store while I went home and fed my white mice and fruit flies and started memorizing maps and all the back issues of *Travel and Leisure Magazine* that dealt with places I liked.

When I drove back to the department store to pick up Sara I found her surrounded by a gaggle of goggle-eyed women whom she completely ignored.

She had a stack of boxes and bags which we carried in one load to the van. She hummed contentedly, stacking the boxes in back.

"How perfect, to be rich and beautiful in a major clothing store. I got attention, I can tell you! People just stared. Envious hens, most of them, and salespeople really helped for a change. Whatever I wanted, someone ran to get. It was lovely!"

And so we spent the next few days, buying, selling, discarding things, adjusting our lives to new conditions like a couple of butterflies escaping their drab old cocoons to start a new life of natural splendor.

We made it a point to spend part of each day at the local library, where we built up mountains of anxiety among the quiet, efficient ladies in charge as we went among stacks like a couple of grazing cows, pulling out books, flipping through them, sometimes discussing them, but more often simply scanning, memorizing and returning to the stack book after book, methodically soaking up hundreds of years of accumulated human knowledge.

We both read history (and disagreed as to what we'd read)and a smattering of biography (extraordinary lives often reported by very ordinary observers) and philosophy (oh, what convolutions of language to express simple thoughts) and all the sciences except economics (no wonder they call it the "dismal science") and poetry (sometimes most sublime but often pretentious mouthings and fakery) and novels, of course. Hundreds of novels. We both ate them up, the good and the bad alike.

I remember someone saying that the first thing a young child says when he begins to talk and the last thing an old person says before he dies is: "Tell me a story."

So, we read stories.

We had our differences. I read Thomas Paine's "The Rights of Man" and the U.S. Bill of Rights and Constitution and marveled at puny mankind's vision and constructive ability.

"How sublime is mankind," I said to Sara. "With the handicap of his pitiful, forgetful brain, his weak little body, his short attention span, his endless emotional distractions, his sudden rages and unholy desires—just look at all he has accomplished! Look at the civilization he has created out of savagery."

But Sara was reading the history of warfare, stories of great despots, endless killings, famines, destructions of former civilizations, and for every good thing I could mention about man she would counter with a dozen foolish or cruel things that our species had also done.

For my Sistine Chapel she would give me a civil war, a Turk vs. Greek tragedy, a Cambodia, a Battle of the Somme, an entire ancient civilization destroyed because some hairy ruler had an itch in his private parts and a bigger itch of ambition in his heart.

And the priests! The righteous ones of all the world's religions. What horrors in the name of good!

Sarah said, "Do you know what wonderful thing happened a thousand years ago in Jerusalem? Let me tell you one nice story from the Crusades. It happened in 1096—it was the time they finally broke down the walls of the city and poured inside with swords at the ready for all the Infidels—you know the Jews and the Arabs, just like today. Well, they killed them all. Men, women, and children. The streets ran with blood. Then these religious creeps prayed and praised each other for having done the work of the Lord."

So Sara would goad me with her vision of mankind while I saw the profusion of consumer goods produced and distributed almost universally and the good life that by and large all civilized communities offered, and I saw the first steps into space and the amazing Voyager II sailing endlessly, billions of miles away, collecting data for an over-eager group of scientists and...Sara saw the crack houses, the shooting galleries of dope pushers, the prostitutes working not for money, but for a fix that would need still more hustling to buy still another fix, and the hard ugliness of cities and...oh, well, there you are, the bright and the dark side of that strange ape called man.

The morning we left our home (now under sales contract to a young couple who "just adored it," as well they might at the give-away price we'd accepted) it was empty and clean, with the sounds of our voices bouncing off walls and everywhere a soapy, just washed smell that made our home so foreign to us that we were glad to leave it.

Outside, the van was coupled to a brightly painted trailer with signs that told the world it was owned by the U-Haul people and that we were merely temporary renters. Inside were only our clothes (mostly Sara's new ones) and cassette tapes and CDs and sheet music and Sara's piano, plus cages of my white mice and fruit flies.

"Why don't you kill them off?" asked Sara. "You don't need them anymore. Do you?"

"Well, maybe. Who knows? You know me: the old researcher."

"Not so old," Sara smiled. "Not after last night."

The van itself was stacked with cases of canned goods: survival rations in case we got hungry between fast food shops. And, oh, yes, I'd paid a visit to the dealer and the van now had a new bumper and a new ignition lock with a couple of brand new keys. No more twisting wires together.

Progress.

So we set out to drive towards a new chapter in our lives. But as we backed out of our driveway and left our home for the last time we both felt a twinge of unease and Sara said, "Why do I feel that we're running away from something? What can there be to fear for people like us?"

I thought about the Wiseass. The immortal Wiseass that I hadn't mentioned yet to Sara, and I replied, "We're going out into the big, big world to see what we can see. We're going out for romance and adventure, nothing less."

"Romance and adventure," Sara echoed. "How nice. So let's get going."

chapter thirteen

I-95 South. You could call it boring. Ugly. Dangerous, even. But to us, it was a fascinating journey through a wax figure world of late twentieth century strip highway. Our van labored along at sixty-five or seventy, just keeping up with the traffic around us, and that seemed to us so slow as to be almost dream-like. We floated down the highway and other cars floated by us or towards us and inside these other cars and trucks the strangely alive-yet-not-alive figures presented themselves for our viewing, like museum figures on a conveyor belt.

We needed only a small fraction of our time to keep the van on course, so we could give full attention to each new person or family floating toward us, could discuss each in detail like scientists at twin microscopes, could then switch off the entire scene and concentrate on each other when we felt like it.

We were the ultimate spectators, and that was exactly what suited me.

Then we came to Fredricksburg, Va. and turned west, following Route 3, and the scene changed abruptly. We were wrapped in the green of grass and tree and covered by a deep sky blue. Man-made ugliness became diluted and almost disappeared in vast reaches of natural beauty.

"This is what I was thinking of when I picked this region," I said. "This and the mountains beyond. Just wait until you see them."

"Do you have a plan?" Sara asked, suddenly. "A plan for the rest of our lives? Are we going towards something you've thought out?"

"Oh, sure," I said. "You know me. Old Doctor Logic. I've got a dream-life planned for us. You'll love it. You'll see."

Sara smiled at me with the indulgence of one who has found you out but is being kind.

Simply sitting in the van as it droned along at sixty-five or so, lugging its U-Haul trailer behind it up hills and down hills towards the distant mountains, became an intolerable bore, even if the scenery was beautiful.

"I think I'll step outside," said Sara, and she opened the passenger door of the van, now laboring up a steep hill at no more than fifty, and in an instant she was running alongside, smiling and waving at me, now running ahead, now running back, then circling the van as she stuck her thumb to her nose, waggled her fingers and made faces at me.

"Two can play at that game," I said, and set the cruise control at just under wide open, then rolled down my window and opened the door and bounced out of the driver's side of the van, running alongside and putting my hand inside now and then to give the steering wheel a small nudge to keep it between the white lines.

Soon Sara and I were both running far off the road, then running back to nudge the van in a tiny correction, then chasing down and catching a rabbit which we tossed gently from one to the other before releasing, then back to the van, then jumping a stream and racing up a hill to turn and watch the van reach a crest and turn downhill, screaming at an ever-increasing speed toward a ditch.

"My piano," Sara shrieked, and streaked after the van, a blur of movement.

I followed, equally as fast, and the game of "save the van" became just a game, but it was a game we won.

Up ahead, there were other cars coming and I saw no reason to startle anyone by running alongside a driverless van, so I opened the driver's door and jumped in, taking over the wheel again.

Sara ran around to the U-Haul, opened the back door and climbed in, and soon I heard music from her piano.

"Better than the radio," I shouted back, and she banged the keys in a crash of chords to answer me, then began to play whatever came into her mind. To me, it was a most happy time. I drove along, jerking the wheel to make the van sway from side to side in big swoops to keep time with her music and hitting the horn to emphasize parts that I particularly liked.

So it went as we made our way through Culpepper and toward the Blue Ridge Mountains of Virginia.

About two in the afternoon, we spied a Burger King and stopped for a snack, ordering four dozen hamburgers, a dozen fries, and four large chocolate shakes, all to go.

Later, sitting at a roadside rest area and eating our lunch and basking in the brilliant sun of a blue-skied June day, I told Sara, "I have a good feeling about this. I think we're going in the right direction with our lives."

She nodded. "Maybe. I hope so."

Then she turned to look me right in the eye and said: "Fair warning. I'm just itching to use all the powers we've got. Don't let me get bored."

Later, we turned south along the skyline drive and were headed towards the Shenandoah National Park when I saw a small sign that attracted me. "Just the ticket, I said. Let's go have a look."

"You can't be serious," said Sara.

"Surrounded by all this beauty? Why not? What better place could we find?"

"But, a condo?"

"No harm in just looking."

"Plenty of harm," muttered Sara.

So we followed the signs, we found the sales office, we looked, we liked (I liked. Sara grunted.) and that afternoon, with the salesman busy calling our bank back in Rhode Island we signed a check and we bought the condo overlooking the Blue Ridge mountains of Virginia.

"So, OK, you get to make the first decision," said Sara. "But for the next thousand years the choices are all mine."

"But this won't be 'home' for us," I explained. "Only the base camp."

Sara gave an indulgent, wifely smile. "Whatever you say. We'll give it a fling. For a while."

There were twenty-four "units," as our salesman had explained. Ours had three bedrooms, three baths, the usual living room, utility room, kitchen, etc. and two large balconies, one facing west, the other, in the rear, facing the tennis courts and pool. The front balcony, on the third floor, opened to the master bedroom. It was high and wide and gave us a beautiful view of the mountains just beyond.

While Sara explored the rooms in our new home I wandered the grounds below, hungry to explore the big world I saw before me.

But soon Sara called, and I saw her on the front balcony, the one facing the mountains, and she said, "Let's unload the trailer. Just toss everything up to me. I'll catch it!"

How nice, to make a game of the nastiest chores, the ones I'd always hated before.

So I did. Piece by piece, I tossed up everything we had in the trailer and van and Sara caught each one and slid it into the next room. My last toss was Sara's piano, and when she'd picked that out of the air someone on another balcony, who must have been watching all along, said softly, "Oh, holy Christ!"

But said softly or not, we heard him and both Sara and I turned toward that voice, catching sight of a very fat man of about fifty just as he slid back into his own front room, hiding from what he'd seen.

"How are we going to live among all those prying eyes!" Sara asked, after I had joined her in the condo.

"We'll manage, I said. But, listening now carefully, I could hear doors clicking shut and footsteps sounding in condos all around us and whispers, persistent whispers. We had been seen, watched, examined, wondered-at, judged by a dozen soon-to-be neighbors. We had assumed that in the middle of the afternoon people would be busy at whatever they did, not hanging by their windows.

Shrugging off this annoyance, (after all, when it really came down to it, what did we care, either of us, about what these wax figured, slow-brained, barely-alive other people thought? We might try to hide our obvious difference from them because of the trouble it might cause, but really, it didn't matter. If we felt like doing something, we'd damned well do it.) I wandered, hand in hand with Sara, opening closets, turning on the water in the kitchen, flushing new toilets, exclaiming over the view from each room, nodding at the tennis courts that were just down the hill, persuading myself and Sara that we had a lovely new place to live. It was bright and airy, with soft creamy white walls that blended into the green world outside.

100

"But *infested* with people!" Sara hissed at me, gesturing right and left of our new walls and down toward the floor.

"Isn't that what the word 'condominium' implies?" I asked. "Didn't we know?"

"Oh, but knowing in one thing. *Knowing* is another. Oh, to hell with it! Let's enjoy."

We returned the U-Haul to the nearest dealer. We found a furniture store, and Sara, who had already decided exactly what she wanted, gave them a list of things to be delivered.

She ordered six king-sized mattresses, two for each bedroom ("No bedsteads, we'd only splinter them again," she said in an aside to me) heavy drapes and curtains, a couple of sofas and chairs for the living room, and… room by room, she furnished our new home. She knew the measurements, had thought out the colors and textures and knew in advance exactly what she wanted and didn't want.

For my part, I was impatient until we found a restaurant supply house. There, I bought a ten-burner West Bend gas stove, a commercial sized refrigerator and freezer and a set of cooking pots and utensils to fit our appetite.

"God! It makes me hungry to think of it!" I told Sara when we got back home and were waiting for everything to be delivered. "Let's pull the tops off a few cans of pork and beans. We can eat them cold."

Before she could answer, there was a knock on our door. A soft, tentative knock. Then, after a pause, a firmer, more confident knock. Sara answered the door, swinging it open as I peered over her shoulder. Our caller was a blonde woman, a neighbor of about forty, with the cheesy, pore-filled skin we had already come to expect from everyone, with flakes of dandruff on the shoulder of her light blue blouse. Her lips were a little cracked under her lipstick and there was an obvious overlap with two front teeth but I realized that she would always have been considered pretty and all I could see now were her imperfections. How sad of me! I'd have to get used to looking at people differently.

"Oh!" said our caller, with the nervousness that came from meeting new people, "I just wanted to invite you to the pool party tonight. You know, to meet everyone? I'm sort of a one-woman welcoming committee, you know? We'd all just love to meet you."

I started to make an excuse when Sara spoke over me, "We'll be there. About eightish? See you! Thanks for asking!"

"*Infested* with people," I muttered to Sara after I'd closed the door.

That night, walking toward the pool where others were already gathered, I said, "This is the last thing I had in mind. The very last. The less we have to do with other people, the better."

"Oh, don't be such a stick! If we're to live here, we have to."

"But we won't *be* living here. At least, not regularly.

"No? Then, where?"

"You'll see. You'll love it."

So, we met the neighbors. And for once in my life, I could remember their names, their faces, what each did or had done for a living, and who was married to whom. Not that it was important to me, just easy to remember.

They stood loosely grouped by age, it seemed. Young, white collar couples here; older, mid-life manager types there. Then the retired; gray, short of hair, but exuding success because they'd made it nearly to the end of their life-road and still had the money to live in a certain style.

I wandered over towards a skinny brunette girl with prominent hip and collar bones and tightly curled hair and a quick, nervous laugh. Her husband, a plump, soon-to-be-bald thirty-something with bad front teeth, was standing nearby talking with another young husband about sports, but watching Sara.

There, by the pool, was the fat man who had seen the piano toss. His wife, about the same fiftieth age, was cutting her eyes sharply from Sara to me, back and forth, her mouth twitching tightly, almost angrily. They had talked, she and her fatty, and they knew something was wrong about us.

The questions! Everyone had them. Who were we? Where had we lived before? What did I do for a living? Did Sara work? At what? Did we have children? Had we ever?

But their questions masked their real question: who and what were we? How could we be so obviously different? Were we dangerous or desirable? How could they, each of them, get involved with what they saw and felt? Could some of what we obviously had rub off on them?

I tried to stay in the shadows, where my strength and vitality wouldn't attract attention, but they sought me out. The wives, most of them controlled and asking tight, innocent little questions while their eyes burned intently, but several others openly inviting, standing just so with legs spread apart, using body language that was flagrant while they smiled and flirted and made remarks that they thought to be suggestive.

And I found it, oh, so painful. Embarrassingly so. I felt I couldn't reject these women out of hand and humiliate them, but I couldn't give encouragement, either, because I just couldn't.

Not so, Sara. She deliberately turned on the light of her sensuality and began to shine it on selected males like a glowing beam.

They responded, each in their turn, like petted puppies, radiating pleasure and yipping for more.

In particular, I watched one healthy young husband with a blond crew cut and bulging biceps. He looked like one of those men who had lived all his life waiting to go out for a critical, game-winning forward pass and run for a touchdown to the violent cheers of all.

And, just now, his pass would be at Sara, as soon as he thought of a way to make it, and one glance at his hurt and furious wife told me that would cause nothing but trouble all around, so I went over and took him by the arm and said, "Tell me about yourself. What do you do for a living!" as I walked him, gently but firmly, away from the pool, away from the flame that was about to destroy this moth.

Then, in a burst of words too fast to be deciphered by anyone else, I shot back, "Sara! What're you doing? Behave yourself!"

She answered equally as fast, so that it must have sounded like no more than a cough to the others, "Don't you like that blond with the big tits? Don't be such a stick! Don't you know how to have fun at a party?"

I was instantly shocked.

Softly, almost casually at first, Sara began to sing. Soon she had taken her place near the pool where the lights shone full on her and she began giving a performance. There was no other word for it. With all the improbability of a movie star in a 1940's film, she simply gathered a circle of people around her and began to entertain. Judy Garland rides again, I thought, a little sourly.

Why? Why does she have the compulsion to do this? How could she, my female half for over fifty years, be so unlike me? And where would it all lead us?

Later that night, when all around us were in bed, I asked Sara, "Why do you do it?"

"You have your fruit flies and white mice," she replied. "I have my audience. Same thing."

chapter fourteen

Scraps of thought at dawn:

"Something is wrong with Sara," I said to myself. I watched her sleep, naked and beautiful, the most startling creature my eyes had even seen. Yet if I had not been made the same way myself I would have run away in fear, knowing that I had seen something unnatural and dangerous.

I try to follow the rules and Sara doesn't, I mused. I say, "Let's not make waves," and she says, "What's wrong with waves?" But really we're both the same. God help the people who get in our way. How can you take them seriously? Really, now.

I've always been in love, I thought, Ever since the moment I first saw Sara in that crappy little night club, trying to sing and dance and not being very good at it, so that my heart went out to her in sympathy and stayed with her in love.

But now I've fallen into infatuation. A violent teenage crazy infatuation. I look at this fantastic creature sleeping on our bare gray striped mattress with the sheet a twisted, useless rope on the floor beside her, and my eyes simply can't get enough.

I was glad that Sara slept her small sleep so that I could have this chance to gaze, when suddenly her eyes opened and she said immediately, "Look at me, Andy. Really give me a good look, all over... now, what'd you think? Am I getting older?" I know you said a thousand, ten thousand years, but it seems to me I may already have these little lines. Really now. Pay attention, be honest. What do you think?"

"No!" she said a few moments later, looking at the growing evidence of my interest. "That's not the answer to everything. Now, tell me the truth: it's all I can think about sometimes and its driving me crazy: am I getting old again?"

Of course she didn't believe me when I told her she wasn't.

So I swore to her in the name of all that might be holy that she was not one moment older than she had been.

I was almost certain that it was true.

chapter fifteen

We were sitting on our favorite mountain peak, eating Snickers bars and watching a brilliant sunset when Sara spoke suddenly.

"What was it that Crick and Watson discovered?"

"The double helix. The basic shape of all life forms. And they didn't discover it, they described it, which left hundreds of researchers free to build on their description. As you know, I'm one of those."

"Then let's call your Blue Pill the Blue Helix. Sounds loads better. Who wants to work for years like you did just to make a stupid pill."

"But Sara, a single helix makes no sense. Never mind a blue one."

"Does to me, so that's what we'll call it."

I shrugged. So long as Sara was happy, I was happy. After all, we weren't putting my blue pill—or Sara's Blue Helix—on drugstore shelves. Sara and I were the only two legitimate customers in the universe (never mind the Wiseass, he was an accident) so we could call it whatever we liked.

I said, "So there we are: The Blue Helix. Sounds great, scientifically ignorant though it is. So that's the new name."

Privately, I thought: *Get used to it, Andy. Blue Helix, Blue Helix, Blue Helix. Whatever Sara wants, Sara gets.*

chapter sixteen

Oh, joyous days! Oh, loving nights! What a glorious month was June in our mountain home!

The two of us were the world, all the rest was phantom. It was a honeymoon. A honey, honey, honeymoon.

We slept only a few minutes each night, around dawn, and the only reason we slept at all was to break the night into the new day so we'd have the familiar sensation of yesterday, today and tomorrow.

Up at first light. Breakfast (ahhhhh! The best meal of the day!) on our big, ten burner stove, and then we'd be off to the hills, gamboling like a pair of supernatural lambs.

Jumping, running, climbing, oh, you can't know the joy of sheer fluid movement when there's no sweat, no stress, no pain. The air rushes by you sweetly, laden with scent, a river of odors, each with meaning.

"This is how it is to be a hunting dog," I yelled once to Sara, covering an area with geometric precision, running with my nose in the air until I scented a bird or a squirrel.

"I'd rather be a lioness!" She replied, swiftly stalking bigger game, a deer, then creeping up on it and flushing it, making it run, then running alongside it neck and neck, jump for jump, as it stared at her, wild eyed and afraid. Finally, she gave it a pat on the rump and let it go.

Childish? Of course. But we didn't mind being children. At least not for a while. We'd been old, responsible and death laden long enough.

One day I said to Sara: "A little work today, then a nice surprise."

I took her to a deserted gas station a few miles north of our condo where we waited for a truck delivery I'd ordered. When the truck pulled in, the driver and his helper slid out of the cab and confronted the two of us, eyes rolling at our strangeness.

"Man, we got this delivery, but it's heavy. Real heavy. Took a fork lift to put it in my truck. Ain't no way you two are goin' to handle it!"

I reached into my wallet and gave them a bill apiece and said, "Keep your eyes glued to that tree over there until you count to one hundred out loud and the twenty you hold in your hand is yours."

By the time they counted and looked around, their load was gone and Sara and I were running through the forest a mile away, carrying the big bundle between us and giggling.

"Over here!" I said, after a few more miles. "It's a great spot I found."

What an understatement! I'd found, not merely a great spot, but home. Home itself. Home its ownself.

About ten acres of clearing, covered with grass and wildflowers, mostly flat. All around it, the vivid green of a healthy forest. A mountain stream running through it in a curving, rushing path, filling a small, knee-deep pool with clear, quiet water before rushing on again to the other side.

We dropped our bundle beside this pool and I began to untie it and spread it out.

"Oh! Its gold! A rich shade of gold! How nice among the green!" Sara said, helping me unfold the tent we'd lugged in.

"Huge! How big is it!" she asked.

"I ordered a forty by sixty. It was the biggest they had in a brand new tent, the biggest I could get without a special order and a wait."

"Big enough. Big enough to live in."

"That's the idea. The idea from the beginning. From now on, the condo is a way station. This is home."

Sara pulled one end and I pulled the other and the tent stretched between us. Then I tossed Sara two of the poles and some of the metal stakes and we started erecting our new home. Once standing, leaning and sagging, we were able to move it, straighten it, tighten it, stretch it, until it was strong and well-placed and just right.

We needed no sledgehammers to drive the metal stakes, we'd just push then into the ground.

When the tent was finished we unrolled and spread the white tarp I'd ordered with it, giving us a fabric floor to keep out the grassy damp.

"Tomorrow, we go to town," I said, "And order what we need to furnish it. I was thinking, maybe a big oriental rug and a couple of mattresses and what they used to call hassocks. Do they still make hassocks?"

"I could learn to love it," Sara said, gazing up at the golden tent, now lit warmly by the sun. "And you're right: an oriental would be perfect. Tomorrow, we shop. I think I'll buy a lute!"

I thought, as I had a million times in the last few days, how very strange it was. At every glance at Sara I saw a supernaturally beautiful, vital creature, a shock to the eyes. I would think that I was used to the way we were, then I'd look again at Sara or at a reflection of myself in the pool outside and get a new shock every time. A shock of pleasure, but a shock, nevertheless.

And yet, with all our lightning-fast thought, our extra-human abilities, our undeniable strength and beauty, we were still basically the same old Sara and Andy Camp. That was a startling thing. Was the set of conditioned reflexes and reinforced opinions instilled during early childhood so strong that nothing could change them? Was the "me" and the "she" inside us so powerful that not even a new superego could recreate them? Was I doomed to be Andrew Camp even if I got sick of being Andrew Camp? It certainly looked it.

We were trapped, like all humans, in the prison of our own personalities. But, what the hell. I liked being Andy Camp. Most of the time.

The first time we used our bathing pool beside our golden tent the water rose over our flesh like a dream liquid, light and insubstantial, like liquid air.

"You know, its not the water that's changed," I said. "It's us. I think we've gotten dense."

"Dense? You, maybe, not me!"

"No. Dense, as in heavy."

"Heavy? Don't you know? For a girl, heavy is worse than dense."

"Oh, the hell with it!." I gave Sara a splash with this new light-weight water. "Fun, isn't it?"

"Delightful. Absolutely delightful. The whole world made new, just for us."

July followed June as we settled into our new mountain home beside the stream and pool, amid the wildflowers.

Now and then we'd slip back to the condo to feed my white mice and fruit flies and to bring back food or other supplies, but we lived day by day in the golden tent. One night we liberated Sara's piano from the condo and set it up in the middle of the tent where it would have the best chance of staying dry.

Then, every couple of days we'd make a trip to town. We brought back huge supplies of canned food, a jumbled pile of musical instruments, which we both learned to play, and we brought back other furniture and supplies as needed until our tent was filled with our possessions and was truly home.

The golden days of summer. I would watch every fiery nuance of the sunrise, committing each instant of it to memory day after day. I just couldn't get enough of sunrises in the green world beyond the golden tent that was our home.

I'd say, "Look, Sara! My God, look at that corona! What a beautiful world we live in!"

Then, the sunrise would fade into day and I'd love that, as well. The sparkling morning, dew evaporating from grass, birds eating worms and bugs, hawks circling for mice, all the beautiful sweet drama of eat-or-be-eaten that is life on our earth.

Sometimes it rained, and I loved the feeding of the green with soft water as well. Sometimes the skies gave us the melodrama of a thunder and lightning storm and what better theater to watch it from than our tent under the skies?

Whatever came, that summer, I was fascinated. I was in a fever of excitement. I couldn't get enough of looking, smelling, touch-ing, understanding.

I felt that I was inhabiting multiple worlds. Wherever I turned, there was another world to understand. The world from the viewpoint of the ant. The world as the turkey buzzard saw it. The sweet, grassy world of the grazing cow. The world from the

111

vantage point of a blade of grass, anchored to the ground, unable to speak, unable to think in the sense that we think of thinking, yet a major part of this complex universe, fed by rain and rotted vegetation, bathed by a sunlight that made its chlorophyll factory flourish, supremely successful in every grassy way until it was stepped upon by a man or eaten by a deer. And even then, with roots that would put forth a new blade of grass within days.

Oh, I understood it all. One day I would close my eyes and say: "I think I'll just live by smell for a while." And then I'd know what the dogs know, the foxes, the cats, the successful predators of the world. I'd sit, eyes closed, and smell a symphony of odors. Some were (in human terms) sweet, some sour, some rancid and harsh. But these were only the minor keys of a complex whole. Great crashing chords of odors outlined the animal world as surely as an infrared photo in the night.

At other times I'd turn off all the senses except hearing, and with ears keener than a cat's I'd listen to the natural world around me and interpret every footfall, every brush against a tree or leaf.

"The perfect time." That's how I always think of it, those long sweet summer months that we spent in our nomad tent beside the mountain pool.

It was like an ancestral memory of happiness. A time when there was no dark, only light. A time when to wish was to have and the having was never less than the desire had been.

I would run up our mountain, Sara beside me, and we would not be breathing hard, nor sweating, nor bruised or strained in any human way, but rather transported to the top of our mountain.

Once on top, we'd sit and survey the world spread out below us like our private paradise, with none of man's ugliness. And there sometimes we'd simply sit and talk. I was thinking a lot these days about black holes and quarks and antimatter and other components of the universe as the modern physicists saw it.

Sara had read the same library books I had and she could hold her own in any discussion I wanted on the shape of the expanding universe as understood through quantum mechanics, but her heart really wasn't in it.

"I'd rather watch an ant drag away a grasshopper leg," she said. "Now, there's a real piece of work!"

112

At other times, we'd find a nice, round rock, a big one weighing a couple of hundred pounds, and stand a half mile apart on twin peaks and play catch with it.

Our rock would go, "whooooosh! from my hand to hers and then back again, thrown at me with what seemed to be sheer destruction, but I'd catch it easily and whirl around like a discus thrower and send it whooooshing back as fast as it came.

Silly? Certainly. But hasn't man always thrown things? Caught things? There's a great satisfaction in it. I said to Sara once, "When I get around to doing research again I'm going to examine the human genome to see if our species has a ballgame gene built in. All this baseball, soccer, football, handball, volley ball and tennis can't be an accident."

For answer she slung our rock at my head like a bullet. "Catch it!" she screamed. "Catch it or die young!"

Looking up at the stars. Looking down on the earth. Throwing rocks. Eating the flesh of animals (now killed, cooked and canned by someone else, of course) and roots and berries and seed and leaves of plants. All exactly like the cave people before us. We talked about this, Sara and I, and got nowhere, except general agreement.

We could imagine ourselves three thousand years ago, sitting on Mount Parnassus and living our lives exactly as we were now, and those mortal men who saw us would call us gods and give us names and write poems and dramas about us. And we could imagine sitting here a thousand years in the future and we'd be the same and mankind would be the same. It would think it had learned a lot but it wouldn't have. The only real change might be in the mountain itself. Mankind would probably have bulldozed it down for some reason.

"Do you think they'll still have wars a thousand years from now?"

"God, I hope not. But one thing I know for sure." I picked up our rock and sent it sailing into the valley below. "If there are still men and women they'll still be making love and still throw and catch things for sport."

Oh, yes. We'd both read philosophy. We could have discussed the tangled rhetoric of Schopenhauer or Kant or we could have gotten into the thousand and one gods and religions that mankind has fought and died for, but somehow this summer on our mountain peak, this was about as deeply as we wanted to delve into manmade mysteries.

It was a most happy time. Sunny and brilliant. A time of extreme awareness. Literally, not a leaf moved without our knowledge and understanding.

I, who had scarcely ever thought of them before, became a flower fanatic. I was caught one day by a perfect pink rose growing in a planter at the condo. It drew my eye, so I snatched it off the bush and ran with it, bounding over tree and rock, to our tent in the wilderness, where I threw myself down beside the stream and began to examine it.

The geometry of its shape was perfect. I found my eyes filling with tears of wonder. The smell, of course, was beautiful, yet to me it was a cliché' of odors. "Do you have to be so obvious with your rose smell?" I questioned it. It was the shape, the mathematical purity of the design of each petal and of all the petals together that choked me up.

But then I saw my rose begin to wither, ever so slightly, and I crushed it with one hand and tossed it away and began looking for more miracles.

They were everywhere. I found wildflowers wherever I looked, and taking them up one at a time I looked deeply within each bloom, so concentrating my attention that I almost lost contact with the world around.

So it went. For those few days I was immersed in flowers. Then I discovered squirrels. I was in a frenzy of discovery.

And Sara? She found her interests, too. The geology of individual rocks. The age of the upthrust mountain range we lived on, the delicate construction of wild mushrooms. There was no end to the beauty and mystery of our universe.

"I could spend a thousand years here," I said, one day.

"Let's don't stretch it *that* far," she replied.

The nights were magic. We could see quite well in the smallest light and all the other animals came alive at night. We roamed far from our tent and only came back to it when we wanted something we'd left there, or wanted to use a mattress for play or sleep.

Ahhh…sleep! Even if it were only five minutes toward dawn, I loved it because I loved the mystery of my dreams. And so, I thought, did Sara. But one night she gave a cry of horror and sat upright, the victim of a nightmare. "Tell me about it," I said, taking her hand and rubbing her back gently, soothingly.

"I dreamed we were old again." Sara shuttered with distaste. "I dreamed that I couldn't get out of bed without laboring to roll onto my side, then working hard to get my feet over the edge of the bed, then asking you to 'give me a boost' to sit upright on the bed. I dreamed that my back ached and my heart fluttered with the effort and I could smell my own bad breath as I labored to shift my weight and then when I had gotten my feet on the floor and managed to stand up, the arches in my feet didn't want to support my weight and my legs trembled and I knew I only weighed ninety-seven pounds, for God's sake, even though I was puffy and soft looking, and then I realized that I would only get worse and I said to myself, 'Sara, if you were a horse, they'd shoot you', yet I still wanted to live, oh, how I wanted to live!

"Can you imagine? Why, my very *guts* were old! Filled with pockets of diverticulosis. Disgusting to have old blown-out guts inside you!

"And then I looked between my legs and the hair was gray and wispy and my little thing was dry and closed tight, with no juices left. My eyes burned. My very teeth were old and coated yellow and sore at the gum line. Disgusting! Old! Disgusting!

"Yet I *still* wanted to live and I thought everyone owed it to me to keep me alive, no matter what, and thank God they thought so, too, or at least they said they did and that's almost the same thing.

"I don't want to ever dream that dream again! I don't really need to sleep and I won't sleep. I'll never be old again, not even in my dreams."

I put my arms around Sara and gave her what comfort I could. I didn't tell her that I'd had the same dreams myself, but that I didn't really mind them that much. Oh, I feared old age because it meant the Dark Angel of death was ever near but it was such a pleasure to dream myself old and then awake to find us as we were, sparkling with life. But I never saw Sara sleep again, not

115

even for a moment, and I was sad to see her reject it because to me it seemed that sleep was necessary to let our dreams sort out our problems and resolve them. Otherwise, like a geological plate that's constrained too long so that internal pressure builds up, there could be an earthquake.

One day Sara came bounding out of the woods with something small and round nestled on a piece of tree bark.

"Look at that!," she demanded. "Do you know what it is?"

"Sure," I said. "I did one like that myself a couple of days ago."

"How can it be? With all we eat, how can we do only this little gray, harmless looking thing? Why, it doesn't even smell!"

I laughed. "Would you feel better if it stank? The thing is, our bodies seem to use everything we eat, to waste nothing that can be used, and what you see here is only truly useless scrap. Sand from our food, mainly. Maybe a little cellulose. Just inert matter. Why don't you toss it away and forget it?

"It's cute," said Sara. "I think I'll have it bronzed." But she didn't. She gave the tree bark a flip over her shoulder and the little gray ball went with it, adding its tiny speck of mass back to the mass of the earth.

chapter seventeen

Sara came back from shopping one day with a small round mirror on a gold chain which she wore around her neck.

"Nice chain," I said, pretending not to notice that she'd already picked up the new habit of glancing into the mirror at odd times. It seemed to me that she was not so much admiring herself as searching for defects. Searching for wrinkles, searching for anything that might show age.

"Sorry, Sara," I said. "But I look at you all the time and I can't find anything wrong. Not a single jot or tittle."

"Huh!" she replied, glancing automatically into her mirror. "You wouldn't tell me anyway. Now, would you?"

Age. Damned old age, followed inexorably by stench and dissolution. The last and worst enemy. No wonder Sara feared it.

I saw people all around us who were like other growing things: here a peach, there a banana, easily bruised, and over there a walnut, tough and hard, but all of them, *all* of them aging in the same inescapable way.

People. They start out new and unformed and then begin their growth toward physical maturity. For one perfect moment they are the best they can ever be. Then, after only the shortest dwell-period they start down the deadly path, traveling the highway that has but one end, and like victims of mass hypnotism, they seem not to know their fate. They go, pushing and fighting or laughing and playing up to the point of death, growing more feeble and age-ugly at each step, and when they at last see the eternal headsman's ax they look shocked. Surprised, Say, "Oh? So soon? Me? Really? Me?

Already? Are you *sure?*"

Sara was right to be age-obsessed. And I never let her know, but I had my share of the cold sweats, too, when I thought of what we'd so narrowly escaped; when I wondered whether we had really escaped for all time or whether I had overlooked something simple and obvious and awful that might destroy us.

"We'll live forever," I assured Sara, wishing that I knew, absolutely, that it was true.

*   *   *   *   *

One August morning Sara and I were bounding along our mountain, enjoying the steamy heat left over from a rainstorm the night before, when a solid-looking rock about six feet in diameter turned under my foot.

"Hey! Wait up. There's something strange here," I yelled. Then I rolled the rock away, giving it a kick for good measure that sent it crashing downhill, bumping into other rocks as it went.

"Look!" I called. "I knew there ought to be one around here somewhere. A cave. A damned big cave, looks like it." I was on my knees, now, peering inside.

The rock had fallen from above to hide the entrance almost as though someone had placed it there, and there were other fallen rocks on either side of the opening that I quickly cleared away to enlarge the entrance to about ten feet. "Come look," I said. "Let's explore!"

The two of us crept into the cave, smelling musty air and a rank animal smell that I mentally identified as belonging to a large animal, perhaps a bear, probably one who had spent the previous winter there.

The floor of the cave pitched downward for a half-dozen steps, then turned and leveled off to bring us to a squarish chamber roughly one hundred feet by one-fifty. The ceiling, low at the entrance, became high and craggy over the large chamber, varying from about fifty to eighty feet. Toward the back, there was another hole, slanting downward, where the cave continued deep into the mountain. I looked into this hole, but the light was dim, even to my eyes, and besides, even if it went to the bowels of the earth and hid marvelous treasures, it didn't interest me just now.

What did interest me was the large chamber in which we stood

"It's a perfect room underground," I said. "Strong and stable, just the right size, exactly what I've been looking for."

118

"Didn't know you were looking," said Sara. She was prowling around, looking at everything closely, just as I was.

"I didn't know it either, until now. But now that I see it, this is exactly what we need." I was growing more and more excited as I circled the chamber of the cave poking at rocks here and there to test their stability.

"Do me a favor," I continued, "Take a run into town, it'll be faster than driving, and get a couple of those big flashlights with extra batteries. You know, those big six cell lights the cops hit you over the head with. I'd go myself, but I need to look."

Sara muttered something, but soon I noticed I was alone, so I kept looking and kicking rocks toward a pile in the back of the chamber as I came to them.

When I had first seen the chamber I had gotten an idea. By now the idea was a full blown plan. My brain was seething with activity. Detail after detail. Lists of things to do, all in order. What to buy. Where to buy it. Where to store things. How to make my underground chamber perfect for my needs.

"Vacation is over for a while," I told myself, happily. *No more flower-sniffing for you. Things to do, things to do.*

Just to keep busy, I swept the stone floor with my feet, piling all the rocks near the back and all the bones and animal debris near the front, where it could be swept out the entrance.

I was humming to myself and working away, sometimes jumping up forty or fifty feet into the gloom to knock a loose rock down from the ceiling, when Sara appeared with an armful of equipment from town.

"A flashlight would be lost in here," she said, "So I brought you a generator and a string of lights. Where do you want it?"

Immediately, I was cooing over my new generator like a proud parent. It was small, only a five kilowatt, and I knew immediately that I'd need a much bigger one eventually, but this was perfect for temporary lights.

So, I filled the gas tank with the can she'd brought, gave the starter a pull, and started stringing lights from rock to rock across the ceiling, jumping up, time after time to reach a likely spot to hang a wire.

Soon my cave was lit. The little generator hummed along, making more noise than need be in the hollow echo chamber of the cave, and some two dozen hundred-watt bulbs glowed, casting harsh white light in some places, leaving black shadows in others. But never mind, I could see every inch of my chamber.

"I'll whitewash it," I told Sara, "That's the easy way, just spray the whole damned thing inside with whitewash, make the lights reflect better, make everything bright and clean."

"How about wall-to-wall carpet!" she asked, with more than a touch of sarcasm.

"Not a bad idea! Really, it isn't. Take care of some of the bumps and holes in the floor, keep everything clean, too. A layer of plywood first, then carpet. Great idea!"

"We had a nice, roomy home. Then a condo. Then a tent. Now a cave. D'you think there's a pattern here, maybe?"

I ignored her. "What we need, first off, is a telephone. Time to order stuff. Lots of stuff. Come on. Let's run to the condo."

By the time I got to the phone I had it all organized in my head. Then I started calling building supply companies, giving them my list. Cement in bags (truck loads of it), reinforcing rods, reels of electric cable, lumber, nails, bolts, air conditioning equipment, duct work, tools (a long list), a big new generator, water and gasoline tanks, plywood for forms, a concrete mixer, paint sprayer, white concrete paint (better than whitewash after I thought about it), and the list went on.

"Good thing we're flush with money," said Sara, listening to me order things over the phone.

I waved that away. Money? Surely I could make more any time I wanted.

"Don't worry about it," I said.

"I won't. Just an observation."

I got back on the phone, working the yellow pages, buying things, running down my mental list, telling everyone I ordered from that I'd run in this afternoon and give them a check but to go ahead and get my order loaded on a truck for delivery.

Then I turned to Sara. "Listen, honey, we've got work to do. Come on! It'll be fun."

"I'll indulge you one more time," Sara muttered as we loped

off down the road toward the mountain and our new cave "Just one more time. This is crazy for people like us."

But she went along. God knows, I knew how she felt. Why should we waste our time doing simple physical things? Simple, simple things that anyone could do when we could do anything?

By noon we had finished. The cave was empty and clean, with all loose rocks removed and piled neatly in the rear.

"I'm starved!" Sara said. "I haven't been this hungry since the first time."

We were running back to the condo, where we had the kitchen stacked with canned food. "I think it's the work. It doesn't make us tired but we do get hungry as we use up energy."

"Don't explain," said Sara, "Run! Let's eat!" And soon we were home, pulling the tops off cans, eating some cold to take the edge off our appetite and dumping the rest into large pots to heat and eat later.

Then, while the stove was doing its work, we jumped into the shower together to wash away the morning's dirt.

"Do you remember that day, forty years ago, when we'd been raking leaves, autumn leaves, and you went inside and had your shower and then you called me to come in? Do you remember that, Sara?"

"Oh, sure," she said. And of course she would, because we could remember anything if we tried. But I knew immediately that her memory was not exactly like my memory.

"I was thinking about our child," I said, gently.

"You were thinking about death," she replied. Then, with a sad, wry smile, "Mamma ain't goin' study death no more."

"Let's talk about something else."

"Let's eat!"

Next day, the trucks rolled in and when they were unloaded we carried everything to the cave, taking a different route with each load so we didn't make an obvious trail for others to follow.

"This is to be the holy-of-holies," I said. "No one but me and thee can ever know. No one in all the world."

I went to work. Sara would help when I asked, but this was my project and I didn't want or need help. I wanted to do it my way, with no discussion.

First, the concrete. Sara carried water, then watched as I put up reinforcing rod, slathered on mortar mix, and improved upon the walls and ceiling, strengthening and smoothing out nature's crags. Then I used the cement and the rocks I'd piled there to close off the small cave at the rear, leaving my chamber with a rectangular perfection that nature never intended.

"Do you remember that Jules Verne book, *Mysterious Island,* I asked Sara.

"Of course. Wonderful story."

"That's how I feel. Isn't it great building things out here all by ourselves where no one will ever see?"

"I'm sorry, Andy. It's more like shooting fish in a barrel. Those men in the book couldn't use the Yellow Pages to order whatever they wanted and they didn't have your strength and mental power. That's what made them so heroic—small man winning against overwhelming odds."

"Killjoy," I muttered to myself. Then, with a spray gun, I turned everything white inside. The difference in light reflection was startling: even one lit match would carry vision from wall to wall.

Laying lines of two-by-fours on the ground, I nailed plywood to them to make a floor, then spread rolls of blue wall-to-wall carpet over that and tacked it down.

Sara had a big bag of Snickers bars we'd brought in on our last trip to town and she sat on a rock she's carried in from the outside and peeled candy bars while she watched me work. Every now and then she'd pop one into her mouth and toss me one, too, but most of the candy went back into the bag, ready for a fast nibble when we wanted. The wrappers went into a trash bag. No littering for our mountain.

"Homey," Sara said, when the walls and floor were finished. Then she watched with eyes growing bigger as I installed the larger generator and air conditioning ductwork and installed a wooden framework for permanent lights and built rows of strong workbenches and tables. Everything was going up, frip-frip-frip, like an impossibly speeded-up movie.

When she saw the tables go up she said, "No. My mistake. Not homey. Not homey at all. You're building a laboratory. And I want to know why."

"I'm building the safest, most secure laboratory in the world," I said. "Safe from prying eyes."

"But, why?"

"Why? Because that's what I do. That's who I *am*."

Sara got up from her perch on the rock she'd brought in for a chair and gave it a sudden backward kick that made shattered gravel and stone dust out of it and began stalking me like a predator. "What do you have hidden away in that mind of yours? What are you up to? *What* haven't you told me?"

"Oh, just a little biological research. You know, like I've always done."

I was surprised at myself. Here I was, being evasive with Sara, as she well knew, and I hadn't planned it, hadn't even thought of it until now.

"What type of research?"

"Oh, you know. On the Blue Helix. What makes it work. How to make more of it if I want to. Things like that."

"More of it?" Sara now had her face almost nose to nose with mine, "Why? Why, for God's sake? What are you up to, Andy Camp?"

"Well, I don't know. Who knows? I might as well make more. Maybe we'll find a use for it. Besides, goddamnit, I can make it if I want to, can't I? Who says I can't?"

"Who'll you give it to? *We* don't need it, do we? Are you hiding something from me? Do we need periodic doses to keep us young?" She was the fierce wife, forced once again to depend upon frail man and hating her dependence. "You tell me!"

What to tell? Tell her that I could only assume we'd never need another dose? How could anyone know for sure? Tell her that I wasn't even really sure that I knew how to make the Blue Helix? Yes, my white mice were alive and doing fine, but they certainly weren't supermice. Then, they hadn't gotten my last batch of Blue Helix, so maybe that was it. But on the other hand, maybe that crap of Henry Fowles' had been important after all. Who knows? Worse yet, who knows what it really was? Some kind of screwed-up accident? And me with not even a sample of it to analyze?

Things I had to find out, and I'd be damned if I'd discuss it with Sara, get her all excited and yelling into my ear like a wife, until I knew what I had to know.

So, I did what husbands have done for eons: I stalled.

To an outside observer, we would have been two vital spirits, each shimmering with strength and elemental force, facing each other with one spirit (me) bent backward, and one (Sara) bent forward in the attack mode as we moved about the squarish chamber I'd fashioned from the cave.

"A-n-d-y! Tell! Tell meeee!"

"This is intolerable. I will not be grilled. Listen, let's go outside and run up the top of our mountain and talk."

I picked up our bag of Snickers bars and then whirled and left the chamber with Sara in pursuit. We climbed, bounding from rock to rock, up the mountainside, as we'd done a thousand times before. "It's going to rain," Sara said from behind me as we ran, "We had to leave a nice dry cave for this."

And indeed, she was right. The day had become dark, cloudy and gusty, and there was a distant rumble of thunder. But we made it to the top and the rain held off. I had been thinking during our climb, trying to understand my own mind.

Sara sat on a small peak and faced me as I sat about fifty feet away on another peak. We came here often because we could look out over the world spread below us like a scale model. I tossed Sara a few Snickers bars and popped a few into my mouth myself and gave them a quick chew and a swallow as I began talking

"I've been thinking about sick people in hospitals," I said. "About babies born with terrible birth defects. About brilliant old men and women about to die and take their spirits and all their accumulated knowledge and memory to the grave. About cruel, thick-headed people who could be made better. About stupid politicians who have immense power and no idea what to do with it. About people in terrible, unbearable, screaming pain. (Sara was looking at me now with shocked intensity, but I plunged on.) I've been thinking about weak, pitiful, ugly, wrong-headed yet noble mankind and how I could help it become something better, finer."

"No," Sara hissed. "Absolutely not! Wipe it from your mind!"

124

I chewed a Snickers and thought. I didn't really want to argue with Sara just now. Fact was, I wasn't all that sure myself what to do. But I knew I wanted to do something. Something to make things better.

"*Don't* you understand? *Won't* you understand?" Sara's eyes bored into mine. "Mankind is the scourge of the earth. A *disease.* A disease that's spread over the earth like a black fungus on a peach.

"Our human disease is choking the earth. We killed each other for millions of years; killed each other and killed all other species that got in our way; killed for profit and killed for fun, killed for God and killed for country and now we're killing the earth itself.

"And you want to give this disease new power? It would only kill more, kill faster, praying to its gods and singing praises to itself while it went along killing and destroying."

"Oh, we're not all like that!"

"Make 'em weaker! If you have to interfere, make mankind less than it is, not more."

"Here," I said, tossing her a handful of candy. "Have a Snickers and calm down. Nothing could be weaker than man, anyway. Do you know just how weak we are? Oh, not us. Them. One-quarter horsepower. That's the maximum, understand? One-quarter horsepower is the very most a trained athlete can develop over any period of time. No more than the little electric motor that drives a refrigerator or a washing machine. That's *all.*

"And that's an athlete, mind you. A strong, strong man. Most people are only half of that, a tenth of that, even. Most people don't have the sustained power of a vacuum cleaner.

Sara sailed a rock at my head, knowing I would catch it or dodge it harmlessly, but wanting to show her anger anyway. "You fool!" she screamed. "Let puny mankind alone! It'll destroy the earth and destroy us. D'you think they'll love you for it? Whatever you give them they'll want more. More and more. And the more you give them the more they'll hate you for not giving them everything."

"But, Sara, we have to do something with what we have. We can't just hog it to ourselves forever."

"Then what? What? Tell me!"

How could I say, "I don't know." How could the computer-brained, all-seeing, all-knowing Andy Camp, Ph.d. and superbeing say, "I don't know." But I said it anyway, because it was true.

"I don't know. I haven't got the foggiest what I want to do, what I ought to do. But I know I want my factory right here in this cave."

"AAAAAAAAAGH!" screamed Sara, and she jumped suddenly off the top of our mountain, landing on a solid outcrop of rock and then with another leap and another going down to the foot of the mountain, and from there she made a streaking run towards our condo, not dodging between the bushes and trees as we always did, but running full tilt with both arms outstretched, destroying everything in her path, making a road through the woods that would be there to mark her passage for years.

I sat on the mountain peak eating the last of the Snickers bars and watching her leave. Some show.

*　　*　　*　　*　　*

A couple of days later Sara sat on a small rise overlooking the old gas station and watched two trucks pull in with the laboratory equipment I'd ordered.

She pointedly refused to help me carry the equipment to the cave and set it up.

"Your problem. Not mine," she said.

Our arguments had grown bitter, with each of us refusing to budge, yet each of us privately understanding the weakness in our own logic. That very understanding of our illogic made us the more vehement.

"Maybe I'll pick out only a few top people. Leaders and future leaders," I said.

"And establish an aristocracy!" she threw back at me.

"I don't know. Maybe just heal the sick. I haven't figured it out yet."

"When the sick get well they're just as bastardly as anyone else."

"Damnit! Sara. I'll find a way. I don't know. Let me think. Maybe I'll make a race of people who're almost perfect but sterile and with short lives. Maybe…"

126

"Andy the castrator, eh? A perfect world in which you're the only perfect stud. Is that it?"

So it went. The skies were filled, not with the sound of music, but with our anger and confrontation. A husband and wife cat-fight. The nastiest kind, because only our spouses truly know our weaknesses.

In and among the emotions a cooler part of my brain wondered: why did Sara and I not think and talk in profundities? Our comments were quick and to the point, but no deeper than they had ever been and just as scarred with the illogic of human emotion. Why? With our new computerpower brains, why were we not philosophical prodigies?

I remembered days when Sara and I had sat on top of our mountain looking down on the earth, our own private garden, and played chess without a board, calling out our moves, or had had deep discussions of the Bertram Russell book, *Mathematica Principia,* which I had studied years before and had coerced Sara into reading at one of our library binges.

Did this understanding of symbolic logic which only an elite handful of humans had ever bothered to learn make us deeper than other humans? Sadly, I thought not. Only quicker, and able to remember and process vastly more information. After all, weak and pitiful mankind had already created every thought we now manipulated. We merely processed them over and over, faster and faster, like a computer set in an endless computation mode.

After watching me move a few crates to the cave Sara called out: "You work! I'm going to town and buy something I've always wanted." And with that, she ran towards the condo with those long, loping steps we both used to cover ground quickly and I turned my back and went to work with a vengeance.

By late afternoon I had everything uncrated and in place in the cave and the broken-down crates stacked neatly outside to be carried off and disposed of.

I stood there, at the cave entrance, flicking the main switch off and on and looking happily at my beautiful laboratory. Then I would turn the lights off again to make blackness so that I could please myself once again by flicking the switch on. To put it simply, I loved the place. The contrast between the natural rocky, woodsy emptiness outside the cave and the brilliant manmade glass and stainless steel world inside was perfect, to my way of thinking. Every time I flicked the switch I not only saw this vision of technology appear, but heard the generator cut on, heard the soft purr of air conditioning, saw digital instruments light up (I'd left them switched on, purposefully, just to see them glow) and knew that I had a research facility that would work with me any time I wanted to use it.

chapter eighteen

Morning. Sudden brightness under our golden tent as the red sun peeped over the edge of the earth. I opened my eyes after a five minute sleep and immediately saw Sara looking down at me.

Such a sight! Every morning, the same thrill, always undiminished, always a delight.

"You ought to sleep," I said. "If nothing else, just for the joy of waking up and seeing us. Seeing what we've become. It's shocking. Beautifully, wonderfully shocking."

"No sleep for me," Sara said. "No old-folks dreams. But I do enjoy watching you sleep. You make faces and sometimes I give you a grab and you smile and squirm in your sleep and I wonder what your dreams are."

"You know what they are when you do that," I said, springing up and taking Sara by the hand. "Let's take a dip in our pool."

So started another day, like the hundred-odd days we'd already spent in our tent.

Sara played some of her favorite Gershwin selections while I spread a breakfast of bread and cheese and cold sausages and preserves. Later in the morning we'd return to the condo where our stove would give us a hot meal, but this early morning snack took the edge off and it was more than pleasant to eat with the chirping of birds and the stirring of all nature around us as the sun rose.

"What're you doing today?" Sara asked, smearing her bread with jam and cocking an eye at me. "Playing scientist in your secret laboratory?"

"You could call it that. I thought I'd just see what the Blue Helix is all about. We need to know that, Sara."

"You do. I don't. We're self-evident. All you can do is cause trouble. Big trouble. *Leave it,* for Christ's sakes. *Leave it.* Don't dabble," she continued earnestly, almost pleadingly, "You don't have to know everything. You know enough already."

I chewed on that thought for a while, then said: "And when man first learned that fermented grape juice was drinkable, and gave him a funny, pleasant feeling, should he have stopped at that? Is that as far as the science of chemistry should have gone?"

"Never mind this goody-goody Andy-the-boy-scientist crap," Sara replied, her eyes boring into mine, "You know what we're both talking about: other people. Let them alone. Don't interfere. *Don't* screw up the world.

"At the very least," she continued, taking my hand and forcing me to look into her eyes, "at the very least, wait a hundred years or five hundred. Promise me that, Andy. Promise me you'll wait and look at ugly mankind for another hundred years before you do anything foolish."

"Not a bad thought," I said, carefully noncommittal. "Come on, let's run. Let's go scare up the birds and rabbits." And, without waiting for her, I began to run up our mountain, bounding from rock to rock, enjoying, as always, the sheer ease of movement. For one who had spent years as an arthritic old man, this was bliss.

But I soon discovered that Sara was not behind me and turning to look I saw that she was walking purposefully back to the condo. I stood and watched her go, feeling helpless to change a situation that seemed, sadly, to be coming apart.

"I'll just make a new batch of my blue liquid," I said, talking out loud to myself. "See what it could have been before the Wiseass contaminated it with that crap of Henry Fowles's. Christ, I have to do that. Anyone would do that. Then I'll just put it right back on the shelf and forget it."

What the hell, I thought suddenly, remembering another year in our lives, *Maybe Sara and I ought to take a trip. Go to Europe again. Why not? She'd love that.*

So, with peace with Sara already made in my own mind if not in hers, I climbed easily up to my laboratory and pushed aside the rock that guarded the entrance and flipped my main switch.

My beautiful factory appeared instantly, all glass and stainless steel and blue light, like a dream from *Scientific American* magazine. I sniffed the filtered air, one part of my brain thinking, *How silly to air-condition the purest of mountain air,* but another part approving completely, knowing that everything in my laboratory had to be under the tightest control.

I entered the cave, found my white smock, washed my hands with disinfectant soap, opened my notebook and put a ball point pen open beside it, glanced at the clock out of habit to mark my starting time, and reached for the first of the 500-ml flasks I would need.

It felt good to be back at work. My hands flew. My body seemed to know every step of the cloning process, so that it moved ever faster. Ever more purposefully. My eyes noted, fingers jotted notes, then stopped: why keep notes? Couldn't I remember everything? With a small shrug at this change in my lifelong work habits, I dropped the notebook into a wastebasket and moved even faster through my ballet of science.

Days passed. Happy, productive days. I was re-creating my Blue Helix in my special lab where every piece of equipment, every chemical, every biological reagent, was chosen to do just this one job.

It all culminated one afternoon when I watched the slow drip, drip, drip of the blue liquid into a beaker. Was it exactly the same material I had created months ago in the Germ Factory? I was certain that it was.

I filled a syringe with the blue liquid and caught a couple of white mice and gave them each a shot. As I held them in my hand to watch the reaction I noticed that one was male and the other female. "I think I'll name you Andy and Sara" I told them. "But no matter how smart and strong you become, you'll still have to live in a cage."

Minutes after the injection I saw them try to fight their way out of my fingers and grow quickly into beautiful, healthy mice.

So I put them into their specially designed all-steel cage and filled their water and food trays and watched them nibble and nudge each other happily and I knew what I had to do.

I walked out of the cave, leaving the lights on, leaving the generator purring, the digital lights blinking, and sat down on a rock outside, staring down at the valley below me.

God bless that stumbling damned fool, Henry Fowles, I thought. No amount of applied intelligence can equal a single stroke of blind, stupid luck.

My white mice, Andy and Sara, were perfectly beautiful specimens: young, strong and frisky. But they were not supermice. Not even close.

I knew now that if everything had gone as planned that night in the Germ Factory—if the Wiseass had not appeared to tell me that he had contaminated my wonderful blue liquid with that awful crap of Henry Fowles'—then Sara and I would have been just as the Sara and Andy mice were.

I would have rescued Sara and we would have been healthy and handsome people, but ordinary. And healthy for how long?

*   *   *   *   *

I went and found Sara. "Can you amuse yourself for a couple of days?"

"Sure," she said, with a piercing appraisal of my face. "Why? What's the boy scientist up to now?"

"I have to pay a visit to the Germ Factory."

"Really?" with upraised eyebrows.

"Don't ask."

"I didn't. Why should I? Obviously, things didn't work out in your lab of all labs."

"Well, they did and they didn't."

"They didn't, or you wouldn't be visiting the Germ Factory."

"Now that you put it that way. See you in a couple of days?"

"Andy—we're not in any danger, are we? I'm not about to grow old again or anything like that?"

"Of course not!"

"If you thought I was, would you tell me?"

"Of course not!"

"But I'm not, am I?"

"Of course not!"

After a long pause: "Andy... I hope you find whatever it is you're looking for."

"Of course I will. I know just where to put my finger on it."

So I left Sara looking as anxious as her new face would allow and made my way back to Rhode Island, to the marvelous laboratory I had always called The Germ Factory.

132

And did I know exactly where to put my finger on the complex manmade protein that I needed?

Of course not.

chapter nineteen

Late night, the moon was down. Almost black dark. The velvet breeze blew off Narraganset Bay as I approached the Germ Factory.

I had seen this bay in all its' moods and had found it soft, warm, pretty, frightening, harsh, life-giving, life-threatening. Everything except boring. Never boring. That's why it had been my choice for the location of the Germ Factory, years ago.

Also, I had wanted my Germ Factory beside the sea because the sea is the soup of life and that was what our work was all about, even if it never involved the sea directly. Try explaining that to a Board of Directors.

I didn't have to wait until the shift change. Maybe I used to be the phantom of the Germ Factory but now I was whatever I chose to be. Yet I didn't want to answer silly questions either. So I left my rented car outside the gate and hopped over the fence and streaked across the blacktop at a speed that would make me a blur to the guard if he saw me at all and entered Building Sixteen out of habit. My old hangout.

Sure enough, there with his back to me, shrugging into blue coveralls, was Fred Rainey. He had the inevitable cigarette burning on a window ledge and turning the white paint a sticky brown. The cigarette smell, to my sensitive nose, was surface sweet and enticingly aromatic, yet harsh and death-dealing underneath. Self-induced suffocation.

"Well, Fred," I said to his back, and watched him turn and look at me with startled curiosity.

"Who you?" he grunted. Then squinting, concentrating, "D'I know you?"

It was strange. This slow moving, slow thinking wax figure of a man used to be important to me. I studied the mole on his cheek, the deep dirty lines on either side of his nose, the blackheads and the beard stubble, the broken veins, the stooped shoulders and yellow teeth. This had been a soft, smooth-skinned baby once, a baby with promise, like all babies. What had happened to make it so hard and worn and ugly?

Yet I knew that only months before Fred had been in far better shape than me and he had thought scornfully of me as an old man.

"Take care of yourself, Fred," I said, walking past him faster than he could believe and disappearing down the darkened corridor while he shouted after me, "Hey! Hey you with the suit!"

I was home. It was lovely, just strolling and looking. The rich colors of the liquids in the glass reaction vessels, the brushed metal perfection of the high tech apparatus around me, what beauty! I stroked a DNA sequencer, admired a Nucleic Acid Extractor that was new since I was here last, noticed that a Protein Sequencer I had used many times in the past had now been updated by adding a Data Analysis Module.

"So, things are moving along," I told myself. "But of course they are," myself answered, "There is always change here, has to be."

One big change: here it was, approaching midnight when all self-respecting yuppie scientists should have been home in bed storing up strength for tomorrow and too many of them were still here, unshaven, weary, slump shouldered, drinking cold coffee from foam cups and talking in monotones as they went about the business of doing what researchers do.

I had scarfed a white smock from a shelf of clean linen and by slumping my own shoulders and walking slowly, with careful back turning when needed, I was able to blend in with the scenery and listen, and I realized after only minutes of nosing about that I didn't much care for what I was hearing.

Things had changed.

The white coated men and women going through the slow dance of research tonight were weary, almost brain-numb from long hours of work. They had no sparkle left and were obviously ineffective. As I moved about they showed little interest in me and I learned by judicious listening that many of those I saw were not regular employees but outside experts, many of them from foreign universities or research labs. I learned that the groups and teams were no longer groups and teams: there was now only one big team, with only one task.

I thought of a well-known scientific parable: "most women, given nine months to do it, can produce a baby. But no nine women, no matter how hard they try, can produce a baby in one month."

But that's what was happening here. Someone had decreed that nine women would produce that baby in one month, so to speak, and it was "work until you drop" time, as well.

It didn't take a genius to know who that someone was or what the problem was that he had commanded them to solve.

So, the Wiseass wanted the Blue Helix and was ready to do anything to get it. Nothing unexpected about that. My job now was to find out what chance he had of success.

I started a systematic search. I settled in behind a computer terminal and flicked through the last several months of recorded work, my eyes scooping the information off the screen faster than the computer could feed it to them, impatient with this methodical machine but realizing that it was at least better than rows of filing cabinets filled with flimsy paper.

Then I toured every lab area but one, listening in on conversations from a distance with my cat ears, flipping through pages of notes wherever I found them, reading labels attached to equipment, examining new reagents, checking the temperature of reaction vessels; sniffing, poking, looking, thinking, assessing as I went.

Within an hour, I was up to speed. I knew whatever anyone knew in this place. I knew everything except the personal pressure put on every shoulder here by the Wiseasss and I could surmise that from the way everyone reacted.

I knew everything except what was happening in the one area I hadn't visited because I had deliberately chosen to look there last.

So I slipped through the corridors toward Building One to the area that had been my own personal lab when the Germ Factory had been first built; my office, my workplace, my home of homes. It was the place from which I had been evicted on the day that I had been said to have "retired."

It was a mess. My old desk was stacked high with papers and floppy disks and scrawled notes on yellow pads.

In the lab area every bit of glassware was dirty and used, the lab sinks filled with unwashed utensils, things spilled on the floor, sticky to walk upon, and there on the sofa, half covered by a copy of *The Wall Street Journal* he had dropped across his chest when he nodded off was a body that snored loudly with each intake, then whistled tunelessly with each outpouring of breath, dreams of stock options dancing, no doubt, in his head.

Henry Fowles.

So, the Wiseass had rewarded Henry for his services by giving him my old office, his own personal lab. I took advantage of his snores to look around, read his scrawls, check the setup and the sequence of his latest attempts at science.

Henry could keep no secrets from me, except one: the secret of which possible foul-up he'd commit next.

He was still at his favorite study: *neuropeptides.* Just where he was when I had seen him last. I wondered why. Why would the Wiseass, who was no fool even if he was a wiseass, have poor clumsy Henry doing the same thing over and over? It made no sense. But then again, maybe it did.

I thought of another old analogy: if you put a million monkeys into a room with a million typewriters for a million years, one of them, purely by chance, would write an intelligent book.

I could feel the hair on my neck rise. It was possible. If anything was possible, this was possible.

I didn't fear discovery by the Wisesass. He was an administrator who had always bluffed his way through the science. I didn't fear the real scientists. They, in spite of the example of the Wiseass before their eyes, would not believe in what they had seen. Ordered to produce a cure for aging, they'd take years, decades, centuries, even, to make the slow, solid, perfect science toward a goal they really didn't believe to be possible.

The only one I feared now was good old bumbling Henry Fowles. Scientist enough to at least know the procedures, coward enough to fear the Wiseasss and be truly driven by him and fumble-fisted enough to make the same mistake twice, if given enough time.

Yes, Henry Fowles was my monkey at the typewriter. But had he managed to make the right mistake once again?

Who knows? Certainly I won't, just by looking at it, and neither will Henry or anyone else here, I'll bet.

Because...when the Wiseass poured "some of Henry's junk" into my blue liquid, both of them thought of it as just that: junk. Why bother to find out exactly what kind of junk?

To them, my blue liquid was a complete unknown. They knew now what I had been trying to do, but had no idea how I had gone about it.

But I knew exactly what I had done, and I had already reproduced it, back in my cave-laboratory.

And to both of us, Henry's crap was an unknown. Both of us knew that he would probably reproduce it again through accident—but neither of us would know it when we saw it.

So, the only answer was experimental: mix the two together and inject a test animal and see what happened.

I had one known and one unknown. Not so bad. Mathematically, my chances were very good. How many variations of his mistake could Henry make, anyway? Five or six? A dozen, maybe? I thought, even fewer, because a mistake once made forms a pattern that's easy to repeat.

They had *two* unknowns. Very, very long odds, particularly when they had no idea at all of what my blue liquid had been.

I searched through a cabinet and found a new package of test tubes and filled six of them with samples of junk that Henry had made and had left standing around in beakers. Then I jammed a rubber stopper into the mouth of each tube and ran a line of transparent tape a couple of times around the middle of the six tubes to make a package and tucked the package safely away in my pocket.

What was in my six samples? Who knows? But just the fact that Henry had saved these six and left them lined up on a counter while the rest of the glassware was piled up, dirty, in the lab sink, made me want to have a look, back home in my mountain lab.

Then I moved back into the general lab area where I spent the next hour fixing things. No smash and destroy. Nothing obvious. Just turn up the heat a little here, add a little something there, change the calibration on an instrument here, contaminate a gel there, wipe a promising bit of information from a computer here and substitute something just slightly wrong. I knew exactly how to invalidate everything useful without leaving an obvious trace.

Oh, I'll just pay a little visit every month or so, I thought, *and soon this place will be so useless they'll sell it to a soap works.* But all my instincts told me it wouldn't really be that easy, not with a super-intelligent Wiseass stalking around, hungry for my blue liquid and a small army at work trying to rediscover it.

The monkeys were typing.

 chapter twenty

A hawk circled. Down below in the green grassy softness a brown mouse scurried from his hole, intent on food just ahead from a dried seed pod that had popped open with the morning's first heat. The mouse found his rich, oily seed and chewed quickly, tasting and approving, then finding another and another. The hawk dropped like a stone until he was inches above the mouse, then recovered, swooped, scooped and ate.

I was home in my golden tent in the mountains of Virginia, where everything in my world was peaceful and beautiful unless you were a recently-swallowed mouse.

But where was Sara? I had taken my small predawn nap and when I had waked, she had been gone.

A head-sized rock whistled past and smashed on a stone outcropping nearby, turning to gray dust as it shattered.

"*A-n-d-y!*" Sara appeared over a small rise, coming at a rapid trot from the direction of my cave. What had she been doing there? She had never dabbled in my stuff. Never.

"*A-n-d-y!* Your damned mice are dead. Sara and Andy, you named them. Both of them dead. *Am I next?*" Then she screamed it at me, screamed not only in fear but in blind, furious anger: "Am I next?"

So I went to work in my mountain lab sooner than I had planned, setting out six numbered beakers of my blue liquid on a work bench and then carefully mixing in a sample from each test tube of Henry Fowles' mistakes.

How to know if any one of the mixtures actually had the key protein?

Only one way: I had to inject a test animal, or rather, six of them. Then, if I got a super-mouse from any one of the six, I'd be able to analyze the new protein and reproduce it as often as I liked.

Small problem: I only had three white mice left. No problem at all: the woods were filled with field mice, down on the plains below. Why not go down and catch a few?

So, taking a small wire mesh cage with me, and leaving the six beakers behind, I ran down the mountain to a spot I knew near the golden tent to go mouse-hunting.

Good thing Sara isn't here, I thought as I went scurrying around on my knees, sniffing out mice under leaves and clumps of grass and popping them into my cage, squirming and squealing.

I collected a dozen or so. Best to have enough, I thought. I'll start a colony of them.

I looked around for Sara for a few minutes without expecting to find her, then started back up the mountain to my cave-lab. "Which of you will be Mr. Supermouse?" I asked my cage full of squealing animals. "And if one of you does get lucky, what'll I do about it?"

chapter twenty-one

I was bounding along, with my long, gliding stride, enjoying each step up the mountain and whistling softly to myself, when I came almost face to face with the bear.

"Hello, bear," I said to him, good-naturedly, "Hello, Mr. *Ursus Americanus* (remembering my encyclopedia's description of the American Black Bear) "My, you look perky this morning!"

It occurred to me that most humans, meeting a fully grown five hundred pound wild bear walking toward them on its hind legs, would be afraid. But, of course, I was beyond all that.

"Be careful, bear," I told him. "I don't want to have to hurt you."

But the bear didn't listen to my logic. He came running toward me, growling and staring intently into my eyes, hair raised slightly on his neck, ears somewhat aback, teeth exposed, clearly intent on combat.

"Oh, don't be stupid, bear," I told him, realizing now that he was going to cause trouble, like it or not. "My encyclopedia tells me that you bears don't usually attack humans unprovoked," I reasoned with my bear. "What's gotten into you, anyway?"

For answer, the bear reared to his full height and made a vicious swipe at my head with his forepaw, claws exposed to rake away my face.

I dodged the blow, but realized with the most intense surprise that I just did dodge him. He had barely missed me.

Fast! How did this bear get to be this fast? Instantly I dropped my cage of mice and ran around him and grabbed his feet from behind and pulled his legs out from under him. But almost as quickly he was up again, standing on his feet and whirling to meet me, both forepaws back for another swipe.

Then I looked, really looked, at his face, and what I saw there raised my own neck hairs. Because he was perfect. Too perfect. He was a dream of a bear, his features every bit as beautiful as Sara's or mine, and with the same shimmering intensity.

The Blue Helix! There were drops of it all around his mouth and nose! He had buried his snout in my blue liquid! I could see him now in my mind's eye, back in the cave that had once been his cave and was now mine, sampling and destroying whatever he found there, sticking his nose into one or all of the six beakers I'd left out.

Swipe! He reached for my head again, and it seemed to me that he was even faster than before.

"Oh, bear," I said aloud, "That head of yours has to come off! Sorry, but I've got to kill you *now* before you eat!"

That, of course, was what he was up to: he had to eat, just as I had, just as Sara had, and he saw me as his nearest meal. To him, I was no more than a giant walking hamburger, and he had to have me. Every cell in his body must have cried out with the need to eat me.

When he had eaten, his strength complete, he would be stronger than I had been, stronger than Sara, stronger and more ferocious than any creature that had ever lived; and he would be absolutely unkillable from now until eternity, a monster let loose upon the earth.

I set to work, grimly and frantically. Running around him again, I jumped onto his back and dug my fingers into his throat. He whirled in a wild and furious dance as I clung to him and dug into his hairy flesh with my fingers.

It wasn't easy! I, who could crush rocks with my fingers, was totally unable to reach into this tough flesh. What to do? What to do?

I began pulling out his neck hair, trying to get down to bare flesh. Even this was difficult. Thank God he hadn't eaten and wasn't up to full strength!

Now, handful after handful, I was getting the hair pulled out, leaving him with a naked ring of pink skin around his neck

Oh, did he hate that! I was flung from side to side, still clinging to his back. But I did hold on. I was still stronger, smarter, than my bear; but I was not, and never would be, the killer that he was. I had to do with rational and unwilling thought what he did gladly and unthinkingly.

His neck skin exposed, I had to use my teeth to tear into the meat at the back of his neck. Then, with the flesh torn, I could finally get my fingers inside to rip and tear.

How he growled! How he roared, screamed with hatred! And I didn't blame him a bit. "Sorry, bear," I muttered as I ripped out one side of his neck. Then I added, "I'll be through in a minute" as I used my thumbs to break his cervical vertebrae and then began ripping the other side of his neck with my fingers.

Strange! I thought to myself, *Here I have his head much more than half off and he seems as strong as ever.*

Nothing for it but to keep ripping. Tough flesh, that, and getting tougher by the second, it seemed to me. I had to use my teeth and fingers together to tear through the last of it, and I knew that if I hadn't been who I was, with the strength I had now, that head would have been safe from any attack on earth.

The last strand ripped. I still rode the bear's upright back and now held his severed head in one bloody hand. With the back of the other hand I wiped my equally bloody mouth and split out bear blood and bits of flesh in disgust at myself.

The bear's body fell forward and I stepped off, still holding the head. Forced to be a killer, I had been a killer, but now I was a scientist again, watching my bear intently.

I rolled the body over onto its back and then put the severed head in the correct relative position, but just a little higher than normal, so that there was a gap of about an inch between head and body.

Fascinating!

Both the head and body stopped pumping blood from the torn flesh. I watched as blood vessels closed, pinched shut at the ends, and then seemed to grope with intelligent movement towards mating blood vessels. Bits of torn flesh reached out for like pieces of flesh. Nerves searched for nerves.

The thing was trying to rejoin.

Oh, Sara, if you could only see this! I thought. Horrible, maybe, but reassuring, too. Because this is what we'd do under the same circumstances. We'd live. We had a compulsion to live, above all else.

Would the head and body actually join and rebuild? I thought so, and I couldn't allow it, even in the interest of science. I moved the head a foot further away from the body and when I did, the bear's eyes opened and he looked right into my face. His lips curled backward in a grimace of hatred, and still watching me intently, he began to wave his ears in the air like small legs. When I experimentally put my hand behind his waving ears he used them to push his head along, pushing against my fingers and slowly but surely walking the head down towards the body again by ear power.

I grabbed the feet and pulled the body a yard or so away from the head and the head immediately stopped its earcrawling. Looking into the eyes, I could almost see a decision being made to save energy now that I had shown the effort to be useless.

Some smart bear!

He was working now in cold desperation, thinking, thinking, thinking, and even after losing his head he wasn't losing his head, so to speak. I had to admire him.

The body twitched uncontrollably. Arms and legs moved. Turning over, the body got all four feet under it, but couldn't coordinate. There was still some strength there, even though most of the blood must have been lost before veins and arteries clamped down.

On impulse, I grabbed the head by the top hair and ran about a quarter mile away, so there would be no possibility of the two rejoining. The eyes opened briefly, took in the new situation, then closed again. There was no other movement. The bear was conserving energy while he thought.

"Mr. Bear," I said, addressing the head almost as an equal, "I'm sure your blood, what remains of it, is crying out for oxygen, and unfortunately you have no lungs. That sort of limits things, doesn't it?"

The bear opened one eye for the merest flicker, then sank back into his contemplation.

"How does he think?" I wondered. "Even with a computer strength brain, he has no language that I know of. Maybe I ought to teach him mine." But there was no time for that, of course.

I had to deal with death. Quite literally, I had to put him out of his misery, and it seemed to me that I had an idea that might work.

Leaving the bear's head on a rock outcropping. I ran down to the bottom of the valley, and using my nose like a dog, found the scent of a rabbit, which I soon traced down and caught.

Then I ran back up to my bear's head and said: "Wake up, bear. I've brought you something." The head opened one eye a crack, then closed it again.

"Truly sorry," I said to the rabbit, and with one motion jerked off its head and instantly rammed the rabbit body neck-to-bloody-neck with the bear's head.

Sure enough, just as I had hoped, the bear's torn neck flesh and blood vessel system began to reach out and join with the rabbit's torn neck. Sizewise, they were no match, but a hasty accommodation was made.

The bear's eyes opened wide now. You could see new energy flowing into the face and it even gave me a low growl of hatred.

Then, for a few awful seconds, the bear-rabbit began to move, jumping rabbit-like toward me while the bear-mouth opened. I backed slowly away, watching intently. It quickly slowed, then stopped.

"If you had studied hematology, as I have, you'd know that rabbit blood isn't good for you, Mr. Bear. It won't mix at all, you know."

I think my bear did know, in a way. At least it knew that it was dying. The eyes grew listless and they looked at me as from far away, all hope gone. I didn't feel victory. I had too much kinship with the bear for that. So, just to give him what peace I could in his last moments, I put one finger into his mouth. He opened both eyes briefly, looking up at me, and bit down as hard as he could, then gnawed on my finger, his jaws getting weaker moment by moment. I let him chew on the finger for as long as he was able, for whatever comfort it gave him.

After a couple of minutes my bear-head was dead, killed by an overdose of rabbit blood which had flooded in and replaced his own oxygen-starved but super-bear blood. And I had to think that even if my bear had known hematology and had known that the rabbit blood was certain death he would have had to take it. When you're facing suffocation, what else can you do?

I carefully buried the head as deeply as the soil allowed in this rocky place, then piled large boulders on top so that no predator could get at it.

Then I took the body, which still twitched with life but whose blood had to be running entirely out of oxygen soon, to the other side of the mountain, far away from the head, and dug a similar deep hole and buried it, then covered it with another cairn of rocks carefully piled on top.

Then I raced up the mountain to my laboratory to see what was left of the Blue Helix. I had a sudden vision of a bird, a mouse, even an insect, getting into it and becoming like the bear. Or like me. Perhaps Sara was right. The very thought of *anything*, man, woman or bug, getting into my Blue Helix was frightening.

*   *   *   *   *

The laboratory was messy, but not a shambles. The bear had pushed a few things around, broken a little glass, but hadn't ruined any of the equipment.

Just the Blue Helix. Just the most important manmade protein in the world today. The entire line of six beakers (at least one of them had to be *the* beaker) had been pushed over, their contents sampled by the bear, and the rest spilled into the carpet below.

I stood gazing at the destruction. "Back to square one," I muttered. Yet…I had learned something important: at least one of these six beakers had held the answer. And if only Henry Fowles would keep doing the same stupid thing over and over, I would find it again. And when I had found it again and had a chance to examine it, I could make more any time and add it to my own blue liquid to create as much of the life-giving Blue Helix as I wanted.

*   *   *   *   *

Looking around, one thing was obvious: my cave badly needed a door; a door that no one and no thing could open. And I had an idea for a door that seemed to me to be perfect.

Whistling to myself, I trotted back to the condo to use the phone. I had to order another truck load of cement and then I had to wait until night when all the world was asleep because my perfect door was not something that anyone would sell to me willingly. I had no choice but to take it.

chapter twenty-two

A couple of days later I was in town at our local supermarket buying groceries—a chore that Sara and I shared these days because both of us liked to do it. The proximity of all that food was exciting. Our mouths dripped as we walked the aisles and we had to keep wiping them, but it was a small nuisance, really.

I had recently discovered Dinty Moore stew. Glorious stuff! It came in two and a half pound cans, which endeared it to me, so I had ten cases of it piled neatly in two pushcarts and another push-cart filled with fruit cocktail and I was pushing the three like a train around the aisles.

Sara and I seldom got around to real cooking. It seemed so slow and tedious and the minuscule difference in taste simply wasn't worth it to us. Volume! That was the ticket. Glorious volume!

So there I was, listening to the soft canned music and standing in line looking over the shoulders of the other standees, watching the strange things that they had bought spread out on the checkout counter. So little food! So much soap and paper! I was playing my usual mental games as I added up each person's purchases in my head and then waited to see how well I agreed with the electronic checker.

Hah, I thought to myself when there were minor differences, *Those damned coupons confuse the issue.*

Then my eyes wandered to the racks of newspapers and magazines and the one nearest me, the local paper, caught my eye with its headline:

NO NEW LEADS ON BANK VAULT THEFT

Investigation continues. A senseless, impossible crime say police. Money left untouched in vault. Door torn from foundation.

I took the paper from its rack to bring home and show Sara. Also, I was hoping that somewhere in the story they would give an estimate of damages. I was anxious to send this bank some cash to cover their loss.

It was a pain, you know? I couldn't very well give them a check with my name on it, and who knows what a bank vault door costs, anyway?

This one had been perfect for my needs. It was now smeared with concrete on the outside and had split rocks fastened to it in such a clever way that you'd never guess that it wasn't just one more section of the mountain. Perfect camouflage. But if you knew exactly where to look you could find the combination knob, now painted a stone color, and if you knew the combination, (which I had carefully reset after listening to the tumblers), you could swing away an opening into the seemingly blank face of the mountain and find a brightly lit and exceptionally beautiful laboratory that no one in all the universe knew about except Sara and me.

I was next in line at the checkout, shuffling through my newspaper trying to find the comics, when I stumbled upon a headline in the sports section that riveted me to the floor, struck almost dumb with shock. It read:

CLIFFORD CLIPS CUBS.
COMMISSIONER CRAWFORD COMPLAINS

Chicago: The Amazing Clifford, TV's game show master now turned sports figure, last night gave a demonstration of baseball prowess that left a crowd of forty-five thousand completely stunned.

Describing himself as "the world's only one-man team," the TV personality used exactly eighty-one pitches during the nine innings to strike out the entire Cubs team. By contrast, his own times at bat consisted solely of home runs, which he hit, seemingly at will, after pointing out the direction of each hit in advance.

The crowd, normally loyal and vocal Cubs fans at first laughed and good-naturedly cheered the one-man team, but grew quiet and finally became belligerent as their hometown team was humiliated.

Baseball Commissioner Crawford, who attended the well-publicized game as an official observer, deplored the performance, saying: "This will kill baseball." Commissioner Crawford went on to explain that...

150

But I didn't care to read what the good commissioner had explained. I was staring, completely transfixed, at the photo of "The Amazing Clifford." I was staring at the Wiseass. None other. The Wiseass himself in a silly-looking baseball suit with his own design, an interwoven T-A-C, embroidered on one breast and on his cap.

"Oh, good Christ!" I exclaimed to myself. "What *have* you allowed to happen? This could be worse than the damned bear!"

When I got back to our tent Sara was there, bathing in our pool, looking so like a fantasy that my heart ached to see her. I held the newspaper clutched in my hand and I knew that the time had come when I would simply have to tell her about the Wiseass, and I felt such a fool for not doing it sooner.

But she was smiling in a beguiling way and when she said, "Join me," I thought, *What the hell...another hour or so won't matter.*

So I was soon in the pool with Sara and then we were back at the tent on the mattress and time passed in our favorite occupation.

Afterwards, in the late September afternoon, with the sun that shone through our golden tent becoming less warm on our bare bodies, Sara slipped closer to me and put her arm under my neck and held me close. But when I whispered a question she began to cry, first softly, then with great heaving sobs.

I grew sad myself and teary without knowing why I should be unhappy, simply reflecting Sara's sadness. "Why?" I asked after a while, "Why are we crying?"

"Because I love you," Sara answered. "I really, really love you, and I hope you'll always remember that, always believe."

Then, before I could answer, she put a finger on my lips and said: "Dance with me, Andy. Come on, let's dance while I tell you something important." She sprang up and opened her arms and began to hum a dance tune as she smiled invitingly at me.

We danced, but to call it that you would have had to stand way back, watching us from a distance, because the hills were wooded and rocky and smooth footholds were hard to find.

So we danced, to the tune of Sara's singing, by flicking a foot here and bouncing there, from clearing to clearing, over small trees, sometimes fifteen feet to a step, sometimes more. From your distance, you would have seen two people in perfect rhythm, but on a grand scale, floating like huge dust motes in the golden sun.

"*Is this all there is?*" sang Sara.

"Ah! Peggy Lee!" I said. "I've always loved that song."

"No! *This* is Peggy Lee," said Sara, lowering her voice one octave and giving a perfect Peggy Lee imitation.

> "*Is this all there is?*
> *if this is all there is,*

"See," said Sarah, "Peggy Lee. Now this is me." She sang the song again, a little higher, a little sweeter, a little more hauntingly and (to me) a little more ominously. I had a premonitory chill at the sound.

> "*Is this all there is?*
> *if this is all there is*
> *my friend, then*
> *let's keep on dancing...* "

Sara drew back and looked me in the eyes as we danced. "Is this *all* there is? Do we spend the next thousand years looking at flowers? Do we spend an eternity tossing rocks? Do we discuss black holes for a century over cases of Dinty Moore stew? Do we dance and dance like the girl in Red Shoes? Is this *really* all there is?"

I tried to answer, but Sara put her finger on my lips again and almost whispered: "I have to get out into the world again, Andy. I can't sniff your flowers forever, no matter how much I love you. I'm burning with impatience to be gone."

"But, Sara," I exclaimed, "There's nothing out there! It'll be empty out there with other people. They're all ghost people to us. Wax figures. You'll be chasing a chimera!"

In answer, she simply looked at me, directly into my eyes, for a very long time. "Isn't it strange," she finally said, again almost in a whisper, "That you who believe in mankind and want to give it your medicine shun any contact with people while I, who mistrust and even despise our entire species, long to be involved with them?"

We danced a few more moments and I made my decision. "If that's what you want, then we'll go," I said. "You were nice enough to go along with me in my wilderness, so I can certainly do what you want for a while."

Sara didn't answer, but gave me a reassuring squeeze, and then, after a long pause said, "I've got something to show you, Andy. I've got something back at the condo."

She stepped out of my arms and slipped on a loose blue dress and a pair of shoes for the trip back to the condo. I picked up my own clothes, then thought better of it and dropped them and found the newspaper. "I've got something to show you, too, Sara. Show-and-tell time!" I said, trying to put a little false gaiety into something I dreaded.

"Later," she said, turning and leaving the tent fully dressed while I had to find my clothes again to follow. "My secret first," she said over her shoulder, moving swiftly toward the condo, "then yours, if you still want to…"

"I ordered it two weeks ago," Sara said, standing beside the red Jaguar in the parking lot of our condo. "Isn't it a beauty? They had to ship it in from another dealer to get me just the one I wanted."

Sara watched my reaction intently, a tremulous smile on her lips.

"Do you like it, Andy? It's my magic carpet to take me out into the world."

Then, eyes sliding past mine, "My chariot to take me away from you, Andy."

"But, why!" I asked, completely shaken by what she'd said. "Together we can do anything. Anything you want…"

Sara was shaking her head from side to side slowly in big, definite sweeps.

"It came to me like a shock a couple of weeks ago that maybe you were wrong, that maybe we didn't have ten thousand years to live, that maybe I'd better do my thing while I still could. But then, you know, crazy thing, that got me to thinking just the opposite—what if you were right? What about living forever? Could it be that that's even worse? A thousand years or ten thousand always in your shadow? Am I always to be just a wife?"

"Am I that hard to live with?" I said. "I never realized. I could change if you taught me." God! I hated to hear that pleading whine in my voice, but I was terrified at what was happening.

"It won't be a divorce, Andy, only a short separation. Maybe just a few years, you know. Even if its a hundred or two hundred years, what's that to us? Just a blink in the eye of time if you're right. I'll always know that you're there, that you're the earth to my moon, so to speak, and one day when I've had my own chance to grow into whatever I'll grow into I'll be back and we'll be together again forever. Or maybe not. Maybe we'll spend an eternity coming together and then moving apart and then coming together again.

"Do you know what it is to be a wife? It's a golden, fur lined trap at best, and sometimes it's an iron hell. And yet, I did marry the man I loved. I wouldn't trade you, I don't blame you, that's not it at all. But this is the way it is: a woman marries and after that she's a success if her man is a success and a failure if he is one. She can nudge and guide and nag him, even scream at him and push him, but in the end she has to live or die with him and that's just the way it is.

"I can't be a reflection any more. Even the reflection of a good man that I love." She let that sink in for a moment, then said, brightly, with a sweep of her hand toward the expensive beige fabric and leather-trimmed stack in the back seat, "Like my new luggage?"

"No," I muttered. "I hate it." Then, with an afterthought, "Why don't you have it in the trunk, where it belongs?"

"Oh," she laughed with mock gaiety, "The trunk's full of your Dinty Moore stew. You don't mind, do you? I've got *miles* to go before I eat."

I watched glumly as she started the Jaguar, backed it around to put it on the road, then stopped the car beside me to ask, "By the way, what was your news?"

I shrugged, not wanting to discuss it. "Where will you go, Sara?"

"West," she answered. "That's all I know just now. West. All good Americans go west sooner or later, don't they?" She leaned out of the little red car, gave my cheek a peck of a kiss and said, "Goodbye, Andy. I'll be back one day." The engine noise rose to a loud but civilized mutter and the red Jaguar took Sara away from me as I watched, my stomach as empty as if it had been torn away.

Maybe she didn't need to be my wife, but I certainly did need to be her husband.

*　*　*　*　*

As I stood, trying to imagine that I could still hear the voice of the Jaguar in the growing darkness, I began to shiver and realized that I was feeling the first chill of fall.

chapter twenty-three

I knew a family once with an old, well-loved and very sick cat. One day, down in the cellar where no one could see, lying in the privacy of her own specially made pet bed, the old cat died.

Within hours, another cat, a stray they'd never seen before, began coming around, purring and rubbing against legs and crying out for cat food.

So it goes in the cat world. Mysterious. Like a vibration in the air that only other cats can hear. A vibration saying: "There's an opening in this family for a cat. Be quick about it!"

So it went in my world, too. The first to appear was Elaine Cummings, the blonde that Sara had tried to shove in my direction the night of the pool party. She was at the door with a casserole and a smile, saying: "Oh, my poor Harry had to go to Chicago for a week on business (he calls me every night so I always know exactly where he is, the darling), and I have no man to cook for and I just thought, maybe you could use this?" Standing just so, scrunching her breasts invitingly between her arms as she held out the casserole, smiling prettily, her every action an offer.

"I *do* believe your sweet Sara had to go away, too?" She continued, "How long will she be gone?" splitting her bee-stung lips into a huge smile.

Looking at the casserole I knew exactly how a fish must feel seeing a tasty worm on a hook.

How to take the casserole without also taking the body that offered it?

But I lied out of this one easily: "Is that tuna? Oh, it looks just great! But I mustn't. Just one bite of fish of any kind and I'd be taken with projectile vomiting, spewing all over the walls! It's an allergy I have. Sorry!"

And, with an added, "Awfully kind of you," I closed the door on her shocked face, wishing I could have found a way to keep the casserole. I love tuna.

There were phone calls. There were knocks on my door with veiled and not so veiled invitations. But all of it was useless. Tedious. Embarrassing.

All I really felt like doing was to curl up on my mattress and suck my thumb. All I really wanted was Sara back and I couldn't believe she was actually gone. Every morning when I woke from my five minute nap I'd feel a sharp new sense of loss.

"Damn," I muttered to myself. "I really don't know how to live without being Sara's husband. All those years I was making money and making a name and riding high on the science trail while she stayed home and yet I was more dependent on her than she on me and neither of us knew it."

To get away from the neighbors I ran up to the top of our mountain and sat and thought sick thoughts. I saw Sara with other men (how could she, when they were all so weak and slow and ugly and simple minded?) and then I told myself that this was silly, that Sara wouldn't do that, that she'd gone away for other reasons. ("*What* other reasons, you fool?")

One day I took everything out of our tent and dropped the canvas on the ground and folded it into a tight bundle. Then, after the neighbors were asleep, or should have been. I carried the piano and everything else back to the condo and put it away. The folded tent went into the garage.

The next morning I drove to town in the van and bought every paperback book on the rack. When I got back I separated them into categories and began reading: first, ten or twelve mysteries, then three Westerns (hard to find now and they used to be so common) and then a dozen romances (oh, what junk, I thought, even though I was, myself, love sick) and then a few police procedural thrillers (an overdose of aggression) and finally a few literary efforts. I read until I was sick of reading, only a few minutes to a book, then drop it on the floor and read another. "Such a way to clutter your memory," I told myself with disgust. "You could be filling it with the elegant purity of mathematics or physics." But I didn't want science, either.

Then, out of boredom and curiosity, I began plinking out tunes on the piano. Soon, without really meaning to do it, I learned to play. My teacher was Sara. I simply remembered how she had played and what she had played. I got great comfort out of it, remembering with careful intensity exactly how her hands were placed, how her fingers moved for each note or chord. I'd sit, just as she would, hands spread, fingers curved, and become Sara for a little while, aping her music with utmost precision. In my mind's eye I would see her play and hear her voice as I played.

But my playing brought new knocks at my door. "Oh! Is Sara home again? Didn't I hear her playing?"

So I drifted, a boat dead in the water, for more than two months.

One day I realized that I hadn't even had a knock on my door for a week or more and, perversely, I was annoyed to be so soon forgotten.

"You can't just stay here," I told myself, so I began to wander the mountains again, this time in cold, wet and windy weather. Time after time I went by the door to my laboratory. I'd search it out, find the stone-colored knob for the combination lock, touch it with a finger, perhaps, then move on. It gave me some pleasure to know what was inside, but I had no need to open the door. What would I do there? How could I save the world when I couldn't even make a life for myself?

Now and again a thought about the Germ Factory with its hundreds of sleepy, irritable scientists milling about trying to duplicate my blue liquid without knowing what they were trying to duplicate would cross my mind, but then the thought would flit away, somehow unimportant to me at the time.

Oh well, I thought. *I've got time. I'll heal and do great things yet.*

But the words were only words. I was empty.

One day, sitting on a rock beside our pool, where our golden tent had been, it began to snow, and in my mind I designed a truly beautiful glass house. It would be solar heated, with triple panes and stones in the floor to gather and hold the heat. It would have one huge, high-ceilinged living room with nothing in it but a glass piano and large, vividly colored cushions thrown about.

It would have one large bedroom with a pneumatic, room-sized mattress and one bath and one large kitchen. Nothing else. And it would be all glass, every wall and roof, every appliance and fixture, and would be built beside our pool so that we could sit in our living room and watch the water ripple and flow outside.

And I designed for it, in my mind, a tempered glass stove with a glass stove pipe, and the stove was designed to burn so hot and to burn the wood so completely that there would be no smoke or black soot inside. In this stove we would build a roaring fire, my Sara and I, and we would watch the snow come down outside and sizzle into our pond and build up beautifully on the tree limbs and the rocks and the grass outside while we were warm and snug inside and...(oh, shit! *Pop* went another daydream...).

"Enough!" I said to myself, angrily. "You've got to pull it together, stop moping. Be somebody, somehow. Whether you like it or not, you've got to go out into the world, be with people, as Sara did, as even the Wiseass did.

"Maybe you can go out there and find the Wiseass and pull his goddamned head off, as you did with the bear," I muttered to myself, and when a voice inside me asked, "why?" I yelled back at it, "Because its something to do, that's why! Something constructive."

That night, with dawn almost ready to break on the horizon, I was about to sink into my usual five minute sleep when something that had been tugging at my mind for weeks popped out, demanding to be looked at and thought about. It was a vision of Sara riding away. From the rear, the Jaguar had sagged to the left. The driver's side was a good four inches lower than the passenger side. How could this have been?

I had a sudden thought and hopped out of bed and found a case of Dinty Moore stew. There were a dozen to the case and each can weighed two and a half pounds so that was thirty pounds, net, say a little for the cans and a little more for the carton, let's make it thirty-two pounds altogether as a close guess.

So, grabbing this thirty-two pound case of stew under my arm I ran to the balcony and jumped down and began running to the staging area, where I knew there was a stack of lumber.

When I got there, I pulled out a short block of wood to be my fulcrum and kicked a hole and buried it diagonally, so a sharp edge was on top, then balanced a twenty-four foot timber beam on this block, then put my case of stew far out on one end of the balanced beam, then found a much bigger rock, which I put nearer the fulcrum on the other side until it balanced my stew, and

159

from that a simple calculation gave me the weight of the rock; then I used that rock to weigh a still bigger rock and used the final rock to weigh myself. Finally, I had the figure that any high school physics student could have calculated: I weighed just over sixteen-hundred pounds.

This meant that Sara must weigh at least twelve-hundred maybe fourteen-hundred pounds. So, that's why her Jaguar had sagged!

My mind raced with this new information. All the eating we'd done was not just for immediate energy, it was to build dense bone and muscle, to make us stronger with each passing day. Stronger and heavier. Heavier because we were stronger and strength requires denseness.

Where would it all end? Would we eventually stop eating? Or would we just get heavier and stronger forever? And why the compulsion, the absolute need to eat so much? Things to think about.

chapter twenty-four

With an effort of sheer will, I began to pull myself together. "There's no joy in Mudville tonight," I told myself, "but maybe, if you just pretend there's a spark of some kind inside you, you can build on it, force something to work."

I had tried scorn. Tried reason. Tried laughing at myself. "What's the matter, buddy? Isn't being forever young, strong, rich, handsome, intelligent and incredibly attractive to women enough for you? What more could you want?"

Breakfast. That's what I wanted. I opened up a case of pork and beans and got a gallon of ice cream out of the freezer for desert and began making a mental list of the immediate possibilities.

I could:
A. Take a trip around the world. Be a supertourist.
B. Go kill the Wiseass.
C. Find a new woman and make her like me, like Sara.
D. Make more of the Blue Helix and heal the sick.
E. Buy a sailboat and head for the South Seas.
F. Learn rocket science and blast off to a new planet.
G. Become a rock star and wow the world.
H. Find a high mountain, stock the top with food, become a mystic and meditate for a thousand years.
I. Create a small army of superbeings and send them around the world to settle wars, bring about peace and prosperity.
J. Open up another case of pork and beans.

I made the only intelligent decision: option J, and when breakfast was over I fired up the van and drove to town and bought all the supermarket tabloids on the newsstand plus copies of *TV Guide* and *People* magazine. It was time, I thought, for me to learn something about the outside world.

What I read there filled me with amazement. How had all this been going on while I had buried myself in my mountain home? Obviously, now, I had a mission. Like it or not, I had to go to New

York, Los Angeles, Las Vegas and the other vortexes of popular culture and get involved. What a prospect for a reputable scientist like me! I felt like an unwilling teenager being pushed into his first sock hop. (Do they still have them? Do they really dance in their socks? Is this something from another era? Am I showing my age again? Too bad I couldn't ask Sara. She would know.)

So, one snowy morning in December I quit my hibernation in the condo and climbed into a plane, bound for New York, Gotham itself, where (according to *People* magazine) the Wiseass lived and did what the Wiseass did.

 chapter twenty-five

Rockefeller Center. I had watched the skaters skate (very badly, most of then, but still nice to watch), I had gone to see the Rockettes and admired their precision (it would have been fun to be among them, dancing along, keeping perfect rhythm, amazing everyone with my leaps and twirls) and I was now window shopping, killing time, waiting for "The Amazing Clifford Show" to go on.

I had a ticket, bought for sixty dollars from a woman who had gotten it free by writing for it a month in advance and who gave it up reluctantly even for the three twenties I paid her.

"I wanted so much to see Clifford in the flesh," she had said sadly, folding away my money in her wallet, "But I'll write in again," she added, putting on a long-suffering face, "I'll get new tickets. I'll see our darling Cliffie yet!" she smiled up at me bravely, asking me to appreciate her loss.

Standing in line to get into "The Amazing Clifford" show, I noticed a tree, a small scarred red maple standing in a circle of dirt in the concrete on the sidewalk and I fell to musing about trees and other plants here in this city of all cities and how they had no choice, no choice at all, as to where they spent their lives.

"Someone planted you here, tree," I muttered to myself, "… and from then on it was live or die with you. Auto exhaust, frightful noise, idiots with knives carving initials, dogs peeing on you, people bumping into you, kids leaning bicycles against you and chaining them around your tender bark, there's nothing you can do about any of it, is there? Your roots have to keep searching under all this concrete for the food and water to keep you alive and your leaves, in summer, have to fight the smog and dust. Some life."

The tree considered all this, no doubt, but didn't answer. Having a strange man talk to it was perhaps a harmless enough occurrence among all the silly things it had to endure to be a tree in a non-tree world.

I shuffled along the line, edging towards the magic door where I would be privileged to watch the Amazing Wiseass do whatever the Wiseass did. There was an air of excitement all around as my fellow line-people pressed onward.

Maybe I'll go back to my cave-laboratory and do a little genetic tinkering on trees, I mused to myself. *I'll tinker around with one tree, let's say a fast growing evergreen like pine or a spruce. I'll make it grow much faster, let's say a couple of feet a week. No, hell, let's say a foot a day, that would shake them up, over three hundred feet a year, say, and I'll make just this one tree completely impervious to attack by insect or chain saw or anything else, and pretty soon this one damned tree will be as tall as one of these buildings, say in two or three years a thousand feet or more and wide enough at the bottom to push everything aside, all the buildings near it, and the roots will reach down and block the subway system and break water mains for a drink and lap up the sewerage to make more tree. And sooner or later everyone in the world, the entire damned world, will know about this one killer tree and they'll worship it and they'll fear it and TV hosts will have experts explaining it and other experts explaining the danger to mankind if the tree ever thinks about reproducing itself and spreading big new trees all over Manhattan and every now and then the tree will drop one enormous pine cone, big enough to crush a bus, and scientists will drag it away to study and then burn the seed in a special furnace, a kind of high tech crematorium paid for by special congressional appropriation just for this one tree, and...*

But about this time I had reached the magic door and my tree dream faded away as a uniformed girl took my ticket and gestured with a small nod of her head toward the aisle I would take to find a seat.

The T.A.C. show was about to begin. The excitement among the audience was so intense that I found myself picking up a little of it, too. "You idiot!" I lectured myself sternly. "Don't let me catch you with one heart beat above normal."

So I settled down to watch, with not a thought in my head but this piece of mediocrity I was about to see, when without a word of warning something shouted inside my head, just as it did now many, many times during each day, and the familiar shout was, "Where is Sara? What is she doing? Who is she doing it with?"

There was no answer to my Sara-question. Just an echo of pain and loss. I squirmed in my seat and looked for something else to focus on. Presently, I found it: a small man, balding, with the sharp, worldly show business face of a Catskills comedian, bounded out onto the stage and began to warm up the audience, first telling a few well worn jokes, then telling us what to expect and what was expected of us as an audience: when we were to laugh and when to applaud. I noticed that most of my fellow audience members were leaning forward in their seats, listening intently to the warm-up man and whispering short, anxious asides to each other, obviously hoping to please The Amazing Clifford by being a good audience.

I watched the three TV cameramen push their soft wheeled-machines around with a worldly, knowing air. All of them needed a shave, all wore casual, almost dirty clothes to further their act of bored sophistication. Behind us, I could see the control room where a team of men and women watched their monitors and spoke with quiet authority into minute microphones to give directions to the cameramen. The audience, thrilled to be a part of this TV professionalism, almost shivered with anticipation.

Then there was a countdown as the warm-up man pointed to the hands of a big studio clock and cued the audience for its opening applause as the curtain parted precisely as the second hand hit the top of the hour and The Amazing Clifford (AKA The Wiseass) was revealed at center stage standing upside down, supported by one index finger on top of a balance beam.

The audience went wild and the Wiseass bounced up and down on his finger in time to their rhythmic applause, going higher and higher as the applause increased. The act was new to me but obviously not new to them. Presently T.A.C. gave an extra flip with his finger and bounced upright to stand and bow briefly to the audience, which now outdid itself cheering and whistling.

I hated that face. Yet, I had to be attracted to it, just as the audience so obviously was, because it was my face, Sara's face, in its intensity, its shimmering strength and intelligence, in its eerily alive skin and burning, piercing eyes.

The audience literally couldn't get enough of him. What he said, what he did, mattered less than what he obviously was.

165

What a beautiful creature was my Wiseass! What a mistake to have made him so when he had been so ordinary to begin with.

Oh, well. Sit back and enjoy the show.

The Amazing Clifford had jumped up onto a sort of show business throne on the stage and stood there beaming out at the audience and into the camera and then there was an expectant hush as a spotlight suddenly stabbed through the manufactured darkness at the foot of the stage to reveal a striking-looking blond girl in a tight, glittery dress. She had a wide, smiling mouth and heavily made-up eyes and she was leading the audience in an act of adoration as she gazed up at my Wiseass. The audience applauded wildly again at the set-up scene that it obviously knew and expected.

Then, when there was again an obedient hush, the girl announced in her throaty, greatly amplified voice: "Our first panel of experts today is from the Astrophysics Department of the University of Colorado, and they will have ten questions."

At this, another spotlight stabbed on and four men and one woman were revealed sitting at a fakey-looking desk, each with a microphone.

The show began. Each member of the panel of experts asked a question, which The Amazing Clifford not only answered, but answered in such a way as to make the expert look slightly foolish for asking it.

At each correct answer the glittery girl led the applause and swooned up at the Wiseass, giving her emotional all each time.

The questions built in difficulty and had obviously been arranged to seem more and more impossible to answer, giving as much dramatic intensity as possible to this reverse-quiz show. It was a display of smug superiority.

The Amazing Clifford's answers were, I soon realized, quoted straight out of several textbooks. I had read many of the same books and could see them now, page by page, in my memory.

After the panel of experts had asked its ten questions there was a commercial break and when the lights came on again the fakey horseshoe desk was filled with a new panel of experts, this time from the Harvard Medical School, and the next ten questions were from the field I knew best.

The Amazing Clifford's answers were, again, textbook correct, and no one could fault them. Yet, I could feel a certain insensitivity to real understanding in his answers. It was like listening to a well-rehearsed parrot. But if that was the way it seemed to me, then I was the only one who thought so. The audience, even the panel of experts, went wild with enthusiasm at each answer, and to reward their applause T-A-C would sometimes dive off his throne and do one-finger handsprings around the stage, ending with a one-finger leap back onto his throne.

There was one strange segment, which the audience obviously expected, where T-A-C did his one-finger jump toward the front of the stage and then flipped upright, gave an imperious wave of his hand to quiet the audience, and launched into a little talk, lasting no more than two minutes.

The audience was rapt. Not a sound, not a move, not an eyeblink as the Wiseass told them some incident from his early life ("Lies. All lies," I thought) and then reminded them of what he was today. He bragged about his real estate empire, his investment banking house with hundreds of experts slaving away, making him richer than a third world nation, his two-hundred-and-fifty-foot yacht with the helicopter pad on top and all his other toys. He told them especially about his girls, girls, girls, giving broad winks and smirks that set them laughing and nudging each other.

The audience died and went to heaven. I watched them watching their Clifford and thought, surely, they must see? Why can't they see? How can they be so blind? But then I thought of TV evangelists and how so many people wanted desperately to believe about TV wrestling. About shallow situation comedies with laugh tracks and how each person in such an audience becomes the willing architect of his own deception.

So, the Wiseass was shallow, but our TV crowd gloried in his shallowness; they literally dived into his glib nothingness and rolled around in it.

Then another thought: what about me?

It seemed strange. I was certainly as physically striking in every way as the Wiseass, yet I sat in the audience unnoticed. I could have bounced up onto the stage and competed for attention and won, shocking the audience as I outshone the Wiseass in jumping and twirling.

But I chose to recede, to hide, even in plain view, so I did and they scarcely saw me at all. He chose to dominate, so he did. The way of the world.

The show ended after thirty minutes with The Amazing Clifford giving the glittery girl a kiss that must have unsettled her breakfast and then he bounced off the stage in big gliding leaps, waving gaily to the audience as he went.

The applause was as loud as hands could create and as the studio lights went on people began buzzing to each other as they stood up and shuffled out.

I made my way against traffic to the front, walking through the cameras and their wires and hopped onto the stage and walked into the wings, following the departing Wiseass. A guard made as if to stop me once, but I simply stuck out my hand as if it held a badge or something and muttered "Network-PR" as I continued walking past him. He didn't challenge me further.

When I found the great man's dressing room I found that, quick as I'd been, a dozen young girls had been quicker. They crowded around the door, smiling wildly, calling out to The Amazing Clifford through his partly open door, jabbing and pushing each other for best position, desperately wanting to be inside the dressing room but waiting for an invitation because they dared not enter without it.

With a "Sorry," I brushed past them and slipped through the door. The Wiseass was seated at a dressing table, not removing makeup because he had needed none, but simply staring at his reflection in the mirror, obviously deeply in love with what he saw.

Hearing my footstep he glanced back and saw me and for one small tick, went perfectly still. Then he bounded up and grabbed me by the elbows, with every appearance of pleasure. "Andy! he cried loudly, for everyone to hear, "My old friend, Andy!"

Then, facing the door of his dressing room he called out gaily, "Don't go away, girls! I'm with an old friend! I'll be out soon to give you what you came for!" There was loud tittering from behind the door.

Turning to me again and speaking too quietly for anyone else to hear: "So, you old fart. I knew you'd come. I've been waiting for you."

I glanced around his dressing room. It was larger than I had expected, with a private bath and a small kitchenette at one end and a king-sized bed at the other. The bed, surrounded by mirrors, was sturdily built, a simple strong board box rising from the floor and capped by a thick mattress spread with pink sheets. There were spotlights in the ceiling and walls, nestled among the mirrors, and a table beside the bed held glasses, bottles and an ice bucket.

"Like my casting couch!" he asked, grinning at me. "Like to try it out? Want me to call in a couple of girls?" Then, seeing my expression, "No? Then what say I call them all in, we'll take five or six apiece, have a contest?"

I shook my head slightly, dismissing the thought. "I came here to see how you turned out, Clifford. I wanted to see what kind of man I'd created."

"*Huuhhhgh!*" he exclaimed, "Don't tell me you're going to take credit for that, not after what the great Henry Fowles did for both of us!"

I watched him watch me for a reaction. So, he was fishing.

"Well, Clifford," I parried, "Did the Great Henry Fowles take his own medicine? Is he one of us, too?

The Wiseass waved this away with impatience. "Think I'm a damned fool? Think I'd tell him?" Then, dropping the thought, "I've got a lot of questions to ask you, Andy, old friend. First off, how long do you think this thing will last?"

"Old friend. Old fart." How could he be so transparent? How could he think that I'd be so stupid as to give him anything of value? Let the bastard squirm. I smiled beatifically and said nothing.

I listened to the girls shove and giggle outside. The Wiseass seemed to ignore them, but if you watched his face you could see a twitch or an eye movement from time to time that betrayed his interest.

"What's happening at the Germ Factory," I asked him. "Have you got them working on my new protein?"

"*Yours!* Hahhh! Without that wonderful material I added from Henry Fowles, it would have been—"

169

"Far purer," I interrupted. "You almost ruined my stuff with that crap you added."

I watched the Wiseass search my face carefully for lies. He was still fishing and I was still muddying his waters.

"We've got a few problems at the lab," he admitted, "But we're working on it. We're getting there. I go down now and then myself and lend a hand when I've got the time."

"Your problem is," I answered for him, "that you have no sample to work from. You have no idea what you're looking for or how it works. You don't even know what my basic approach was, so you're just stumbling around blind. Isn't that about it, Clifford?"

He looked annoyed and waved his hand toward me, dismissing the subject. "What the hell, it doesn't matter," he said. "There're just the two of us like this and I wouldn't want to give it to anyone anyway, would you? So why worry about it?"

So. He had forgotten Sara. To him, she had been just a useless old woman, not worth remembering. I said nothing.

The girls at the door had gotten together and were using their fingernails to scratch slowly at the door while they chorused: "Oh, Clifford...Oh, *Clifford*...Oh, *Clifford*" in rising tones.

"Listen to them!" he grinned, delighted. "I like to let them get excited, get their juices flowing." He gave a doglike sniff. "Can you smell 'em? I can!"

And indeed there was a strong female odor coming in from under and around the door. *"Oh Cliffie!"* they sang.

"Do you ever injure girls like these?" I asked.

"Oh, some of them rip," he said. "You know how it is, like they're made of wet paper or something and you get a little excited and maybe give an extra jerk and then there's nothing but blood, shit, and tears. You know how it is."

He waved the thought away, impatient with it. "It doesn't matter, anyway," he added as an afterthought. "God knows there's always plenty more where they came from. Miles and miles of them, lined up wherever I go."

I had a sudden vision of daybreak on our mountain, Sara's and mine, with dew on the grass and rabbits feeding on tender greens and a hawk circling lazily in the sky and I wanted nothing so much as to be out of here, away from this Wiseass and his foolish

170

girls. But I knew I'd have to ask a few questions that'd plague me if I didn't.

"What's in your future, Clifford? What will you do next?"

"Next? Who knows? Right now, I'm reviewing my options, that's what. The whole damned world is open to me. You, too, if you had the guts, but you don't, of course."

"What kind of guts would I need?"

"Take-charge guts! But you never will. I know you. Always in the background, sniping at people. Always the observer, and the observer never wins. Can't win."

"Are you talking politics, Clifford? You want to get elected to something? Is that your ambition?"

"Elected? Are you out of it? You think I want to be President of the U.S. of A.? I could do that. Dead easy. Just like on my TV show, I could have these fools eating out of my hand. Give me a month, they'd think I was God Almighty with a blue ribbon around my ass. But you gotta say, what comes next? Think I want to spend my good time arguing with that stupid Congress? Sit at a desk and sign bills about child care? Eat State dinners with foreign turkeys and make speeches? Who wants that? Do you?"

I admitted that I didn't.

"You know what a politician does?" he continued. "You know how they get what they want? Every one of them works the same damned way and people never catch on because they don't want to catch on. They'd rather shut their eyes and hope."

"What they do is take some money or some power away from one small group and give it to another, much larger group with more votes, and then they say, 'Love me. Love me for my generosity!'

"A little promise, a little power," said the Wiseass. "Or if you want to get right down to it, it's more like, 'a little promise, a *lot* of power', you know?

"Did you ever listen to what those turkeys running for President promise? Damned little. Damned little. They give a hundred speeches and say nothing. You gotta listen with both ears to hear anything at all, but people elect them anyway on the basis of what they think they said.

"Now, you take me. *If* I wanted to run it, mind you, because I don't. Well, hell, look what I could promise if I wanted to: a cure for cancer? Sure. Why not? A cure for AIDS? Dead easy. I can hear it now, my slogan, you know: *'I want to be your biotech president!'* Or, maybe something that has a cute little rhyme, like: *'Clifford The Cancer Curer!'* And if I wanted the old fart vote I could hint at extra long life, too, maybe. You know?"

"So, Clifford. All you need is my blue liquid."

"Oh, nooo!" But he gave me a sharp look as he said it. "I said 'promise', not 'give'. You think I want to give away my own secret? Make them as good as I am?"

Strange, I thought. He's looking right at me. He knows as well as I do that I created him and that I'm all that he is and maybe more. Yet, he simply can't admit it to me or to himself. What a strange and evasive being is my Wiseass!

I said, "What you need, Clifford, is me. You need me in a laboratory producing miracles for you to buy votes with. Is that it?"

"Oh, well. What a thing to say. What a point of view!"

"My only question is, Clifford, why on earth do you think I ever would?"

"Oh, hey, listen," he said. "I'm above all that. If I want power over the people I'll just take it, to hell with this vote business anyway. And maybe I will, if I decide that's what I want. But I don't know. It could be a pain. You've got to think before you start things rolling: is that what you really want? That's where I am now, trying to decide, but if I do decide to do it, then, *whammo!* I'll do it. Look out world, here comes The Amazing Clifford!" He gave me a slow wink and poked me in the ribs with his finger. "See what I mean?

"In the meantime," he continued, poking away, "pussy's plentiful and the world's at my feet fighting for a chance to give my toes a kiss, so what's the rush? Eh? Eh? Isn't that the way of it? *Eh?*

"But now," he said with another slow wink at me, "My girls have waited long enough, they're heated up enough to chew nails, so I'm going to open this door and let them have their Amazing Clifford. You can stay and watch, you can join in, or you can leave." He glided towards the door, put his hand on the knob and called out, "Get set, girls!" and flung it open. The girls streamed into the room, laughing and chattering and squealing as they came.

I examined them as they entered. Some mother's daughter, I thought, looking into each eager face. Some father's little girl.

There was one girl: a small brunette with a heart-shaped, very white and tender face and startling blue eyes, who seemed to be masking an innate softness with a bold bravado. I caught her by the upper arm and held her back briefly as the others flew past her. She struggled, then looked into my face and drew back slightly, shocked by what she saw. Slowly the realization dawned that she was being held by another being equally as compelling as The Amazing Clifford and you could see the emotion flicker through her face as she tried to digest this new information.

"You're going with me," I told her. "Don't worry, you'll love it." And I whirled her around and walked her out of the room, where I could already hear the rip of clothes and the laugh-scream of the women behind me.

I simply couldn't leave him like this. So I stopped, turned, and called out through the now-closed door:

"Clifford! It won't last! Only I know how much time you have left and only I know how to make it last forever—if I want to. So enjoy!"

There was dead silence for a moment, then a furious snarl of "Back off, bitch! Leave me alone!" and then a series of slapping sounds, followed by anguished cries from one of the women and anxious indrawn breath from the others.

"You're a liar, old man!" came the answer from the other side of the door, over the sobs and mutters of the women.

Then, after another pause, my Wiseass recovered his poise. "Let's show 'em girls!" he urged, gaiety forced back into his voice. "Let's show 'em how The Amazing Clifford got his name!"

Reluctant, grudging laughter faded into real laughter as the girls allowed themselves to be won over, the little incident forgotten, their Clifford still a dream of love and excitement.

We walked out of the building and into the alley, my brunette girl and I, then down a side street and across another street and into a small, dusty-looking park where we could stand for a few minutes under a tree and out of the foot traffic while I talked to her. Taxi horns blew in a constant irritable fury and the mingled voices and foot cloppings of a thousand nearby humans made it difficult to hear or think.

"I think you're a sweet girl," I began, and she smiled, pleased but uncertain. "Too sweet to be left behind in that zoo." Her face fell.

"Look," I said, and swinging her around to face the small. gnarled oak tree where we stood, I poked my finger deep into the living wood and ripped it up and down, leaving a nasty splintery gash several inches long. A traffic light changed and hordes of pedestrians walked beside us. The girl's face was white and set as she stared at the injured tree.

"That could have been you," I told her. "Some of the girls who were with you may be getting ripped like that right now. I know that man. When he gets excited he won't care who he hurts. Maybe some of those girls are tough enough to stay with him, but you aren't. If you resisted, you'd be ripped."

She was staring at me in ultimate horror. I'm not sure she understood or believed one word. But she did understand the torn tree and the unnaturally strong grip on her arm and this brought, first a piteous whimper, then a small scream and finally frantic calls of, *"Police! Police!"*

I put my mouth to her ear so she couldn't shut me out and said: "Go home to mother! Don't go back in there!"

I turned and walked away, leaving her, wild eyed and shuddering beside the ripped tree, a small girl, surrounded by the hurrying crowd, more afraid of the one who had saved her than of the one who would have ruined her.

chapter twenty-six

When I'd located the address I'd found in the phone book and used the small, scarred elevator to reach the ninth floor I almost turned away. The atmosphere was grubby, uninviting. It reminded you that the world was dirty.

My detective was middleaged, a little heavy and soft around the middle, with thinning white hair and startlingly blue eyes behind rimless glasses. There was a framed family group photo on his desk sitting beside an IBM PC with a modem and printer.

"That's my principal weapon," said the detective. "With a telephone and a computer today you can find out a whole lot more than you ever could from peeking in windows. Be surprised what people tell you on the phone, you know how to ask. Course, I do get out, nose around, wouldn't want you to think I just sit here sending out bills, you know?

"I don't point guns at people," he went on, "cause a lot of people point them back at you. But I sure can find out whatever you need to know."

No Sam Spade, he, but maybe exactly the investigator I needed.

I wrote him a retainer check for five thousand dollars (totally surprising him) and said that I wanted to know everything there was to know about The Amazing Clifford.

"Christ, mister, just buy a newspaper. What d'you need with me?" He was looking at me strangely, sure he had a freak on his hands. I couldn't blame him.

"No... I mean everything. Assets, liabilities, business associates, girl friends, where he sleeps, what he eats and how much, where he buys his clothes, where he travels, where he is at all times, what you think he's going to do next...that kind of thing. Everything.

"I'm going to call you from time to time," I continued, "and I want to be able to ask you whatever pops into my mind about this Amazing Clifford and I want you to have an answer. Just send me a bill, anytime, and I'll send money. OK?"

My detective took off his rimless glasses and wiped them on his tie and stared at me with his electric blue eyes and asked, frankly curious: "You got a thing for this guy? Lots have, you know. Women and men too, I guess. I'm just asking."

"I've got a thing *against* this guy," I told him. "But I won't say more. You just keep your eyes on him for me."

We completed our arrangements. My detective was intrigued, not only because he smelled money, but because he was about to investigate a legend and I had implied that he might find dirt.

How easy to find an ally, I thought. *Just write out some numbers on a piece of paper and you've got a friend. Sort of.*

I left my plump detective secure in the knowledge that he would watch my Wiseass for me. Better him than me.

I started back to my hotel, deliberately walking through Central Park with the belligerent thought, *Mug me, someone. Go ahead. Make my day!* But no one obliged. The world around me was sweet and harmless as I walked toward the terminal boredom of my room.

Going up the elevator with a fold of newspapers under my arm, the loud, clear voice sounded unbidden in my head again:

"Where is Sara? What is she doing? Who is she doing it with?"

chapter twenty-seven

Alone, Alone, Alone. I was so alone. A miasma of loneliness had me by the throat like a sickness. I thought that if I had found myself alone on top of our mountain I could have found joy and peace, but here in a hotel room with millions of strangers streaming by like ants below I felt such a depression that breathing itself seemed superfluous.

Trying to break the depression, I called room service and ordered lunch for eight. Then, waiting for it to come, I took a long hot shower and settled down with the newspapers I'd brought up with me, deliberately reading every word on every page, from the fall of foreign governments to homemaker hints for removing stains from linen napkins.

One story about our exploding world population (two billion fifty years ago was now five billion and in another twenty years would be ten billion, most of them starving and ravaging the world for scraps) put me even further into depression. How could this disaster be averted? Suppose I tried? What could I do? Produce millions of tons of food that contained a birth control substance, maybe? And then catch hell from everyone for invading the civil rights of those I saved?

I daydreamed about this for a while, but knew that I would do nothing and that no one else would, either. We were watching an enormous catastrophe in the making. The earth would be denuded, billions would die. Many of the fortunate ones who stood by, watching and deploring and wringing their hands, would also be killed as the have-nots took from the haves.

Oh, well. I had food for eight coming up soon. All was right with my world, except that I was desperately lonely. Almost suicidal.

So, nothing for me to do but read on. What else was new in the newspaper world? The comics? Usually, they make more sense than the rest of the paper. Given only the comic page and "Dear Abby" or "Ann Landers," one might survive.

Now the entertainment section: maybe I ought to go to the movies, get my mind off my troubles. But the movies would be so slow now. I'd be forced to watch them at their own pace. I couldn't speed-read them like a book. Sara and I used to love the movies.

I see they've got a new star in Hollywood. A new singer-dancer-actress, an all around fabulous creature everyone is foolish about. She's not only the newest glamour girl, the new Jackie, Liz and Di, she's also an activist, a new Fonda. And this one seems to be an activist people love.

Now, that's class! This new female star won't give her name, just one initial, and the mystery of this has everyone wildly excited.

A knock at the door by the room service waiter interrupted my reverie and I dropped the newspaper and turned my attention to the food, but as I was chewing away, eating enough to feed a third world family for a month, an idle question came to me: what was this new actress's initial? I picked up the newspaper and scanned the story. Her name, or rather, her initial, was "S."

Oh, my good Christ! "S."

I had found Sara!

Without another thought I picked up the phone and called the hotel's transportation desk. "Get me a one-way ticket to Las Vegas. And hurry."

chapter twenty-eight

Slot machines at the airport, set to capture your first and last dollar: Las Vegas introducing itself to the traveler.

The taxi took me through this neon blossom of the desert just before nine at night, when the town was pulsing with gambling, with shows, with all that makes Vegas Vegas. The extravaganza of light and color here in the desert sand made you grin involuntarily. Here was man, thumbing his nose at nature and making you like it in spite of yourself.

I hurried the driver, dropping a couple of twenties into his lap as I talked, leaning over the seat and urging him on. I told him he'd have a fistful of those twenties if he could get me a ticket to the show at Caesar's

"You mean, 'S'? Man, those are sold out. Always sold out, you know? Every time she comes to town, *wham!* a sellout. People crawling for tickets."

"Never mind. Find me a scalper. You'll know how to do it." I dropped another twenty to emphasize my point.

We whirled into the entry to Caesar's Palace. It was a scene to make you laugh out loud. A Hollywood vision of Roman excess. White columns and colored lights around a huge reflecting pool, fake statuary everywhere. Yet, it commanded your respect: anyone who would go to such exuberant lengths to create his dreamscape out here on the desert sand had to be admired.

My taxi driver, temporarily moved to action by my constant drip, drip, drip of twenties, parked at the rear of the cab line and saying, "just wait," to me over his shoulder, trotted into the lobby and found a uniformed bellman who listened, palmed one of my twenties, then pointed out another man who was collecting tickets at the head of a line deep inside the lobby. My driver looked back, gave me a "come on" wave and as I caught up with him, was talking earnestly with the line handler, who was shaking his head in denial.

I slipped up behind my driver and put a small stack of twenties into his hand for ammunition and stepped back to let him do his job.

Walking just a few feet from the crowded line and turning his back on the standees, the line handler pocketed a folded packet of my twenties with practiced ease and shook hands with my driver, passing him my ticket, all the while shaking his head in mock denial for the sake of any standees who might be watching.

"Don't worry," my driver said to me, winking broadly, "you'll have to stand back here at the tail end of the line, but he'll take good care of you, see that you get a good seat and all that. OK?"

I passed him the promised stack of twenties and he gave me a smile and a wave and left, proud of his ability to get things done in his town.

So it was that I ended up at a table about two feet square, sitting in a semi-circular seat crowded leg-against-leg with a somewhat beefy man I'd never met but who, like me, was unattached. The line handler had made us a couple.

Drinks were ordered (I gave him mine) and steaks were brought, which I ate with my usual speed, and with an almost ruthless efficiency the dinner part of the dinner theater was created and almost as quickly, the remains removed. The lights dimmed. There was an expectant quiet as people "shushed" each other, and my seatmate leaned over and whispered to me, "This 'S,' she's hot shit, you know? Gets you all excited but the truth is, she scares the hell out of me."

I smiled at him and turned my head away in dismissal. Why should I discuss Sara with this balding, heavy stranger? I could smell the stink of cigar smoke on his breath, mixed with the scotch he'd just finished.

The house lights went from dim to black and a series of spotlights flashed on, lighting the orchestra pit, where music roared out in a sudden burst, surprising and pleasing everyone.

My seatmate, hell bent on saying what he had to say, ignored the music and cupped his hand to his mouth and directed it into my ear as he shouted against the music: "I know a guy, good-looking guy, a regular Clark Gable type, with a little black mustache and built like a boxer, he got involved with this 'S,' you know what I mean?"

I smiled and moved my head back slightly, dismissing him again, but he hardly noticed. I realized I was almost in a panic to have him shut up.

"All the women went for this guy, you know. All he had to do was pick and choose, but not any more!"

I forced a smile again. "Let's listen to the music, OK?" And I started moving my hand to the beat, smiling and acting out my lack of interest in what he had to say.

"Not any more!" He finished his story despite me. "He went with this woman, this 'S' and now he's emasculated. Mashed his privates to a jelly, that's what she did! They had to trim them off. Hamburger, that's all. It's like she must have a vise down there, you know? A regular steel trap.

"You wouldn't catch me trusting *my* little peter to a woman like that," shouted my seatmate. "Not after all the tales I've been hearing. Nosiree, not me!"

I started to smile my dismissal of him again but then I knew I'd have to be rid of him. I couldn't watch Sara with this man beside me.

How could she? I thought, sickly. *How could she act so much like the Wiseass?*

The spotlight swept across stage and stopped at the wing, where Sara would enter. Her voice, now just offstage, was pouring out of this corner and we in the audience knew she would be step-ping into the spotlight within seconds. The anticipation built. I had to act.

"Give me your left hand," I said to my seatmate, and before he could react I took it and held it palm up on the small table between us. "Grab that napkin with your right hand," I told him, and I had to take the napkin and shove it in to his free hand.

"Now," I said, hissing the words to him, "Look into my face. Look into my unnatural face!" and I took his little finger, left hand, which I had already decided he could most easily do without, and with my thumb and forefinger pinched the end of it into ham-burger and then immediately covered his mouth with my hand, preventing his scream. "Cover it with that napkin!" I commanded him. "Don't drip blood and cause a scene! And now, get out. Get out! Leave me!"

He backed out of the small booth, eyes wide, lip trembling, breath coming in gasps.

"Run," I hissed at him again. "Run before I mash your fat ass off."

Sara bounded on stage as he turned and, holding his hand in the napkin, shuffled out as fast as the crowded room would allow.

All eyes were on "S," my Sara. The moment she reached center stage all music stopped and her voice stopped and there was intense silence until the audience, suddenly realizing what was expected of it, began a deafening applause.

Sara swept the audience with her eyes, stopping momentarily with each person, staring almost into each individual soul. The effect was profound. Each audience member felt that he or she had been seen, had been examined, recognized and understood. It was an intensely personal search, with a small, bright spotlight directed from the back of the stage to pinpoint each audience member in turn as Sara searched them with her eyes. And to each there was a small nod, a smile, an individual reaction that seemed to say, "I see you. I know you. I understand you. I'll know you and greet you next time I see you." Her mobile face, shimmering in intensity, spoke a private thought to each.

As her gaze neared me I ducked as though to retrieve something fallen on the floor and she swept by me. But an expression of puzzlement flickered across her features. I knew she'd dart a look in my direction again, and I went on guard against it.

There was a low sweet sound from Sara that turned quickly into a song from a Victor Herbert operetta. She whirled gracefully around the stage on her toes while the song soared. Then, with another stab of spotlight, a handsome baritone was revealed on stage and hand-in-hand the two whirled with the music while his rich male voice entwined with hers in a duet of love. Each of them stared longingly into the eyes of the other.

I was jealous down to my socks.

I thought briefly about my former seatmate with the mashed finger and was sick, not only for him, but for myself. In a long life I'd never hurt anyone before. Not deliberately. He had lost the end of his finger. I had lost a vision of myself as a peaceful, kindly man. Now my fingers itched to tear the vocal cords out of this baritone and get him out of my Sara's arms.

High on a sugar-sweet Victor Herbert note of innocent passion Sara's voice slid into a low-down Janis Joplin country rock whine and when she whirled her pretty baritone out of the spotlight with an outstretched hand another hand out of the dark instantly grasped hers and she pulled into the spotlight another male singer/dancer, this one with the sideburns and the idiot leer of a country-western stud.

Together they danced and sang the sort of Joplin-like sweaty-sex trash that had me grinding my teeth in a jealous rage. How could she? Where was my sweet Sara?

Then it was a Latin rhythm and a stylized dance with still another partner. They were obviously standing all around the stage in the dark, these male partners, and Sara could simply stick out her hand and choose any man she wanted to suit her song. How convenient.

And so it went through hard rock, soft rock, easy listening, New Orleans Jazz, operetta, and big band sound. Each segment brought a new dancing partner and Sara used them all and outshone them all.

The wax-figured, slow-minded audience had become a single mass being that swayed with her music and giggled and grinned madly to itself, lost in shared enjoyment.

I was not amused.

From time to time Sara searched the crowd with quick, sharp eyes. She covered my space over and over and each time, quicker than she, I ducked or turned or put a handkerchief to my nose to evade her. But she knew. Or suspected.

Once, in the speeded-up special language that we used, so fast that no one else could have heard it, she burst out in the very middle of a complicated lyric, *"Andy? Andy? Are you there?"*

I didn't answer. Again, minutes later, in the midst of another song with another man, thus time with such a long sentence that the audience must have heard it in spite of its speed, heard it perhaps as a staccato bark, "Andy...I know you're there. Come backstage after the show. We'll make a night of it. Have a ball. Say you will, Andy!"

I didn't answer. Instead, my eyes began to pick out my escape route through the crowded audience and before her song was finished I jumped up and ran for it in a blur of motion.

"Forget it, bitch!" I screamed back over my shoulder as I ran through the crowd and out the door.

I streaked through the corridors and the gaming rooms filled with blue haired women at slot machines and more knowing types losing their money at roulette wheels and crap tables and then I was through the lobby of Caesar's Palace and out into the sweet-smelling desert night. A few blocks of pulsating neon glitter and then I was out in the dry desert kicking up sand as I ran, twenty feet to a stride and my legs a blur of motion.

Faintly, over my shoulder, I could hear a speeded-up cry that must have brought pain to half a thousand eardrums: "… Oh, Andy! Don't ruin both our lives. Don't be such a stick! Come back, Andy!"

I ran. And ran. I ran towards nothingness as I ran away from Sara. Later that night, after her show, I heard her in the desert calling and searching for me, but I had found a small gully far from town where there was room only for me and a frustrated rattlesnake, and here I hid and waited until she was gone, letting the snake strike me again and again until he gave up and crawled away, no doubt with a sore mouth and broken fangs.

I didn't know which made me feel sicker: for me to have called Sara a bitch or for her to so obviously be one.

chapter twenty-nine

So began my forty days in the desert, more or less. At first I stayed roughly in touch with Las Vegas, coming in at night to eat at cheap restaurants and fast food shops and buying cases of canned hash and stew to take back with me to the hills. Every day during this time I watched the "S" name in lights on the big electronic billboard outside Caesar's Palace and mooned about my lost Sara like a lovesick teenager.

I constantly wondered where she was staying, what her room looked like, what she did with her time during the day, why she wore that strange looking white toga she'd had on the night I'd seen her performance. Was the toga part of the Caesar's Palace motif? I doubted it. If Sara wore a toga it was only because Sara wanted to wear a toga for reasons of her own. I was just surprised that she didn't want a more figure-revealing costume. Surprised, but glad, too.

To hell with the toga. The thing I really wondered was, who was Sara with all night after her show? One of the male singer/dancers? All of them? Someone else? Some Las Vegas gangster, maybe? Some movie star? How the hell could she do it? How could she do this to sweet old me?

How could she even *want* to do it with one of these soft, slow, mushroom tender men? She had to know there was the danger of destroying any man she touched. Didn't she have any sympathy for them?

Oh, to hell with these unknown men! Back to the honest question: "How could she treat me this way when she knew I loved her so?"

I'd stack my two or three cases of canned goods on one shoulder and grab my five gallon water jug with a free hand and lope off into the desert to a spot I'd found that I could call home.

It was up in the hills, a little cave under an outcropping of solid rock, with an eight by ten foot flat area in front that I thought of as my verandah. From it I could look down on Las Vegas. I felt that I was standing guard over Sara, in a loose, ineffectual way, even though I couldn't see her or she me.

185

And here, just to keep my sanity, I began to look around me, to try to understand the complex geology of the area, and I realized almost with a shock that I had chanced upon a part of the world that was sheer magic in its sterile beauty.

Why if Sara were only with me, I thought, *we could live in these hills as peacefully as we did in our green mountain home. A different kind of beauty, but beauty no less.*

I began to wander, filling my eyes and my memory with the fantastic shapes and colors of the eroded desert. I was constantly reminded that I could see constantly reminded that I could see a hundred million years, more or less, in the layers of earth that were everywhere revealed.

I could read the upturned strata that showed how two earth-plates had jammed together, eons ago, to form a mountain or a rolling hill. I remembered what geology I'd read in my previous library binges, but it wasn't enough to satisfy me now. "I'll have to visit the Colorado School of Mines," I told myself, "or the geology departments of the University of Nevada or Arizona. I really need to get into this stuff. Ignorance is not bliss."

I felt as though I were living in an x-ray picture of the earth. All my life the world had been covered with grass and trees and concrete and people, but now I was seeing its true skeleton, understanding how it had been made.

It was beautiful, yes. Beautiful enough to make your eyes water as the subtle earth colors blended into a symphony of visual pleasure. Yet, the desert was harsh and alien to a being like me who depended upon huge food and water intakes.

Only those species who had learned to live sparingly could survive.

If I had been turned loose here with no civilized food handy I'd be forced to kill and eat a bighorn sheep a day, or a mule deer or a pronghorn antelope. Within a month I would clear all the large wildlife off this corner of the desert and be forced into eating the desert tortoise or dozens of jack rabbits and snakes each day. Soon, all by myself, I would ravage this harsh land and make a true desert of the desert.

So I rambled on, the born-again geologist, learning for the first time, as though it was my own discovery, what millions of others had seen and understood before me and saved by cases of Dinty

Moore stew from having to face the moral choice of either pre-serving or destroying all life around me.

"What in God's name is Sara doing right now? And who is she doing it with?"

Now and again, without my bidding, the desert rang with the sad, bitter song of the cuckold. My helpless rage put me to smashing stones with my fists. The loneliness made me cry out in shock waves of anguished sound. The shame. The shame. That was it, the sheer magnitude of the shame that I felt as my symbolic horns grew was almost too much. "How could she? How could she do this to me?" Thus wailed the foolish wronged husband in an impotent tantrum, aware of his own weakness even in the face of crushed rocks as his mind's eye showed him in graphic and pornographic detail exactly what his wife of more than fifty years had undoubtedly done in bed with another man, or with men without numbers.

The fact that she had crushed them with her weight and pinched off some of their parts was of no real matter to me. To hell with fragile and foolish mankind. It was Sara who had made me a cuckold, not the men.

Geology flew from my mind as these Sara-thoughts invaded. "Back to shale, damnit! Concentrate on the Jurassic!" I'd order myself sternly.

So it went. An interesting time, but, overall, a miserable time. I tried to make the best of it.

One day I trotted over the hills to the impossibly blue waters of Lake Mead and along with a gang of tourists, watched the mouths of a thousand carp open obscenely to demand food, which the tourist children dutifully bought from the concession stand and threw to the round O's of open-mouthed fish.

Then I bought a ticket and went out on the tourist boat to look at the entrance to drowned caves and to hear the guide recite the cute names that man has given to geological shapes because he cannot otherwise deal with their beauty and complexity. What man can't understand he trivializes.

Afterward, I trotted over the desert to Hoover Dam to admire the engineering marvel that it is: a striking manmade beauty with its simple, powerful shape; as utilitarian as a needle, as perfect in form as an egg, as audacious in sheer mass as the great pyramid of Cheops.

All this, the damming of the Colorado to drown a fantastically beautiful land and create Lake Mead, the dam itself and the complicated irrigation system stretching for hundreds of miles below it, all were a tribute to puny man's ambition and creative force—and also a perfect example of man's rapacious need to reshape the world to suit himself.

But who was I to argue? Wasn't I a man myself? And hadn't I performed at least the potential for the ultimate rape of the earth by creating myself and Sara, the ultimate rapers if we chose to do it?

So I sat on a hill overlooking Hoover Dam and watched as the tourists with their cameras and kids moved about the dam showing it proper awe, and I thought my thoughts.

I thought about hunger, the great driving force of all life, and satiety, modern man's answer to hunger that makes much of our race fat and diet-crazed while millions of other species die and become extinct…and about sex, that primal itch that every species must have to survive and how we had turned it into such an elaborate game…and about aggression, that ugly and cruel cause of wars and murder, but absolutely needed for survival (just show me a completely happy, gentle people and I'll show you a cemetery) and I thought about anger…and killing… and history… and guilt… and beauty…and religion… and all those other big questions that keep college sophomores up nights earnestly attacking cases of beer.

But mainly I thought about perspective. About point-of-view. About relative truth.

I thought about how everything is true and everything is false, depending upon the position of the observer. Einstein said it mathematically in his general theory of relativity. We can say it more simply with the fable of the six blind men and the elephant. But say it however we like, truth has a million faces and your truth is only my truth if we stand in the same spot and look in the same direction at the same time.

I thought about man and woman and how weak they really are and I looked at Hoover Dam below me and thought about the swarm of man-ants who had created it in five years, which was two years ahead of schedule because it was Great Depression time and people were hungry for jobs and they had worked frantically, these weak little quarter-horsepower creatures, and they had poured over three million cubic yards of concrete to make it six hundred and sixty feet thick at the base and twelve hundred forty-four feet high, and they had fifteen hundred injuries a month but they only outright killed ninety-six men on the whole project, which is not bad at all unless one of the ninety-six was your Uncle Charlie, and Las Vegas needs the electricity for its neon lights so let's not quibble about details.

I made myself look down at the tourists who were swarming over Hoover Dam and I thought: If you really, really believe that these people are a plague on the earth, why not just wipe out a few of them the same way you'd spray bathroom cleaner on a grimy, germy tub? How about that, Andy, big scientist? Where is the strength of your convictions?

Why don't you just throw down a few tons of rocks and wipe out all these tourists, then go to India, Africa, China, New York City, London, here and there where the biggest hordes are and clean up the earth by wiping out some of these pests who are killing it. Say a million here a hundred million there. If you really worked at it you could make a real difference. The newly green earth would smile at you, call you savior.

But the vision of myself as a mass-murderer—and the earth without my species—did not appeal, no matter how beautiful some future summer morning might be with grasses waving gently in the breeze and a million other species copulating happily in the vacuum left by greedy man's departure.

So then I was left with the opposite question: "Then why not mass-produce the Blue Helix (as soon as you get the missing ingredient from stupid Henry Fowles, of course) and give it to everyone?

189

What kind of man am I, with the power to lift the whole human race out of the muck and not do it?

But just because I can run and jump and crush rocks and do great gobs of arithmetic in my head, does that mean I'm out of the muck myself? Aren't I dangerous? Sweet old me? Look at the way I crushed that guy's finger with scarcely a second thought just because he wouldn't shut up. And if innocent Andy is dangerous, just think what a danger many other people might be. But that's a childish thought. Simplistic. Of course I'd create a new hell on earth. No doubt about it. I'd take a rapacious weak species and make it a rapacious monster species

But there is beauty, goddamnit, there is music, and mankind created it all and there are gentle poets and dedicated life-saving doctors and honest priests and soft, loving wives and mothers and people who plant trees and sing about the earth and of course a lot of them are saints and a lot more are sentimental bores but not really bad people...and goddamnit, Sara, why'd you have to run off and sing your songs for other men?

So here I sit, the strongest, most capable man who ever lived on this earth and I don't have a single clue as to what to do.

You talk about Jesus on the mountaintop with the devil at his side urging him to earthly power, well at least he had a clear cut choice, or thought he did, and I can't even figure out what my choices are.

What about the great philosophers? I'll bet if you had an even dozen of them, from Socrates to Schopenhauer, from Kant to Kierkgaard, sitting on a special jury and you put the question to them: "What must Andy do about giving his Blue Helix to mankind?" they'd look at each other, shrug, and cry out in one unified chorus: "Search me!"

Look at this outpouring of words as I sit on my rock and not a new thought in the bunch, nothing beautiful and true, nothing shining and pure to uplift the spirit, just the same old human muddle. It reminds me of an old Southern song I heard once, and the song had a couple of lines in it that went:

"Oh, I ain't got enough to pass around,
so I'll just keep it all for myself…"

That about sums it up. I'll just hop off this rock and go about my business and let humanity go along its merry miserable way a few years or a few centuries longer until I figure it all out.

So I didn't stone the tourists. I didn't save the earth from man or mankind from itself. I jumped down the hill from rock to rock and trotted into a little touristy shop near the dam and bought a case of Snickers candy bars. Then, peeling and eating a Snickers from time to time (with the nuisance of having to stuff the damned wrappers into my pocket where they kept trying to expand and crawl out) I ran for miles across the barren landscape towards the Valley of Fire, a special place I had always wanted to visit.

I was running, jumping from rock to rock, thinking dark Sara-thoughts, almost oblivious to the special beauty around me, a strange and fanciful landscape of vivid red wind sculptured stone, when I kicked up something half-buried in sandstone that had a different feel to it. When I really looked at it I found it was no rock at all but a bone fragment of some kind and thinking back on my library binge of paleontology it looked like a part of the fossilized skull of a giant metoposaur; one who had roamed this land in the Triassic period when all around us was a huge shallow swamp. I held the skull fragment and looked into an empty eyehole and shivered with a kind of fright at the strangeness of it.

"Will I still be here two million years from now?" I asked myself, "Still looking at rocks and bones and still wondering what to do when I grow up? Is this skull my Yorick and am I to be a Hamlet, forever unable to make up my mind?"

But then I looked around me and the red of the rock at the Valley of Fire and the blue of Lake Mead beyond it were so vivid, with such a clean, sterile beauty, that I could for a little while at least, accept the world I saw with pleasure.

I waited for the sun to set, watching each detail of the changing kaleidoscope and remembering Delacroix's statement that "… colors are the music of the eyes. They combine like sounds to produce harmonics…" and by that logic I was standing in the midst of a crashing color symphony.

So be it. Enjoy.

*   *   *   *   *

Next morning I had a sudden thought that started me loping off towards Las Vegas, driving holes in the soft surface with each step.

How long had I been away from New York? Over a month?

Plenty long enough for my hired sleuth to do his job.

I dreaded making the phone call. I wanted no part of the Wiseass and his grubby world, but knew I had to know what he was up to, like it or not.

By and by, having worked up a great hunger during the slipping, sliding run in soft sand, I stopped at a Burger King on the outskirts of Las Vegas and ate a dozen cheeseburgers and drank a couple of chocolate shakes to wet my throat for the call. Breakfast would have to come later, when my business was done.

I used a phone booth outside the Burger King and through the modern miracle of a dime, a nickel and a credit card, I was soon talking to my detective over more than two thousand miles of copper wire.

"You're calling from Vegas, eh? Didn't figure you for the type! Well, what do you know. Put a dollar in the slot for me, eh?"

"Tell me about the Amazing Clifford."

"Tell you the truth, I liked the guy until that day you came into my shop and laid out that check. Then I said to myself, 'what the hell, Harry, you got the client's money, won't hurt to look around and give him a report, everybody's entitled to what they pay for, never mind why anybody would want to investigate a national hero like that, so I started looking, doing my job, you know?

"I put together all the news clips, all the public records I could find. Then I started talking to everyone around him you

192

know? Everybody involved in his business or his personal life. Most of them thought he was great, just great, but not all, you know. I was surprised. Really, really surprised. I ought to know better, as many people as I've looked at, you always find a little dirt, you know where to look...

"Say," he went on, "did you know he was an officer of Fairmont Pharmaceuticals? Now, who would expect that from a show-biz type like The Amazing Clifford? They got one laboratory he practically runs. He's there every time you turn around and he really cracks the whip over those guys."

I admitted that I did know about Fairmont.

"Well you could have fooled me. Say, do you know about his airplane? No? Well he's got this nice little Lear jet, loaded with electronics, the works. Flies it himself, you know, goes everywhere in it, usually has a couple of giggling girls with him, he's not the nice, nice boy I thought he was, you know, actually I don't like the guy at all now I know more about him, the things he's done to some of those girls, a lot of it illegal and some of it criminal, you ask me. Guy like that, he gets away with murder, I mean plain old nasty murder, but the people he's got around him, the money, you know, the PR people and the lawyers, the lawyers like a pack of damned rats, cover up anything, cops in his pocket, too, probably, who knows what actually goes on? But then, hell, the rest of the world loves him, so what's my opinion?

"But listen," he said. "I've got a full report already written up so where can I mail it to you?"

"Never mind," I said, "Just read it to me. But first, tell me: where does he go in this plane?"

"Well, I'd say its strange. He just bats around the country. No pattern I can see. Looks to me like he's looking for something or looking for somebody, you know? Always on the move. But then I can't actually follow him, you know, not with him in that plane and me on the ground."

"Of course you can. I'll send a check. A big one. You charter a plane and a pilot, keep your eye on him every minute. Right?"

He read me his report, with details that obviously amazed him, but didn't surprise me. Then he began building up and justi-fying the size of the bill he would have to send me for the plane and pilot. He was stunned into silent acceptance by the even larger size of the check I promised to mail.

"Tell you what," he said, after a long pause, "Even before I do any flying around, I'm goin' to do some digging. There's a place I've got to look into, bet I need a shovel before I'm through, me and my beer belly and all, digging up dirt on this Clifford. You'll see next time we talk."

I hung up and trotted into Vegas for a few plates of scrambled eggs with bacon and toast dripping with butter before running back to my home in the hills.

With thoughts of the Wiseass invading my head, the clean and sterile beauty of the desert never looked more inviting.

What is Sara doing? And who is she doing it with? And what in hell will I do about it all?

chapter thirty

A couple of weeks later, after I had watched the sunrise from my rock-strewn veranda, I started down the mountain in a series of large jumps, heading for Las Vegas and breakfast. As I neared the city I looked automatically towards the Caesar's Palace billboard with the huge "S," as I did every morning about this time.

But the "S" was gone. A man in white coveralls was working on the sign from a long ladder. I watched, filled with apprehension, as he began to slip in new letters announcing a new star attraction.

So, Sara was gone. I felt a sharp new loneliness. Until now I had known that I could come down out of my mountain to see her if I chose, but now I couldn't. Her very presence was missing.

Instead of continuing on to the diner where I had been used to ordering a couple of dozen scrambled eggs plus pancakes and all the fixings (regulars there were making bets on how much I'd order and how long it would take me to eat it) I went instead to a super market and bought a couple of cases of Campbell's Pork and Beans (Dinty Moore stew had recently lost some of its appeal) to eat on my veranda up in the mountains while I thought.

Suddenly the desert I had loved was empty and bare again and geology held no charm. Where to go? What to do? After all, I had centuries to kill. I'd be damned if I'd chase after Sara. I told myself it was a good thing she'd skipped town. Healthier for me to go my own way. Take her at her word and see her again a century or so from now, when we'd both established a new and independent life. Maybe have a new fling with her then. Come together, then pull apart, over and over again through the ages ahead like two asteroids on intersecting orbits.

That is what I told myself. I said it aloud for all the hundred varieties of cactus that surrounded me to hear. But of course I didn't believe a word of it.

So, I ate the beans and buried the cans in the hot, dry sand and loped down to town again to buy an airline ticket to "some place back East," which was as, far as my thoughts had gone.

On the way, I stopped again to watch the workman arrange new letters on what I still thought of as 'Sara's sign' and when I saw that he had already spelled out the name of an over-the-hill comic I went into a kind of blind fury to think that Sara could be so casually replaced by this mediocrity. I came roaring down on his ladder and knocked it out from under his feet and caught him in the air just before he would have hit the blacktop and put him down gently. "Don't finish that sign!" I yelled into his ear. "Don't let me see that name in lights or I'll fold you up like this ladder," and to demonstrate, I rolled his aluminum ladder into a metal ball.

Stupid. Stupid. Of course he'd finish the sign. Of course I had no right to stop him. Of course the world would turn as usual and just because I could break rocks with my hands I couldn't do much to change it. Slow moving, slow thinking mankind would do exactly as it pleased, despite me.

"The cuckold's revenge," I muttered to myself. "Don't bother your wife. Don't seek out her lovers. Just make a fool of yourself with the sign man. Nice going, Andy."

So I dropped a handful of twenties on the sign man to buy a new ladder and ran in a dust-raising blur to the airport.

"A one-way ticket to Providence, Rhode Island," I told the ticket agent, making a snap decision. From the report I'd gotten from my detective it was well past time to visit the Germ Factory again. The Wiseass had been busy while I had been mooning around, lovesick in the desert.

"Stick to business, stupid Andy," I told myself. "Things are happening."

196

chapter thirty-one

Narragansett Bay was cold, windy and unfriendly. I remembered my last visit to the Germ Factory, only months ago, when the soft summer night breeze had been like warm velvet. I stood outside the gate now, late at night, looking in at the lighted buildings.

Change. The inevitable change of seasons. I shivered in the cold and thought about time, that strange dimension that we all know yet can't define. I thought about the relatively few thousand years that man has been man (not nearly as long as the cockroach has been a cockroach) and yet how far he has come. I thought in particular about this last century that was now ending and how fast we seemed to have moved in these ten short decades, no more than an eyeblink of history.

What a century! I was born soon after the Wright brothers flew the first airplane and now we are well into space travel and the great airlines have already blossomed, grown seedy, and dived into bankruptcy even as they fly increasing millions to every spot on earth.

The computer age has already gone from gee-whiz to ho-hum, even as it daily expands and controls more of our world.

Now, biotechnology takes over, and look at us go! We've already tried the first official gene transplant and we're charting the human genome (a mammoth job with an importance that few understand) and when that's done… there will be no limit. No limit at all to the ways we can change and control life.

So. We're about to step into tomorrow. The future—the marvelous, fearful, bright and scary future, where we all step off into the abyss of trackless time—is almost upon us.

I, for one, am ready for it. Just as soon as I patch things up with Sara and find, once again, the missing ingredient for the Blue

Helix that stupid old Henry Fowles keeps making over and over again by mistake.

*   *   *   *   *

I jumped over the fence and ran past the gatekeeper, who probably saw me as a blur and then denied in his mind what he had seen, and darted into the first open door to escape the cruel wind. Then I began my search.

Just as on the last visit, I first checked out the progress of the team of legitimate scientists. In an hour of intensive looking, zilch.

These were the ones who were attempting to duplicate my own blue liquid. Since they had no sample to work with and no clear idea even of what I had been trying to do, how could they duplicate it?

But still, with such a large team of intelligent researchers stumbling around, who knows what they might come up with?

The monkeys were typing. So far they were typing gibberish, but they had to be watched. But of course my only real objective tonight was the Henry Fowles factory of fruitful screw-ups.

So, I streaked through the darkened corridors to Building Number One, to my old office and lab, which was mercifully empty.

Things were neater this time. Someone (not Henry, I'd bet) had straightened up, washed the glassware, put things away.

But, sure enough, on one clean lab table there were four beakers, each labeled with code numbers.

So, I thought. *Some system has been added. These four are numbered for an evaluation of some kind. I wonder how they test them since they still don't know what they're looking for? Obviously they have to use test animals of some kind. Mice, flies, or something.*

I found four new test tubes, poured a generous sample from each beaker, numbered them, stoppered them, wrapped the four with tape as before, and slipped them into my pocket.

Then I left, slipping through the corridors like a ghost until I reached the outside door nearest my rented car so that I could dash across the blacktop and hop over the fence without being too long in the cold wind. You may be strong, Andy, I thought, *But you shiver and shake in the cold like everyone else.*

I opened the door of my rented car and jumped in, anxious to escape the wind. But as I started the engine to get the heater going, I heard the breathing of another being in the back seat and spun around to face it.

"Hi!" said the Wiseass. "Have a good visit?" My heart dropped. It wasn't fear. It was the overwhelming nuisance of having to deal with him. The disgust at having to enter his world, to talk on his terms.

"Well, now, Andy, I want to thank you for this visit to the facility. It'll be a big help, I have to admit it."

"I did nothing to help you."

"Course you did!" he said, cheerfully. "Just like you did before. Just like I planned it. I knew you'd stick your damned old finger in the pie, like you always do. All I have to do now is see what you changed, then I know what's important and what isn't. Big help, Andy! I've got a crew at work on it right now."

"Then this whole place is a trap?"

"Oh, don't flatter yourself. Catching you was just a sideline. This place is really cooking, don't you know that?"

Cooking, hell. Except for Henry's carefully orchestrated screw-ups, they were doing nothing of value.

"The reason I waited out here in the cold was to tell you something, Andy. I wanted to tell you what I've decided. Wait a minute now. I don't want to say this from the back seat." He opened his door, got out and slipped into the front seat beside me.

"I want to see your face when I tell you, Andy, old boy, and I want to give you something cute. You'll get a kick out of it, guaranteed.

"By the way," he said. "That was some dinky little condo you had up in the mountains. I had thought for sure you'd do better than that." He was watching my face for the reaction and in spite of myself I knew that he saw one.

"Your neighbors tell me you didn't even use it," he continued. "Said you slept out in the woods in some kind of a damned pup tent like a boy scout. Now, Andy, you got to admit that's crazy for a fella with your possibilities. Eh? Right? Wouldn't you say so?"

How could he have the ability to make me sick with impotent rage every time we met? How could he know exactly where to put his grubby finger to degrade everything I loved?

"But, hey! that's not what I wanted to tell you," he continued. I hardly heard him. I had already jumped to a new and terrible thought: if he had found the condo, could he possibly have found my laboratory in the cave? I thought not. I was certain not. It was too well hidden, and if he had, why would he bother with this charade? But just knowing that he had been there nosing around was enough to shake my world. I felt defiled.

"What I wanted you to know was this: I've decided what to do when I grow up." He grinned at me like a naughty boy trying to be charming. "Yep, I've decided that I might just as well leave politics up to all those turkeys who're screwing it up now. No office-holding for me. Just a pain, you know? Now, power, that's something else. The thought of complete power has a nice healthy ring to it, you know? Now maybe that's something I can use. Cut out all the red tape, get right to the meat of things."

He continued: "All I really want is, when I say, 'Shit,' I want to see a billion asses squat."

"The world now has five billion. Soon to be ten."

"Whatever." He waved the thought away. "Who's counting?"

"Anyway," he continued, "I've got a little scheme, you'll see it soon enough, start with the U.S.of A., get all the bugs in my game-plan worked out, then before you know it, I'll move on, have the whole damned world marching in lock step, doing what I tell it to do and loving it. I mean, *loving* it."

"And those who don't love it?" I asked.

"Hey, listen. I brought you something," he said. "To hell with politics. You'll see soon enough, idiots will be cheering, heaven come down to earth, The Amazing Clifford our savior, our leader in this new one-world and all that crap but give a look at this.

"I know you like to eat," he continued, "So I brought you something nice." He pulled out of his pocket a tall, slim jar of olives and held it up to the light, turning it this way and that for me to see. The olives were stacked in perfect rows, their red pimentos gleaming from the tops, each olive exactly the same as its neighbor except for the one in the center of the stack that was not an olive at all but a blue eyeball staring out, it seemed to me, in terminal terror.

"Greetings from your private eye," said the Wiseass, smiling into my face and watching it carefully for reaction.

"Oh, yes, I mentioned to him that I'd left him one eye out of the goodness of my heart but if I ever found him prying into my business again, I'd send you the pair."

I was sick, remembering my pudgy, harmless detective. Seeing him now, a broken, frightened man surrounded by the loving family in the photo I'd seen. My every instinct was to grab the Wiseass and pull his nasty head off, but I remembered my bear. I couldn't see myself tearing at his throat with my fingers and teeth. Not just yet, anyway.

I stared at him for a long moment, looking from the olive jar to his smug, superior face, certain of its own invulnerability and scornful of anything that old indecisive Andrew Camp might do.

Then I waved my left hand in a quick, threatening motion that gave him a moment's distraction and at the same instant, in a blur of notion that even his quick reflexes couldn't block, drove my right forefinger knuckle-deep into his left eye socket.

"... and a tooth for a tooth," I murmured.

His face was statue-still, rigid with fear. His hand reached immediately for my wrist to hold it in a desperate vise-grip, protecting his eye from the flip-out he expected.

When I made a tentative tug to break his grip I found what I had expected: that we were roughly equal in strength. "Oh, Cliffie, you're so nice and strong," I mimicked the voice of one of his adoring girls. Then in my own voice, "But I've had experience fighting super-beings like yourself. And killing them. Didn't tell you that, did I? You didn't know I'd made others."

His eye muscles, try as he might to hold them still, were twitching against my finger. I could feel what was coming up and I didn't try to stop it. First, the Wiseass made a supreme effort to tighten his grip on my wrist, then he suddenly jerked his head back, freeing his eye socket from my intruding finger with a soft, wet "plop."

He was audibly panting and his body almost weak with his escape from terror.

"Greetings from my private eye," I said.

His wiseass confidence was slowly returning. "You couldn't do it," he said. "You hate my guts and you had me by the short hairs and you still couldn't do it."

"All I had to do," I said to him, "was crook my finger. That's all. Then, when you jerked your head back…"

He stared at me again, intently. "You thought of that? You thought of that while your finger was still inside my eye?"

"Sure. I'm just a nicer guy than you are. But I'm not a damned fool, either. Now, stay away from me. Stay completely out of my life and I may let you live!"

He didn't budge. "You made others? And killed them?"

"You'll never know. Not from me, you won't. Now get out and take your bloody olives with you!"

The Wiseass got out, backed slowly away from my rental car, wiped his left eye with a nervous finger and shouted back at me, "It's *not* over, old man! If I've got a million years to live, then I've got a million years to make your ass sorry for what you did tonight!"

"But you don't have a million years," I told him quietly. "Only I know how short your time really is." I lied deliberately to terrify him, hating the lie and hating to be a liar but hating him even worse.

He turned and ran for the Germ Factory like a scalded dog. *God help his researchers tonight. I thought. He'll be at them with whips.*

chapter thirty-two

As I drove away through the cold black night I told myself that this time there was no escape. I now had to do something I dreaded.

Exactly as my detective had described to me, no more than five miles away on a road just north and inland from the Germ Factory, I found the gate to the Broadmore Nursing Home and drove through, to the parking lot, where I sat for a moment and looked at the old mansion that had been turned into a geriatric nursery.

I could see that new wings, long and low and modern, had been added on either side, and the entire place, even in the black night, had the look of prosperity. "A healthy growth industry," I remembered reading from a stock prospectus for a nursing home chain that a broker had sent me sometime in the past.

There was a time a couple of years ago when I had sneaked away from Sara to spend afternoons visiting different nursing homes, trying to be "realistic" about our future. It had left me with a mortal dread of being put into such a place, or seeing Sara in one, or even entering the doors.

"Get out of the car. Go do what you have to do." I had to talk to myself, force myself to act. And of course it was black night and that gave me an excuse.

Come back tomorrow, in the daytime, I argued with myself. *No! Do it now. Just take a quick scouting look. See what you can see. Go ahead, you coward.*

So I dropped the argument with myself and ran from the car through the cold wind and quickly circled the building once, searching out the doors and windows and getting a general overview. Then, in a dark corner where I had found a vulnerable door, I punched a small hole with my extended fingers and reached in to unlock the door and enter.

Soon I was out of the wind and slipping through the dark corridors, knowing that I had probably set of a silent alarm with the door business.

But what the hell, I thought. *If the cops come, I'll just leave. Give 'em all a little excitement. Keep their blood flowing. Meanwhile, I can have a little look.*

I was sickened by the smells. The reek of disinfectants, the layer upon layer of food odors that clung to the walls, the smell of medicines, of floor cleaners and waxes, all the normal institutional odors were here but they were pushed far into the background by the smell of people. Old people.

Old bowels had been at work and no exhaust fan could ever completely erase the evidence. Urine had defied rubber sheets to soak bedding that had been changed, washed, dried, and then soaked again until streaked a permanent and pungent yellow.

I was being suffocated by the dry choke of old skin that had sloughed off so many hundreds of bodies to lie in a soft gray, almost invisible powder on every sheet, then to sift through and be buried in mattresses and rugs and draperies over the years and then finally to infiltrate the very air so that I knew that I breathed in hundreds of microscopic flecks of old flesh with every breath as I strode about in the darkness looking.

And the sleep sounds! Groans. Mutterings. Chewing and smacking and swallowing noises and the click of teeth. Sometimes disjointed nonsensical conversations with long remembered family. "Come out here, Maud! I want you to see this! I want you to see what that brother of yours has done! Maud! D'you hear me, Maud?" Followed by snuffling snores and stentorian breathing. Somewhere a persistent cough, with the breath scarcely caught between coughs, then finally a pause in the coughing with the cougher muttering, "Oh, shit, shit, shit what a life."

I walked the halls swiftly, keeping to the shadows and staying on my toes, glancing this way and that, memorizing the layout. At the head of each corridor, a nurses's station, all but one unoccupied at this time of night.

Then, as I slipped past the one nurse on duty and turned down another corridor, a light around a door frame and a mutter of conversation from inside. Young, strong male voices, so out of place in this warehouse for the old.

"Easy now, push it in slowly. Not too fast! Damn! It's happening already! Who'd believe it? Go ahead, finish it. Give her the full dose. Might as well…. Look at that! Look at those arms! Feel that skin! Goddamn exciting, eh?"

Another voice, more concerned. "Pulse erratic. Crazy. Close to fibrillation. Pressure gone to hell. And listen to that breathing."

"Screw the pulse. What'd you expect? Look at those legs. We're getting there, I tell you!"

I listened, filled with horror. My every impulse was to break down the door and yell and throw things as I scattered these midnight riders of science, but I didn't. I told myself that the person they were using for a white mouse had already been injected, was already beyond my help, and they wouldn't be injecting anyone else until Henry Fowles came up with a new batch of mistakes to try.

Why pretend surprise? I asked myself.

Why else would the Wiseass own a nursing home?

Also, somewhere hidden away in the very back of my mind was a tiny thought that said maybe I really needed to know what they had found out.

Disgusting! Be ashamed, Andy. But keep your eyes and ears open, because this is where it's at.

I turned and ran, streaking down the corridors on silent feet, keeping well into the shadows until I found my broken back door and went out into the night, running towards the shelter of my car.

*   *   *   *   *

I had to wait until ten the next morning for the costume shop to open, so it was almost noon before I appeared at the nursing home dressed in my finery.

"But we didn't order a clown," protested the activities director, a tall, rangy blond woman of about fifty with a huge lipstick smile and an atmosphere of perpetual, incurable gaiety.

"Fairmont Pharmaceuticals," I told her. "They're paying. They think I might cheer up the patients. See?" I continued, giving my red clown nose a squeeze that made a loud 'honk!' "I'll let 'em squeeze my nose, I'll tell jokes, sing, play the piano if you've got one. Entertain them. Help them pass the time."

"Last week it was dogs," she said, throwing up her arms in surrender, "and they did love the dogs when that girl brought them around, and before that it was cats and monkeys. But a clown?"

"Well Fairmont thinks…"

"Oh, I know! Whatever Fairmont thinks, Fairmont gets. So come on in and be a clown. Just keep out of the way of the people who do the work around here!"

Without warning, she threw herself into action, crying, "Oh, look, people, look at the nice clown!" and she reached up and gave my red rubber nose a big squeeze, crying out again as loudly as she could, "Now who'll squeeze the clown's nose? Come Mrs. Partridge! You can be first! Squeeze his nose and make it honk! Come on! Come on! Push that walker before Mr. Hancock beats you to it!"

And, as the two bore down on me, one shuffling along with grim determination behind her walker, the other, a man, pushing his wheel chair with gnarled, arthritic hands, I learned what it was to be an entertainer. After they had each had their 'honk' I walked the corridors, now filled with old people, and visited the rooms where those too sick to sit in a wheel chair languished in their beds.

After only a few minutes of embarrassment, I was at home in my costume, knowing that I could come and go as I pleased, seeing all, hearing all without being seen myself. Whatever the Wiseass and his Germ Factory crew had going on here, I'd soon know about in detail.

* * * * *

My clown persona quickly made new friends. Sort of. There was a piano in the rec room, an old out-of-tune grand that must have gone with the original mansion, and I took off my big floppy clown gloves and began to play it, remembering what I'd learned from Sara.

Soon several dozen patients began converging on me, some at a shuffling walk, some in wheel chairs, some with a variety of canes and walkers. "Play *Misty* for me," said one, probably confusing a song with the movie, so I gave him a big red lipped clown smile and went on playing variations of Chopsticks until my audience was complete, then I played and sang songs from the twenties, thirties and forties while they beat time with their hands and feet and sang along as best they could.

206

Meanwhile, I watched them with my sharp eyes peering out of the eyeholes of my clown mask, seeing and assessing all.

Nearest me, leaning on her walker and looking over my shoulder as I played, was an eighty-six year old widow I'd met earlier. Her name was Esther Hall and she had lived all her life only a few miles away, in Portsmouth. She was a fighter and I liked her. "I had to sell my house," she had said. "It made me sick to do it. Belonged to my mamma and poppa before me and I felt like I was selling out the family, but then I was the only family left. Still felt guilty, though.

"So here I am, living up what money I got for my house in this damned place, every day I spend a little more of it, I say to myself, 'Esther, today we spend the kitchen sink. I think how the fireplace went yesterday and the front porch has been long gone and I know when all the house is spent and the yard is used up, too, I'd better be gone myself because that's all there is and nobody loves a pauper."

Beyond the crowd, sitting sideways in his wheelchair with his wasted legs at an unnatural angle, was David Rayola, once a foreman at a fiberglass boat-building plant until his accident. Now seventy-one, he was just a youngster here, but had a special problem: he would constantly wet himself. His bladder control had gradually disappeared with the injury and now was almost totally lost. He had worn diapers for over two years and was still mortally, bitterly ashamed. He would sit, face twisted into a deep frown, mouth tight and working, eyes angry but seeing all behind their rimless glasses. No song for him. He rejected any attempt I might make to spread a little cheer his way. Yet, he did want to talk and resented time I took with others. He had decided that on a man-to-man basis he and I had something in common. After all, he assumed that neither of us was truly old like the others. David Rayola watched. And remembered. He always knew what went on, and maybe he was condemned to sit there peeing his pants in little dribblets but that didn't mean that you could ever fool David Rayola.

Another man, Bill Prentise, would never sit still for my playing. A wanderer, he looked continually for his dead wife. "Ev? Damnit, Ev! Where are you? Did you see Ev, anybody...?

Ev…. ? I don't like it here, Ev…. Let's go home… *Evelyn! I'm calling you now for the last time, d'you hear?"*

A woman, Rose Gorman, with blue white hair and a sprig of long curly hairs growing out of her chin, was a singer of hymns who would earnestly belt out *The Old Rugged Cross*, or, *In the Valley* while I was playing *Roll Out The Barrel* on the piano. "Gentle Jesus!" she would cry out at odd times. "Jesus, lover of my soul!"

"Age," explained Helen Morrow, the floor nurse who looked after this flock for the eight to four-thirty shift. "They can't help it. They're like children. That's why they like your clown suit."

I started to argue with her, to say that if you could just see the world their way, you'd see that inside their heads they were still young and strong, and that the calamities of age would seem to them to have been artificially imposed from the outside, clouding brain and crippling limb like some awful disease. But why try to explain this to nurse Morrow? Who appointed me God?

Lunch time. Bells rang and feet shuffled. I went into the dining room with the rest, even though I couldn't eat with my clown mask on and I wouldn't take it off.

The dining room was not filled and no one ate with appetite. "Only about a fourth of them bother to eat here," Nurse Morrow had said. "We have to feed the rest—some with spoons and some with tubes."

I sat beside Esther Hall, who spooned apple sauce into her mouth slowly, with long pauses to nibble a bite of bread or sip tea that had grown lukewarm from her neglect.

"Do you feel silly in that clown suit?" She asked, looking up at me over her empty spoon. "I hope not, because I sort of like it."

"Actually, I've always hated clowns," I admitted.

She made a small face to acknowledge my comment and then continued, "You sound kind. And intelligent. And I can talk to you because you have that silly suit on so I don't have to watch your expression and wonder at every moment what you're thinking about this ugly old woman."

"I'm thinking that you were never ugly," I said as gallantly as I could, seeing clearly the wrinkled skin, the sagging double chin,

208

the humped shoulders, the cloudy eyes, the arthritic hands and knees, all the cruel signs of age.

And I thought to myself that just as she could talk freely to me behind the anonymity of my clown suit, I could just as freely approach her. Age had become her clown suit and most people she would meet for the rest of her life would never see beyond it.

"Oh, you must have been a beautiful baby…" I hummed the old tune, and she gave a quick, quirky smile.

"Actually, I was," she said. "You should have seen the young men who used to run after me. All this hot sexy stuff wasn't just invented yesterday by the yuppies, you know, even if they do think so. We had our turn. See? I can say that to your clown face. I wouldn't say it to one of these young Fairmont doctors who're always running around here."

Looking at her, peering now for the first time behind her mask of oldness to see the girl she must have been, just as an archaeologist will reconstruct a complete individual from a skull and a hip bone, I saw a young Esther, a redhead with white, lightly freckled skin, with full, fleshy lips, with a charming little ridge just under her nose, on the upper lip, that gave her smile a nice quirky look that people would remember.

Her eyes had been green, gold flecked. Her voice—even now strong and not quavery with age like most of those here—would have been well modulated and pleasant.

An honest girl that one could love and depend upon.

"Married?" I asked.

"Oh, yes. Gene. A nice man. Very likeable. Good to me. Died of pneumonia after he insisted on going clamming one February day. I told him not to go, but he did anyway. That was Gene. He felt guilty about our store burning down to the ground. Not his fault, no one ever blamed him, but the insurance had lapsed and that was his fault. He said he forgot to pay it but I know he spent the money on a necklace I didn't need for my birthday and thought he could make enough to catch up on the insurance later. A sweet man and smart too, but his timing was always off. So he went out on the bay in raw February to dig some quahogs for me because I liked them. Next thing you know the doctor and the undertaker and no more Gene. My love. A really sweet man. Maybe I make him sound foolish but times were hard and he kept trying different things and his timing was bad, mainly...

"And now this damned place," she continued. "And these damned doctors. My Gene would have told them off, the way they act."

I had to ask. "Did you ever cheat on him, Esther?"

"Cheat? What! You mean with another man? We didn't do things like that, not when I was young."

"Some did," I urged. "Some always did. You never wanted to?"

"Why...you embarrass me! Talking to an old lady like that." Then, after a pause, turning slightly to look directly into the eye-holes of my clown mask, "The answer is 'no'. None of your business but 'no'. Because that's what it would have been: 'cheating'. Cheating on a promise. Cheating on a friend. I couldn't stand to live with that kind of a lie and neither could Gene."

"Tell me about the Fairmont doctors," I asked.

"You're not from Fairmont? Then who hired you?"

I waved the question away. "Tell me."

"I don't think they bother you until your money runs out," she said. "That's the way it seems, anyway. Long as you can pay, you're a private patient and you stay in 'A' wing and you have some rights. But when you can't pay, they make you sign papers and you move to 'B' wing and then they think they own you."

"What happens in room two-twenty?"

"Who are you, really, behind that clown suit?" She put her spoon down very precisely beside her plate and turned her head away. "I think I talk too much."

"You can tell me."

"Talk to someone else."

"Are you afraid?" Then I had an idea. One that had been in the back of my mind since I had first met and learned to like Esther. I dropped my voice to a whisper. "I have to go away for a few days, to a place I have in the mountains of Virginia. But if everything I'm doing works out right, maybe I'll bring something back with me. Just suppose that I could come in some night when everything was quiet and give you a simple injection... and it would make you feel much better. Maybe even make you young again, so I could see how pretty you used to look. Wouldn't you like that, Esther?"

210

Her eyes snapped opened in a quick fury: "You dirty clown! I trusted you, and you're one of them!"

Shrugging off my help with a contemptuous wave of her hand, Esther levered herself erect and into position behind her walker and began to shuffle off, her every motion an expression of anger.

"But just the same," I said quietly to her departing back, which was still rigid with disdain, "I'll be back and whether you like it or not, I may bring a little something with me."

Inside my head a small voice said distinctly: "You fool. You're playing with disaster. Leave her be."

chapter thirty-three

I checked out the newest batch of Henry Fowles' mistakes at my mountain cave laboratory. Three of them, when mixed with my own blue liquid, killed fruit flies. But the fourth sample, when mixed, produced a fruit fly that even I had trouble killing.

I spent a week with this fly, a lifetime in fly years, and decided that in his own fruit fly way he was strong and intelligent and probably immortal. Superfly.

I would have loved to have kept him alive and with me as a pet, feeding him fruit just to watch the show. You ought to see him gulp down a spoon-sized chunk of banana, chewing it and swallowing it while you watched, his speeded-up metabolism turning the banana instantly into increased weight and energy, so that the banana seemed to disappear into the small fly-body like a magician's conjuring trick. Amazing! It was like watching a rerun of myself in the diner.

But the thought of my fly getting loose to breed with other flies and produce a race of super fruit flies to decimate the entire world's fruit crop while human babies cried for orange juice made me cautious. So, reluctantly, I killed my fruit fly by putting him to sleep with chloroform and then encasing him in a cube of plastic, where he died from a lack of oxygen. I kept the plastic cube with my fruit fly inside as a sort of souvenir, in my mountain lab.

Anyway. I now *knew*. I now knew it *all*.

It was no trick to analyze the one successful version of Henry's crap, his magical crap, once I found out which one worked. I now could make more of it any time I wanted, and by combining it with my own blue liquid, I could make as much of the complete Blue Helix (as I still thought of it) as I pleased.

More than that. Now that I knew, finally, exactly what the two combined proteins were, I understood how and why they worked, and my mind raced with this new knowledge.

I knew now that it was silly to think of the Blue Helix as two different proteins combined. When I made more, I'd make one somewhat different blue liquid to do the same job.

But more. Much more, my excited brain thought, racing ahead. I could now see so many ways to make intermediate materials to do specific jobs. It had to be tested, of course, and may take weeks or even months of work, but I could now see possibilities for a complete family of new proteins: some to cure disease only, some for longevity, some to increase intelligence, perhaps, or strength. Who knows what I could produce if I put my mind to the task of altering the human genome, our collection of over fifty-thousand genes?

So I sat on a rock outside my lab and played God inside my head. Oh, I could do *this,* I thought, Or *that.*

Enjoying the sound of it.

I watched a squirrel in a hickory tree swing from limb to limb, going about his squirrel business. "I can make you a far better squirrel!" I shouted to him, but the squirrel swung away, unimpressed.

More to the point, I thought, *I can make Esther a far better Esther.*

"Don't even consider it!" my rational brain shouted back at me."

"But I'm lonely," I answered, "...and I like that little ridge under her nose and her nice, warm smile. Besides, I know she'd be a nice girl. I like the sound of her voice."

"Oh, you fool! You silly, maudlin fool!" answered my brain. "You know better. You really do know better!"

"But I like being around her. I feel comfortable."

"There are a million women, ten million, a hundred million, billion of women out there, so why pick out one old woman that you know nothing about?"

"I like the way she didn't talk down that silly husband of hers. That was kind."

"So you make her young and you don't like the way she turns out. Maybe she bores the hell out of you. Then what? A million years with the wrong woman? Or do you encase her in plastic like the fly?"

"And what about Sara!" the inner voice added.

"Yes...what about Sara? *What is Sara doing right now? And who is she doing it with?"*

So went the debate. A useless dialogue. I'm sure I did know better. All the same, when I left my mountain lab bound for Rhode

Island that afternoon I had a syringe packed in a protective case in my pocket and it was filled with the Blue Helix.

"Just in case I do decide to do it," I told myself. "But of course I won't. I know I won't. I'd have to be an idiot to do that."

chapter thirty-four

Night. A cold wind was still blowing but there was no ice on the ponds, just slushy, nasty winter misery in southern New England.

I had slipped silently through the dark corridors to her room, wondering what I would do when I found her there asleep, perhaps with open mouth and fetid breath, an old and tired woman to whom I had somehow become attached.

Her room was empty. Her bed was stripped, her closet empty. Her room was no longer her room at all. Even her smell was gone, covered by a mask of strong disinfectant.

I turned and ran for another room I knew and was bent over his bed and about to shake him awake when David Rayola's voice came up to me out of the darkness: "Is that you, clown?"

In spite of myself I turned my head away and held my breath at the stench of urine from his diapers. "Where is she? Where is Esther?"

"They took her. Right after you left."

"Room two-twenty?"

"Sure. You know about that, eh?"

"But she still had money. She should have been safe. I wouldn't have left her, otherwise."

"Didn't matter. Guy cane in here, guy I've never seen here before, madder than hell he was, he didn't care about anything except what he wanted to know, and he went from one to the other of us asking: 'Where is that damned clown? Where'd he go? What'd he want? Who'd he talk to? Who was he especially friendly with?'

"I never said a word," David continued, anxious to have me believe him, "But a lot of these old yahoos in here don't understand things that well and they all said, 'Esther. He talked a lot to Esther. He liked Esther.'

"So, when this guy heard that he said to some of these young Fairmont doctors who run around here, he said, 'Take her! Take her to that room and fix her!'

"When one of the young doctors tried to tell him Esther wasn't a charity case he just screamed at them to take her, so they did."

The Wiseass! There was no need to describe him to David.

I knew.

"What happened to her? Did she get an injection, like the others?"

"Oh, you know about that. Thought you would. Sure. I slipped down there in my wheelchair, listened at the door. They had to hold her down. It was awful. I liked Esther, too, you know, and I saw her come out of that room, she was tied onto a gurney, one guy pushing her and one with his hand over her mouth, she was screaming and biting and tossing her head and strong, you wouldn't believe how strong she looked tied down like that and this guy struggling with her, until two more of them came to help and all three were struggling with Esther while the fourth one pushed the gurney along.

"And she was different-looking, a lot different. All twisted up. Scary looking. Younger looking, too, I'd hardly know her, but crazy. Screaming crazy. Something was just awful about her, her face all twisted and her body too. I tell you, I wouldn't have known her if I hadn't seen her go in."

"Where is Esther now? Can I see her?"

David Rayola snorted. "You may know something about this place but you don't know it like I do, now do you?"

So, David Rayola told me where to find Esther. The thought flitted through my mind that I could, if I wanted, give him the injection I had in my pocket and turn him into my eternal, immortal friend. But I listened to the rational part of my brain that screamed, "Don't be such a fool!" and I left David squirming in his own pungent dampness and ran out back of the building to the small field he had described with the oak tree in the center and the stone wall all around.

There, in the northwest corner, just as David had said, I found a short-handled shovel, a garden spade, sticking out of a mound of earth.

I pulled the shovel out of the cold and wet but still unfrozen winter ground and was looking for a place to start digging when a small yellow price tag on the shovel handle caught my eye and I turned it towards the moonlight to read the name of a hardware store in Mount Vernon, New York.

What had my detective said to me? "I think I'll buy a shovel and do a little digging?" Was this the very spot where he had lost his eye?

The dirt flew in a long, muddy stream as I used the shovel in thousands of quick, hard strokes. It was a blur of digging that soon uncovered twenty-eight identical gray caskets, each no more than inches away from its neighbor.

Each gray casket had a number written across the top in big, angular letters with a red Magic Marker, and under each number, a name and a date.

I stood there in the cold moonlight, knowing that I had to look. Dreading to look. Why look now?" I tried to weasel out. "You've got the Blue Helix now. You know exactly how and why it works. You don't need to see their mistakes. There's no scientific reason to look."

Starting with the first casket and a name I didn't know, I used the spade to pry open the lid of each coffin in the row, determined not to look at the contents until I had them all open for viewing.

If there's no scientific reason then maybe there's a moral reason I have to look, I thought, grimly, bending to the task.

I forced my head to turn, my eyes to focus, my brain to understand and record.

Here, I thought with a shudder, is *my enemy.*

Old nasty Death itself, the Dark Angel. The real and final enemy of us all. Horrible. Horrible. Horrible.

There was no neat progression. They did not go from bad to good, from failure to success, or from the ugly to the beautiful. Instead, they were, each of these naked bodies, a shuddery mixture of success and non-success. Here was young skin, perhaps, on twisted and distorted limbs. There was a well-formed face on a monster body, not young, not old, just grossly distended. In one casket an old woman with strangely young legs had been buried with one hand between her legs and a self-absorbed leer still on her face, with the lower lip bitten through by her yellow teeth in what must have been an orgiastic frenzy.

I got down into the trench with the gray coffins and made myself examine each one in detail. At coffin #5 a hand suddenly snaked out and caught my ankle and a crazed male face followed the hand out of the coffin, eyes wild, mouth working and a voice making frantic "Eh! eh! eh! eeeehhhh!" as a young-old body, as white and slickly puffy as a slug, with narrow shoulders and a bulging white belly and legs that were almost useless white strings, tried to use my ankle to pull himself out of the grave.

I took a good look at the body, the face, the absolutely mindless blankness of this grave-creature who had somehow survived burial and in my revulsion I raised my shovel to cuts its head off when a better thought hit me and I slammed down the lid to his coffin. "See you later," I muttered to answer his scratching and keening from inside the gray box.

Quickly, now, sick with disgust, I examined and mentally cataloged each corpse (for I found no more alive). The last was Esther Hall and she was the only one I refused to examine in detail. One glance confirmed that she was truly dead and also truly distorted, a horrible caricature of the young, pretty girl she had been, could have been again.

Without looking at her face or twisted body, I pulled one hand out of the coffin and took it between mine. It was stiff and cold, but well formed, just as I had imagined. The hand of a young, pretty girl. "But there are millions like her out there," my rational brain urged. "Don't get soupy, sloppy sentimental on me."

To spite my rational brain and shut it up I thought briefly of giving Esther's cold, stiff arm the injection of the Blue Helix that I still had in the case in my pocket. "Now that would truly be a stupid gesture," my rationality answered back. "It would just sit there, a magic puddle inside an arm without circulation, until both the arm and the blue liquid dried up. A useless idealism. What kind of scientist are you, to moon about this girl you never knew?"

So I closed the lid to Esther's coffin, leaving all the others open to the harsh winter moonlight. Then I pulled the one coffin out of the trench that held my still-alive, still scratching, still-muttering monster and took it back to the nursing home, perched on my shoulder. I ran down the dark corridor to Room 220 and put my monster's coffin on the table they had used for their experiments and opened the coffin lid and pressed my detective's shovel into its grasping hands and closed the lid again and left, locking the door.

I ran to the nearest nurse's station (deserted at this time of night) and used the phone to call the local police and tell them to hurry to the field behind the nursing home where they would find an open trench filled with illegal corpses, all put there by the Fairmont Pharmaceutical Corporation.

"And who am I? Why I'm sort of a corpse myself," I lied to the incredulous policeman on the other end of the phone. "You'll find me in my coffin in Room 220, with the shovel I used to dig up the others."

chapter thirty-five

I drove to Providence, turned in my rental car, trotted across town to Federal Hill and picked one of the really fine restaurants there and had a meal. Oh, my God, how Italian cooking suited my appetite! I ate with the tears running down my face as the waiter brought me more, more and more. As I ate, my mood lifted and I knew that I was free from that damned nursing home forever. It was like waking from a nightmare. OK, so I had to do something about destroying the Germ Factory and I wanted to give a helping hand to David Rayola and maybe a couple of others. So I would. I'd take care of things like this after I had done what I had to do next. But I'd do what I had to do through lawyers and bankers. I'd never set foot in that living cemetery again.

Pleasantly satisfied after the meal, I ran through the dark streets and down a highway about fifteen miles south, keeping well into the shadows at the edge of the road when cars approached.

When I reached the place I'd planned to visit, I jumped over the metal fence and started roaming the big blacktop parking lot looking at RVs.

By the time morning came and salespeople started straggling in to work I had already found one that cried out, "Buy me!"

It was thirty-four foot Winnebago Elandan. It had a rear bedroom with a queen-sized bed which I really didn't need (no queen) and a nice little bathroom and a kitchen that caught my eye immediately.

Then there were just the details of paperwork. "Call my bank, verify my check...how do I get it registered?" Details, most of them solved with a checkbook.

By noon the Winnebago was legally mine and I had driven it less than a mile to a supermarket, where I filled my new home with the necessary.

I stacked the rear bedroom ceiling high with cases of Dinty Moore stew and Campbell's pork and beans; filled the refrigerator and freezer with milk and eggs and bacon and sausage and frozen dinners (damn the cholesterol, full speed ahead) and I bought a case of candy and another one of nuts to keep on the seat beside me for snacking while I drove.

My Winnebago scooted down the road like a deer. It looked so huge, compared to a car, but it drove so smoothly, once I got it moving. I swooped from lane to lane like a native son, cutting off sports cars and watching in my huge rearview mirrors as their drivers gave me unfriendly fingers. My faithful 454 V8 engine pulled us along at an easy seventy, my airhorn helped clear a path before me and the cassette player blasted away with a tape I'd found of Willie Nelson singing *On the Road Again*.

My RV had a TV, a regular radio and a CB radio. I was in touch with the world, yet snugly private in my mobile habitat. Best of all, I had become invisible.

I had bought sunglasses and a long billed cap and I knew that I would just fade into the woodwork for most people.

Try it sometime: just get behind the wheel of a RV. No one will ever see you again except the driver of another RV, and he will wave and smile beautifully, certain that in all the world only you and he have found truth and freedom.

I headed south with the cruise control set, reading a stack of mysteries I'd bought in the supermarket and stepping back to the refrigerator every now and then for a snack. The Winnebago cruised smoothly down the road with only minimum supervision from me. Just a glance and a twitch of the wheel now and then kept it on the road.

South for a thousand or so miles to Jacksonville, I thought, *Get past this winter weather, then head west on Route 10, all the way across the damned country. Stop when I feel like it. Take a little sightseeing detour when I feel like it. Do whatever I feel like doing.*

Somewhere in the back of my head a voice murmured, "What an ambition for a super-being! The stupid Wiseass is flying around in his own plane and planning to rule the world, Sara drives her red Jaguar wherever she pleases and wraps everyone around her finger, and all you can find to do is to scuttle across the country in your RV like some huge brown cockroach, dodging and hiding from everyone on earth like a criminal on the loose. Tell me, how did all this happen?"

I didn't answer myself. I drove, heading south until I got below Washington, then, almost on impulse, I turned west toward my mountain home in Virginia, and drove until I found the abandoned filling station and then took a run up the mountain to my laboratory, where I unloaded the syringe I had carried in my pocket to Rhode Island, squirting the ounce of pale blue liquid back into the flask it had come from, then stoppering the flask and washing out the syringe.

With a final glance around the lab (oh, how beautiful to my eyes!) I closed the disguised bank vault door and left, trotting down the mountain to my Winnebago. It would have been foolhardy, traveling around with a loaded syringe that anyone could find and use, or, worse still, that my own sentimental self might use on some impulse of loneliness.

I followed the Skyline Drive south for a few miles, then found a fork that let me veer off to the southeast and work my way back to I-95, trading travel efficiency for beauty.

In spite of my resolve to ignore the Wiseass I found myself glancing up every time I heard a small plane overhead.

Next time, I promised myself, *Next time I crook my finger.*

So it went. No matter how much I might protest to myself, thoughts of the Wiseass couldn't be driven completely away. Like it or not, he was my imaginary vulture in the sky, circling and waiting.

Two days later my Winnebago and I crossed the Mississippi near Baton Rouge and entered what I considered to be "The West." I still thought of the Wiseass every time I heard a plane overhead but he was becoming more annoyance than threat. "Careful how you catch me," I murmured up at the sky, "Because when you do catch me, I'll catch you harder."

The Wiseass would have to wait until I could get around to dealing with him. But deal with him, I would, I promised myself. After I took care of my other, more important problem, the Wiseass had to be the very next in line.

chapter thirty-six

Southern California, land of Tacoburgers (I ate 'em by the dozen and loved them) and fun in the sun. Why do some Easterners come west and embrace everything they see as if it were a long-sought corner of heaven while others carp and criticize and feel endlessly out of tune?

Is California, more than most places, a giant Rorschach test blot that affects each viewer according to his vision? I thought so, as I wandered the streets and beaches, blinking in the eternal brightness, smiling at the hype and almost overcome by the cult of youth.

Faced with an orgy of pleasure-seekers one can either laugh and point and decry, or one can jump right in, join the crowd, enjoy.

I could do neither. I liked the place, but I was not here for fun. Should I go down to muscle beach and confound the weight lifters? Should I buy a skateboard and zip through the crowds and raise envy among the initiate?

Oh, no. I had a higher, more noble purpose: I was here to spy on my wife.

It wasn't difficult to keep an eye on Sara, because in a land where everyone followed every fad and where each fad flowed into another in natural progression, Sara had become the ultimate fad. She was as pervasive in Southern California as soft ice cream. Her presence, her influence, was everywhere. Back East, she probably made the papers and the TV news about once a week. Out here she was a daily event, with her own paparazzi, her own journalistic cadre and millions of eager followers.

*   *   *   *   *

… the evening news shows the fabulous "S" at a sewerage outfall at the edge of the Pacific. She has arranged for six concrete mixer trucks, for a trailer load of steel bars and plate, and as the enthusiastic crowd watches she plugs the sewerage pipe with steel and concrete and then stands on top of the plugged pipe and makes a little speech about the ecology and how only greedy man pours such filth into our oceans and sings a few songs about the earth. Wild applause. Everyone feels purged and good and happy …and later that night the news story has to be expanded as toilets overflow throughout the county and the sewerage backup is so bad the day becomes known among the polite as "Brown Sunday."

*   *   *   *   *

… three night later, "S" is on the *Tonight Show* capturing her audience with song and dance, making them love her, then smiling and laughing aloud in her Leno interview as she tells him just how stupid she considers those who watched her plug the sewer pipe and how she laughed when the toilets overflowed… And when Leno didn't understand her reasoning and the audience didn't understand it either, she laughed in their faces and after a while they all pretended to laugh with her because the force of her beauty and her personality carried them all away…

*   *   *   *   *

… the fabulous "S" in the pacific Northwest, in the forests of Oregon, driving steel spikes into trees to damage chain saws and shoving log skidders and bulldozers down ravines and laughing, singing and laughing, as she leads the crowd of earth-firsters in logging destruction to save the forests…

*   *   *   *   *

… a laughing, singing, lecturing "S" as she prods the wives and children of out-of-work loggers in a lumbering community into a righteous frenzy over the actions of do-good owl-savers who have destroyed their jobs… Thousands of you are out of work. Why? why? To save *this*?" And she throws a bunch of gray feathers into the air as the crowd cheers…

*   *   *   *   *

224

So it went, from the Brazilian rain forest (the destruction exactly like the destruction of our own northwestern forest lands and for the same selfish economic reasons) to Alaska and big oil. From industrial wastes to political graft. From the U.S. Congress with its endless committees and its huge labyrinth of self-serving staff members and its incredibly myopic ways...to the military, those exceptionally intelligent, well-motivated men and women, truly the best of mankind in many ways, who were, with their clean and beautiful uniforms and their mentality of true patriots, hired killers all, prattling about their commitment to peace like an army of PR men gone wild.

Sara took a verbal swipe at them all, and then had a laugh at them all and with them all...

*   *   *   *   *

...Oh, yes, "S" was in the news and her news was always on a million lips as people tried mightily to understand her. The dewy-eyed thought she was one of them, dreamed that she was, yet were rebuffed by her constant carping laugh. Those who called themselves conservatives couldn't stomach her earth-first demonstrations, yet took heart at her cynicism towards the liberals...

In the end, people did what they always do: they chose to see the part of "S" that suited them and to ignore the parts that didn't. And for all of them, Sara put on a show; they simply couldn't ignore her. She was the female rampant, the indomitable, triumphant "S."

And, oh, the supermarket tabloids! Did they have what they had always dreamed about! The single "S" fit so snugly into a headline and any outrageous thing they could imagine became believable, maybe even true.

*   *   *   *   *

There were editorials about "S" in serious newspapers. "What *can* she want?" read one plaintive headline. The writer labored through each of Sara's twists and turns in public pronouncements over the months, then described her as a brilliant woman, fascinating to watch and to hear in full song, but obviously on the verge of ecological and political schizophrenia.

It was to laugh. Sara knew exactly what she was doing. She had no interest in persuading, lecturing or leading public opinion. They just thought she did because one-by-one she had trotted out every standard argument and then later rebutted each of them with a counter argument.

I knew that she truly believed none of them. She had no hope for mankind but she couldn't leave it alone. She had to prod it, push it, show it the error of any way it chose to take, laugh as it moved this way, laugh as it moved that way.

No, Sara wasn't trying to improve or save mankind. She was merely having fun.

* * * * *

Fun. It seemed to me that Sara was in a frenzy of fun seeking. How many cheering, foot-stamping, love-exuding groups can you enjoy? What's the thrill, day after day, in seeing your name in the papers? Where is the challenge in doing anything when you can do everything?

Did someone say, "Poor little rich girl?" Who could be richer than Sara?

* * * * *

She lived (so my supermarket tabloid told me) in a great California house on a cliff overlooking the Pacific. A dramatically beautiful home, bathed in the sound of crashing waves.

I lived in my Winnabago, which I drove through the streets of Los Angeles and surrounding towns, stopping off here and there to try a new fast food treat or to take in a tourist attraction. A useless shuffle.

One morning I found myself in Anaheim, and there just ahead of me was the huge parking lot for Disneyland, the American Mecca. "Why not?" I said, as I bought a ticket.

226

So I went on all the rides, watched all the shows, ate hot dogs and avoided having my picture taken with Mickey Mouse.

I looked around me at all the thousands out for fun and thought that no one in this manufactured world of escapism was running away from his everyday problems faster than Andrew Camp, scientist, super-being and cuckold extraordinaire.

I was, in truth, getting sick of being Dr. Andrew Camp, with his peculiar problem.

"But you've got to get down to it," I lectured myself.

"Down to what?" I answered.

"Spying! What else?"

I was filled with self-disgust.

When I reached Santa Monica I swung through town, roaming through the palm-lined, flower-filled streets in my Winnebago as other drivers blew their horns and told me rudely to "move that thing!"

What a nice place to live! I thought as I drove down San Vincenti Boulevard, admiring the graceful apartment buildings there and the lushly beautiful foliage. Then I swung by the public pier, scene of so many movies, and watched the couples strolling, many of them hand in hand. I watched one couple, both past seventy, both showing the curse of age in the way they walked and stood, and yet as I watched them smile and talk in long familiar patterns, I was filled with envy.

I followed Route 1 north, admiring the views, lazing along in my mobile habitat, in no particular hurry even if the cars behind me always were.

My supermarket tabloids had told me approximately where Sara lived in her big house on the ocean bluff and it was easy enough to find it. Impressive! Dramatic! Who wouldn't want to live in such a place?

I drove past it a couple of miles, then turned and drove back again, fixing every detail of the home in my mind, then turning again, I found a little used road, almost a trail, on the land side of the road and about a mile south.

I took this trail in the RV, climbing slowly in low gear.

My top heavy home swayed from side to side, but still, in spite of the ruts and ridges, the Winnebago was remarkably surefooted.

The road curved slightly to the north, as I had hoped it would, and after ten minutes of climbing and twisting I found a flat spot where I could park. I was high in a grove of stunted trees looking down toward Sara's home, about a half mile away. I backed the RV this way and that, threading it among the trees to camouflage its outline. I got out to check my work and decided it was acceptable. Just as important, I had a line of sight to the house, and the ocean beyond.

The sound of the waves beating their ceaseless roar on the rocks and the complex smell of the ocean were both with me from where I sat.

I peeled a half dozen candy bars and took a stroll through the trees, munching candy and fixing the scene in my mind. The air was dry and clear and perfect. A half mile away, just beyond Sara's home, sea gulls whirled over the water, calling out with their impatient, demanding tones and dropping, wings folded, to capture yet another fish, or rising to squirt out the white liquid remains of a previously eaten one onto the rocks below.

A beautiful, graceful bird, I thought, but I certainly wouldn't want to know one.

So I lived for a dozen days and nights, eating my beans and stew and watching Sara live.

I played games with her; one sided games she never knew were being played. Mr. Supersleuth, sliding from here to there among the bushes like a wraith, learning to walk without noise, every footstep planned, learning every angle from every location that would give me a line of sight while hiding my body from Sara if she should happen to glance up.

Oh, simple-minded Andy, a boy playing detective. I watched myself watch Sara and I was amused and disgusted, but I still watched.

She had a routine of sorts. There were engagements, public activities to attend. Eco-demonstrations, political activism groups, singing engagements, photo sessions, press opportunities and the like. The public side of Sara. These events took her away from home for a few hours at a time, usually in the late afternoon or early night. I would watch as she backed out her little red convertible and scooted down the road, cutting through traffic with disdain for the other drivers, but I saw that she always made it back home before daybreak, and of course she never slept.

The supermarket tabloids had warned me that Sara would be surrounded at home by an ever-changing coterie of beautiful people. She was said to be the society hostess for a hottub crowd and it was said that during the long nights she would reward them for their adoration by performing on the great patio overlooking the Pacific. My tabloids had hinted that dark things had happened. Men, and sometimes women, were mysteriously injured and carried away and nothing more was said; they just weren't around the group anymore. New ones, from an endless store of eager hopefuls, always took their places.

One tabloid saw UFOs landing on her patio and decided that the key to all her powers was extraterrestrial.

Another scum-sheet invented stories of satanic rituals, of black masses held on her patio overlooking the roaring Pacific on dark nights when the moon was down, of sacrificial blood on stones and screams of terror from fresh young virgins (virgins, yet, in trendy California!) and other editorial daydreams to sell newspapers.

So said the gutter press.

None of it ever happened. None of it. At least, not while I was watching.

The Sara I saw each night on her great stone patio overlooking the Pacific was deliberately and intensely alone.

She did play her piano (a new Steinway grand, all white), sending a cascade of music out to sea where the waves could batter it and silence it, but she played for herself alone, and when she sang it was more like intense vocalizing than singing. She released trills and yells and yips and even screams and shouts. Expressing herself. Amusing herself. Just hollering to hear herself holler. I wanted to yell down to her, "Is this the great 'S'? The golden voice so many cherish?" But of course, I didn't. I listened. I watched.

One night I noticed a new sound, a quiet, deliberate clicking noise. It was not musical and was too quiet for anyone to hear but me.

I jumped down in big, swooping leaps until I was almost on the road, then ran north a few hundred yards until I was lined up with the window to the room where the clicking came from.

Sara was typing. That was it. She had a computer, a word processor, and she was clicking away at it, fingers flying faster than anyone ever typed before, faster than the computer keyboard could absorb it, so she'd have to pause briefly now and then to let it catch up.

I crossed the road and crept closer, fascinated by this new insight into Sara. We could both remember any thought we wanted, so why bother to write anything down?

I crept even closer, almost to the window. Sara was a dream as she sat at her computer. I had forgotten the depth of the shock I felt each time I saw her. If she had this effect on me, who understood what she was and why, how must she appear to others? Like an elemental spirit, shimmering with vitality, radiating beauty?

Sara was concentrating, typing with blinding speed, eyes glued to the monitor.

I ached to step into the room through the window and throw my arms around her from behind. Why not? Why the hell not? I knew she'd welcome it. I knew what would happen moments later and how we'd both enjoy the reunion as we smashed her new furniture and scared the seagulls.

But after that... another parting? I simply wouldn't face it. So I watched her type for a while longer, then crept away on quiet feet and climbed back up to my Winnebago.

Two days later. My TV had told me that there would be a gigantic 'save the redwoods' rally in the Muir Woods, near Sausalito. Of course the fabulous "S" was expected, along with a gaggle of movie greats.

Roughly what? Hundred and fifty, sixty miles? Two hours there, two back, an hour or two to do the performance? We're talking five, six hours, easily, more time than I could possibly use.

So, I watched as Sara drove her little red convertible (hated that damned car!) onto the Pacific Coast Highway, headed north. I was parked beside the road just south of her, just another RVer that no one sees, peering out of my sunglasses under my long billed cap as I pretended to tinker with my engine until I saw her, then a quick slam of the hood and a laborious rollout of the Winnebago.

Why try to follow her? No good reason, except that I wanted to. It was hopeless, anyway. Sara averaged ninety miles-per-hour while I followed at a sedate seventy, straining to catch a glimpse of her on the road ahead. Cans of hash rattled and crashed against canned peas as I flung the Winnebago around curves and when I found a long downhill run I almost hit ninety myself as the 454 Chevy engine screamed and the plastic covered body swayed in the wind of its own passage.

After a dozen miles I slowed and stopped at a turnout and backed the RV into position for a U-turn. What was the point? To make sure she was really going? Or just to participate once more in something Sara was doing? At any rate, it was over. I turned back towards the big house beside the sea.

The spy was ready to do some spying.

Sara's new home was a dream out of *Architectural Digest*. Cream and gold with a deliberate accent of vermilion here and there and always the blue seas outside to give a restless living picture. Great sofas and pillows, vivid oriental rugs, mirrors and glass. Modern opulence. Nothing old. Absolutely nothing. And there was no one defined cultural style. Yet an Arab sheik would have been right at home.

I thought wryly of my RV, my mobile habitat, as I moved about, fingering a vase or admiring an abstract painting.

The computer was in a glassed area overlooking the sea. I sat behind it in the freeform chair Sara used and looked about me, seeing the scene she saw as she typed. I felt in command of the world, with the great private home behind me and the ever-changing sea before me and an obedient, semi-intelligent machine at my finger tips.

I thought, This is how it feels to be Sara.

But of course I was wrong. I only knew how it felt to be Andrew Camp spying on Sara.

I turned her computer on, watched the screen brighten, punched up the word processor and scanned the directory to find the only files that made sense, then started to read the contents of the first file off the screen with all the excitement of the discoverer of stolen secrets and all the guilt of a diary sneak.

Sara had started right in, with no hesitation:

Hello, computer. This is Sara, the girl-child, signing in. I am a woman and that is my central problem, or my central strength or whatever. Let's say the central fact of my being, OK?

Are you a male computer or a female? I get the idea of maleness, somehow. Your stupid rigid logicallity, probably. Tell you what we're going to do, computer. I'm going to write whatever pops into my mind, no order, no logic, just what I feel like and when I'm through I'm going to hit a couple of keys and erase you and then you'll be as empty and stupid as ever.

Fair warning, computer, I'm going to shock your circuits now and then. Or maybe I won't. What does a computer care?

I remember being a girl even before I knew for sure I was one. I had a little friend, when we were four, on a hot summer day and I remember it as clear as clear and he took me behind a big beech tree in the back yard and said, "I can pee further than you, I bet' and I saw his little tube squirting and I was shocked. Jealous? No, I don't think so, just shocked that we could be so different like that and later on I did use an empty thread spool I took out of Mama's sewing basket to try to pee like him, but it just made a mess.

Well computer, when you were on the assembly line back in your factory with a thousand other computers I don't think you were thinking that some crazy woman would be telling you about peeing, now did you? And I won't anymore. Enough of that.

If you think this is going to be another one of those women vs. men diatribes then you've got another permutation coming, computer. That's one of the big fashions these days, part of the politics of life as we know it, but its mainly crap, you know, part of the endless chatter we live with.

Speaking of chatter, it's like someone said to me, 'get a life, Sara,' so I did. I got a life, all right, some life I got. I sort of took on the whole damned world, or at least what I wanted of it, but now that I've got it all in my very own hands the world has vanished into triviality. That's why I laugh and cry and scream at it sometimes and no one seems to understand and the reason is simple: the world I wanted so badly all my life isn't there anymore.

It has all become one big tiresome Donahue-Ophra show for the chronically complaining victim and the politically correct expert. All we hear is one big whine.

But I suppose it's just a passing fad. If Andy and I are to really live a thousand or so years, this demoralized end of the empire America will be history in the blink of an eye anyway. It has the smell of defeat about it. Too bad. Politicized to death, and we were almost great.

The thing is, computer, we people, all of us, have got a soup of millions of memories floating around and you stir up that soup and God only knows what lumps will float to the top. Some of them will be enough to gag a maggot as we used to say, and some so sweet they're almost worse.

I sat down to write something sublime. I think I did, after all I'm the fabulous 'S' and everyone knows I can do anything, so why did I start with this kind of stuff? I just let my fingers do the talking and this is what they said. Don't blame me, blame my fingers.

The thing is, women are different, computer. Men have been saying that forever and they say it as sort of a whiny complaint as though we've wronged them by being women, but the truth is, we are different and we aren't different just to annoy men, but because we just are. So we can either feel guilty and apologize for being female or we can love it and I've just in the past year, since Andy made me what I am, learned truly to love it. And yet at the same time I'll have to admit that it would be a lot easier for me right now with the weight and strength that I have to be a man. I could just run through society like a knight of old, lance out to spear whatever got in my way. 'Oh, ho! Fair lady forsooth and what did you expect from this errant knight?'

But here I am again sending obscene surges through your motherboard and I promised.

"Sara! You've got a nasty mouth!" My dear sweet mother talking all those years ago, and she was something, I can tell you, my mother. Maybe she was all right once, before she got married to him. Women do have special problems and if they don't have problems, they marry them.

I stopped reading the computer screen and looked out to sea for a while. I remembered the difficult mother. I remembered the sly man, the father, whom I had tracked down and talked to in St. Louis years ago, and I didn't want to get involved with either of them again. I dreaded what I was about to read. "Sara, for God's sake, why can't you just keep it to yourself," I muttered. And in my mind, her voice answered: "Just turn off the computer, Andy, and you'll be rid of it. But I won't." So I hit the page down key a few times to skip this section and continued reading.

But there is another thing, computer. If you had eyes to see right now, you'd see that I am so beautiful that it would blow all of your circuits just to look at me.

But it wasn't always like that, computer. I used to hate the way I looked. I used to say to myself, looking in the mirror, "'Sara how can this be?" Because I would look and look and I would just get furious at what I saw and I'd say to myself, "'How're you going to change it?"

The only one who didn't see my problem was Andy. He actually seemed to think I was perfect. At first. I didn't believe him. Then when I knew he meant it, I said to myself, "Sara, what did you do to deserve all this luck?"

Painful! Sara ought to realize that I knew the problems she saw but they simply didn't matter. Love is not blind, no matter what the poets say, but love sees what love wants to see. I hit the page down key a few times to skip some more and then got on with it.

Oh, well. Another subject computer. One of those maggot-memories I told you about. Went out to breakfast with Daddy once when Mama had the flu and I watched Daddy and the waitress kid around and flirt and I realized that Daddy had what they used to call "a line" that he used on the waitress and that he probably used that same line every day of his life on, say, a secretary or whatever other female he found on his travels, and young as I was then, I realized right there in the restaurant over a bowl of Rice Crispies that Daddy had always used his line on me.

And I didn't lose my smile or move one single hair, but my world dropped right out from under me the moment I saw that all Daddy's talk about how pretty I was and what a lovely woman I would be and so forth and so on had just been part of his line to get what he wanted and didn't mean any more than what he was saying to this waitress.

Then I looked at Daddy and saw that his face didn't quite fit together right, either. He had the same awkward look that I had and it was easy to see where I had gotten my look that I hated so much and I thought, well maybe it used to drive him crazy too, when he was my age, and maybe still does, and that's why he has to do the waitress, but I didn't care. I wasn't overflowing with sympathy for Daddy right then.

And yet, the thought hit me that I must have known somewhere inside me all along that Daddy's line was just a line, but I needed to hear it like a desert needs water.

"Just like the story of the three little pigs and the wolf," I thought. "My house is built of straw."

I felt that sometimes even after Andy came along, but he did change things. He put the solid world back under my feet, because there was no line from him. I used to listen hard and with Andy, whatever he said, it was the truth as he saw it and Andy's truth was ever so much better for me than Daddy's line.

Am I being simpleminded, computer? Is this silly meandering the best I can do? The fabulous 'S'? The great brain who could rule the world if she wanted?

I could, you know. Rule the world. I've got a good piece of it wrapped around my finger now, not even trying. Sometimes I think it would be fun, establish a worldwide matriarchy, you know, make all the men of the world kowtow to the women for change or I'd knock some sense in their heads, but then I'd have to spend my time running things, all the details, and if you think women would run things better than men, you are no smarter than any other computer. Things would be different all right, but better? Make the men all worker bees and

235

let the women hold court and send out great wafts of pheromones to drive the men crazy, or maybe the men become useless drones and the women throw away their lipstick and underarm deodorant and become hard-eyed competitors like men and what's the good of that?

I used to tell Andy that people were just a disease on this earth anyway and he believed that I believed that and maybe I did or maybe I still do. Anyway, it's one truth among many, many truths, and you can't deny it.

Well, I certainly didn't set out to write this kind of stuff. Blame my wandering fingers.

Once upon a time, when I was thirteen, my father was away on business most of the time but he came home on weekends and one time he and my mother had this big shouting screaming fight that went on for days and a little later my mother went to the doctor's office and took me with her and for the next two or three weeks we had to go to the doctor's every day for a treatment I thought was awful and my father said to us both, next time he was home, smirking and shamefaced, trying to make a joke because, as I know now even if I didn't then, he was mortified, and he said, "I see I brought you both a present from New Orleans," and I was stupid enough then to think I'd go looking for my present in hiding places around the house when my mother screamed at me, "I had no choice. It was my marriage duty! But you, you little slut!"

And that was the last time we saw Daddy. He sent money now and then and life got grimmer and my mother and I were never friends again and she got old and mean and I always wondered after Andy and I got married and I had all those miscarriages if maybe I had scars inside or something but damned if I was going to bring that up to my doctor, open that old can of worms and so what, happens to girls all the time, or so I read. No big deal unless you make it one.

And then, forty years or so later, I got the word that she was dying and I went to see her at the hospital hundreds of miles away and she turned her face away from me. Just one glance at me and she turned away and I said to myself, "It's now or never," so I put my mouth right up to her ear where she couldn't help hearing me or ever be able to claim she didn't and her skin I remember was soft and velvety old ladies skin against my lips, and I said, "Mama…I was just a little girl. I couldn't help what he did." But she just tightened her lips and closed her eyes, shutting me out and by and by she died.

The first time I saw Andy I got the giggles. He took one look at me and got cow-eyed, and you could just see it, he was hooked on me. Of course, I liked that, but I didn't know what I'd do about it because Andy was no dreamboat.

I could feel my face burn. Damnit, Sara! Did you have to rub my nose in this? I thought I was pretty special back then and I thought you thought so, too. Do you have to ruin my dreams? The voice in the back of my head said, "Just turn off the computer, Andy. Stop snooping and you won't know."

But, of course, I didn't stop. I just speeded up the scrolling and tried to skip the details.

All the girls said Andy was "cute"so I said so, too, and I looked around me with my eyes wide open and it was during the Depression, a really scary time before World War II, and I said to myself, "Sara, that Andy Camp is cute enough, and what's more you love him madly, don't you? And the name, Sara Camp, sounds all right, too, don't you think? At least it won't be something funny like Sara Snicklesnapper and he thinks you're just the cat's pajamas and that's all right, too, isn't it?"

And then there is the business of getting married. Not elaborate the way it is today when everyone has more money, but still pretty dramatic, the bride is the star of the show any way you want to look at it and the groom just staggers around dumb and white-faced while the bride radiates and all the girls are envious. Nice.

So we were married and you know what? Surprise! We both, the two of us, discovered what they used to call "married love" and we were good at it, really good, like Fred Astaire and Ginger Rogers dancing together and I said to myself, "Well, Sara, well now, you just fell into it, didn't you?" And one day when I had nothing else to think about I thought and realized that I was probably in love for real and it seemed to me that I had been building a shell around myself for years like a big, hard walnut and Andy was the only one who could break my shell and eat my meat.

He adored me, mind and body, and I adored his adoration. You might ask, computer, in human logic is this any basis for love? The answer is, what basis could possibly be better?

It was great to have someone take care of me and earn the money, too, but it was hard to give up my independence, so I didn't. I made it plain to Andy that I'd do whatever I damned well pleased, within reason, and he didn't mind that either. He just needed me to love like a child needs his teddy bear. Hooray!

Painful! I deliberately closed my eyes and hit the page down key many times, refusing to ruin my own sweet memories of that part of our life by reading Sara's. When I started reading again, I saw that I'd skipped about a dozen years.

...sometimes Andy talked about his work and I didn't even know how he could think such difficult things like that. How could I sleep right beside another person who had things like that in his head I didn't know about? Words, even, that I couldn't spell or pronounce, much less understand. I said to myself, "Sara, why don't you learn Russian or German? Andy will never know about that and you can have your secrets in your head safe from him, too." So I did. Lots of things, languages, history, literature. Lots of subjects. Whatever I felt like, and Andy didn't know about any of them so it was my own sweet knowledge.

Andy and I used to dance together and we'd sing sometimes and the truth is, we both knew we weren't very good at singing. Better at dancing, but still not great, you know, and I'd play the piano after we saved the money to buy me one. I loved that piano and I was really frustrated that I didn't play it better. I had a few lessons way back before Daddy left and then, no more lessons, no more piano, but I could still pick out a tune and thump my way through it and Andy and I were happy signing and dancing and it was the one time outside of bed that we really felt completely together.

....and yet...and yet..it seemed to me that we had love all around, plenty of love, but I did feel I'd missed out on Romance, Romance with a capital 'R' and I just kept looking over my shoulder for it like a person who's had a great meal but is hungry for dessert.

I hit the page down key a few times. Those memories were too sweet to me to take a chance on reading a different version of them. Besides, I was searching for something...

Beauty. Boy and girl beauty. I used to think I knew about it exactly. Then, as I grew older, I got so I couldn't tell anymore. Is this girl called beautiful just because she's young and has regular features? But then, everyone's young once. And this male movie heartthrob they're all screaming about. Looks like a punk kid to me. Mean eyes. Scaly skin. Can't they see? So I got confused, I really did, trying to remember why I used to think I knew what beauty was and it was a sad thing to me because I'd always thought beauty was important and I'd thought I'd had it. Then, after my change, after Andy gave me the shot and made me what I am, I thought that all other people were cheesy and ugly, slow and stupid, just wax figures, Andy used to call them, creeping around, barely alive. But now I'm beginning to see beauty in them again. Oh, I laugh and poke fun, but you've got to admire their guts to do so much with such slow brains and skimpy muscles.

But enough of that, let's get down to something important which is my diet. I've simply got to lose a lot of weight.

Diet? "No, Sara!" I could feel my neck hair rising. "We've got to eat!" I had always known that our compulsion to eat was real, but Sara and I had never really talked about it. It had been too obvious to discuss, like the law of gravity. I kept reading, eyes glued to the monitor.

The thing is, computer, I've got these really strong urges. Needs, really. Andy and I used to have a great time rolling around on those mattresses and I needed that like I needed to breathe and I still do, and God knows men are attracted like flies to honey, but then I weigh twelve-hundred pounds so that makes me a monster. They're like mushroom men, you know, can you imagine making violent, passionate love to a six-foot mushroom. Too bad for the mushroom, parts and pieces, and bloody crumbs lying all over. Not much fun for me either.

So I'll just have to do what women have always done. I'll go on a diet. Women have always shaped themselves to fit the ideal picture men have of them, you know. When they wanted us fat to prove they were the big brave food providers, we'd look like a hippopotamus and when they wanted us thin we'd diet down like a skinny boy with only a couple of soft bumps just to please them, but I've got a problem: I've got an appetite like you wouldn't believe.

No, no, no, computer. I'm not going to diet down until I'm weak or something. I'm just going to knock off seven, eight hundred pounds, maybe just a little more, try to get to the point where I don't crush people by accident.

I left the computer running and ran to Sara's kitchen, frantic with the idea that she'd done something stupid, life threatening, even. But they were all there, cases and cases of canned foods stacked in a storage room off the kitchen. Not my hashes and stews and beans, but still substantial foods. Tuna and crab meat. Endive. Asparagus. French onion soup, and many others.

She has plenty of food, I told myself, but is she eating it? So I ran out to the concrete apron where a dozen garbage cans were lined up and lifted all the lids. Oh, thank God! Hundreds of empty cans, some of them freshly opened, with the smear of food inside still soft and edible. Certainly she was eating. The tops of all the cans had been ripped off, not cut. Sara's trademark, hers and mine.

Then what was she up to? I ran back to the computer.

I've got a secret. Actually, two secrets. No, I won't tell you computer, you or anyone else, but one of those secrets is a sweet secret and one of them is simply awful. Degrading. It really makes me ashamed of myself so that I don't even like to think of what I've done, but then, what is the old saying from the bible? "'I return, like a dog to its vomit" and do the same old disgusting thing again and again. What is it? A secret: that's what it is. Mine to know and yours to never find out. Forget I mentioned either one. The sweet secret or the shitty secret. On to another subject which is the sea.

I have to tell you, computer, that I live beside the sea, the glorious, fearful Pacific that sends waves crashing against my cliff. And you can't smell, but I can. They say dogs smell five hundred times better than humans and I can out-smell a dog anytime, so the symphony of smells I get out of the ocean is almost indescribable. But the ocean I love is also the one thing I'm afraid of and I don't know exactly why. Some of its smells are simply awful and one thing that keeps popping into my mind is that if the ocean is the birthplace of all life, then it is the ancient graveyard of almost everything that has ever lived, miles deep in places, they tell me, with the slime of other times, other beings. So I look at the Pacific and I love it like a child loves its mother and at the same time I tell it, "You don't fool me, old ocean. Deep down, you're tricky and mean."

So much for salt water. Let's come back to something I mentioned before because it's the one big thing that stands between Andy and me and that one thing is called, "Romance." That's right, it has a capital 'R.' No matter where you put it in a sentence, you've got to put a capital R on Romance because that's the kind of word it is.

I've been waiting for Andy to grow up and I think he will if he ever learns to stop playing boy-scientist. He can be such a joy. But such a jerk, too, sometimes. My prescription for Andy is to let him wallow in his own misery for a few years. He needs to be alone, but by my desertion, maybe, and I'm sorry about that, but shocked into thinking things through, seeing the world with bigger eyes. If he ever does grow up in the man-woman sense then he'd be the perfect mate for me. But first he has to learn Romance.

Maybe some other woman will teach it to him before I do but he's totally pig-headed when it comes to loyalty, except maybe for what I've heard lately.

My cheeks were burning, my teeth were grinding in frustration, and I was furious. "I deserve better!" I shouted to the computer monitor.

But one way or another, Andy just has to learn about Romance and Romance always seems to involve other people. For Romance to truly happen, there must be a contest where Fair Lady is won, swept off her feet, in competition against others—even if the others are not really competing except in the Fair Lady's mind. Romance is unreal, a game involving the drama of winning or losing, and it is the only game between men and women that's worth playing.

"All right!" I shouted to the computer and to Sara. I'll learn Romance! Love, true love itself, is not enough for you, so I'll learn to play your silly games. What must I do? Bring flowers? Write sonnets? Defeat rivals? Wear a tuxedo? What is the etiology of this thing you call Romance?"

Listen, computer, you ought to watch the nature shows on TV, any of them. You'll see a little male bird fanning his tail feathers out in a display, strutting before his female, trying to win her favor. Same with the monkeys and apes, the fish even. So is mankind any different? Why, no. We're the most romantic of them all.

I could feel the blood rise to my face and brain in an almost blind fury. Goddamnit, I'd had enough of her Romance crap with the capital 'R.' Yes, I'd dance to her tune, but damned if I'd read any more about it. So I scrolled down rapidly, skipping pages as my eye took in key phrases and rejected them.

Some pages I did read but I won't repeat them. Painful. About her several miscarriages. About the one child who went almost full term and was then born dead, our little boy for whom I still grieved.

Oh, yes, and the joys of living in our green mountain home in our golden tent. Even though she appeared to have loved it, she did leave it, so I skipped most of this. Why risk having my sweetest memories destroyed?

242

Finally, I switched the computer off. There were still hundreds of pages to be read and I could have done it as fast as the computer could scroll, but why? Pain lurked for me on every page. "You snooped and were paid the snoop's reward," I told myself.

I sat staring at the now lifeless computer. My strongest inclination was to toss it over the stone wall and into the ocean. "How'd you like to be the first computer to grow barnacles!" I asked it. But it was Sara's, not mine, and I didn't want to fight about her lost computer, so I did nothing.

After a few minutes, I looked around, removed all traces of having been there, and left Sara's great modern house beside the sea for the protection of my own snug Winnebago, where I could open a case of Dinty Moore stew and think.

And what I thought was this: Go to her tomorrow morning. Woo her like a swain. Do whatever you must, but get her back and create a new life together or you're both the loser.

I waited through the night. Saw Sara's red car come home. Heard doors slam. Heard the tops ripped off a dozen cans. Heard her toilet flush. Heard her play a few chords and then run a stiff finger up the keyboard and slam the lid shut. Saw her leaning over the seawall, watching the crashing waves. Said to myself, "Tomorrow morning. In the daylight. Talk it all out. Bring wildflowers. Practice grinning. Modulate your voice. Choose your words. Think Romance."

So it went. I had my five minute nap just after daybreak, then I went for a twenty mile run to work the anger out of my system. I had a shower in my Winnebago and then dressed in my best. My courting clothes. Then I started trotting down the hill towards the road. Towards Sara and a new life devoted to Romance. Romance with a capital R.

chapter thirty-seven

As I got near the road I noticed two things that seemed strange. Near the front driveway there was a tank truck with a sign that read, "Sam The Sewer Man" with an advertising slogan, "Let us suck your troubles away," and then under that a phone number plus the message, "Radio Dispatched" with little electrical zig zags radiating out from the words. Then there was Sam himself, I presumed, or one of his helpers, dressed in brown coveralls and wielding a big black flexible hose that was stuck into Sara's septic tank. He was obviously pumping the contents into his tank truck.

The other strangeness was a nondescript black car with a small Avis sticker on the back. What was it doing here?

"Morning!" said the sewer man, gaily, waving to me with a free hand, obviously a man who took pride in his work and liked to talk about it. "You ought to see what I'm pumping here. It's not what you think!"

But I ignored him. Because over the sound of his pump, over his cheerful voice, over the sound of the waves crashing against the seawall, over the sound of the seagulls wheeling over the surf calling out incessantly as they searched for fish, I heard a soft, rhythmic thudding sound that only my sharp ears could pick out among all the other noises around me.

Romance, capital "R" Romance, so carefully nurtured by a night of deliberate preparation, flew out of my soul abruptly, replaced by bloody anger and blind fury. Soon my nose confirmed what my ears had heard and I ran into the house wildly, with only one thought: "Who? Who in hell was doing this thing with my Sara?"

I gave the bedroom door a quick backhand that splintered it and there in front of my eyes was the scene of scenes: the scene above all scenes that could be dreaded.

There upon the mattress covering the floor was Sara, caught in the act, as I had known for moments now she would be, with the naked, scared, defiant and somehow triumphant Wiseass.

244

The Wiseass! The Wiseass! "How could you?" I screamed at Sara. "How could you do this with The Wiseass? With The *Wiseass*, no less! Couldn't you have picked another prick? At least saved me from this?"

Oh, this sense of smell. Oh, how miserable to have it now. Better to shove hot coals up my nose than to smell Wiseass semen; to not only smell it, but to know with bird dog surety where the smell came from, to know without the ability to fool myself that this pungent stink of Wiseass semen came from every orifice of Sara's body.

"Hey, don't get so excited," said the Wiseass, looking at me now with a mixture of defiance and cunning. "You want to join in? There's plenty for all, you know."

My eyes were locked onto Sara's. She was not afraid but intensely curious as she watched me watch her. You could see her thought: "What will Andy do, confronted with this?"

The scene was frozen. A tableau that had been repeated through the ages: the two lovers (lovers? How could these two be lovers?) caught in the act. The offended husband, furious, helpless to know what to do. The deliberately placed mattresses on the floor, not for sleeping, never for sleeping. The nakedness. The sexual slime. The smell. The fear and the fury. The certain knowledge that the world would never again be the same for any of the three after this moment.

Did it make a difference that they were beautiful in their perfect nakedness? That the cheating pair and the cheated-on husband were all three shimmering creatures of physical perfection... elemental forces of nature... demigods in a human world...a sight to shock an ordinary mortal?

No, it didn't. The pain was the same. The pain was, if anything, more intensely felt.

I couldn't stand and watch this scene a moment longer. So quickly that I was a blur of motion even to them, I reached for the Wiseass and got him by the throat and jerked his face up to mine and was about to say something that would destroy him when I realized that in my fury I could find nothing at all to say. The inside of my head was a red whirlwind of hate, with no room left for words or reason.

That face, that hated face, so close now, to mine, was contorted by my choking hand, but strangely unafraid. The Wiseass grabbed my wrist with one hand and began trying to peel my fingers away with the other, then as I watched, furious and unbelieving, his now-perfect mouth twisted in a little circle and then pursed quickly and exploded with a load of saliva. The son-of-a-bitch had spit into my eye.

The surprise made me loosen my grip, just for a few naoseconds, and that was enough for him to free his throat from my choking fingers and then immediately knee me in the crotch.

I was only vaguely aware of Sara in the background watching us fight.

I reached down and caught him by the ankles and whirled, flinging him head-first through the wall of Sara's house, so that he landed on the patio in a shower of stone dust. But while the wall was badly damaged the Wiseass was not.

"Your turn," he yelled as he lunged at me, and before I could decide what to do, he had me around the head with one arm wrapped around it as the other hand began exploring my eyes, then, as I closed them tightly, he ran a finger up each nostril, trying to find a vulnerable spot to probe or tear.

I was disgusted at the feel of his naked, sex-slimy body now intertwined with mine as we tested each other for weakness and maneuvered for leverage, each against the other.

"I'm going to kill your ass and take your woman," he breathed into my ear. "How do you like that, you old fart?"

I immediately stamped on his instep and when I felt the smallest relaxation of his hold on my head I reached down and caught him quickly in the one place I hated most to touch but knew that he would hate even more: I had grabbed the Wiseasss, quite literally, by the balls, and I squeezed them until he let out a high undulating, "Dooonnn'ttt!" and put both his hands to work tearing at my hands, trying to free himself as he repeated, "Oh, nooo! Dooonnnn'ttt!"

As the seagulls circled over us, curiously, I began to whirl the Wiseass around and around on Sara's patio overlooking the ocean. I turned in a tight circle on my feet like an Olympic athlete, hearing a pitiful *"ohh, ohh, don't,"* as his body went around my head, both arms rigid as they converged at his crotch, fingers frantically working against mine, trying to tear them away from his testicles. When his body was a blur of motion I gave an extra tug and let him go like a thrown discus and watched as his scrambling arm-waving, leg-waving body flew through the air, yelling *"Heyyy!!! Hey!!! What-the-hellllll!"* and splashed down among the waves about a half mile out to sea.

Sara came up behind me, still naked, still stinking of Wiseass. "I was only having fun, Andy."

"My sweet Sara, the whore," I replied, watching the spot where the Wiseass had landed and wiping my hands, over and over, on my pants. He was not to be seen, as I knew he wouldn't be.

"He was the only one who was really equipped to scratch my itch. Besides, there was another reason. A good reason."

"My sweet whore, Sara," I replied.

"But he didn't *mean* anything."

"My whorey sweet, Sara."

"You know I never *loved* anyone but you."

"My Sara whores sweetly."

The Wiseass had been under water for over a minute, now. I wondered how he would handle it.

"Ah-ha!" I said, as his body shot high above the water like a super dolphin, breath whistling, and then splashed in again, heavily.

"He weighs fifteen-hundred pounds," I told Sara over my shoulder. "He can't possibly swim."

"But...he's strong."

"Doesn't matter. He can beat the water to a froth but he can't support his weight. Don't try to argue physics with me!" I shouted back at her. "Not with that stink on you!"

Neither of us spoke. We watched the Wiseass. Every couple of minutes he would surface, shooting way into the air, breathing heavily, then splashing back. Each time he was nearer to the shore. Obviously, he was crawling along the bottom towards the shore, then finding a rock strong enough to support his weight and jumping to the surface to breathe, then crawling again.

Just what I had expected. Just what I had wanted. Let the son-of-a-bitch crawl on the slimy undersea rocks forever, scared and fighting for his miserable life.

"What'll you do when he climbs out?" asked Sara, over my shoulder.

"I'll show you." I waited, grim-lipped, as he made jump after jump, each time getting nearer the shore.

As he made the last jump I hopped over the seawall and ran down the beach to meet him as soon as he stepped out, cold and shaking and panting for breath. Before he could speak, before he could move, I had him by an ear, whirling around in a blur of motion, then sailing through the blue sky to the same spot in the ocean he'd entered before.

"That's cruel," muttered Sara.

"I haven't even begun to show you cruel," I muttered back.

Six times more the Wiseass jumped his way ashore and six times more I slung him back, each time grabbing him by a new body part. It seemed to me that he was getting lighter with each toss and each time he sailed further out to sea. The desperation in his eyes each time he saw me about to grab him was enough to melt the proverbial heart of stone. I was not moved. My answer to his fear was not pity but scorn. For the first time in my long life I knew that I was not only able to kill a living being but to torture it before killing, and I intended to do just that.

The seventh time the Wiseass fought for shore he jumped for air twice and then was under for much longer than usual, at least three minutes.

"Don't tell me the bastard's finally drowned," I muttered.

But sure enough, he came up, this time riding on the back of a large shark. He had his fingers hooked into the shark's mouth and rode him, bending the shark's head in the direction he wanted him to go. At least that was his theory. But the shark had other ideas and would not be ridden like a horse. The shark broke the surface, rolled violently, then dove again, twisting and turning and heading out to sea, completely out of control.

Soon there was a cloud of blood where the Wiseass had ripped the shark's head open and left it to die and soon after that, another Wiseass jump like the rest.

248

"So much for Mr. Shark," I said. "He had the bad luck to meet a bigger one."

"Ingenious," said Sara softly from behind. "Even if it didn't work. You've got to give him that."

"I knew a bear once who was smarter," I told her, as we waited for the Wiseass to drag himself ashore once again, panting heavily and looking around wild-eyed for me, knowing that he was too tired to prevent me grabbing him. I waited just long enough for him to gain a little hope, then I jumped off the ledge and caught the Wiseass and threw him out again.

"You *have* to stop this!" said Sara. "You can't be a murderer."

"You've lost the right to tell me what I can't be."

"Oh, Andy! I was only curious, for God's sake! And I didn't realize that the Amazing Clifford was the one you used to call the Wiseass until he told me how he got the way he is. He looks so different. So much better."

"What did he tell you?"

"Listen to me!" she said, ignoring my question. "He and I were featured in the same issue of the *National Enquirer* once, for God's sake, you know how it is. Celebrities get to know each other. People put you together. They say, 'You ought to get to know so and so'. I was just fooling around, exploring my world. He was nothing, really."

"What did he tell you?"

"Well, he said a lot. He said you weren't the one who really invented the Blue Helix, said it was a brilliant man who worked for him, under his direction, a man named Henry Fowles. He said you kept breaking into the laboratory, kept trying the steal the secret from this Henry Fowles. Said you were really just some kind of a fake, Andy."

I went from fury to sick fury. I turned and stared at Sara's face as if she'd spoken ancient Greek. To take even that away from me! To take away the right to my own Blue Pill. Her damned *Blue Helix.*

"And you believed him?"

"Oh, Andy! You know I still love you. Always will. And I know you're not really a fake. You've tried hard. You're brilliant, I know that. But look at what we both know to be the truth: you did try to save me over and over again before I went to the hospital and it never worked, you always thought it would but it wouldn't, and then you came in that last night with that Henry Fowles stuff and it did save me. Then you tried to make more of it at your lab and those Sara and Andy rats looked good for a while and then they died. And I know you went back to the Germ Factory at least once, just like he said, and maybe more than once. So don't ask me what I believe, ask me what I know.

"Besides," she continued, "He could give me the one thing I had to have, the one thing you couldn't. Now—you can't blame me, Andy, you just can't blame me. I bet that's why you've been breaking into the Germ Factory, to get the same thing I had to have, those booster shots."

"Booster shots?"

"Yes. To keep us from growing old. Don't tell me you don't know. I used to ask you and ask you about growing old and you'd claim we didn't need anything because you didn't have whatever we needed and you wouldn't tell me the truth but all the time you were breaking into the Germ Factory trying to find the booster shots this Henry Fowles had developed."

"So the Wiseass has been giving you these shots? And you've been giving him what he wants to pay for them? You sucker! You rube! You mark! Here you are, the queen of the universe for a million years without doing one damned thing because I put it all into your hands and you fall for the first carnival pitchman who comes along selling colored water and pipedreams."

I wouldn't look, couldn't look at Sara. In my fury I was afraid I couldn't keep control. In the back of my mind some rational part said, "Oh, God, don't let her argue this. Let her accept it quietly or there'll be an explosion. If she puts up any kind of an argument terrible things will happen."

Over a minute passed. I could hear Sara breathing behind me. I still refused to look at her or to say more.

"A placebo?" she asked, finally.

"Worse. An absolute fraud. A fool's medicine. Probably just saline solution and vegetable dye. That's just what that bastard would do. Just how his tricky little mind would work."

"You have to understand," Sara said, after a longer pause, speaking over my shoulder because I kept turning away, refusing to look at her, "Let's say for the sake of argument that you're right.

Let's say that maybe he did fool me with the booster shots. I don't know. You have to understand how terrified I was of losing all this. I'd do anything. Anyone would. You would, too, I'll bet, if you were in my shoes.

"You know, I didn't really like him," she continued. "I mean, its not like I was in love or anything. I know he's really sort of ordinary. Certainly no one you'd want to spend an eternity with. Strong, of course. Well equipped and plenty of staying power, but no imagination. Not nearly the lover you are."

To be compared. Weighed. Evaluated like a draft horse or a slave at auction. It was too much. It was all too much.

"Do I know you?" I asked. "Did I ever know you?" And before she could answer I turned and grabbed Sara by an ankle, and whirling just once, slung her far out to sea.

"See if this washes some of the Wiseass stink out of your body," I called out after her as she sailed through the air.

"*Annnndddddyyyy!*" was her only reply as she splashed down.

The Wiseass made one of his periodic leaps for air and I saw that Sara had landed far beyond him, much further out to sea.

But why? I thought. *I didn't toss her that hard.* Then I remembered how her body had felt, whirling around my head before I let her go, and an alarm went off in my head. She had felt so light. She should have weighed twelve-hundred pounds or more, but it seemed to me that she must now be no more than two hundred. Maybe much less. How could that be? I knew she'd eaten. I knew she *had* to eat, just as she had to breathe.

Then I looked again and Sara was swimming. *Swimming on the surface!*

I ran back to the house and found Sara's cordless phone and ran back to the sea again, watching Sara swim the mile or so towards shore as I dialed the number I remembered from "Sam The Sewer Man's" truck. I got his wife on the first ring and insisted that she patch me through to his mobile phone.

His message was clear "… I tried to tell you… you wouldn't listen… the thing was, there was no shit, understand? Just puke… can you believe it? Fifteen-hundred gallons of puke? Ain't that something?"

I slammed the phone down on Sam The Sewer Man without thinking of thanks.

Bulemia! Sara was bulemic and anorexic! So that's how she was losing weight!

I watched her swim strongly towards the shore, furious with myself for throwing her in but knowing that she was in no real danger. Then there was a rush of water under her and something that I first took to be another shark fastened onto her body and I saw that it was no shark, it was the Wiseass, hitching a ride home on Sara.

The damned Wiseass. Trouble to the last. He had caught her around the legs, where he held with a death grip so that she had to swim with her arms alone, and he was not only heavy, but terrified. Beyond reasoning.

She had a cruel load to pull but I could see that she was pulling it. Slowly, she made progress, fighting hard to keep the two of them afloat and just inching forward as she beat the water furiously to stay on top.

Could I have helped? At my own sixteen-hundred pounds I couldn't swim either, so it would have been difficult and I really didn't want to help, anyway. "Let her suffer through it," I told myself. "If the bear could cope and the silly Wiseass could cope, then Sara can damned well cope, too, lightweight or not."

So I sat and watched. My wild anger was fading but there was nothing positive to take its place. I thought, dully, that if the waves should happen to close over Sara and the Wiseass I would probably watch the blank spot in the ocean for a while and then trudge away, too numb to care. It was not that I really wanted the waves to close over her, I was just indifferent.

It seemed to me that I still loved a woman named Sara with all my being. But somehow, the Sara who struggled so before my eyes was not that Sara.

As far as the Wiseasss was concerned, I'd be delighted to watch him inhale water, eyes bulging in his final terror.

After a long, hard swim, Sara made it to the shore, the Wiseass still clinging to her legs. I jumped of my perch and walked down to the beach to meet them.

"Do you plan to throw me in again, Andy!" Sara asked, head down in the sand, heaving for breath.

The Wiseass grunted softly and unwrapped his arms from Sara's legs, looking up at me beseechingly. "Noooo... don't!" he said. "I couldn't... I just couldn't."

His dangling Wiseass lip hung down. I hated his weak, silly face. His eyes, (oh, my God, his eyes!) were burned and blind as he tried to find me with them, crooning again, "Noooo...don't."

Sara's back was toward me. It had freckles I hadn't seen in almost a year. Freckles and wrinkles and wet, wispy white hair at the nape of her neck.

I reached and turned her over as gently as I could. She was a woman of eighty. A woman I had spent a lifetime loving. She was exactly as I had seen her on that awful last night in the hospital except for one thing.

From the looks of the living, kicking bulge in her stomach, the bulge that she had been able to control until now and hide in the plump sweetness of her marvelous body, I would say that my Sara was now pregnant.

She was very far along.

She lay now on her back on the sand, one hand drawn up with an effort and propped to shade her eyes as she looked up at me wonderingly. "Andy," she just managed to breathe. "You're still so beautiful. You must find me hideous now."

I touched her stomach. "How long?"

There was a hint of a smile. "Seven months. Don't you remember seven months ago?"

I shook my head. Unable to think. Stunned.

"A great math brain like yours!" she whispered, working hard to say it. "Surely you don't have to count on your fingers like a suspicious mother-in-law... seven months ago we were in our pool beside our golden tent and, I was just about to make my little speech about loving you and leaving you."

"Oh, yes," I murmured. "I remember exactly what we'd just-done. It was lovely. I've relived it a thousand times since."

"So, I took a little of you away with me, Andy. I knew it almost right away. Never doubt that its yours, or that the two of us were coming back to you, and soon."

The Wiseass was moaning again. His only vocabulary seemed to be a wailing, "Nooooooo…nooooooo!"

I picked up Sara's cordless phone again and dialed 911 while she smiled weakly up at me and shook her head slowly from side to side.

"Too late. Too late. Don't bother."

I spoke into the phone, to the emergency ward of the hospital, told them where to come, told them to 'hurry, hurry', told them it was a life or death matter, told them that there were two people, told them that they would be alone, to please hurry, to please…

"Who are they!" I was asked. "What is their problem? An accident? A fight? A killing? What, exactly, is wrong?"

I said, "You'll find an old woman, just past eighty, dying of heart failure and the complications of age. She's also seven months pregnant," I added. "Please save the baby.

"Beside her you'll find a stupid young man who's blind and badly burned. Burned by the sea."

"What? What did you say?" The voice demanded.

"But never mind him. Save my wife and baby!"

Before they could argue, I slammed the phone down and turned to Sara.

"Now listen: I told you before I'd come with my Blue Helix and save you and you didn't believe me but I did. This time, I'll do it again. Believe!"

She managed a small smile. "I believe, Andy," she said, choking the words around her swollen tongue, "I believe that this time I'll really die. But never mind."

Her eyes closed. She turned her head slightly away, deliberately dismissing me.

So I turned and ran.

chapter thirty-eight

You don't need to know the details. How I left the Winnebago forgotten in the woods and ran north towards San Francisco because I remembered a better plane schedule at this hour than at LAX.

You don't need to know about the stubborn woman at the ticket counter who kept saying they were all sold out even after I offered to stand or ride with the baggage.

I don't want to tell you about the young businessman I followed into the men's room after I saw him with a ticket on the same plane where I'd been refused. I didn't hurt him. I did strip him naked and take his ticket and flush his shredded clothes down the toilet. That kept him for a long time shivering in a stall, pleading for help while everyone ignored him, assuming he was strange in some way.

And the plane, like all planes going cross country, thought it had to stop in Chicago and that was a waste of time, there was plenty of fuel, just a matter of picking up paying customers and letting others off and I had no time for that, so I did a bit of hijacking, who can blame me, wife dying?

They got so excited! Here I was up in the cockpit with the pilot and the copilot with the stewardess screaming at me to leave when I pushed her out and said, "OK, now, everything's OK, we're just skipping Chicago, an emergency or I wouldn't bother you, so plot your course for Dulles International."

Of course they couldn't leave well enough alone, I knew in advance they couldn't, so it was no surprise when I heard on the radio that they had Dulles swarming with police and SWAT teams and dogs and whatever they could muster.

So I took over the controls (easy to do, I'd been watching them for hours) and flew us into the Richmond airport, leaving all the police at loose ends in Washington.

No time to rent a car. I could just imagine the red tape and the local police at my elbow. So I ran.

It was night and it was cold, nothing like California beach weather. So what, I thought. *Just a dose of cold reality.*

I streaked over the blacktop roads faster than a rented car could have made it. I was following a road map in my head that I remembered from months ago, heading for my condo, my mountain. My cave. My Blue Helix.

Sara could turn her head away and deny me all she pleased, but I was going to save her again and we three would make a new life together. If that didn't work, then it would be baby and me and Sara could go free.

As I ran through the black night on the cold black roads I thought: this business of Sara and the Wiseass reverting, could it happen to me? Of course it could. Fair warning.

I had always known our eating was important, now I knew how important. Sara had lost it through deliberate starvation. Bulimia and anorexia. The Wiseass through too much work and fear in the ocean. He'd simply burned his vitality away. Now, if he'd eaten that shark instead of wasting it, he'd still be what he was.

I ran north and west, following highways 33 and 522 towards Culpepper. Houses were dark. Chickens were quietly sleeping. Dogs barked now and then as I passed. I could hear and smell them better than they could me. Once I heard two cats fighting: a terrible sound. Pigs grunted contentedly at one farm. At another there were lights and the sounds of a TV tuned to the *Tonight Show*. A country night owl.

Now and then I'd meet a car or pass one and each time I would see the car sway as the driver saw me as a blur in his headlights and had to deal with what he saw, or thought he saw.

No matter. I ran. And ran. And got hungry. And hungrier. I told myself, "It doesn't matter. You've got plenty of energy left and besides… there's food in the cave. Food and the Blue Helix. Enough Blue Helix for Sara and for me, too, if it ever came to that, and cases and cases of Dinty Moore stew.

It began to rain. A cold, wet and windy night. But by now I was only about thirty miles away. "A mere bag of shells," I said, remembering TV's Ed Norton.

The cold rain began to freeze in a slushy mess on the road and I felt myself begin to slip. "Weight and strength mean nothing on ice." I reminded myself, taking more care. After a while I got off the blacktop and ran on the grass beside the road. A little slower but less slipping, a little more work, a little less progress. Whoever said it was a beautiful world?

I came, finally, to the small town just south of our condo. Dead of night, the town was asleep, but I was very pleased. "Almost home. A few miles to the condo, then a dash through the woods, then a short climb up the mountain. Nothing to it, Andy!"

So I started the final leg. Starving! But not really dangerous yet, it seemed to me. I was like a car with a broken fuel gauge: you may know its low on fuel, but just how low?

I ran on. It really doesn't matter, I told myself. With both food and the Blue Helix in the cave, all you have to do it get there.

I thought of Sara as I ran. By now she would be in a hospital hooked up to tubes, doctors standing around amazed. Would they take the baby? A Cesarean section would kill Sara just now. There'd be no next of kin to authorize it. What would they do? How could they even believe what their eyes told them, an eighty year-old with a baby?

What about the baby? Would it be what Sara and I had become? Of course it would. All its life in the womb it had been superhuman. It still had food, the last of Sara's life force that it was surely sucking away, so why wouldn't it remain strong?

What would a super-strong, super-intelligent baby do if it were endangered? Why, it would survive, that's what. Survive at all costs.

If Sara began to die would it rip its way out to breathe? I thought so. Every organism fights to live and this baby had developed no special affection for Sara. It hadn't even gotten to know her yet, or at least, not from the outside.

I ran past our condo. Did I leave food there? No. I remember cleaning it out, eating the last can, before I left. Besides, it didn't matter. It really didn't. I ran to the abandoned gas station that we had used as a staging area.

From there I took a path through the woods that was familiar even in the dark. Familiar, but not friendly. Last summer I had loved this path. Now it was wet and cold. The trees had lost their leaves. The softness was gone. Beauty was gone. Hard, cruel winter ugliness remained.

I fixed my thoughts on the cave up ahead. I longed to open the steel bank vault door, flick the switch and see the clean beauty of the laboratory. I knew that the electric heat would come on and soon I'd be warm and contentedly feeding my hunger as I ripped the tops off Dinty Moore stew cans and got ready to cope with the problems of getting back to the west coast and Sara with my Blue Helix.

It was just ahead. The rain was freezing on the mountain stone and I slipped and skidded and had to use fingers and toes to climb the path where I was used to running, but never mind. I was getting there. I was still strong. I was still the new me. Everything I needed was just ahead.

I made it.

I stood in front of the disguised door. There was a gleam of light from a moon slipping from behind clouds for a moment and I found the knob, twirled the combination by sound and feel, felt the click of tumblers falling into place, gave a tug, and the door swung open. Warm, filtered air wafted out to meet my face in the dark. Home!

I flicked the switch. Lights appeared immediately and I stepped inside the cave, inside my mountain lab.

Shambles! A complete shambles! I stood, transfixed, unable to believe the destruction. Not a single instrument had been spared. Not one piece of laboratory glass was unbroken. The very lab tables I had built were smashed into splinters. There was not, literally, one single item in the cave that I could point to and say, "This, at least, escaped."

Except the generator and the lights and the electric heat. These had been left; left it would almost seem, just so that the rest of the shambles could be plainly seen.

The Wiseass? No. Impossible. Besides, he'd take what he wanted, not smash things up. The bear! The goddamned bear! Somehow it had joined its head and body and done this! Why hadn't I destroyed it more completely?

I walked through the destruction, tears streaming down my face. Exactly where I had expected to find it I found the flask that had once held the Blue Helix. It was smashed and the carpet under it had long since soaked up the blue liquid, which had then dried and dissipated.

Gone.

Of course I could make more. But not here. Never again here, and not anywhere in a short time. The process would take days, at best, even in a well-equipped lab with no one to bother me.

Why? Why would the bear, even it its fury, destroy this place so completely? How would it know enough? Why not just eat my Dinty Moore stew (I could see that the tops were ripped off all the cans and I knew there was nothing left for me) and go to sleep for the winter in my nice, warm cave? Don't bears like caves?

So I raved at the bear, hating the bear for what it had done. But of course I knew all along that it hadn't been the bear. It was just that I couldn't immediately face what I knew it had been.

I wandered about, picking up this and that smashed item, remembering how it used to look, thinking vaguely that I'd have to get moving, I'd have to go back, find civilization, eat, make new plans, when I saw the mirror over the sink and all my bear illusions were ripped away.

The message was written in the bold script that I knew so well. It was written in vivid red lipstick on the glass. It read:

> *Sorry, Andy, but…*
> *you will not play*
> *boy-scientist in your*
> *secret lab, pretending*
> *to save mankind when you*
> *can't even save me.*
> *You will not!*
> *You don't fool me! Not*
> *any longer you don't!*
> *S*
> *And you won't save that*
> *stupid Esther, either!*

Oh, shit! Oh, Sara! Look what you've done! You've outsmarted yourself, you've killed yourself, you've killed our baby maybe, you've ruined my life for a thousand thousand years, you've been so stupid, Sara, how could you, Sara? Why didn't you save the Blue Helix at least, Sara? Steal it. Keep it for yourself? A thing that precious? To pour it on the floor? Stamp on it? Destroy what I had created? Oh, I know, you didn't believe. You thought you were destroying trash, garbage. But how could you have been that certain that I was wrong? Why couldn't you have had a little blind faith in me? When? When? When did you do this thing? I was here only two weeks ago, so you must have come destroying while I was driving west in the Winnebago. Why? What set you off? Did winning our stupid argument about mankind really mean that much to you? Were you actually afraid that I'd do it? Didn't you know I was just as confused about that as you? Goddamnit, Sara, look what you've done!

But Sara didn't smash all this because of our argument about mankind," a more sober part of my brain accepted. *She did it because the Wiseass, like the serpent in the garden, told her lies and she believed them.*

My world had changed.

It had turned a full revolution and left me in the bitter cold outside, looking in a broken window at the shambles of my life.

I leaned against a rocky wall and took in the scene, deliberately moving my eyes from glass shard to glass shard, from broken instrument to smashed table, memorizing every detail. When I came to the smashed flask that had contained the Blue Helix I lingered, fixing every particle of glass powder in my memory.

I knew I would have to leave. There was nothing for me here, not even food, which I needed. But where would I go? What would I do? Who would I do it with? Or for?

Or for: that was the thing. Who for? For more than fifty years the answer to that had been Sara. She had never been entirely out of my mind, no matter what else I may have been thinking or doing. Was she only a habit? It seemed to me that she had been the trellis that my vine had grown upon and without her I was no more than a tangled pile with no pattern, no purpose.

Our baby! I could stand amid the broken glass and cry about this, too. After our early years with the miscarriages, then the little boy almost brought to term but to die like the rest, then the long years of denial, putting our babymaking behind us, trying to say it really didn't matter, and now a real live perfect baby who would surely be as strong and as beautiful as we were, to be nurtured,

260

taught, loved, guided into responsible adulthood. But could I build a new life around someone I'd never actually seen?

Hunger! That was my only new reality. The million billion cells in my body cried out, "Never mind your maudlin grief. Feed us!"

Hunger finally got me moving again. I walked through the crunching glass to the door, flicked the light switch off for the last time, heard the generator die because the lights no longer needed it, listened to the utter silence in the black dark of the cave where even my eyes couldn't pick up a glimmer of light, then stepped outside into the cold wet night and swung the bank vault door shut and spun the combination for the last time. Then I found rocks and piled them around the door to make a final disguise.

I started down the mountain in the cold, wet and windy night. Outside, I could see like a cat, still, and just for my own reassurance I found a fist-sized stone and crushed it to a powder with one hand. Then I started making my way down, taking small leaps in the dark from ledge to ledge, doing a little slipping and sliding from time to time but what the hell did I care about that?

I had reached the bottom of our mountain and was running through the underbrush near our pool, where our golden tent had been, when my nose suddenly said, "rabbit!" and my body said, "Eat!"

So I followed my nose and sure enough, under a pile of brush, in a nest of leaves, digging down with my hands I found a nice, plump rabbit. I took him out of his winter home and held him in the dim light, feeling his warmth and feeling his heart pound in fear. I soon realized that he was a she and that there were four smaller rabbits in the nest waiting for my rabbit to come and warm and feed them.

While my mind coolly surveyed the rabbit, my body lusted for it. Every fiber called out, "Eat! Eat! Eat the rabbit, you damned fool!" and the saliva poured from my mouth, running in two sticky streams down my chin.

The rabbit saw my face and knew with the old eat-or-be-eaten certainty that is everyday life in the wild, that she was a dead rabbit. She shuddered in my hand, her face making frantic twitching motions, teeth ready to bite if they got a chance.

I simply couldn't.

I told myself that I wasn't sentimental, but hungry or not, I couldn't kill this rabbit and eat it raw. If someone had given me a hot pot of rabbit stew, well, beautiful. Pass the salt. But the thought of gulping raw, quivering rabbit meat with the blood running down my chin was too much. So, with my nose and my mouth and stomach all disagreeing strongly with my emotions, I put the rabbit back in the nest with her babies and covered them again with leaves.

As I began a fast trot to the northeast, cutting through fields, sometimes following roads, sometimes not, my nose kept finding and reporting to my other senses the exact location of squirrels and rabbits and mice and birds and pigs (I heard some contented 'oinking' from a pen)—all good things to eat that I refused. After a while my mouth stopped salivating and my body settled into a long, disappointed wait for food. "When do we eat?" my million billion body cells cried out. "Only when his stupid brain lets us," was the sad answer.

What my body cells didn't know but my brain did, was that I was experimenting in a crude sort of way with the agony Sara must have felt as her already starved body tried to fight its way to shore with the Wiseass wrapped around her legs. A self-inflicted hell.

After a while I intersected I-95 and turned north, following it through Maryland and then to the New Jersey Turnpike, passing cars and trucks as I ran, a human figure coming out of the rain and mist of black dark and startling tourists by the hundreds as I appeared beside them like a ghost and then sped past, knowing that they would think about what they'd seen, then find some rational but wrong explanation for it and go along undisturbed in a view of life where only reasonable things happened.

About half way up the turnpike, still thinking dark Sara thoughts, still unsure of the future, still ravenous, I said to myself, "This running is stupid. When does your tank run out of gas? Are you half full? Or running on empty? You haven't got a fuel gauge, you know."

"Of course it's stupid," myself answered back. "Its simple, old fashioned punishment, and punishment is the only answer for guilt.

"But what are you guilty of?" I asked.

The answer: "I'm not sure. Keep running."

After a while I started to pass a truck, a loaded eighteen-wheel semi that was barreling down an incline at about eighty. When I was running even with the cab, on the passenger side, I muttered, "Oh, the hell with this running," and opened the cab door and stepped inside.

The driver was bug-eyed, shrinking back against his door, foot standing on the brake pedal. He was a huge, fat man, bald on top and whiskery. I could smell his stale sweat and fear.

"Hi!" I said to him, brightly, trying to be reassuring. "I'm going your way. Thanks for the lift!"

"Don't stop!" I reached down as gently as I could and lifted his foot off the brake pedal. "You don't want to jacknife us now. Never mind me, just keep driving."

And he did. Glancing at me continually, eyes still wild, body odor coming at me in waves, heart pounding audibly, breath whistling.

"Man, don't hurt yourself," I said as soothingly as I could. "You'll get used to me. I'm harmless. Going to New York?"

"Bbbboston." Rolling his eyes, staring at me.

"Great! So am I. Or at least, most of the way. Just keep driving."

I settled down in my seat, looking straight ahead, ignoring my driver, giving him a chance to adjust and thinking my own black thoughts.

I thought suddenly, completely out of the blue, of Thomas Jefferson. I thought of his great house, Monticello, his five thousand acre plantation, his inventions, his enormous production of writing—the sublime Declaration of Independence among it—his presidency, his belief in the perfectibility of mankind and in a republic based upon democracy at a time when this thought was new. I thought of Thomas Jefferson and was ashamed.

There were so many of them. So many great men and women who had taken their weak bodies and faulty brains and made so much out of them while I had taken my enormous powers and diddled them away.

I had smelled the flowers. I had watched the squirrels. I had run and jumped and crushed rocks with my hands and chased after Sara like a sick calf—and Thomas Jefferson, with so much less, had helped to create a new world.

"But I did intend to do great things," I defended myself. "I was taking the long view, the ten thousand year approach, and I had less than one year. It was just a vacation, a time to look around. Besides, I still can. I'm still strong, still smart. I can still do it, if I ever figure out what to do."

"Hey!" said my driver, his courage recovered, seeing that I was safely hunched down in my seat, "Hey! Young strong fella like you, you like football?"

We blasted through the night, headlights boring into the dark gloom while I searched my memory banks for football. "Don't know much about it," I admitted. Then, trying to be a regular guy for him, "Baseball's my game."

"Baseball!" he cried out. "I love it! Let's talk baseball!"

In one of my library binges I had come across a book or two of sports statistics and the names and figures were handy in my head to recite if I wanted them.

So we drove well into Connecticut while I thought my dark thoughts and now and then threw out a baseball stat to please my driver.

Our baby! I thought. If only Sara and I could raise it, teach it how to live among frail mankind, it could be a marvel. But suppose Sara died while I was gone? Suppose the baby tore its way out or the doctors performed a Caesarean section, what then? It would need to eat, but have no teeth. It would learn to walk, to run, almost immediately. It would search out milk by smell. I could just see it, like a small monster, searching the maternity ward for new mothers with fresh milk and then attacking them, draining them dry while they wailed with fear and loathing.

There would be no one to teach it human restraint. It would want, it would find, it would take. Eventually, it would grow and learn, but it would learn first that humans were inferior beings to be fed upon, used, and it would learn that no one could deny it, and it would be beautiful beyond imagining. Men and women alike would fear and adore it. Normal children would hold it up as example and emulate it. I knew this was not a daydream, but would be happening just as I imagined it as I blasted through the night headed for Rhode Island and the Germ Factory.

"Mickey Mantle's number was seven when he played for the New York Yankees," I muttered to my driver, answering his question.

"Jesus!" He answered in admiration. "How d'you do it?" For this was perhaps the fifteenth baseball question I'd answered for him, reading the facts right out of my memory, not knowing, for example, what a shortstop was, but knowing with statistical certainty what particular shortstops had done.

Hunger gnawed at my entrails. Every cell cried out for food. My body raged at my stubborn brain and my brain raged back. "I'll tell you when you can eat! Who made you? I made you! In all the world, who understands you? I understand you. No one else!"

"Holy Jesus," my driver said. "Oh, shit, look at that. There goes my schedule!"

The sign blinking up ahead read:

Weigh station is open

My driver started tapping his brakes, slowing smoothly and cursing steadily as he headed for the offramp that would take us to the weigh station.

"I've *got* to eat," I blurted out suddenly, surprising myself.

"Well, you can't do it here. Not in the goddamn weigh station. We'll stop soon. Place up ahead."

I had an idea. Who said I didn't have a fuel gauge? Who said I didn't know whether my energy was half gone or running on empty? Sure I did. Easy. All I had to do was weigh myself.

I had weighed about sixteen-hundred pounds only yesterday. A normal man my size would weigh just under two hundred. So, why wouldn't a simple scale tell me how close I was to disaster?

I opened my door and hopped out and ran to the weigh station ahead of my truck and watched the procedure. By the time my truck reached the head of the line I knew exactly what to do.

I dug a couple of twenties out of my pocket and flashed them at the inspector. "Humor me," I said. "Just take a minute. No harm. I want to get weighed."

My truck driver got out of his cab now, standing behind me. "He's a funny fella, stubborn as hell but harmless." He told the

265

inspector. "Easiest way to get rid of him is, why doncha just weigh him?"

I ran over and dropped my two twenties in front of the inspector while up ahead a state trooper yelled, "Move it, back there!"

I stood on the scale. "Just tell me what it reads and I'll get off."

"Four-seventy," the inspector said, grudgingly. "Unless my scale is broke, you weigh four hundred and seventy, which is impossible. Now, get off!" His hand closed on my twenties and he winked over my shoulder at my driver. "Let's move it, now. Out of here!"

I jumped back into the cab, still starving, but relieved. So, I'd lost a lot of weight and my body was crying about it, but there was plenty left. All I had to do was sit here and do nothing for another fifty, sixty miles and I'd be back at my truck stop, back where it all began almost a year ago.

"Now they's a McDonald's up ahead," said my driver when we were once again on the road, boring through the night. "About three miles, and I could go for a couple Big Mac's myself, whatdyousay?"

"No. Don't stop. Stop and I'll break your leg."

"You crazy? First you say you got to eat and now you say don't stop. You crazy or what?"

My body agreed. "I'm suffering!" it screamed at me. "You're killing me! What's wrong with you?"

"I want you to suffer," I answered my body back. "I want you to remember this a thousand years. Because I know best. Who's the scientist here, anyway? I know you weigh four hundred and seventy pounds and that's almost three hundred pounds of sheer energy, so don't get smart with me. Suffer if you must, but be quiet about it."

"Goddamnit," I told myself. Life has got to have a pattern. There has to be some rhyme or reason to it or else everything is just random chance. So, I started my new life eating everything they had at this one truck stop and that's where I'll go back. That's my pattern. An almost-circle is nothing. *Nothing*, understand? To eat just one Big Mac before I got to my old truck stop would be like stopping ten yards short of the top of Mount Everest.

WILLIAM B. EIDSON

We zoomed past McDonalds. My driver yelled, "So long, Big Mac" as we passed. "A crazy man. A crazy man done hopped into my truck. Sheeeeeiiiit!"

He looked at me. "They's other places, up the road."

"Near the Rhode Island border," I told him, "on the right hand side of the road, there's a place, not a chain, a big, old fashioned truck stop where they really know how to cook scrambled eggs (my mouth began to drool uncontrollably) and bacon and fried ham and sausage that's dripping grease but crisp on the outside and hotcakes and mashed potatoes with a thick sausage gravy and steak, I could go for a steak and a gallon of milk and ice cream and a couple of pies and..."

"Christ! Mister. You are hungry. You're strange, too." But I noticed that he stepped down on the gas pedal and hunched his shoulders purposefully for the drive.

I made my plans. First, to eat; eat everything they had, just like the last time. Then run again. Leave my trucker here with his mouth open and run the last twenty or thirty miles cross country, heading northeast, towards the sea, towards the Germ Factory.

When I got there, throw Henry Fowles out of my old office and lab. Throw everyone out. My Germ Factory. Not theirs. Never was theirs. Always mine. I dreamed it. I built it. They stole it.

Then get a new batch of Sara's Blue Helix going. It would take at least three days for all the reactions to work their way through. No way to hurry it beyond that. It wasn't just mixing up chemicals, for God's sake, I had to make complex organisms grow and almost die, then change into something else, over and over again. So, three days.

Maybe Sara could hang on. Surely Sara could hang on if she tried, if she didn't give up. Right now, she'd be choking, trying to breathe. Last time, she hung on, waiting for me. Not believing, but hoping. This time? Maybe she wasn't even hoping.

The baby. A new equation. Would it wait? Would it sense Sara's near death and tear itself out? Would the doctors, curious about this baby in an eighty year-old woman, cut it out? Or would the baby stay in Sara's stomach, eating her last reserves of energy until they both died?

No way! That baby would want to live and God help anything that got in its way.

The sky was getting lighter. Still dark, but the end of night was near. We passed Mystic, heading north, boring down the highway.

"What'd you think?" I said. "Another ten miles?"

"About that. Maybe fifteen. Still hungry!" he cut his eyes at me, split his mouth in an ugly grin. "You know what? You're a silly bastid. Oh, you know your baseball, but for a guy so smart you can be so dumb, you know?"

I didn't answer. I was holding my hungry gut with both arms. It ached like a wound.

"Don't you know you don't weigh no four hundred and seventy pounds? Just look at you! Why, you ain't got no waist to speak of, not much ass, nice shoulders and chest, I grant you. Strong looking, sure, but how you figure you weigh four hundred and seventy pounds when I'm so big and fat, yes, fat, I'll say it myself, fat, a whole lot fatter than you, and I weigh only about two-eighty myself so how do you get off with four-seventy? Crazy!"

I humored him. "Well, you saw it yourself. You saw what the scale read."

"Sure! I saw it all right. I was right there. Right behind you, you silly peckerhead. Standing right on the scale with you. Adding my weight to yours. On the scale, right? Didn't you know?"

"So," he continued, "Take away my two-eighty pounds, what do it leave? I make it about one-ninety pounds for you. Right? Right? And just looking at you, I'd say that's just about right. Right? What d'you say to that?"

I scrunched down in my seat. My body said, "See?" Experimentally, I reached over to the window crank and pinched off a piece of the shiny metal. "See, yourself," I mentally argued with my body. "You're still strong."

"Just drive," I told my driver. "Hurry." My world was melting before my eyes.

I practiced breathing shallow breaths to conserve energy, as Sara had done. I calculated the energy I'd just wasted by pinching off the window crank and then regretted the mental energy I'd used making the calculation. "Don't move, don't breathe, don't think," I ordered myself. "Only a few miles now."

The truck droned on. I refused to answer my driver's questions. I refused to move. "I'll be like the bear," I told myself, and closed my eyes.

After a few minutes I felt the truck slow, heard the turn signal go on, then felt the sway as we turned into the parking lot.

I can't wait to order from a waitress, I thought. I'll have to take their food again, just like last time.

The air brakes made their chuffing noise. We rolled to a stop. I opened my eyes. We were no more than fifty feet from the door.

"Made it," said the driver, cheerfully. "Now we eat, and I am by-God ready." He opened his door and stepped down, waited a moment, then said peevishly, "You coming or not? All that eat. eat, eat talk and you just sit there?"

"Go ahead," I told him. "I'll be in a minute."

And with one disgusted glance at me he turned and headed for the lights, the smells, the human feeding noises of the diner.

I watched him go and I wanted to follow. But my back hurt. My breath was hard to draw. I could feel my shoulders slump forward and my belly grow. My eyes needed glasses. My brain was numb and slow moving. My ears… it felt as though someone had clamped a pillow over each ear, muffling the hundreds of sharp sounds I was used to hearing.

I held up the back of my hand to catch the light and saw what I expected: age spots and wrinkles. I felt ashamed.

Shame. That was the first reaction to age. How could I, used to admiring glances, return to old-manhood? How could I learn to creep around again, muscles reduced to strings, every step an uncertain totter?

Shame. I knew I couldn't let the driver catch me sitting here in his cab when he returned from feeding. "What're you doin' here, old fella? Where's the young guy?"

So I opened the door and stepped down from the cab. It seemed such a long way down, dangerous for old limbs. Why, I could fall, break a bone, just getting out of this truck.

I was no longer hungry and I knew that food now would not restore my vitality. My cells, my million billion trillion cells, were just what they had been almost a year ago: those of an old, worn out man.

I started off down the highway, walking slowly, then getting into the rhythm of it and moving a little faster, feeling my heart pound, my breath come faster but always short and whistling.

"You're not through yet!" I said through deliberately clinched teeth. "This is a setback, but you can make it. You still know what no one else knows. All you have to do is make it to the Germ Factory."

chapter thirty-nine

So I walked, terrified that I wouldn't make the twenty-five or thirty miles to the Germ Factory. At my old-man speed, what was that? Twelve, fifteen hours? Would my legs, my heart hold out?

And suppose you do make it, I thought, *You've still got to get past the guard. Then you've got to find Fred Rainy and pay him off, then you've got to have at least three days of uninterrupted work somehow, dodging Henry Fowles and all the others every minute. If you can do all that, you'll make the Blue Helix again, and if Sara's still alive you can fix everything. Except there's still one other little problem—can you remember how? Can you still remember how to make the Blue Helix?"*

I could feel my mushy old-man's brain fade in and out like an Atwater Kent radio. One minute I knew exactly how to make the Blue Helix, the next, I didn't.

Panic time.

The morning light appeared, grew stronger. Cars passed with early workers. I stuck out my thumb and was ignored. I trudged on, the miles ahead of me growing more impossible with each step.

All I need is a simple ride, I thought. *Any one of these cars can do it.*

From behind I could hear another car. From the sound of it, this one was driving slowly, stopping often, then going again.

My savior, I thought, and turned to meet it, thumb outstretched, my broadest smile plastered on my face.

About a city block away, the car stopped beside a mailbox. A beer can was thrown out the passenger window, and a moment later, a heavy shouldered, straw-headed teenager stepped out of the car with a baseball bat. He wiped his mouth with the back of his hand, and then swung the bat, beating the metal mailbox until he had killed it. He jumped back into the car, yelling, "Whoooeeee! Whooooeeeee!"

The car crept up to the next mailbox, the one just beside me, and the door was flung open for another bash. The young man with the bat jumped out again, looked at me for what seemed to be the first time, and yelled: "What are *you* looking at?"

He looked back in the car at his buddy, the driver, laughed, and then turned back to me. He flipped the bat in the air, catching it at the fat end and made as if to offer it to me. "How about you, old fart? You want a turn? You ever cut loose one day in your whole frigging life?"

When my tired brain couldn't think of an answer, he grinned, and flipped the bat back with careless ease, and then rose on his toes to bash in the mailbox in as if it were his mortal enemy.

From inside the car the driver leaned across the seat to shout at me, "Hey, *move it,* old man! Move your slow old ass out of my face!"

My pimpled friend with the bat jumped back into the car, yelling his "Whooooeeeee!" again. Before they moved down the road to the next box, he stuck his head out of the window and it seemed he was going to yell something else at me. But instead, I saw pity in his eyes for this old man who didn't understand "cutting loose."

Pity for this old man who had refused his turn at bat.

I put my head down, watching the road move slowly under my feet as I walked deliberately but without real hope towards a Germ Factory that seemed endless miles away. I thought that perhaps the young man had a point.

I just felt so damned old.

Everyone and everything around me seemed filled with energy. The world was rushing toward me with such frightening speed that I was helpless to deal with it.

Sara and I had thought we'd left age behind, and in every physical way, we had. But our attitudes, our opinions, our dreams, our points of view: all were based upon a life that started around 1915, when the world was different. By the time World War I came along I had been a big boy, with a vision of life that was set, almost unchangeable, no matter what I learned afterwards. Sara, and even the silly Wiseass were each set in their own patterns too. I remembered voices from my childhood, saying of an old man, "He's set in his ways." What I didn't understand then was that we all are.

If Sara and I could have gone ahead the thousand or ten thousand years we had expected, what antiques we'd have been! The people of that time would have marveled at our strangeness.

We were as caught in our own past as a fly in amber, unable to be anything except what we were.

But...by now Sara and I have a son or a daughter and that son or daughter will have no past. It will have no ties with anyone. No family to love. No patriotism. No religion. No loyalty. No inherited vision of what the world should be. No ingrained morality. No code of civilization. It will be a free and fearful thing, our child.

I had a vision of Sara in the operating room, either cut open by the doctors or ripped open by our hungry child. I saw the baby, boy or girl, covered in blood and slime, toothless, only eighteen or twenty inches long at most, but weighing perhaps a hundred pounds already; able to walk and run and jump, straight from the womb; and hungry, hungry, for food, for knowledge, for growth and for everything that human animals prize; running down hospital corridors, doctors and nurses in pursuit, trailing behind it the umbilical cord that the doctors had found too tough to cut with their puny scissors and scalpels, the cord still attached to the afterbirth; the child looking for all the world like an unholy succubus as it scours the hospital for milk, seizing upon new mothers with full breasts and draining them amid their screams and then finding bottles of infant formula already made in nurseries and drinking these greedily also; perhaps running off with armloads of bottles and jars of Gerber's baby food to stockpile them somewhere, just as I had with Dinty Moore stew.

I saw clearly that our child would decide almost immediately that the people around it were either friends or enemies, and the chase through the hospital, with shouts and attempts to corner and catch, would hardly seem the acts of friends.

This child would quickly develop, both mentally and physically, so it would need no caregiver, no mother, father or nanny to survive and grow. But emotionally, oh, how it would need and cry out for companionship!

So our child, born with no point of view except survival, would quickly began to develop one based upon experience, and quite soon it would develop its own ineluctable personality and begin to work its way with the world.

I so much hoped that it would find love, somewhere, from someone, for its own sake and for the sake of what it could become with love...or the fear what it would become without it.

My steps are getting slower and shorter, and as hope fades for me and for Sara, my foolish brain laughs and laughs and I find a silly smile fixed on my face as I realize that I may have become the father, and Sara the mother, of the new Christ. Or, if human love is missing, the Antichrist.

So I walk. Then I rest awhile and talk to myself. Then I walk again. I hope, for my sake and perhaps even for yours, that I make it. If not, then all I can say is, "God help the world."